I0562013

THE HONEST LAWYER

BY THE SAME AUTHOR

HIS GRACE OF GRUB STREET
THE PREVENTIVE MAN
THE TRUSTY SERVANT
NARCISSUS IN THE WAY
THE TURNING SWORD
SHERIFF'S DEPUTY

THE BODLEY HEAD

THE
HONEST LAWYER
BY G. V. McFADDEN

JOHN LANE THE BODLEY HEAD LIMITED
LONDON   VIGO STREET, W. 1

First Published in 1916
Popular Crown 8vo Edition, 1924

MADE AND PRINTED IN GREAT BRITAIN BY MORRISON AND GIBB LTD., EDINBURGH

TO

THE MEMORY OF

MY MOTHER

CONTENTS

PART I

THE JUSTICE

CHAP.   PAGE

   I. A Dog with a Bad Name   3

  II. The First Time of Asking   11

 III. The Response   20

 IV. All the Fun of the Fair   25

  V. In the Dark   34

 VI. The Game Continued.   .   .   .   42

 VII Sabbath-Breaking   51

VIII. Declaration of War   61

 IX A Gazing-Stock   69

  X. A Branch of the Chideocks   .   .   81

PART II

THE SENTENCE

  XI. The Lawyer at Home.   93

 XII. A Delicate Proposal   102

XIII. Parchment and Paper   .   .   .   110

 XIV. Her Kingdom   120

 XV. A Game of Shuttlecock   .   .   .   135

 XVI. The End of her Trust   .   .   .   150

XVII. A White Stone   157

XVIII By Night.   170

 XIX. Ridley calls the Tune   .   .   .   179

CONTENTS

PART III

THE FELON

CHAP.		PAGE
XX.	RESOLVE	197
XXI.	HER SHADOW	206
XXII.	MOVE AND COUNTER-MOVE	220
XXIII.	THE LAWYER PAYS	230
XXIV.	SOPHY'S HOUR	240
XXV.	A BUNCH OF SEALS	254
XXVI.	LOVE-LETTERS	265
XXVII.	WINNING ALL ROUND	273
XXVIII.	HER PART	282
XXIX.	TWO AND TWO ARE FOUR	296
XXX.	HIS SHADOW	307
XXXI.	THE PASSER-BY	318
XXXII.	TO HAVE AND TO HOLD	326
XXXIII.	THE WAY OF A MAID	338
XXXIV.	COMMITTAL	349
XXXV.	MANY TONGUES	360
XXXVI.	THE SECOND TIME OF ASKING	369
XXXVII.	COLD COMFORT	377
XXXVIII.	THE GOVERNOR'S TOAST	383
XXXIX.	LOVE GOES A-MARKETING	388
XL.	A CLAPPING OF HANDS	398
XLI.	THE THIRD TIME OF ASKING	410
XLII.	"AND THE DAY SHALL HAVE A SUN——"	422
XLIII.	FOR EVER AND EVER	430

PART I

THE JUSTICE

" A little romantic interlude of this sort comes in so refreshingly among the drier details which make up the life of—
a common lawyer ! "

THE HONEST LAWYER

CHAPTER I

A DOG WITH A BAD NAME

IT was said that Lawyer Ridley never lost his temper, which statement was only true in so far that the deeper his annoyance, the cooler became his manner, the choicer his words. And the manner left his adversary with a vague feeling of having been insulted, while the words, often only dimly understood, stung. He was not popular in the town. His personality carried on the prejudice induced by his calling. He was not one to veil his opinions on superficial matters—which is to say, that if he thought a man a fool, he managed to convey the impression in that elegant diction of his. But his more human emotions, if such there were, he concealed in a strictly non-committal way, and what lay beneath the surface never rose to view. Many of the townsfolk had grievances against him, but none that enlisted the sympathy of the whole community, which was a point in the lawyer's favour. Moreover, no man had ever found him out in a lie. He knew himself to be honest in his dealings with all, and, if the virtue brought him less credit than he might have looked for, his own good opinion apparently compensated for his neighbours' lack of perception. To have been hurt would have been to compliment them, and Lawyer Ridley flattered no one.

His ways of dealing with men were somewhat original. As thus :

" Fiander," he said to his clerk—he kept but one, a tow-

haired youth, with a womanish mouth and pale blue eyes—
"go and ask Mrs. Channing to give you my shaving-
mirror."

The youth obeyed, and presented the glass to his employer,
who pushed it aside.

"I don't want it, man ! Look in it yourself."

Fiander did so, and saw a very pink face looking back at
him.

"Well ? "

"Well, sir ? "

"Find yourself a handsome fellow ? "

The clerk was understood to murmur that he had never
thought about it.

"Don't upset theories ! You ought to be the best-
looking lad alive ! "

"I'm afraid I don't follow you, sir."

"One has got to be either useful or good to look at in this
world, Fiander. Have I made it clear ? "

Undoubtedly he had. The young clerk went back to his
high stool, and Ridley had no need to complain of his lack of
application for the rest of the day. Thus the lawyer got what
he wanted, without raising his voice above its ordinary level
tones.

When, a few days later, an outlying farmer jogged into
Dorchester and brought a whisper of coming disaster, slow
tongues were moved in speculation as to how the lawyer
would take it. It was not a market-day, but there were
enough idlers to fill the parlour of the *King's Arms*, and
throats grew rapidly dry with unwonted exertion.

"'Tis a tidy bit o' misfortune for a man o' his standing,"
said one, in the judicial tone of an onlooker. "No doubt
he'll feel it sore."

"You med well say that, neighbo'r," assented another,
setting down his mug with a clink of finality, intended to
express the moribund condition of Lawyer Ridley's career.
"No manner o' doubt he'll feel it, though a's such a close
fox that I reckon he'll not say much."

"'Twill take the pride out o' he ! " cried a woman's thin
voice from the background. "The set-up twoad ! "

"For my part," said he who had brought the tidings,
"I bain't sorry."

The speaker was a man of substance. Everything about
him spoke of prosperity. It was indicated no less by his
manner than by his appearance. When he opened his lips

it was apparent that he expected folks to listen. His assertions were addressed not to a chosen few, but were intended to catch the interest of the whole company. He showed this by a trick of glancing round before making any statement, and by standing like a rock when it was uttered, pugnaciously challenging anyone to contradict it. He wore much the same clothes as those which had covered his grandfather, and his mental outlook had advanced at no greater stride. A town-bred man would have shown more difference in his own opinions in ten years than Farmer Pouncey did from the modes of thought of two generations back. Oats where there had been barley, a new barton or two, an old hedge levelled, a flower garden snatched from a cabbage-bed to please his wife, only in such ways did he deviate from the well-worn track of his forebears. Any dead-and-gone Pouncey might have come back and found his favourite seat still in the old corner.

The present representative of the family was a well-preserved man nearing sixty, strong of limb, tough as his own gaiters, self-willed, obstinate. He could be fair-minded where his prejudices were not involved, but they were easily aroused, and were exceedingly tenacious. At this particular time, Lawyer Ridley was the most firmly-rooted one of them all. When he expressed approval of the fate which was to chasten that young man, every one looked serious, and emptied his mug quickly, so as to give an undivided attention to what the farmer had to say.

" If ever a man do desarve a set-back, 'tis that same young rogue," he said. " And what I do say is this—he needn't look for me to pity en ! "

" True. Sure," assented the rest. Then the woman who had spoken before raised her voice in a shriek.

" Lard ha' marcy ! " she cried. " And him owing me nigh on two pound for bacon and cheese and what not. If what Farmer do say be true, how'll I ever get my money ? "

" An' thy Robin'll ha' to look out for another master ! " croaked an old man at her side.

" Love us all ! " cried the woman. " I never thought o' that ! Wa'n't it enough to turn the lad into a laughing-stock afore the town, so as every silly maid goes playing peep-bo over t'other's shoulder to see if he's handsome or no—why, I do declare the poor boy couldn't sit still in church last Sunday for the eyes of the wenches on him, and him as hot as fire wi' blushing ! An' now he's to be turned out o' his place, and my money I'll never get ! "

" Come, come, woman," said the farmer, laying a broad forefinger on her arm, and checking the others with a look, " the knave owes a tidy bit all round, I reckon, but he shan't cheat ye if I can help it. As to that young jackanapes of a lad o' thine, he shan't starve. I'll find en a job myself first."

The woman, who was a small shopkeeper and the mother of the lawyer's lanky young clerk, looked up gratefully.

" Ay, danged if I won't ! " assented her champion generously. " I'm looking for a lad to clean out the pigsties."

Betsy Fiander wailed anew.

" Well, 'tis honest work, I take it," declared the other. " A deal better for the loon than l'arning to rob and cheat, from a dangerous rogue who owns he's a Radical, and shouts for Reform ! "

" A Radical's money's so good as another man's," asserted some one boldly. " The point is, since Lawyer's been and lost his, how be we to get ours ? "

" Seems to me," said Farmer Pouncey, " that if ye don't look smart, ye'll not get a penny."

A new-comer looked in, and asked to be enlightened as to the state of affairs. Glum faces greeted him on all sides. Only Pouncey seemed to be enjoying the situation. He it was who explained.

" 'Tis Lawyer Ridley," he said, with a nod up-street. " Lost all his money, they be saying, and these pore souls reckon to lose theirs. The Weymouth Bank's broke, and there's little doubt that he's a ruined man. Sorry I am for all the folks he's owing money to, but for his own sake, I'm glad. There's naught like a smarting back to learn a man to keep the whip off t'other folk's. Twenty-five pounds did he cheat me out o', and, if he's lost the six thousand as his skinflint wold wort of an uncle left en, 'tis a lesson and a triumph for all honest souls."

" 'Tis the wicked man in the Bible," murmured a woman piously. " ' He heapeth up riches, but cannot tell who shall gather 'em.' "

A clamour of voices rose. The news had spread—fresh faces blocked the doorway. Interest vied with the sense of personal discomfiture. It was found that the lawyer had a healthy appetite and a discriminating taste, joined to a reprehensible habit of paying bills once a month—some-

where about the middle, and September was already a
week old.

"Tell 'ee what," cried Farmer Pouncey, at length, moved
apparently by the woebegone faces of his companions, "I'll
go up-along, and ha' a word wi' the man, and see what can
be done. 'Twould be a crying shame if harm came to any
o' ye for lack o' a man to speak out."

His attitude being much applauded, the whole roomful
swayed towards the door, and crowding like a flock of sheep
—which in truth they greatly resembled—got themselves
out into the street. The sight of so large a concourse, on a
day that promised neither a market nor a fair, was so unusual
a sight that it was presently augmented by as many curious
and idle townspeople as could add to it. At the head of the
procession marched Farmer Pouncey, with Mrs. Fiander at
his side. After these came a huddled group of men and
women, united by a wonderful bond of sympathy. In all
the company there was not found one voice to say a word of
pity for the victim of financial failure. To the disinterested,
the affair offered just the amount of appositeness to turn it
into a good joke—as if a fowler should be caught in his own
gin, or a constable sent to gaol. They were apprehensive
only of two things: that if the lawyer could cheat them, he
would; and that if any man could successfully battle for
their rights, it was the one who had undertaken to see the
matter through.

The procession had merely to walk in a straight line to
reach its goal. The air was still, and the town, in a general
sense, quiet enough. The sound of many feet was distinctly
audible in the lawyer's office some few moments before,
raising his head somewhat heavily, he became aware of the
concourse that had gathered outside his house.

The roadway, to his circumscribed vision, seemed full
of sunburnt faces and curious eyes. While he watched, the
crowd surged forward, pressed itself against the iron railings,
and craned towards the window. It was a positive invasion.
He leant back in his chair, and eyed the intruders coolly.
If a ruined, he was apparently not a broken man. For three
minutes he sat so, staring out as they stared in. For so long,
nothing happened. Outside, though Ridley was unaware
of this, the Widow Fiander was timidly exhorting Farmer
Pouncey not to anger her son's employer.

" 'Tchut! ma'am," cried he, "d'ye think I'm going out
o' my way to harm you or your lad? Bain't it certain the

boy won't ha' Master Ridley's wages in any case ? What's he got to lose ? "

" Maybe the story isn't true," she ventured.

The farmer turned from her with contempt, and pushed his way to the door. It was recessed in a quasi-Grecian portico, after the style of the preceding century, and was hung with a heavy knocker of a more antique type. There was about the whole house a suggestion of solidity and prosperity. Wedged in between less pretentious dwelling-places, it gained in importance from its humbler neighbours, and looked from its second-storey windows upon the mossy tiles of the smaller houses. Its somewhat severe architecture was relieved only by a high-pitched gable and a few mouldings of Purbeck stone. No bow window broke the flatness of its façade, which would have been plain to austerity but for the crimsoning leaves of the creeper, which reached to the roof of the portico, and the medley of late summer flowers that filled the tiny space between the wall and the railings.

" Be I to go on with this ? " demanded the farmer, as he grasped the knocker in his great hand.

An instant later, the quietude of the house was broken by a series of loud bangs. Ridley scarcely moved an eyelid. Robin Fiander was squirming uneasily on his stool. He had caught a glimpse of the farmer, and knew that no friendly errand brought him to this house.

They heard the door opened—the sound of voices. Then came a tap at the office door.

" Well ? " asked Ridley, as his housekeeper looked in.

Farmer Pouncey's request for an interview was repeated —shorn of the many embellishments, which had been perfectly audible through the open window.

" I can't see him," said Ridley. " You may go, Mrs. Channing. Don't interrupt me again."

Fiander breathed heavily.

A moment later the farmer was heard asserting his determination not to move from the step until the interview had been granted. Mrs. Channing came back, and reported timidly.

" That'll do," said her master. " Fiander will deal with him."

" I—I, sir ? " stammered the clerk.

" Yes. Go and present my compliments to Mr.

Pouncey "—Robin slid from the stool—" and tell him to go to the devil."

" Sir, if you please—really—I——"

" And tell that grinning crew outside that, if they don't go off in a couple of minutes, I'll come out and read the Riot Act."

" Yes, sir, I'll tell them. Only, please, about Farmer Pouncey. He's a temperish kind o' man."

" Well ? "

" If you don't mind, I'd really much sooner—that—that you gave the message yourself ! "

Ridley rose.

" As you please, Fiander." He walked to the door. His clear-cut regular features were quite composed, his pleasant voice as even as usual. His eyes were almost smiling. With his fingers on the handle, he spoke again. " I'll pay you what's due to you when I come back," he said.

Fiander, crimson with mortification, clutched his arm. To him, Ridley was admirable—more than a master—an example of culture, of firmness, of a hundred and one qualities which he himself longed for, besides being possessed of an inexplicable personal attraction which Fiander was most conscious of when smarting under the other's displeasure.

" I'll go, sir," he cried. " On my soul, I will. You don't know what you're asking, but I'll do it for you."

Ridley, looking neither surprised nor gratified, stood aside, and Fiander went out. By now, the farmer had advanced into the passage, and here the clerk found him, backed up by some half-dozen forms which were endeavouring to squeeze themselves in after him.

At first sight, Fiander faltered, casting a wistful glance at the door he had just left. But, as the lawyer showed no disposition to relieve him of a distasteful duty, he was forced to go through with the business.

" If you please, sir," he began, a little too respectfully for the success of his errand, " Mr. Ridley really can't see you, and he'd take it as a great favour if you'd all go away at once."

" And who told you to come interfering wi' me, my lad ? " demanded Pouncey, with anger in his eyes.

Fiander retreated a pace or so.

" Mr. Ridley did," he said, from a comparatively safe distance. " You've really no right, if I may say so—to—to—

come inside a gentleman's house without his leave. Mr. Ridley isn't at all pleased—and, sir, you must go."

"Go!" roared the farmer. "Go! Because a little washed-out stripling like you says so! Be I to l'arn manners from a half-starved scarecrow of a swindling lawyer's clerk? I'll tell 'ee what it is, Robin Fiander—if you don't want to feel my boot against your shins, you'll stand out o' my way in double-quick time! I'll deal with your master first, and stop your crowing a'terwards, my lad!"

"Sir," pleaded the clerk, hanging on to his arm, for the farmer had gripped the young fellow's shoulder, and was swinging him aside. "Sir, for pity's sake!—I don't want to anger you——"

"Hey?" cried Pouncey, red and furious, "hey? But you've done it! Lard love 'ee, you young sinner, if ever I catch ye skulking round after my maid again—'tisn't a warning I'll give 'ee next time, but a good sound thrashing as'll knock manners into a young cub as wants to l'arn his betters!"

He ended by striking the tow-coloured head vigorously against the passage wall, and jerking the frail figure contemptuously to one side. Fiander, limp and crushed, more by the other's words than by the rough treatment, swayed helplessly, and fell into his mother's arms. He was almost glad to see the tears in her timid eyes—it was like weeping by proxy.

The farmer marched on, followed by the rest, and without further ceremony, burst open the door of the office.

Then he spluttered and fell back. Lawyer Ridley was looking at him along the barrel of a small pistol.

CHAPTER II

THE FIRST TIME OF ASKING

DURING the next few minutes, much was said and more was thought—particularly by the farmer. His brain was not acute where the niceties of speech were concerned, but he was rapidly convinced of the superiority of the lawyer's tongue. It was all very well to curse it for a lying deceitful member, but it struck him, against his will, as an exceedingly useful one. He himself, with his homely invective, and farmyard bluster, was overborne, beaten back, and put to utter shame by the quietly spoken words of his adversary—which sounded civil enough at first, but were found to hold an unpleasant gibe or an uncomfortably correct statement. And this discomfiture was independent of the silver-barrelled weapon which the lawyer had laid aside as soon as his silence had forced the other into speech.

At the end of five minutes, the original purpose of the interview had been lost sight of completely. Whether Lawyer Ridley was a bankrupt, or Mrs. Fiander likely to lose her money, no one of the gaping onlookers had any idea. The only impression arising out of the affair was the growing one that Farmer Pouncey was not quite as smart as every one had thought him.

"What about the five-and-twenty pounds you robbed me of?" shouted the farmer, at length, in obvious retreat.

"Mr Pouncey," said the other, with his most pleasant smile, "if your perceptive faculties were less of the asinine order, you'd realise that if a litigious fool chooses to go to law, and suppresses an important piece of evidence——"

"Cuss thy long words! You told me we'd win the case!"

"So I did," assented Ridley cheerfully. "Only you misrepresented the facts, you see. You misled me entirely."

"Go on! Call me as big a liar as yourself!"

"I couldn't pay you a greater compliment," said Ridley.

"Hear him!" cried the other, choking with rage, and missing the lawyer's point. "Says I'm as girt a rascal as himself! If I don't warm his skin for him a'ter that, he's welcome to call me all the names he can lay his wicked tongue to!"

Farmer Pouncey being a man of considerable inches and proportionately broad, things looked awkward for a moment for the young lawyer, who was slight of build and had inconveniently separated himself from his weapon. Not that that was more than an empty threat, being unloaded—whereas the farmer carried a stout-handled riding whip, and was gripping it for action, with the butt-end foremost.

Ridley stood very still. Once again the soft look that was almost a smile had come into his eyes. Suddenly he bent slightly forward, his lithe young body at the spring. Then his right fist shot out, and caught the farmer underneath the jaw, and darted from there to the other side of his astonished face. In another minute, Pouncey was seeing stars, wonderfully irradiated from a pair of whirling fists, which so dazzled and bewildered him that his own attempts at retaliation were feeble and misdirected. Not a single blow got home while a well-aimed stroke of the lawyer's cunning arm speedily knocked the wind out of him. Ridley followed up his advantage, and before the spectators had thought of laying their money on either party the farmer was sent sprawling into the passage at the feet of an elderly man who had just entered the house.

Encountering the gaze of the new-comer across the body of his fal'en foe, young Ridley flushed brightly, and showed signs of being more or less ashamed of himself. This elderly soldierly looking man was the last one by whom he cared to be caught milling in his own office with a truculent yokel.

"I didn't look for this pleasure, sir," he said, with an apologetic glance at his bleeding knuckles. "If I had— you may be very sure I wou.dn't have received you in this way."

"It was very neatly done," said the visitor handsomely. He stepped over Farmer Pouncey, and entered the room. "I don't think Jackson himself could have bettered it Still— not quite professional, is it? I don't mean as regards the Fancy, but as regards the Faculty."

Ridley again changed colour.

"I'm very sorry, sir," he said. "I offer a sincere apology. But the truth is, the fellow insulted me, and quite deserved the lesson I gave him."

" I don't doubt it," replied the other, with a reproof in his manner not expressed by the words. " But if your levee is ended, I should like a few minutes alone with you."

" At your service, sir," said Ridley, maintaining composure in an awkward situation. Then he turned to the townsfolk, and raised his voice. " Now then, out you go —all of you! And, if any of you dare to repeat this performance, there'll be trouble! As for you, Pouncey, you're not fit to be let loose outside your own pigsties! You can do your swearing in the road—there! Take him away, some one! His Honour the Governor is kept waiting."

Awed partly by their leader's unexpected fiasco, partly by the personality and traditions of the latest comer, who was the Governor of the adjacent prison, the crowd slunk out. They dragged the still dazed Pouncey with them, and though they hastened they went quietly, with a sheepish scuffle, and an air of wishing that they had not come.

When the door had closed upon them, Ridley, scarcely more at ease, pulled down his cuffs, and smoothed his hair. Then he twisted a handkerchief round his right hand, and turned towards his visitor.

That gentleman was still standing, his fine features settled into an expression of quiet interest, not unmixed with concern.

" Is this true that I hear? " he asked, with customary abruptness.

" About the Bank ? " said Ridley.

" Yes. Is it closed ? "

" Unfortunately, it is, sir."

" Ah! Then you are a ruined man ? "

" I've lost close on six thousand pounds, sir. Yes, 'tis bad enough, I admit. But I'm not exactly the bankrupt these stupid fools take me for. There are a couple of securities left untouched. And the practice remains."

The other nodded gravely.

" Still, it is a loss for a young man like you, Kenelm. You'll be years—even if you improve on your uncle's business —saving six thousand pounds."

" I daresay," said Ridley. " Yes, it's a blow, though not a knock-out one. I shall have to work, that's certain. The worst part of the affair is the damage such a calamity does to a professional man. You saw for yourself a little of it this morning, sir. No sooner do these silly folks get wind of my misfortune than up they all troop, ready to tear the coat off my back."

" Or the skin off your knuckles ! "

Ridley smiled. He was an exceedingly well-favoured young man when he chose to look pleasant.

" I had to do it," he explained. " The fellow called me a liar, and a cheat, and threatened to strike me. They've got a notion into their silly pates that I shan't pay them the trifling sums I owe. That's all nonsense, of course. I'm not a broken man, though it's bound to make a slight difference."

" When did it happen ? " asked the Governor.

" Yesterday. I heard last night. I was thinking of sending to let you know."

" You say that it will make a difference," resumed the other, after a pause, during which he had carefully observed his companion's face. " Do you anticipate any immediate embarrassment ? You were not thinking of marrying ? "

" Heaven forbid ! " cried Ridley, with a short contemptuous laugh. " The fair sex has no attraction for me, I assure you."

There was neither satire nor amusement in the steady eyes which were watching him. When the elder man spoke, there was, for the second time, a hint of reproof in his tones.

" Don't jeer at such things," he said. " Marriage is the goal of a great many men's desires."

" Well, well," said Ridley, " at least I have no such intention, so the calamity is lessened by so much, I suppose."

" Yes—the misfortune. I am sorry about it. I came to say so."

" Thank you heartily, sir."

" Also, I wish to assure you of a more practical sympathy. If it should be necessary, or in any way desirable, I trust that you will not hesitate to draw upon me to any amount. You are a young man, just at the beginning of your career. I am an old one, ending mine. You may take from me without compunction or shame."

" The shame, I fancy, would lie in the refusal," said Ridley, with one of his fine perceptions. He held out his hand. " If I need it, I will not hesitate. 'Tis generous of you to offer it."

" I would do more than that for you, Kenelm," said the other. He laid his hand on the young man's shoulder. " Much more ; and you know it."

There was a great deal in his tone, but more still lay behind the words—things that Ridley guessed at rather than knew —a sentiment deep and unrevealed, an ancient emotion squandered unrequitedly, but grown none the poorer for that. If this set-featured man, now little more than a Government automaton, had missed something in his youth, he did not refuse to gather up what remained to him. Of his friendship Ridley had had ample experience, and he accepted it less as a matter of course than he did most good things that fortune doled out to him. He remembered occasionally that this man had known his mother.

The recollection was very strong upon him at this moment, when the fact seemed likely to bear material fruit. Not devoid of finer feelings himself, he wished that his acceptance of the other's favours could have had a less mercenary flavour about it, but he shrugged the objection away, for the same instinct had already shown him the ungraciousness of rejecting the offer.

He therefore reiterated his provisional promise to accept the proffered aid, and very quickly the veil raised between these two fell again, both thereafter feeling more comfortable. The one had almost outlived the expression of sentiment; the other had not yet attained to it.

" I don't think," said the younger man, in a strictly business tone, " that there is any immediate cause for anxiety. I certainly don't intend to let the loss of the money—it is an intolerable nuisance, though — hamper my capacities. I may not be popular in the town—hang it all, I know I'm not!—but the gentry round about are finding out my value. When I think what the practice must have been worth when it was worked by my uncle, with his last century ideas, and that drunken old clerk of his, why I'm simply amazed that he had six thousand pounds to leave me—What the devil, Fiander! Why don't you knock when his Honour the Governor is here ? "

Fiander, who had blundered in unaware of a visitor, stammered a feeble apology, and held out a letter.

" The man was very urgent that it should be delivered at once, and into your own hands, sir," he explained.

" What man ? Where is it from ? " asked Ridley, as he took the letter.

" A servant, sir. I—I didn't recognise the livery. He will take an answer back."

" Very well. Wait outside till I call you."

The Governor rose.

"Don't leave me because of this," said the younger man, tossing the letter on to his table. "I'm in no hurry. It does these fellows good to be kept waiting. They're such an overbearing breed. If anything, worse than their masters. I dare say 'tis the most trivial business."

"Still," replied the other, "even so, it must be attended to. Don't make mistakes—now of all times."

Ridley looked annoyed. He flicked the letter with his finger-end.

"You wouldn't have me obsequious to these high folks, would you, sir?" he asked. "Such manners are a little old-fashioned at this time of day, I think."

"Courtesy is never old-fashioned," replied the Governor. "You young ones are apt to overlook—facts, sometimes. No! I am going. I have said all that I came to say, and I cannot afford to neglect my duties. I am less fortunate than you."

Ridley shrugged his shoulders, looked obstinate for a moment, then laughed.

"I'll attend to it as soon as I'm alone," he promised. "And from the bottom of my heart I thank you for your generosity, sir."

"It is nothing," replied the other, as their hands met. "Let me know if you have any further trouble, and send to me if you need help."

"I don't deserve your kindness, sir," said Ridley. "If the townsfolk invade me again—which I don't fancy they will!—I'll use your name if other arguments fail. Good morning. Fiander, show this gentleman out."

In the passage a grey-haired man, obviously a servant of some sort, was waiting. Glancing at him as he went by, the Governor decided that it was small wonder that the clerk did not know the livery, since the man wore none. In the roadway, he found his own servant with the horses, and alongside, hooked to the railings, another animal fully as well-conditioned as these. He mounted, and rode off, with no thought of the bit of local history which was forming under his gaze.

Indoors, the young lawyer was opening the letter. At the first words his attention was caught; a moment later, he frowned; then, as his eyes ran along the easily flowing lines, he settled himself in his chair, a cynical kind of amusement deepening in his face.

Presently he rose, and still holding the letter, summoned the clerk.

" The man is waiting ? " he asked. " He must take a verbal answer. I can't write with this hand, and the matter's too private to dictate to you."

" What shall I tell him, sir ? "

A gleam of amusement brightened Ridley's eyes.

" Just this—I'll think it over. Nothing more."

The message was delivered. The servant bowed, and left the house. If anyone had followed him, it would have been noticed that he rode out of the town by a circuitous route, and appeared to be in a hurry. Arriving presently at a secluded spot some half-mile away from Dorchester, he came upon a young lady, mounted on a white horse, who was evidently waiting for him.

He rode up, and saluted.

" Well ? " she cried.

" I handed in your letter, miss."

" You didn't see the gentleman ? "

" No, miss."

She appeared relieved, and sat back in her saddle. Excitement shone in her eyes, but in her manner there was a little shrinking and fear.

" Where is his answer ? " she cried. " Why don't you give it to me, fool ? "

" He says, miss——"

" Says ? " she echoed, and her colour began to rise. Underneath her russet-coloured habit her breast was heaving quickly.

" He says that he will think it over," the servant finished, in a stolid and unheeding way.

" Is that all ? " she demanded. Again she leant towards him. " Did he say anything else ? "

" Ne'er a word, miss. That was all his young chap said."

She wheeled her horse suddenly.

" Home ! " she cried, in a voice all choked with hard breathing. Her face was flaming, her eyes were bright and angry. She was biting her lips in her rage. When presently a tear slid down her cheek, she would have lost a diamond sooner than that drop.

" I shall hate him ! " she muttered, to the trot of the horses' feet. " Hate him for this insult ! But, oh, my God ! how much more I hate myself ! "

And she rode steadily forward, every word in that letter of hers ringing through her head, the whole rapidly becoming distorted in the light of her new perception as to how it had probably been received.

The groom kept his eyes on his mistress's shapely back, and thought no more of his morning's errand. This was precisely the state of mind on which the young lady herself had reckoned.

Meanwhile, as every minute put a further distance between the writer and the recipient of the letter, the missive itself lay on Ridley's table, where he had tossed it aside after a second perusal. It was not until the end of the day brought him time for the leisurely consideration of trifles, that he unearthed it from the mass of papers where it lay half buried, and read it through again.

It ran:

"SIR,—I am a woman of considerable fortune, who, learning with deep regret of the calamity which has overtaken you, is moved to offer you an easy way out of your difficulties. The fact that my position and parentage are far superior to your own, is a sufficient refutation of any unseemliness that might else be brought against me. Your own character should be an additional safeguard. Briefly then—I desire to place my hand at your disposal. I have already said that it is not an empty one. In becoming my husband you will gain the immediate benefit of release from your present embarrassments, and the subsequent advantage of the influence at my command on your future career. Should you be less ambitious than I assume, all necessity for continuing your labours will be removed. I need not remind you that there are many pleasant occupations for a man of leisure. In short, my proposal offers nothing but advancement in every direction. I leave it to your good sense to understand so much.

"Should you be willing to profit by the opportunity so freely held out to you, I am ready to grant you an interview whereat much may be said which I cannot set down here. You will understand my desire for privacy. I therefore request you to meet me at nine o'clock next Saturday evening, on the ramparts at the Eastern side of Wareham. It is immaterial whether I belong to that town or not, since I do not choose to disclose my identity at this early stage of our acquaintance. If I am asking you to take something on trust, you must remember that I am placing in you as much confidence as I expect you to accord to me.

" My servant is waiting to carry your reply. You will please to be quite definite as regards the appointment, and a refusal to keep it will be taken as a termination of the whole matter."

Seldom, since Adam first wooed Eve, had such a strange love-letter been penned. And it was to this imperious missive that Lawyer Ridley had sent back the cavalier verbal answer—that he would think it over.

Small wonder that her face flamed, and that every mile placed between them seemed a precious thing.

CHAPTER III

THE RESPONSE

THE following Saturday, the day named by the lawyer's secretive mistress for the meeting, was an important one to the people of this district. It was the day of the half-yearly fair at Wareham. Ridley had left Dorchester in his boyhood, been educated and started his career at Bath, and had only returned to his native town on the death of his uncle. He had not so much forgotten, as ceased to remember, the traditions of his own county, and the significance of the date fixed in the letter at first escaped him. Learning by accident what the day was to his neighbours, he saw a purpose in the choice. On a fair-day, strangers in even such a quiet town as the old Anglo-Saxon survival of Wareham might pass unnoticed, whereas, on the other three hundred and sixty-three, an unfamiliar face of either sex would create instant comment. The lady, therefore, had chosen next Saturday for her own protection—either, directly, because she was a stranger to the place, or, indirectly, because he was.

" By gad," said Ridley, to himself, " she's thought it all out—the artful schemer ! "

Meanwhile, Friday intervened.

At odd moments, during the day, the young man found his mind reverting to the letter. The persistence of his fancy in this direction annoyed him. But for his cynical humour, he would have destroyed the sheet. As it was, he carefully preserved it, being chiefly influenced by the reflection that, considering the use he intended to make of her proposal, the lady would soon be ready to give one of her ears to get her letter back. That she should have any power at all to catch even his faintest interest, irritated while it surprised him. Women, apart from clients, had no meaning for him, and he was contemptuously tolerant of the weakness in others only because a distressed lover was a subtle compliment to his personal immunity. As usual in such cases, he was unaware that his present attitude of mind was not incompatible with subsequent surrender. The truth was, he was indifferent with the potentiality of becoming ardent, just as he was selfish with the possibility of making sacrifice. Neither quality had quite so firm a grip on him as he led people to suppose.

To divert himself from his own embryo love affair, he took a keener pleasure than usual in rallying young Robin Fiander upon his. Ever since Farmer Pouncey had knocked his head against the wall, the clerk had moved about with a pathetic look of genuine suffering in his pale blue eyes, and Ridley, finding sharp words of no avail, fell at length into a more unbusiness-like mood, and openly laughed at the woebegone youth.

" What a poor-spirited lad it is ! " he cried. " Upon my soul, I'll get some old dame for clerk, and find her the better man of the two ! Why don't you start love-making with one of the town girls ? That would bring t'other hussy to her senses if she cares for you at all."

" Ah," said the youth ingenuously. " Ah, but she don't."

" Then let her go to the devil ! "

Fiander shook his head.

" A smart lad like you—yes, you're not without parts, if you'd only get this silly maid out of your head ! "

" I can't, sir. If you'd ever seen her, you'd understand. She's the prettiest young lady in Dorset."

" Anything like her father ? " inquired Ridley drily.

" No, sir, she's not. She's a deal finer than her own folk. That's where all the trouble lies. There never was such a maid."

" There never is," said Ridley. He kept silent for a moment or so, then he asked, " You blame me, don't you, for this last fiasco ? "

His clerk was at once too honest and too loyal to reply.

" Well," continued Ridley, " I'm sorry if I've damaged your prospects in this quarter. Though, at the same time, if the girl herself doesn't care for you, I don't see that I've done much harm. It may even give you some interest— what do they call it ?—romance, in her eyes, if you have to run the gauntlet of the horse-pond and her father's ash stick, in order to visit her."

" She don't live at home," said Fiander simply.

" Where then ? "

" At Wareham," said the other, and Ridley roused himself, looked as if he were going to speak, and then said nothing.

" But 'tis not easy to see her neither," murmured Fiander miserably. " She's too good for me—that's the truth."

But Ridley seemed no longer interested. He ordered the clerk back to his desk, and took up his own pen. Presently, he fell to biting the end of it, and finally laid it down.

Who was she ? More persistently, what was she ? Some wanton light-o'-love, desiring coverture ? Some wrinkled old maid, eager to capture a husband on this side of the grave ? Or merely some giddy girl, just released from the backboard, as innocent as ignorant, as foolish as pretty, longing sentimentally for a lover to come forward, and baiting her trap as she best knew how ? Which was she ? Rather, was she any of these ?

There was a note struck in the wording of the letter which was at variance with each fancy. Underlying the apparent immodesty of her approach, there was the unmistakable sound of pride. It was this which made the whole such a fantastic piece of reading. The offer she made was not advanced as an appeal—it was given out as a demand. The native pride which could thus insensibly and yet palpably colour such a proposition as hers, was as little consistent with a tarnished name as it was with wrinkles or silliness. If, then, the lady had neither too much experience nor too little, why did she find it necessary to seek a husband in such a roundabout way ? Surely a wealthy woman, without such defects as Ridley was inclined to repudiate, might find many suitors without running after an obscure country lawyer—choosing him too at the very moment when his fortunes were none too staple.

The obvious explanation was one which Ridley, with his avowed contempt for sentiment, passed by without a second thought. The lady's letter itself gave him scant justification for assuming that she was in love with him. The tone was too business-like, the manner too reserved, to suggest to any but an inordinately vain man that the self-abandonment of romantic affection had prompted her advance. Ridley, heart-whole and level-headed, put that idea away from him from the first.

" She's too damned patronising," he said to himself. " A woman in love would never have alluded to her own condescension in the matter."

It was this very air of superiority, combined with her

over-confidence, that irked him, and by so doing, forced his attention to the letter. There were a hundred more important things to think about, greater interests to turn to, for while he threw his personal conjectures up and down in his mind his clients' business was at a standstill. There were bigger fights only waiting for him to lead the charge, yet on this Friday morning he found the man in him getting the better for once of the lawyer. No contested claim, no conflicting evidence, no existing lawsuit, moved his combative qualities with half such fascination as did the possibility of riding rough-shod over the pride of this haughty dame.

The way was easy enough. He had merely to ignore her letter, and allow her to wait for him until she was tired. He had ample excuse in the pressure of business which threatened him. It would be interesting to watch for her next move. An unmannerly course, undoubtedly, but could a man be expected to act as a gentleman towards a woman who had been something less than ladylike ?

Born in an age when Democracy, released from leading-strings, was just beginning to feel its way alone, Ridley had found the new doctrine that Jack has no fewer rights than his master an exceedingly good one. His natural good sense, and somewhat cynical temper, saved him from falling into the error, common with ardent young spirits just aware of their own value, of unconsciously imitating many of the evils which he was campaigning against. While condemning the arrogance of the aristocracy, he never wished to set up a society overruled by a class less educated and fully as tyrannic. While satirically contemptuous of the pride of Birth, he did not unduly glory in his own middle-class lineage. He was cool even in his enthusiasms ; a Radical who knew that mere topsy-turvyism would not necessarily bring about desired Progress.

" It's not a reversing of the classes, but a greater cohesion between them all that we want," he would say.

But, if he gave what he demanded, he also demanded what he gave, and the lady's slighting allusion to his inferiority spurred his own pride in no small degree. Without it, he would have thought neither better nor worse of her for being the gentlewoman she declared herself—as it was, it pleased him to think that he could humiliate such a one.

And it therefore only remained to find the most effectual way of doing this.

Until the moment when Robin Fiander had swept his

thoughts back into the groove, Ridley had decided to take
no notice of the letter. But from that time, for no particular
reason, his inclination swung round. To wound, without
being there to see the effect, was, he decided, poor sport.
He had no intention of trying to pierce the lady's mask, but
why should he not keep the appointment, and tell her plainly
what he thought of her and her audacious proposal? The
notion was alluring; he thought of it many times during
the day. It had the strength of a temptation. He read the
letter over once again. The objectionable phrases stood
out as though written in red ink. Yes! this high and
mighty madam should not be disappointed of a meeting with
the lover whom she had graciously chosen. He would go to
Wareham.

"And, by gad, my dear," he said, as he folded the letter
with a smack on his knee, "you shall go home smarting
for your pains!"

That his own return might be in any way unusual was a
thought which did not occur to him.

CHAPTER IV

ALL THE FUN OF THE FAIR

WAREHAM town, a place of old-world memories and proud traditions, had become hopelessly left behind in these latter days. It had made its history, and almost forgotten it. Its castle, its nunnery, its quays, were things of the past. Its very seaboard had vanished. Of its ancient glory, nothing now remained but a long straggling street, bisecting a ring of Saxon-raised earthworks, a few churches of great antiquity, a ruined convent, and its half-yearly fairs.

The town was picturesque in formation, and pleasantly situated. Lying in the heart of a pastoral and fertile country, it was securely wrapped round by the green slopes of its fortifications, and further isolated by the proximity of a river at either end—an isolation which was, however, rather suggested than actual, for Wareham lay in the march of anyone travelling from the inland town of Wimborne to the little fishing village of Swanage on the adjacent coast. Generally speaking, the place appeared as if a Greek cross had been described upon the meadows between the Puddle and the Frome, and then enclosed in a circle. Within that circle, moved the life of Wareham.

As the ancient glory had departed with the passing of history and the gradual recession of the sea, so the old-time enterprise and fervour of the inhabitants had also declined. It might be that they had been cured of any love of wandering and adventure by the grisly exposures set up on the lower bridge in the days of the Bloody Assize. Whether or no, they had done and seen little since that distressful time. Market-day was an incident ; fair-day an event. Beyond these excitements, the tide of life at Wareham moved forward slowly, like its own rivers, and was untouched by contact with the world without. Radicalism, with Reform written large on one of its many foreheads, might be raising its hydra-

head in some far-off place called vaguely " Lunnon-town,"
but that was a matter of indifference to these quiet rustics.
Superstition yet lingered.   The whisper of machinery made
the deepest thinking among them hold their breath, but not
for long, since the notion was too impracticable to merit
serious alarm.   Besides, something remained of their ancient
sturdiness, and, if it were true that other villages and townlets
were ready to riot for their rights, Wareham promised itself
that it could do the like.   And having so far roused its
slumbering energy, it fell asleep again

The September fair was the more popular of the two held
each year, and on the day when Lawyer Ridley brought his
sub-acid observation to bear upon Wareham men and manners
the little town was astir from one bridge to the other.   All
day long, a trickle of vehicles had entered the circle from
either approach, and had clustered thickly about the lower
end of the town.   Gigs, carts, brightly painted waggons,
droves of cattle, sheep, pigs, and fowls, all crowded together
in the earlier hours of the day.   Presently the pens were set
up, the heifers tethered to their posts, the poultry hustled
into the market-house, and the horses stabled at the various
inns.   While the actual business of the day was going forward
at a leisurely pace, booths and stalls were being got ready
by those to whom belonged the task of providing that light
entertainment which came as an interlude, between the
serious responsibility of buying and selling in the morning,
and the no less important duty of drinking hard all the
evening.   In the open space formed by the intersecting of
the four roads, rows of stalls were placed.   Here were displayed cakes of gingerbread and sticks of barley-sugar,
gimcrack toys and trinkets.   In the unoccupied square of
ground near to the largest church, had been set up a merry-
go-round, and a booth where for the price of one penny might
be seen the finest show in the South of England.   Minor
exhibitions of the instructive and marvellous were squeezed
in wherever room was found, and towards late afternoon
no showman, had he no more than an inverted box for plat-
form, and only a piece of coloured glass for his stock-in-trade,
but had his own special audience.

It was at this time, while this section of amusement-
venders was reaping a satisfactory harvest from the credulity
and ignorance of the rest, that Lawyer Ridley came strolling
into their midst.   He had ridden in at a leisurely pace, with
no purposed deviation from his original plan.   Since he

intended to be master of the situation at the coming interview, he had no desire to conceal his presence beforehand. He therefore left his horse at the best inn, made a hearty meal after his ride, and then walked out into the thronged streets, a little less than interested, a little more than indifferent as regarded the things he saw.

In the jumbled medley of rustic humanity here drawn together, he was a noticeable figure. His sombre clothing, with its lack of ornament, appropriate alike to his profession and to his condition as sole surviving relative of a cantankerous old skinflint, was sufficiently out of place to call for remark, where others were dressed in their gayest and smartest. But the black riding-coat and white breeches had an unmistakable cut and style that the gaudier clothes lacked. The bearing of the wearer, moreover, was no less singular. He neither slouched like the older men nor strutted like the younger. He walked with an easy swing of the body that turned his tall slimness into grace, when a less effective carriage would have laid it open to a charge of mere lankiness. His face showed paler than the ruddy-brown countenances that neighboured it, its expression, though rural perceptions hardly went so far, was more subtle, its capacity of a wider scope than these dreamed of in their ignorance. As far as features went, Nature had turned it out well, with a precision of outline that would suggest beauty to one class of mind, and coldness of temperament to another. It was a face where the emotions, real or assumed, were exhibited chiefly by the mouth and eyes. The latter, dark-hued, and pleasant, even when the lips were twisted cynically, had the physical peculiarity of one being brighter than its fellow, though the defect passed unnoticed by casual observers. Together they kept a sharp look out on the world of men and things, but were, in spite of their play of expression, little given to betraying the secrets of the mind behind. The lips, narrow, and of a good colour, proved a far better criterion of the owner's mind, for those who were wise enough to understand.

On this afternoon, they showed a disposition to curl upwards at the corners. Undoubtedly, he meant to enjoy the interview on the ramparts.

Meanwhile, there was enough to catch and hold his careless attention, as he walked down the street. He was not looking for a possible writer of the letter, since it seemed improbable that she would venture herself out of doors until dusk should cover her identity. But she was in his mind none the less.

The thought of the affair being no more than a hoax had crossed him once or twice without seriously affecting him. The suggestion necessitated no alteration in his plans. Should the lady prove to be none other than a vulgar cheat, he promised himself that he could deal with such, and read her a lesson which she would not forget in a hurry. Naturally, he argued, she would not be far away from the appointed place, since her curiosity would answer for that. And he would find her—yes, by gad, he would!—and after that, his tongue would have lost its cunning if he could not make her cheeks burn with a few quiet words.

Presently the rustic clamour and confusion drew him to itself, and he found that he was hemmed in among a crowd that swayed and craned around a cheap-jack. Mounted on a chair near a glittering stall of imitation jewellery, the man was voluble and persuasive, but the crowd was shy, and held back. Ridley listened with a kind of admiration to the flow of eloquence, almost convincing in its unveraciousness, which declared that only a week ago, an identical bunch of seals to that now offered for the sum of sixpence, had been purchased by the King himself.

"To say nothing of the many members of the nobility and gentry, gentlemen," cried the cheap-jack, pausing a moment to adjust the ancient beaver which was continually slipping down on to the tips of his ears. "All of 'em at this present minute wearing gold seals just the same as these. Going for sixpence, gentlemen! And to-morrow I'm going too! This magnificent offer cannot be repeated. Now then, ladies, don't be shy! Never mind your blushes. I'm a married man myself. Only sixpence—and your sweetheart will have the very smartest bunch of seals in Dorset, a-dangling from his fob, when he walks up the church on the happy day."

As the bait failed to tempt, and the seals had already been reduced from half a crown, the salesman adroitly dropped the trinkets, caught up a shining tin tray, and after banging it vigorously to rivet attention proceeded to lay on it circular pieces of metal. With another delicate adjustment of the hat, he launched forth again :

"Now then, ladies and gentlemen! Watch me! Here we have a dozen genuine half-crowns, all fresh from the Bank of England, and stamped with His Most Gracious Majesty's image. Hard as iron. Watch me!" He affected to bite one of the pieces. "And twenty times as val'able.

Very well ! Just to assure you, gentlemen—and ladies ! "
—with a bow which imperilled the beaver—" of the genuine-
ness of the other bargains, I am going to present these coins
—solid silver, milled and stamped—to anyone who cares to
accept them." A score of dirty hands shot out. The cheap-
jack whisked the tray out of reach, and continued, " For the
sum of three pence, the lucky lady or gentleman who is wise
enough to avail themselves of this remarkable opportunity
becoming the possessor also of a set of di'mond studs, as
recently worn by the Prime Minister at the Opening of
Parli'ment."

As he finished, the cheap-jack was ringed round by hands
of various shapes and sizes, all eager, and all clutching pence
in their fingers. The tray was emptied and generously re-
filled. Interest did not flag. Fresh hands were held out,
conspicuous among these being one of a greater cleanliness
than the rest. It was reached out from a point not far from
the young lawyer. Peering through the crowd to discover
the owner, he saw that it was a respectably dressed woman
nearing middle age, who thus proffered three solid pennies in
exchange for a disc of base metal and a few pieces of glass.
He had hardly traced the connection between hand and
face, and looked back again, when the woman's wrist was
suddenly grasped and pulled down to her side. Ridley became
slightly amused, for the fingers which had performed the
action were small and impetuous, and were daintily gloved
in yellow kid. At the same moment, a rather childish, but
very impatient voice exclaimed a protest. It was perfectly
audible to Ridley, for the crowd, on the whole, was a silent
one.

" How can you, mother ? How can you be so common ? "

" But, my dear, t'others are getting 'em, and they'll be
gone in a minute."

" Well, the idea of the thing ! " exclaimed the first voice.
" Really, mother, I wonder you haven't more pride."

" There ! They're all gone, Dolly. Ev'ry one ! I'll
never get another chance. Such a nice-spoken, handsome
gen'leman, too ! "

" Call that handsome ! " retorted the disdainful young
voice. " Come along ! I'm tired of this ! "

A slight movement in the crowd showed Ridley that the
unwilling parent was being dragged away by the daughter.
The ranks closed up quickly, and the cheap-jack's voice
ran on as volubly as ever. Ridley slipped out of his place,

and edged his way to the outskirts of the crowd. The little incident had interested him—it was so obviously the new running a-tilt the old—and he was in a sufficiently idle mood to care to look a second time.

The woman still stood in the roadway, staring about her. At her side was a girl whose dress and general style offered a sharp contrast to her companion's homely array. The elder woman showed undoubted signs of past good looks, and was dressed with an absence of the gaudy smartness which characterised many of the visitors. The girl was pretty ; not quite so pretty, Ridley decided, as she possibly thought herself, but sufficiently so for any swain on a fair-day. She was wearing a dress of some figured material, and the ribbons that fluttered round her were not of the pink colour affected by most country-girls, but of a delicate shade of mauve. She wore a wide hat, instead of the ordinary bonnet, and went gloved, whereas the other holiday-maids showed bare hands and arms in honest unconcern.

" Out of place ! " was Ridley's comment. " And, therefore, not to be admired."

The pair moved off down the road. Ridley, his idle interest still holding, followed them. A little block of sightseers brought him close upon them, and again snatches of conversation came to him. He never had any scruples in listening to what was uttered in public.

" I thought you wanted to come out," the mother complained, in a tone of gentle remonstrance. " And now you won't look at anything."

" What did you want to see ? " asked the girl.

" That conjurer—now——."

" Why, mother, I could see him stuffing the rabbit into the hat ! And I don't think he'd washed for a week ! "

The woman sighed audibly.

" Perhaps he hasn't much time," she said. " I thought him wonderful. It was a very pretty yellow jacket he had on. Where are you going now, Dolly ? "

" Sophy Hoddinott's down by the church, telling fortunes. I want to go there."

" Dolly ! "

" Well ? Oh, do come on ! Why not ? "

What the objection was, Ridley did not hear, as the crowd, suddenly breaking up, momentarily parted him from the two. But he caught the girl's reply half a minute later, and guessed the context.

" I'm not bound to do everything Miss Chideock likes ! "
she declared, the mauve ribbons all in a whirl, as she flung
her head about. "Because she can't enjoy a bit of fun,
there's no reason why I should mope too."

" I wonder at Sophy daring ! Miss Chideock said
she——"

" Yes, I know ! I can't think why she's so spiteful. Even
people who believe in it never pretend that Sophy's anything
but white."

" I don't hold with it all the same," objected her mother,
with the timid protest that foresees subsequent acquiescence.
" Sophy have said some very queer things at times 'Tis
tempting Providence, I call it."

" Nonsense ! " cried the girl. " She's white, I tell you.
And of course I don't believe in it a bit. Only——"

" Dolly, dear, I do wish you wouldn't. Miss Chideock's
sure to hear of it, and I'm certain she'd not like it. You
should try to please her ; she've been complaining of you
a'ready."

The ribbons fluttered again.

" I know that," said the girl. " 'Tis partly why I brought
you out. I suppose she told you about my burning the
jam ? "

" No—'twasn't that."

" About watering the roses, then ? How was I to know
it would spoil them ? "

" She didn't speak of it, my dear."

The girl appeared to wish that she herself had followed
such an excellent example. A few yards were covered in
silence. Then the girl broke out :

" Well, mother, you may as well tell me ! "

" She said you weren't quite so circum—something or
other, I forget her long word—as you did ought to be with
strangers. There ! Now I've a-told 'ee, my dear, and I'll
say this too, that I do wish as you could find it in your heart
to fancy young Robin Fiander, and let strangers go. There
be no need for you to ask your fortune of Sophy Hoddinott
or anyone else. 'Tis in your own hands it lies, under Providence, my dear."

" Now, mother, don't begin all that again, please ! I'm
sure I don't want a sweetheart worrying me at all, and, if I
did, it wouldn't be Robin. And as for strangers, if Mr.
Alaric likes to talk to me, I don't see that I can help it. Miss
Chideock talks enough to him herself."

" 'Tis different, that.   He's her cousin, you see."

" Well, 'tis no fault of mine !   I don't mean to let it spoil my holiday.   And I do call it unkind of you to scold me on fair-day, when you've not seen me for three months ! "

The woman's arm curved itself round her daughter's waist as they turned the corner that led to the church square. Here was evidently a young lady accustomed to have things very much her own way.

" And I've anathematised you, my dear, for getting into my clerk's weak head, and turning it upside-down ! " Ridley thought, as he continued to follow leisurely in their steps, his casual interest filliped by the discovery.   " And, curse it all, you pretty hussy," he added, " he's a deal too good for you, and so I shall tell him on Monday ! "

A few yards farther on, he again lost sight of them.   At one side of this securely remote space, tucked away from the main street at the extreme limit of the town, a small crowd had collected.   It was composed mostly of young people of both sexes, all wearing a somewhat sheepish air of having merely strolled in without any particular object.   Seated on a stool, with her back to a wall, was the fortune-teller, a dark girl, shabbily dressed and of no special appearance.   What her features were like it was impossible to tell, for she kept her head lowered beneath the hood of her sunbonnet.   At her clients themselves she never glanced.   Palm after palm she examined, while Ridley, recollection stirring in his mind, watched her over the heads of the crowd.   But her eyes went no higher than the hand in her own.   Possibly it was part of her game to pretend that no aid from face or identity was needed.   She appeared to speak glibly, and gave her patrons no more than a few minutes each.   As the crowd diminished, new-comers took the vacant places.   There was no doubt that Sophy Hoddinott was popular.   The square held other attractions, noisy and novel, but the white witch held her little court against the wall, successfully competing with all her rivals.

Ridley, who had sought to charm away warts by the aid of the fraternity in the old days, and who had recalled the fact that this girl's name was the same as that of his late uncle's old bemused clerk, lingered in this corner until Dolly Pouncey had worked her way to the fortune-teller's side, and ostentatiously drawn off her gloves.   With her retirement, red of cheek, and dimpling with smiles, his interest in the scene died down.   He waited until she had dragged her mother off in search of other genteel delights, then he strolled quietly away. He spent an idle hour on the Western side of the town, watching the tail-end of the fair itself. Business proceedings were being wound up with the removal of innumerable pigs in open carts, unsold heifers were loosed and driven away, the trader's remaining stock of whips and harness was packed up, and slow-footed farmers and drovers left the spot to find the most congenial amusement that the day provided.

CHAPTER V

IN THE DARK

THE street had reawakened to a subdued stir when Ridley left his inn for the second time, and stepped out to keep the appointment. Round the door of the house which he had just quitted, and at various illuminated points about the town, small clusters of men and vehicles indicated that Wareham Fair was over for another six months. The outlying farmers were returning home. Such centres of light and conviviality were noisy enough, otherwise the place was silent as usual. This produced the paradoxical effect of making the whole town seem alert and active, inasmuch as to a person standing between two such farewell groups the noise of each came sharply through the still air, striking the listener from either side, and confluxing in his vicinity. There were few foot passengers about, and though Ridley glanced keenly at such as passed by he failed to distinguish a woman's form among them.

It was after nine o'clock, and dark to a degree, when he made his way along the lane-like road that presently brought him out on the ramparts on the Eastern side of the town. He mounted up until he was at a considerable height above the roadway. Short smooth grass deadened his footfall; on one side he found a continuous tangle of bramble and gorse bushes, on the other, only the shelving sides of the earthworks. It was very dark close at hand, but away where the horizon might be supposed to lie a pale radiance illumined the gloom, like dim earthshine. The night was cloudy, and the young moon no match for the masses of vapour stretched across the zenith. From below, on his right hand, Ridley could hear the crisp rattle of the last of the gigs as they crossed the bridge at the upper end of the town.

He had walked along, wary and alert, for more than a

third of the distance before he found anything to arrest his attention. He was forced to watch by sense of hearing alone, and for the first ten minutes the ramparts were apparently his own and no other's. But at the end of that time his ear caught the sound of a slight rustle some little distance ahead. It was soft, suggestively feminine, seductive as a caress in the stillness of the night. Ridley halted instantly.

The sound was repeated, nearer at hand. Undoubtedly there was some one ahead of him. Something in the unusual nature of the situation appealed strongly to him at this moment. The lady, he reflected, with a pleasurable cynicism, was coming to meet him. He would wait where he was— she should make the second advance, even as she had already made the first.

A shape grew out of the gloom all around him. He smiled as he thought he grasped the significance of the fair one's being able to sight him before he distinguished her. His eyes were even now only growing more used to the obscurity. Hers had obviously been straining and peering into the darkness for a far greater length of time.

" If you please, sir——" said a voice at his elbow.

Then Ridley pursed up his lips in a soundless whistle. He recognised the voice. There was in it a childish intonation that a lover would find fascinating, and another woman regard as an irritation. It was, in fact, the voice of Dolly Pouncey.

" Oh, please, sir, will you come this way ? "

" Why ? " asked Ridley, feeling the pressure of fingers on his arm, but not moving. " I'm very comfortable where I am."

" I'm glad to hear you say so ! " the childish voice answered plaintively.

" How's that ? " asked Ridley. " Aren't you ? "

" Not at all ! I'm frightened of the dark."

" Ah ! " he said. " Still—I can't help that, can I ? "

" I didn't say so. But will you please to come ? "

" You can't expect it, unless you give me a good reason," he said.

" You came to meet a lady, didn't you ? "

" A lady, I believe, has come to meet me."

" Yes—that's it ! She's over there, a little farther along."

" Indeed ! "

" You were to come to her."

" The devil I was ! "

" And I'm afraid I shall fall—the brambles tear one so."

" Hold my arm then," said Ridley. " Though, as you know this place so well, I should have thought that you could better have guided me."

" It looks different in the daytime," murmured the girl, as they set forward. Then she suddenly paused. " How do you know I live here ? " she asked.

" I know many things," he said.

" That will do ! " cried a third voice, when they had walked some thirty yards, and Ridley halted. The girl's hand dropped from his arm, where it had clung a little too closely during the walk. He bowed in the darkness, the night hiding the mocking deference of the salutation. " Now, miss," said the stranger, " go—and remember what I told you."

The girl vanished into the immediate gloom, moving with the sure foot of a cat. The other woman remained motionless and silent for half a minute, as though listening to her companion's retreat. Then she spoke.

" Will you walk along the bank with me, sir ? " she asked.

He turned ; she accompanied him, a gliding shape with a voice, no more. When they had gone a certain number of paces, she stood still, and uttered a low call. There was no response. He heard her breathe deeply. The next moment she addressed him.

" Since we are in no danger of being overheard," she said, " this spot will do. Come, sir, let us get to our business. You received my letter, and considered it worth your while to come. That is a good beginning."

" I can find a better," he said, in his pleasant tones.

" State it, sir."

" You received no letter from me, I fancy, yet you also considered it worth while to come."

Then a little sharp sibilant sound, following on his words, told him as clearly as if it had been noonday that the sting had been appreciated. He could imagine the rush of blood to her cheek. He waited for her response. It came at length, cool and dignified.

" Have I led you to suppose, sir, that I am considering myself at all in this affair ? "

" I bow to the correction, Miss Chideock," he said.

" Considering the circumstances, I admit that my suggestion
is scarcely justified."

She leant towards him. He could feel her breath hot
upon his cheek. It was almost like a blow.

" You are infamous ! " she said.

He laughed.

" Did you summon me merely to call me names ? "
he asked.

" Why not ? " she retorted, with a wit as keen as his own.
" You have called me by one—you called me Chideock.
Why ? Why ? "

" A simple love of the truth, my dear lady. What
else ? "

" A trivial ruse to trick me into betraying myself," she
cried. " Oh, I see I must be on my guard with you lawyer
fellows ! "

" Prudence comes a little late, I fancy, madam," he
said.

She was silent at that. In the gloom, he saw her fall back
from him. Presently she answered, with less heat than he
had anticipated.

" You are right there, sir ! I have committed something
to you in allowing this interview. Secretiveness is now
necessary to me for that very reason."

" I have no desire to probe and pry, I assure you, madam,"
said Ridley, who was puzzled as well as amused by the
encounter. " The knowledge of your identity is a question
of mind rather than of matter—since I can swear that I
never set eyes on you in my life."

" Of mind—how ? " she asked.

" By an intelligent working of the same," he told her.

" You are very self-confident," she returned. " Think
what you please. With the workings of your mind, I have
little to do."

" Why did you wish to see me ? " Ridley asked.

She hesitated, taken aback by this call us move of
his.

" My letter—I thought you understood," she muttered.
" That explained."

" Possibly," he said. " But at present I cannot refer to
it. I recollect that it was rather obscure. Perhaps you
would kindly refresh my memory."

Silent again for a moment, she appeared to brace herself
together. He could fancy her throwing back her head.

There resounded in her voice the firmness with which she had opened the interview.

"I made you an offer," she said.

"Ah, yes!" replied Ridley, with an amused laugh, calculated to make her writhe. "So you did. Well?"

"Have you considered it?" she asked, and he could hear the excitement struggling in her throat.

He kept her waiting for a moment.

"It is a matter, madam," he told her, then, "which a man might reasonably be permitted to take his time over."

"You have had three days," she said.

"True. Yet I made up my mind in less than three minutes."

"You are bewildering, sir," she stammered, catching her breath. "I thought you were blaming my haste."

"No," said Ridley. "Only your forwardness."

"Ah!"

"Before I give my answer," he went on, as she remained silent, "I should like to hear what your plans are."

She plucked up spirit, and stamped her foot on the grass.

"Plans!" she cried. "They cannot concern you unless you are going to accept my proposal!"

"And you are beginning to fear that I am not."

"Fear!" she broke out. "Why do you say that?"

"Come!" said Ridley pleasantly. "Let us understand one another. Why do you want to marry me?"

"Why?" she returned, her foot still tapping the grass— he could hear it, throb, throb, like the beating of an over-strained heart—"Why do women ever wish to marry? Because I love you, of course."

The words were uttered with a glibness that lessened their boldness by detracting from their sincerity. Ridley himself stood silent, tricked for the moment into gravity. That spontaneous affection was at the root of her request he had never believed, but her earnestness was such that it might well have sprung from that cause. Here was neither hoyden nor hoaxer. In truth, he was at a loss what to make of her. In all her utterances he recognised that note of pride which had sounded so clearly in her letter. A pride so evidently inborn and natural to her that not even her anxiety could hide it. Her imperiousness saved her name. Ridley ratified his previous decisions, and only regretted their negative quality. It was easy to say what she was not ; less so, to guess at what she was. Here he felt tolerably certain of only one thing. The lady was young—her voice and movements alike indicated youth. He found himself wondering whether she were good-looking. Or had indeed her lack of physical attraction induced her to try this odd mode of obtaining a husband ? Was her pride more consistent with plain features or downright ugliness than with a lost reputation ? The very notion of pride seemed, on the surface, at variance with her present position. Yet there it was, unmistakable. And it put her beyond the pale of ordinary judgments. No, he could make nothing of her. She was a puzzle, a mystery. Meanwhile, she was waiting. He suddenly realised this.

" You say that you love me, madam," he said. " The words are rather amazing, I find."

" Why ? " she asked with a deeper touch of hauteur. " Gentlewomen have loved beneath them before now."

In the darkness Ridley flushed. After that, he resolved not to spare her. The insolence was so delicate, so unconscious, that it was unforgivable.

" I did not mean that," he said. " The immensity of the honour paralyses thought in that direction. But you have hidden your own sentiments so well that only a fool would have so concluded."

" Well, well, accept the statement now," she said, " and be content."

Ridley was silent. When she spoke next, he noted with satisfaction that her voice was sharp with anxiety.

" Surely you can see how very much to your advantage a marriage with me would be ! "

" I understand that so well," he said, " that I confess I am curious to hear the other side."

" How do you mean ? "

" Taken at your own value," he explained, " here is a lady, well-born, and exceedingly wealthy, who wishes to unite herself in marriage with a poor country attorney, of no particular achievements or ancestry. There is no reason to suppose the lady absolutely brainless, and although she claims affection as the basis of her extraordinary desire her every word and tone give the lie to that assumption. Mere disinterestedness would hardly stretch to such a point. It must surely be that she has something to gain. The question of what this may be forms a rather interesting speculation for the fag-end of a busy week."

" Oh, but this is intolerable ! " broke out his companion.
" You will drive me mad ! I was a fool to trust you ! You
shame me utterly ! I will withdraw my offer ! I thought—
I hoped you were a gentleman. Did you only come here to
insult me ? "

" I came," said Ridley, with enough of a drawl to give
point to the words, " to amuse myself."

" At my expense, sir ? "

" Certainly not—at my own."

She drew back, gasping. He had matched insolence with
insolence, carefully and successfully. Whatever her hopes,
they must needs have fallen from her at that moment. There
was a short pause, and into that silence Ridley laughed. He
had promised himself enjoyment at this interview. Standing
there, with three feet of darkness between him and the woman
who had magnificently condescended towards him, to seek
her unknown ends, he was getting his enjoyment thoroughly.
For he heard her sob, even as he laughed.

He would have turned on his heel and left her, contemptuously, rudely, while his laughter still hung in the air, but she
sank her pride to address him again.

" Is this your answer, sir ? " she cried. " Are you so blind
to your own advancement ? "

" I cannot sacrifice my independence to please you," he
said. " Plainly, I do not wish to marry you. If I did——"

" Well ? Well ? "

" I would have done the courting myself. Take a word
of advice from a lawyer, madam, without a fee——"

" Oh," she cried, " do you think that I have not paid—
most heavily ! You are modest, you common lawyers, then !
—you rate your words too low ! Say what you have to—a
last insult, I suppose, a final insolence ! How dared you
come to make a sport of me ? "

" If I had foreseen any regret in the matter," he answered
blandly, " I should not have done so."

She caught at his words.

" Regret ? " she repeated. " Do you regret coming here
to-night ? "

" Not in the least," he told her, as though he spoke the
thing that she would wish to hear. " I shall long remember
this meeting. It has been most amusing. A little romantic
interlude of this sort comes in so refreshingly among
the drier details which make up the life of — a common
lawyer ! "

With that, he bowed towards her in the darkness, gave her a pleasant " Good night," and left her there.

She waited until the silence had swallowed up the echo of his footsteps, then, with bent head, she walked slowly back the way she had come. Anger had for the time been absorbed by some deeper feeling.

CHAPTER VI

THE GAME CONTINUED

RIDLEY spent the night at Wareham, purposing to return home the next day, shake the incident from his mind, and fit himself for the serious business of the following week. From these plans he was diverted by a somewhat freakish fancy of his own.

As a matter of fact, the affair refused to be shaken off.

Whether he would or not, he found his thoughts reverting to it all through breakfast-time, and his meal was enlivened by an occasional reminiscent chuckle of satisfaction. The Chideock Affair, he called it to himself. The name stuck oddly in his mind. He took a pleasure in mouthing it to himself. It had a full round shape, as it were, and brought the muscles of the lips into excellent play.

" It runs in my head," he told himself, presently, " that the Chideocks are clients of mine. If so, it would explain the lady's attack on me——" he drank half a cupful of coffee, and then added—" perhaps. At least, it would account for her knowing of my existence. And, by gad, sirs, I don't think she'll forget it in a hurry ! "

This young man had stepped into his uncle's shoes no longer than eight months ago, and had been too busy reaching out in new directions to pay much attention to the connections already formed. Ambitious and modern in his ideas, he had mingled a little recklessness with his self-sufficiency, and had been more anxious to infuse fresh life into the old practice than to nurse it as an already established concern. At odd moments he had glanced through ancient documents and endeavoured to make himself master of the secrets entrusted to the firm. But it had been a task rendered more difficult by the absence of anyone who could enlighten him. Fiander, an even more recent arrival than himself, naturally knew nothing. The old clerk, whom he had found in sole charge, after his uncle's death, he had speedily sent off. For some months previously, the old fellow had been incapable of doing more than imperil the reputation of his employer.   His retention so long was merely attributable to his master's parsimonious habit of mind.   With his decline of usefulness his salary was lessened.   Thus the respectability of the firm, as evidenced by the presence of an aged clerk, was maintained on next to nothing.   When young Ridley came on the scene, old Amos Hoddinott was engaged in drinking away the few wits left to him.   To have kept him on would have meant maintenance at the expense of the firm in a double sense.   Kenelm Ridley, more generous than most people believed, pensioned the old man off, and selected Robin Fiander in his stead.   Hoddinott retired into the country, the money being conveyed to him by the hand of a carrier once a month, and Ridley thought no more about him.   But his possible connection with the Chideock family, as clerk to their lawyer, made the young man's mind revert to him this morning.   He was inclined to regret not having learned something about his uncle's clients from the old man.

" I suppose it's my own fault," he told himself, presently, as he stood looking out into the quiet street.   " Perhaps I ought to have called on 'em.   I wonder why I didn't !   Too devilish afraid of their patronage, I suppose.   I'm sorry now that I was so uncivil.   It would have paid—I could have estimated last night's interview better, if I had— perhaps ! "

He stood there thinking.   Once he moved with extended hand towards the bell-rope.   But his arm fell to his side before he had touched it.   He had assured the lady that to pry out her identity had no interest for him, and as yet the desire was not overwhelming.   He would learn what he might from possible letters and documents in his own office, which would be a legitimate enough proceeding, but he would not question the townsfolk.   At the same time, there seemed no reason why he should not take a look by daylight at the scene of last night's encounter.

Church bells were ringing, and a thin stream of people was filtering down the main street as he stepped out into the open air.   These were making for the lower end of the town. Ridley, turning in the opposite direction, followed his own tracks of the previous night.   Reaching the walls, he paused and looked about him.   Seen in the fresh morning sunlight, with the mellow tones of ancient bells vibrating the still air, the only impression wrought on a mind attuned to the present was a vivid imagining of the past. Here feudalism had placed its foot upon an Anglo-Saxon civilisation, and left an imprint that had lasted on into the nineteenth century. Here Time might be thought, if not to stand still, at least to slumber, and to dream impressively. Events which had swept away castle and nunnery had spared the older foundation, and these turfed mounds appeared so fresh in form and composition that they might have been supposed to nourish the same grass-blades that had bent beneath the tread of those barbarians who had followed on the sandalled heel of Imperial Rome.

A thin mist hung over the middle distance, and deepened in the shallow hollows of the pasture-land to the left. The position of the sea was a matter of instinct rather than of perception on such a morning as this, but the swelling of the far-off downs, which heaped themselves into a huge shoulder away to the left, marked the line of a broken and rocky coast. On the immediate right of the walls, the ground fell away to the level down sparsely covered slopes, and met the hedges or stone walls of the adjacent gardens. Ahead, beyond the limits of the town, the road to Corfe gave tokens of its existence where sunny patches of white appeared among the outstretching green. The course of the river could be traced only by the density of the mist.

Ridley, though not insensible to either the picturesque or antiquarian aspect of things, was not in a sufficiently detached mood to dwell long on the beauties or impersonal associations of the scene. To appreciate the far-away past needs an isolation from more immediate memories—a contrasted attitude of mind that looks back from the standpoint of to-day over the length of years. Whereas, to be interested in yesterday, pulls the imagination up short, and foregoing centuries have no meaning for it. And Ridley, after the first careless survey of his surroundings, was thinking of last night.

Here was the spot where he had first become aware of a second presence. Here, Dolly Pouncey had joined him. There, the fair unknown had revealed herself by those sharp words of greeting. So his eyes ran over the ground, with an amused look in them, until they suddenly became riveted on one spot, and brightened with a new interest.

He was staring at something that shone as yellow as the gorse flowers above it—some foreign substance that had no place among the grass and brambles. With quick movements he reached the spot, and raised the trinket. It flashed joyously in the sunlight — a gold chain formed of faceted links with a locket attached. Ridley turned it about and whistled softly.

"Ho ho!" he said, and pieced together a pretty theory as to its loss.

He had no doubt that the trinket belonged to Miss Chideock. It was far too costly to be an ornament of little Dolly Pouncey. An intricate monogram was engraved on the face of it. Examining this more closely, he made it out to be O. C. or Q. C.— he could not be certain which. The fine chain had snapped in two. He could picture the anxious imperious woman waiting a full hour before his arrival, pacing up and down, tugging at the chain around her neck in her impatience and doubt. How often, he wondered, had her hand dragged at it, while his words and tones lashed her for her immodesty? How wild must her temper have been, as she fled home, self-humiliated by the failure of her schemes, since she had not discovered her loss, and hastened as soon as possible to search for her treasure.

He held it in his hand while he decided what to do. Restoration was a matter of course. The manner of it, less so. He considered the point leisurely. It was clear, after the shortest period of thinking, that by losing her ornament, Miss Chideock had given him another card to play. It only remained to choose the most effective way of doing so.

The idea of calling openly at her house, and announcing his find, was not sufficiently attractive. It would merely inform her that he was convinced of her identity, and had discovered her residence—no difficult task in a town where she must be well known. She would naturally refuse to see him, and he would be forced to retire with the unpleasant sense of having done her a service. He laughed at the suggestion, and stood weighing the trinket in his palm, as if he were calculating how many grains it contained, whereas he was merely deciding how many additional stings he could pack into the simple act of giving it back to its owner.

At length a way appeared to him that satisfied his ironical temper, and promised no obligation to the lady.

"And she ought to thank me for that!" he thought, with a dry laugh, as he made his decision. "If I read her aright, she'd hate to owe me anything as much as I should hate being of use to her!"

He took out his watch, removed the ribbon, and replaced

it by the gold chain, afterwards knotting the broken ends together, and putting the watch back into his fob. Instead of the customary strip of watered silk and bunch of seals Miss Chideock's chain with the locket attached now dangled from his waist. The alteration was conspicuous enough for his purpose. Should the owner cast eyes on his adornment she could not fail to recognise it. Indignation alone would prompt her to claim it. And could she deny her identity after that ?

Ridley walked on, left the earthworks, and reached the lower end of the town. He was now not far from the spot where the white witch had held her court on the previous day. No one was about. The bells had ceased ringing ten minutes ago. He would probably be the last to enter the church towards which he was walking, but that was an accidental embellishment of his plan.

The outer door stood open. Entering the porch, Ridley took care to let it swing-to heavily behind him, and groped his way in the consequent darkness to the body of the church. With his eyes still full of the sunlight without, obscurity here also seemed to threaten his plan. But his natural assurance suffered no check, and he made his way in his heavy riding-boots to the top of the nave. The building appeared to grow lighter, and before settling down he knew that not a single head in the sparse congregation had remained at its normal angle since his arrival.

Ridley was not an irreligious nor a prayerless young man, and for the present he made no further attempt to disturb the devotions of his neighbours. Having taken a place at the top of the church, he had restricted his own observations, since both decorum and diplomacy alike prevented his staring at those who sat behind him. Whether Miss Chideock was one of these, was a matter of conjecture, and a rather important one—for the success of his scheme depended on the assumption that she was. Still acting on this supposition, Ridley sat, knelt, and stood throughout a somewhat tedious service, with the apparent detachment of a St. Simeon Stylites.

At length the congregation got to its feet, with the unconscious bustle of relief that follows on a more or less enforced inactivity. Ridley turned slowly, threw his outer coat well away from his waist, and took a leisurely survey of the backs of the departing worshippers.

Not a few of the heads were turned again in his direction. He bore the scrutiny without embarrassment, as his manner was. Finding in these near by nothing to interest him, he continued to run his eyes along the multi-coloured stream of townsfolk that was moving down the aisle. A familiar profile suddenly struck on his gaze, arresting it with a sense of amusement, as he recognised his old enemy, Farmer Pouncey. His presence was easily understood, though Ridley had missed meeting him on the previous day. By the side of the farmer's red visage appeared the paler, more refined features of his wife, and Ridley hunted round with his eyes, until he had discovered Dolly's winsome face, peach-like and demure, moving along with the rest, some few paces in advance of her parents.

He waited until the church was nearly empty before taking his own departure, and when he got outside Dolly Pouncey had disappeared. Not much surprised or disconcerted by this hiatus in his plans, he strolled down to the bridge that crossed the river at the lower end of the street. The church-goers had melted away, the quiet associated in a country mind with the Sunday dinner-hour lay over the little town, the time and place alike were well suited to a consideration of events.

The bridge was of stone, five-arched, with a wide parapet, giving at both ends a low drop into the meadows that banked the river. The prospect was broad on either hand, and was, as a whole, a more detailed view of the same country over which Ridley had gazed some two hours earlier. Locally, the position gave him a good sight of this end of the town, and, in turn, made him a conspicuous figure to anyone coming in this direction. The young lawyer leant over the left side of the bridge, and wondered who this would be. While he waited, he removed the locket and chain, and slipped them into the deep pocket of his riding-coat. Should the lady herself come to claim her property, he was determined to give her no lead. Should she depute the errand to another, he would refuse sight of the ornament save to the owner.

That Dolly Pouncey at least had seen and recognised the trinket, he had scarcely a doubt. It was possible that by now its loss had been discovered. She would, so he argued, report its unexpected reappearance to Miss Chideock, and search, either authorised or in person, would be made for him. In view of this, a return to his inn was the obvious course. But Ridley, with his natural bias towards the original, preferred the bridge. Miss Chideock had chosen the first meeting-place ; it was his right to choose the second.

Why should his site be less picturesque than hers ? Moreover, he was minded to lead the lady a dance before she
found him.

Half an hour passed. Beyond a boy driving cows to
fresh pasture, he had seen no one. The fact that he was
growing hungry did not improve his temper, but he stuck
to his post patiently. After his first careless scrutiny of his
surroundings, there was not much to engross his attention.
He counted fishes down below until the occupation was a
weariness. Then he lolled against the side of the bridge,
and read over the words on the iron tablet affixed to the
opposite wall, until he could have repeated them backwards.
They notified a recently passed Law, and were emphatic as
such things usually are.

DORSET

ANY PERSON WILFULLY INJURING
ANY PART OF THIS COUNTY BRIDGE
WILL BE GUILTY OF FELONY AND
UPON CONVICTION LIABLE TO BE
TRANSPORTED FOR LIFE
BY THE COURT

7 & 8 GEO 4 C50 S15   T FOOKS

" A damned wicked Law too ! " thought Ridley at the
first reading. But at the fiftieth the words had lost their
sinister meaning, and his eyes wandered again to the end of
the street. What he saw caused him to turn in an idle
manner, and bend his long lean figure over the parapet once
more.

Footsteps pattered alongside. His attention was fixed
on the river below. Some one touched his shoulder. He
turned to meet the blue eyes of Dolly Pouncey. His hat was
already in his hand, but his sleek black head bowed before her.

" I beg your pardon," she began, with a running glance
over his well-favoured face and form, " but I think I saw
you in church."

" Indeed ! " he said. " That's not unlikely. I was there."

" You came in late."

" I'm afraid I did, Miss Pouncey."

Her eyes ran up to his.

" How do you know my name ? " she asked.

Ridley, leaning easily against the wall, laughed. Miss Chideock, he thought, had chosen a very agreeable delegate after all.

" There was a witch here yesterday," he said.

" Oh, yes. Poor Sophy ! But I don't believe in that nonsense, of course."

" Yet you had your fortune told," Ridley reminded her.

" How do you know that too ? " she cried.

" You did ! " he persisted.

" For the fun of the thing," she admitted. " There was no harm—and Sophy's been very badly used."

" In what way ? " he asked.

" Locked up ! "

" What on earth for ? She seemed a respectable sort of person."

Dolly looked as if she could say much, but made no reply Meanwhile, Ridley remembered.

" Ah, of course," he said. " Your Miss Chideock threatened her."

The girl shot another glance at him.

" What a lot you do know, to be sure ! " she cried.

" Don't I ? " said Ridley.

Dolly Pouncey continued to gaze at him. A genuine regret was showing in her eyes.

" I can't think how I came not to see you yesterday," she remarked.

" It was dark," he said.

" I mean—before that."

Their eyes met again. A confident kind of amusement glowed serenely in his ; hers glittered with half-rueful consternation.

" How you force me to say things that I don't mean to ! " she exclaimed pettishly. " I'm afraid of you. You find out so much."

" I haven't gone out of my way to, I assure you," he replied. " In fact, there's still a deal I don't know."

" Then you'll not learn it from me," she declared. " I ought not to be here at all talking to you. I'm supposed to be lying down with a headache. Father would be angry if he knew."

" Where is he then ? "

" Down at the Pure Drop, having dinner with mother. They're going home to Medley's Croft presently. I slipped away because——"

She paused, a little anxiously.

" Well ? " he asked.

" Sir—I don't know your name, and 'tis not important to me—when you came into church, you were wearing—a chain——"

Again she hesitated. Ridley, wondering in how far she was a cat's-paw, declined to help her out.

" Well," she went on in a moment, " a friend of mine has a locket and chain just like that one, and I thought it very probable she might have lost it last evening, and you have picked it up. Did you find the one you had on ? I'm certain she was wearing hers last night."

" Where did she lose it ? " he asked.

" Oh, I suppose, wherever you found it."

" Did she think she recognised the one I wore ? "

" Dear me ! She knows nothing about it. I've not seen her this morning."

" She hasn't sent you, then ? "

" No, she hasn't. I recognised the locket, and thought I'd better get it back for her without saying anything to anyone. Please let me have it."

" Wait a moment," said Ridley. " How did you find me ? "

" I met the sexton," said Dolly. " And I asked him which way you'd gone. Of course, every one noticed you in church. And he said he'd seen you leaning over the bridge ten minutes ago."

" And you're sure Miss Chideock didn't send you ? "

" No, she didn't."

" But she'll be glad to get it back again ? "

He thrust his fingers into his pocket as he spoke. Dolly's hand flew out.

" Very ! She values it so much."

Ridley withdrew his fingers with a laugh. They were empty.

" Then Miss Chideock must come and ask for it herself," he said.

CHAPTER VII

SABBATH-BREAKING

THE girl beside him gasped at his audacity.
"If you'd only heard what she said last night
you'd not ask it of me," she declared.
"What ? Are you afraid to take the message ? "
"You needn't put it so unpleasantly as that, but——"
"She's got a temper, then ? "
"It is pretty bad at times," Dolly admitted, in con-
fidence. "Oh, yes. Miss Quenride can say things when
she likes."
"That's a mighty odd name," commented Ridley. "Worse
than my own. Quenride ! Smacks too much of feudalism
for my tastes. I suppose she is feudal, by the way ? "
"She's hard to get on with," said the girl.
"And who are you ? What part do you play in the house-
hold ? "
"Whatever she pleases ! Sometimes it's tracing her
embroidery patterns, or else it's helping with the cakes and
pies, or it's playing piquet with her, or reading to poor little
Mr. Gilbert, or walking out with her when she's dull, or——"
"I understand," said Ridley. "A gentlewoman's maiden !
I knew she was feudal ! "
"She may be," said Dolly, without comprehension.
"But she's not always interesting. I sometimes think I'll
go back home. Last night I almost told her so."
"What was she so outrageous about ? " asked Ridley,
with a smile.
"I suppose it was because you found out her name. She
declared that I must have told you. Unreasonable, wasn't
it ? "
"Tell me," he said, "what is the lady like ? A regular
fright, isn't she ? "
A pair of innocent blue eyes stared up at him.
"Why, she's quite the prettiest lady you ever saw ! "

" Ah," said Ridley. " but I haven't seen her, you know. That's what I want to do."

Dolly suddenly wondered whether she were not wasting time. The impulse to run out and recover the locket had been genuine enough. But the episode had undoubtedly been seasoned by the vituperous remarks of her father during the walk from church, which turned a mere incident into an adventure. The young man, she found, was civil, but luke-warm and irresponsive. Moreover, he evinced an unreason-able interest in Miss Chideock. What was between the two, Dolly Pouncey did not know, and was not greatly troubled about. But that he should turn his eyes so persistently in the one direction, was irritating to a degree. She decided that if she could prevent it, he should not see the lady.

" I think it extremely unlikely that you will see her," she told him. " She wasn't well when I left the house this morn-ing, and she doesn't like you, and—really, sir, you had very much better let me have the locket and go ! "

" Not I ! " said Ridley, who had been watching her care-fully, and seeing a good deal more in her face than she guessed at. " Not I, my dear ! "

" Oh ! "   Then, deciding that this was a propitious moment for an affected retreat, " Very well, sir—then I shall go without it ! "

She moved a few steps away, still looking at him. Ridley appeared unconcerned.

" You'll carry my message ? " he asked.

" I'll not promise," she retorted, turning away.

" One moment !   Wait, I say ! "

" I can't !   I mustn't !   'Tis your own fault ! "

" Come back !   Tell Miss Chideock—— "

But Dolly, stimulated by a fancied advantage, had broken into a ladylike run, and shook her head without looking round.

" You little hussy ! " muttered Ridley, under his breath. Were his plans to be upset by this trivial butterfly ? He set his long limbs in motion and caught her before she was well off the bridge. With one arm round her waist and the other hand tilting up her chin, he put his lips to hers with a laugh.

" There, my dear ! " he cried.   " 'Tis what you were wishing for, isn't it ? "

The kiss was flavourless, for it lacked ardour of any sort, being diplomatic, and not emotional. But since that was not to be imagined by an onlooker, the results were sufficiently far-reaching. Dolly herself detected something missing in the episode, but like a wise maiden made the most of what was given. As soon as she could, she uttered a moderately shocked scream, and another more convincing one, on hearing her first drowned in a roar arising not many feet away.

Ridley, still with the tantalising smile on his lips, looked over her startled head, and dropped his arm quickly. Farmer Pouncey was bearing down upon him in a way which promised about as much self-control as might be expected from a mad bull.

" It was your fault ! " gasped Dolly mendaciously.

Something in Ridley was touched. She was so small and pretty—and contemptible.

" He shan't blame you," he promised.

There was no time to say more. The angry father, torn away from his Sunday dinner to search for his missing daughter, was already shaking his leg-o'-mutton fist in the young man's face.

" You owdacious rascal ! " he roared. " What the blazes do 'ee mean by it ? I'll l'arn ye to lay a finger on my maid— roast me if a' don't ! I bain't in your house now—and you shall smart for this, by the living jingo you shall ! "

Ridley stepped back, and answered never a word. The cause of all the trouble had retreated to the edge of the bridge, and was crying with fright.

" Why the blazes don't ye answer ? " cried the farmer, red and furious. " Say some'at, can't ye ? or I'll heist ye over the bridge by your long spindle-shanks, ye black-coated, black-hearted young devil ! "

" Go on," said Ridley.

" Go on—ay ! " cried his enemy. " I'll go on to please 'ee. I'll let 'ee know what I do think o' ye, afore I've done. An' then it shall be *go on*, to another tune, you scoundrel, an' it'll be one as your dandified skin won't like ! "

Ridley flicked a finger at him.

" Can't 'ee speak ? " roared Pouncey. " Be struck dumb ? "

" I'm waiting till you've finished," the young man an-swered. " When you have, I'm going to knock you down."

In his anger, the farmer had circled round, so that their relative positions were now reversed. Ridley had his back to the town. As he made his announcement, he leant his elbow on the parapet of the bridge, in a half-languid, wholly confident manner that drove his heated antagonist to frenzy.

He endeavoured to repeat the lawyer's words. An inarticulate roar was the result. In his distress he rolled his eyes round, and a satisfied gleam sprang into them at once. He threw out his hand.

"Did ye hear him, ma'am?" he cried. "Did ye hear the swindling rogue? Take witness—I call on ye, ma'am—he said he'd knock me down!"

"I heard it," said a voice from behind.

Ridley's natural impulse had been to look round as soon as he was aware of another presence. But the moment was inconvenient, owing to the uncertainty of the farmer's procedure should he be left unwatched for a second. Consequently, Ridley did not move a muscle.

"What is the trouble?" he heard the voice ask, coming closer.

The tones were cool and collected, but not to be mistaken—the speaker was set in authority. So much the young lawyer gathered from the voice itself, and Pouncey's demeanour provided corroboration. He descended, through the several processes of anger, vindictiveness, and defence, from ungovernable rage to the subdued self-confidence of a chastened man about to be justified. His attitude was at once deferential and important.

"Ye do know well enough, ma'am," he began, "what brought me down here. Seems to me 'tis a pity I ha'n't come some time back. There's my darter, as you do see, ma'am, an' here do stand the knave as trapped her to come here to taste his wicked lips. Be a man to put up wi' that? Be I to touch forehead, an' say ' thank 'ee, sir,' to a rogue as I finds kissing an' cuddling my own maid, on the King's Highway, on a Sunday marning? Be I to, ma'am? Or be I to let en feel the weight o' my fist, as a feyther should?"

"It seems reasonable," remarked the new-comer, with a touch of hauteur. "In any case, it is a most disgraceful scene for a Sabbath day, and I am not pleased."

Ridley turned while she was speaking. She finished what she had to say with her eyes locked in his. There was just enough of mocking amusement in his bow to inform her that no introduction was necessary—that he was well aware who she was—that she stood revealed before him as the writer of the cold love-letter, who had developed into the impassioned woman of last night.

But the mockery was an afterthought—almost an instinctive act of self-defence. For at first sight of her, he stood astonished. Questions raced up and down in his mind even after he had recovered his composure. Questions to which there were no answers. If Mystery had cloaked her in the darkness, the broad daylight drew its folds more closely round her. She stood before him, and he wondered at her—wondered that such bright beauty, such a queenly carriage, such a perfect air should ever have stooped—should ever have needed to stoop, to ask for crumbs from his own sparsely-filled hand.

She met his gaze calmly, almost indifferently. Her cheek showed a high colour, but this, he reflected, might be natural to her, since a certain richness of tint seemed to be the dominating note of her beauty. It lay upon her lips, shone in the warm grey of her eyes, and glowed in her hair, which was neither red nor gold, but a ruddy and alluring combination of both. Her mouth was soft and tender, so that, looked at alone, it suggested a gentle and yielding disposition. Taken in conjunction with the other features, it merely prevented pride from deepening into haughtiness, and detachment from hardening into severity.

" She makes a bid for sympathy with her mouth and chin," thought Ridley, " and dares you to offer it with her forehead and eyes."

After a moment's cool scrutiny of her, he spoke.

" If I had known that the Lady of the Manor was approaching," he said, " I would have ended this painful scene five minutes ago."

" You would, would you ? " cried Pouncey, breaking out anew. " Knocked me down then, a' reckon ? "

" Certainly," said Ridley. " I'll do so at once, if the lady pleases."

" You do hear en, ma'am? " So the farmer appealed to her. " You do see for yourself what a damnation Radical it is."

" A very dangerous man," said Quenride Chideock. " But you're surely not afraid of him, Farmer ? You've a remedy. He's used threatening language to you. Why don't you give him in charge ? "

The attack was so unexpected that Ridley was startled into a look at her—a thing which he did not mean to do unless on his own initiative. She appeared unconscious of his glance, and he bit his lip in genuine annoyance.

But Pouncey smacked his thigh gleefully.

" Lard love 'ee, ma'am," he cried, " what a grand head-piece ye've a-got ! 'Tis the very thing ! A day in gaol will cool his hot blood, for sure, an' l'arn en not to meddle wi' my darter no more."

Ridley turned a crimsoning face towards Miss Chideock.

" What devil's folly is this ? " he asked, not wishful to choose his words. " What possible charge can be brought against me ? Do you know who I am ? "

" Very well," she answered ; and for the first time he heard a tremor of anger in her voice.

" Then," he made sharp retort, " you should think twice before you side with this blatant fool ! "

But Quenride Chideock had recovered herself. She met his blazing eyes calmly.

" Surely," she said, " you do not suggest that I should side with—you ? "

Ridley laughed suddenly.

" By heavens, no ! " he said. " Yet it might be prudent not to interfere, madam."

" It is you who have interfered," she answered. " This girl is a member of my—that is, of my grandfather's house-hold. She is therefore under my protection. I do not choose that a maid of mine should be inveigled out by a stranger, and treated in this light way."

" Inveigled ? " repeated Ridley, with a delicate raising of the eyebrows. He would have said more, but he happened to catch a piteous glance from Dolly Pouncey at that moment. So he refrained himself, and threw up his shoulders in a way which suggested that the lady's opinion was nothing to him.

" There is no great harm done," he said. " I have been indiscreet, possibly, since Miss Chideock's regard for the proprieties must surely be well known. Beyond that, I think, there is no more to be said."

She scarcely heard him out. With a quivering lip, and hands which she vainly tried to keep steady, she swung round upon the other man, who had merely decreased his anger from boiling to simmering point, and was ready to fan it into the intenser degree at a word from her.

" After all, Farmer," she cried, " 'tis your affair, not mine ! The man has insulted your daughter and used violent language towards yourself. Moreover, he has broken the peace of the Sabbath with his disgraceful brawling. You are a church-warden in your own parish. If you can forgive him all these things, it will be time for me to speak."

"Madam," cried Ridley, "in the name of my profession, I compliment you! Your talent for perversion would win admiration at the Old Bailey itself!"

She flashed a look at him, but was waiting eagerly for Pouncey to speak. The farmer, backed up by such authority, which went further than Ridley was aware of, was not slow to follow her lead.

"By gemini, ma'am," he cried, "I'll not shame my nation by letting such wickedness go unrebuked. 'Tes my duty to make a public example of the villain. He may beg an' pray for marcy, but he shan't find none. Not till him an' all his thievish kind be given their dues, can honest men hope to lay safe abed. Now then, come along o' me! And when you're laid by the heels, I'll go an' finish my victuals with a better stomach for knowing as you can't do no more mischief to-day."

Ridley took a swift survey of the position. Chagrined at having allowed himself to fall into such a hole, he still knew that, left to himself, he could have managed Farmer Pouncey as successfully as on the previous occasion. To attempt now to appease his more powerful enemy by a more or less detailed account of what had actually taken place, would land Dolly Pouncey into pretty trouble. He had promised to shield the girl, and he would not fail her. Moreover, apart from Dolly, he doubted if such an appeal to Quenride Chideock's sense of justice would be attended to. Even if it were, the inevitable conclusion must be a tame handing up of the locket—a proceeding as distasteful to him in his present inimical mood as an arrest itself. There remained the alternative of knocking down the farmer, and making a rush for it. A hasty reflection convinced him that this was impracticable, since the combined malice of Pouncey and Miss Chideock would pursue him to his own town, where publicity would render the affair doubly annoying. There was nothing for it but to submit.

He looked at the fair face opposite to him. The soft mouth had tightened. There was no probability that she would allow the farmer's anger to cool. Plainly, it was with the lady that Ridley had to reckon, though she snatched at the opportunity of making Pouncey her mouthpiece. Ridley smiled and bowed.

"You are exceedingly eager for my punishment, my dear lady," he said. "One would almost believe that you were moved by private animosity. For my part, I think

3

that quite enough has been said over a trivial affair. If, however, you have any interest in pushing the matter further. I am content to place myself in the hands of your Justice, whoever he may be. No sensible man would think twice about dismissing the case."

A curious expression flittered across Quenride Chideock's face. But the next instant she had turned to lay a silencing finger on the farmer's arm. Only just in time, for already his great mouth was gaping for speech.

" As a person of some authority in this place," she answered Ridley coldly, " I give my full approval to your arrest. I cannot have the town disturbed in this way on a Sunday."

He shrugged his shoulders.

" Then there's nothing more to be said," he conceded, with a fine assumption of indifference. " I'm staying at the *Red Lion,* so you'll know where to find me when you want me. I'm not going to run away ; I'm merely returning to my inn. I wish you good day, madam."

Again he bowed, with a bold, bright glance into her eyes —a look which drew them to his, and held them there, help-less, defiant, with a touch of fear behind. Ridley recognised this, recovered his composure, and laughed lightly as he turned away.

Farmer Pouncey stretched out a hand after him.

" I bain't going to take my eyes off of en ! " he cried.

" Follow him then," said Quenride. " Only don't touch him, if you love your life." She drew herself up with a shiver. " He's a dangerous man—oh, he's dangerous ! "

Ridley was walking quickly away. Pouncey set off after him. As he went, he happened to remember his daughter, and stopped for an instant.

" Do 'ee see to the pore maid, will 'ee, ma'am ? " he called. " She be fair scared to death."

" She'll come home with me," said Quenride.

" Very good, ma'am. I'll send her mother up to her when I've a-settled the rascal."

Quenride stood as if she had not heard. So she remained until Ridley's riding-coat, with the farmer's blue broadcloth in close attendance, had disappeared from view. Then she swept down upon the shrinking Dolly in a very whirlwind of fury.

" You light little creature—you common-minded girl ! " she cried. " When I gave you permission to spend the day with your parents, was it that you might degrade yourself

by flirting on a public highway with a man who's a stranger
to you? Back you go to your dairy for this! I'll bear
no more!"

"I wouldn't be any use in a dairy!" moaned Dolly,
crushed by this tirade, but most heavily by being charged
with a lack of gentility. "Father wouldn't have me there!"

"Your father! If I told your father the part you played
with that man, he'd lay his stick across your shoulders, and
upon my honour, it would do you no harm!"

"I've done no wrong," protested the tearful girl. "I
can't help people kissing me—I never can! And after all,
he only did it to coax me into letting him see you! And
I'm sure I don't know why you came here after me."

"You've no right to be told," retorted Quenride. "But
'tis simple enough. I wanted to speak to you, and when I
got to the inn they told me that you were lying down. You
were called, and could not be found. Your father started
off to look for you, and I followed. I saw Timothy Hutchins,
who told me—as he'd just told your father—that he fancied
you were down on the bridge with a gentleman. That
seemed a matter for looking into! I know you well enough
to guess how you behaved. Your lack of self-respect wearies
me! You will flirt with any man!"

"I don't," said Dolly, with a spark of indignation. "And
if you really think it all my fault, Miss Chideock, I don't know
why you were so hard on the gentleman himself just now."

A wave of colour swept over the other's face. Dolly
dried her eyes, with the perception that she had said something cleverer than she had intended. Her wits cleared a
little more.

"And after all," she went on, vehemently, "I really
don't see that 'tis so much worse to talk to anyone in the
open, in broad daylight, than it is to meet him in a lonely
place, at dead o' night, when no one's looking. Of course,
I'll not tell, as I promised not to——"

Quenride Chideock was furious. Her eyes blazed at the
now frightened girl, who shrank away as from a blow.

"How dare you?" cried the other, quivering no less than
she. "How dare you bring me down to your own level,
you insolent child?"

Then, with a sudden pulling of herself together, she
turned and walked back home, Dolly following at a little
distance. Remorse on Ridley's account, and timidity on
her own, combined to check any elation which she might have

felt at the result of her last sally, the effect of which was to be more wide-reaching than she could foresee. The immediate result was Quenride Chideock's complete reticence as to the secret meeting on the ramparts. From this moment, she never alluded to the occurrence again. As a consequence, she forbore to mention to the girl the loss of the necklace, although she had sought her with that selfsame intention. Dolly, smarting under Quenride's biting words, dismissed all thought of responsibility, and left it to the lawyer himself to restore it when and how he pleased. Thus, the fragile ornament, with its broken chain, remained that day in the young man's pocket, to become a not unimportant link in the bit of local history of which his friend the Governor had seen the beginning, with no suspicion that the latter end should touch even himself.

CHAPTER VIII

DECLARATION OF WAR

HALF-WAY up the street, Ridley became aware that Pouncey was no longer following him. But he built nothing on that. Herein lay wisdom, as the event proved. The farmer had merely diverged into the open doorway of a cottage, in order to command the services of the constable who was to keep the culprit in custody until the morrow. This individual held a variety of offices in the town, and was no other than the sexton who had directed three persons to the bridge within the last hour.

Ridley was waiting in the coffee-room, straddling across a chair, with his arms folded over the back. Having made up his mind that escape was likely to lead to greater disaster, he was ready to put a bold face on his present trouble. But he loved Miss Chideock none the better for her meddling.

Pouncey took the matter in hand at once.

"There he be!" he cried, with denunciatory finger outstretched. "Take him off, constable, and hold him tight. 'Tes my charge, an' there bain't a doubt of his guilt."

The other man advanced slowly, with an air of respect, which Ridley appreciated, angry though he was.

"A' reckon there be some mistake," said the new-comer appealingly.

"Devil a bit!" cried Ridley himself. "I'm your man, officer. But I'd be obliged if I could dine first. I'm as hungry as a hunter."

The point was conceded with alacrity by the constable, and grudgingly agreed to by Pouncey, who insisted on remaining in the room until his enemy left the house. Ridley prolonged the meal to its utmost limit, then rose leisurely, and declared himself ready to accompany Hutchins. There was nothing in his cool well-mannered acceptance of facts to suggest the maelstrom of angry cynicism which he was preparing against his next meeting with Quenride Chideock. For one thing, there was in Ridley a deep vein of honesty, though, like his other virtues, it was seldom recognised. He had no quarrel with this obviously right-minded officer of the law which he himself lived by. In truth, since the moment of the arrest—an informal enough procedure—Hutchins had relinquished his status as constable, and had risen or fallen as the case might be, to the more peaceable rôle of sexton and parochial gossip.

Called back, by the termination of the meal, to his immediate duties, he grew shamefaced and apologetic towards the prisoner, so that, when the pair left the inn, some confusion of identity might easily have arisen.

"Where are you going to take me?" asked Ridley, when Hutchins, with an unexpected show of authority, had sent Pouncey about his business.

"I doubt I must take thee to my home," said the constable. "There's some one a'ready in the lock-up."

"I'd like company," said Ridley, unabashed.

"But, sir, 'tis a young woman!" Hutchins's ecclesiastical side was to the fore again. "'Twouldn't never do!"

"A woman? Then, for heaven's sake," cried Ridley, "put me anywhere but there! I never want to set eyes on one of the sex again!"

"That bain't a Christian way o' looking at things, sir," remonstrated the churchman. "'Male and female created He them.' Who be us pore martels to differ from He?"

"According to that, woman was made while man slept," Ridley reminded him drily. "No doubt, if man had been wide awake, he'd have had a say in the matter. 'Twould be a heavenly world without 'em."

The other shook his head.

"A' don't reckon Adam thought much o' the Garden till he see Eve in it," he said. "We don't know even now that we be in Paradise, until there's two o' us."

Ridley walked a yard or so in silence. Then he said:

"Since there can't be two of us in the lock-up, why don't you take the woman under your roof, and let me make shift?"

"She's only a common body," Hutchins made slow reply. "Besides, to tell 'ee the truth, my wife 'ouldn't hear of it."

"Why not? Isn't she respectable?"

" Nothing against the maid as I knows on, sir. But, you see, they do say she's *wise*, and my wife do think 'tis well to let such folk alone."

" What has the girl done to get herself into this trouble ? " asked Ridley presently. His interest being personal rather than professional, he contrived to throw the latter quality into his tone as he put the question.

" No harm as I knows on," said his informer. " Only Miss Chideock don't hold with her ways, and hev warned her a'ready. She do say 'tis a wicked sart o' a livlihood, and hev put her foot down on pore Sophy."

" Miss Chideock seems to rule the roast here with a vengeance," remarked Ridley drily. " Surely she doesn't believe in the fortune-telling nonsense ? "

" I don't know about it bein' nonsense," protested the sexton, with deferential dissent. " But Miss Quenride don't believe in it, and do say as Sophy shan't cheat the folk in this town."

" Indeed ! A high and mighty madam, I perceive, this Miss Chideock of yours."

" Proud as the devil," affirmed the pillar of the church.

" And the girl—she's some relation of old Amos Hoddinott, I suppose ? "

" Gran'uncle, he be. Nigh childish now, they says, pore soul."

" He was that nearly eight months ago. Well—I hope the girl will get off lightly, and disappoint your fine lady."

The sexton stared.

" Lard love 'ee, sir, don't ye know ? "

" What ? " asked Ridley.

" Miss Chideock—she be our Justice. Leastways, one of 'em, that is."

" What ? " cried Ridley, again.

" 'Tis true, sir. On the Bench she do sit, alongside the Parson and Mr. Mayor, so bold as ninepence, if a common chap may say so. 'Tis an ancient right o' the ladies o' the fam'ly, granted to 'em ages ago by the Vargin Queen. They do say as 'twould take an Act o' Parlyment to dislodge she. As to that, I can't speak, but 'tis true as gospel that Miss Quenride do hear the cases every Monday marning so sure as ever the day do come. And atween me and you, sir, 'tis said as she do twist t'other pair round her pretty finger."

" A female magistrate ! " exclaimed the young lawyer " She ought to be ducked ! "

Then the personal side of this discovery occurred to him, and his brow grew dark.

"Do you mean to tell me," he asked, stopping short on the sexton's doorstep, "that I shall be brought up before this lady to-morrow morning?"

Hutchins looked apologetic, but did not deny it. Ridley swore softly. He understood now why Miss Chideock and Pouncey had exchanged glances at his confidence in the prospective magistrate. Small wonder indeed that the vixen had carried things with so high a hand. An uneasy curiosity took hold of him. It was a concession to Quenride Chideock's authority to put the question, but he could not refrain, though he asked it as indifferently as his smouldering anger would allow.

"And what sentence does Miss Chideock usually give for Sabbath brawling?—which is the charge they are going to bring against me."

His companion stared fixedly at a point several hundred yards away, and had the decency to throw into his voice considerably more of the impersonal quality than Ridley had managed to do, as he replied:

"She gen'rally do give an hour or so in the stocks for that."

"Thank you," said Ridley, and stepped over the threshold.

He followed the man in silence up to a tiny airless attic under the roof, having declared that he preferred solitude when the choice was placed before him. He ordered Hutchins out of the room when he stood fidgeting with his eye on the key. Ridley then locked the door himself, flung the key through the casement, which was open, and shouted out to tell his jailer what he had done. Having thus settled Hutchins's wavering sense of duty, and safe-guarded his own honour against a possible temptation to escape, he sat down on an unfurnished truckle bed and damned Miss Chideock very heartily.

"She'll never dare," he said to himself, presently, when by reason of repetition the futility of his occupation became apparent. "She may bluster a bit; but she'll never dare. After all, I've got the whiphand; and if I was worth wooing as a husband I must be worth conciliating as a friend. At least, I should think so! Hang that little hussy Pouncey! What a fool I was to have anything to do with her! That was the outcome of Fiander's interest in the first place, I suppose. And so, damn Fiander too!"

The afternoon passed slowly. The cottage was situated in a side street, and the view, even when he craned out of the casement, was limited and uninteresting. When a slender meal was brought up to him by the constable's wife, he asked for something to read, was supplied with a Bible and a Culpepper's *Herbal*, and so spent the time until dusk crept into the poorly lit room. He then hammered on the door, which the woman had unblushingly locked, and shouted for candles. These were presently brought by Hutchins himself. He carried a letter in his other hand. This he handed to Ridley with a diffidence that suggested the writer at once.

"'Twas brought a moment back," said the constable. "Very like my lady hev changed her mind."

Ridley broke the seal.

"SIR,"—he read—"It is possible that we can come to an understanding. If you will promise on your word of honour to return the former letter which I addressed to you, you need be under no apprehension of to-morrow. The bearer will convey your written reply. None other will be accepted.

"QUENRIDE CHIDEOCK."

Ridley folded the letter, and whistled softly.

So! She had stooped to bribe—almost to threaten. Had she been playing for this situation ever since the first encounter on the bridge? Whether or no, the move was adroit enough. The pity of it was that she had overshot the mark. Without hesitation, Ridley set about proving that she did not yet know her man.

He humoured her so far in that he wrote the reply, instead of sending it by word of mouth. But this was merely because he knew that if given verbally, through the medium of two or three persons, it would lose some of its neatness. He tore a page from his pocket-book and pencilled a note as brief as her own.

"MADAM,—I find I am unable to comply with your request. You have made it impossible, by seeking to turn a favour into an act of feeble propitiation, which would look like nothing so much as an acknowledgment of fear.—I beg to subscribe myself, Madam, your very humble servant,

"K. RIDLEY."

He knew that she was clever enough to read the double

meaning conveyed in the few lines, to understand his full appreciation of her own position—whose the true desire for propitiation was, and what it indicated. It pleased him to let her see that he knew how weakness and anxiety were masquerading as pride and power. At the same time, he was aware that in a sense he would have been wise to yield, and let her have the satisfaction of thinking him afraid. But Ridley's way was seldom that of other men, and even when the answer had been irrevocably dispatched he still found pleasure in the reflection that he had dared her to do her worst.

When it had grown quite dark, Hutchins again came upstairs, bringing a couple of blankets for the prisoner's bed. Ridley asked if Miss Chideock had sent any other letter for him.

" She hev not," he was told. " Nor won't now. They do shut up early at her place, 'cos of pore Mr. Benjamin."

" Her father ? " asked Ridley, for he was quite ignorant of the family.

" Gran'dad, sir. A pore wold bedridden creature, hardly to be called a man."

" Ah," said Ridley, " that's the reason, I suppose, that the lady takes so much upon herself. Is there no other man about the place ? "

" Only Mr. Gilbert, sir. And bein' a lad, an' crippled at that, he don't count for much, though Miss Quenride thinks the warld o' he."

" A lively household ! " said the young lawyer. " An invalid old man, a cripple boy, and a shrew to govern 'em all ! "

" A' wouldn't care to say that," amended Hutchins slowly, " though she've grown sharp-tempered of late. But there, 'tis likely the pore maid has trouble enough. Mr. Benjamin were always close-fisted and thirtover, and 'tisn't to be believed he should be any sweeter in his sperit now. 'Tis well known a' won't spend a penny on aught, for Miss Quenride do sign the paper money now. I reckon he leads her a sorry life, an' they say Mr. Alaric do worry her a tar'ble lot."

" What ? Another of them ? "

" Her cousin, sir ; not much liked, to speak in your honour's ear. He bides out Bridport way. 'Tis whispered as he be courtin' the lady for the sake o' the wold man's money-bags, for the Chideocks be rich folk, though the

Mohuns be pore as Job. But Dolly Pouncey, she says
' No ' ; they do quarrel so often as they meet."

" Your young lady is an heiress, then ? "

" 'Tis said so. The wold gen'leman hev brought her up,
you must know, sir. And he hev always hated the Mohuns.
When he were on his lags Mr. Alaric dursen't hardly show
his nose in the house."

A sudden thought struck Ridley.

" Good Lord ! " he said. " What a pretty family for a
man to marry into ! "

Hutchins had finished arranging the blankets by now,
and was ready to go. He paused at Ridley's last remark,
and smiled slily.

" An' yet it 'ouldn't be so bad a thing to be Miss Quenride's
husband," he said.

" How do you make that out ? " asked the other.

" She've the power to go again' the law, as well as to
help it," explained the constable. " 'Tis the privilege o' the
Chideock ladies, an' a girt one it be. If any o' their male
folk do get into trouble wi' the Crown, they may claim his
life as their due—so Sovereign Queen Bess did say, her bein'
so pleased wi' the randy they give her in wolden times. It
hev been the savin' o' one or two wild young rakes a'ready,
and will be o' more yet, no doubt."

" They have used the privilege, then ? " said Ridley,
who had never troubled his head much about the bygone
history of the county families.

" You may say that, sir. Back in wold Judge Jeffreys'
time they saved a lad, though his worship were sore again'
it. An' one o' fam'ly—not so long ago, neither !—med ha'
been hanged for bein' too smart wi's pen—God forgie I for
speakin' so of a gen'leman !—only his lady took the matter
up, and 'twas found as neither King, Lards, no, nor yet
Commons, couldn't undo what her Blessed Majesty had signed
an' sealed all they years ago."

" A very nice legal point," commented Ridley, wavering
between irritation and professional interest. " Perhaps the
precedent stood for something. At any rate, it seems that
your young madam can correct her husband with the stocks
and whipping-post, or save him from the gallows, just as she
feels inclined."

Hutchins laughed loudly.

" 'Tis a tidy way o' puttin' it," he said. " Yes, in a
fashion o' speech, 'tis true."

"Is she likely to marry, by the by?" asked Ridley, with assumed carelessness. Do what he would, this perplexing creature of blood and brains moved his interest more strongly the oftener he heard of her.

"She med ha' married at least three times to year," said the constable, shaking his head. "But she sent 'em all away—good county matches every manjack of 'em! No. Our young lady don't seem to hanker after the holy estate at all."

"Don't she?—by Jupiter!" muttered Ridley to himself, as he lay down among the blankets, and thought of Hutchins's last startling declaration. "Sends away three good likely fellows, and throws the handkerchief to a poor devil like me! Bewildering, to say the least of it! What the deuce can her game be? And what's she going to say to me from the Bench to-morrow?"

CHAPTER IX

A GAZING-STOCK

B Y noon the next day, Ridley was taking the situation with a seriousness which he had hitherto denied to the affair. Quenride Chideock, whether from malice or impetuosity, had shown herself capable of a vindictiveness and daring which he had scarcely anticipated. As a result, he was suffering a disgrace which would make him a figure of fun wherever the tale was told, and might even damage him as a professional man at a time when all his resources would be taxed to the uttermost. It was small wonder that he nursed his spirit in bitterness, and cursed the hour when he had taken up her challenge.

He had spent one hour in the stocks already, and two more, according to sentence, were yet to pass. The irksomeness of the ignominious position had hardly so far made itself felt. But he was growing conscious of it, and the effort to maintain his customary easy air under annoyances was becoming momentarily more laboured. He sat very still, reserving his strength as well as he could, knowing, in the grimness of his humour, that he would probably need it before he had played out his own part that day.

The proceedings had been grossly unfair. From the moment of entering the chamber where the court was held, he had felt that his fair enemy meant mischief. He denied the charge—which was that of brawling on the previous Sabbath Day—but refrained from naming Dolly Pouncey as a witness on his behalf. The girl, who might have said enough to make a conviction impossible, was not called. Her father, who between his implanted antagonism to the prisoner and his awe of Miss Chideock was capable only of the most incoherent evidence, gave a heated and incorrect account of the meeting. Ridley listened with an air of insolent toleration, and was daring enough to smile, when the senior Justice conferred with his colleague, who looked very proud and handsome on the Bench. Three hours in the stocks. He knew that she had suggested an extra hour on the strength of that smile. He therefore repeated it— making it a little more pronounced than before—and shot a look of defiance straight into those beautiful eyes of hers, as he turned to leave the court.

But, for all that, he was furious. He had kept his word to the silly child who had helped him to this plight, but the satisfaction was small. The fact itself merely deepened the injustice. Under this he was smarting keenly. But by far the most galling thought was the knowledge that he had pitted himself against a woman—and got the worst of it. This was a new experience for Lawyer Ridley, and one which lacked the proverbial charm.

He had been conducted to the place of punishment by the friendly Hutchins, who had locked his ankles in almost tearfully, and promised to release him a little before the appointed time. Farmer Pouncey came to see the sentence carried out, and was then forced to take a reluctant departure, and return home. A small crowd collected after the constable had gone, to stare at the culprit. The sight itself was not an uncommon one, especially after a fair-day, when much drinking and subsequent quarrelling prevailed. But the circumstances were novel enough to excite a torpid interest in the rustic mind. For the first half-hour, Ridley sat under a fire of eyes, and though he managed to smile, albeit a little rigidly, he could not keep his cheeks from burning. But, on the whole, he carried off the shameful situation with as fine an air as many a better man might have done, and, if his wrath smouldered still more bitterly as his pains increased, his eyes were calm and pleasant, and his manner composed.

Either there had been fewer delinquents at this particular season or Quenride Chideock had been absorbed in her own affairs. It was easy to believe that Hutchins would wink at many things at such a time. At any rate, for the first hour, Ridley had the stocks to himself. After that, the gazers having dispersed, a companion was provided for him in the person of the girl, Sophy Hoddinott. She was placed beside him, sullen and passive, and Hutchins went away again, with a cheerful assurance to her that it was only for an hour, and a commiserating glance at the other victim.

Ridley looked at the girl. Quietly at first, then finding

that she took no notice of him, more boldly. She was young, well under twenty, he judged, but neither graceful nor pretty. A certain colourlessness weakened her into insignificance, and lent a pinched look to features of no marked characteristics in themselves. Her figure was undeveloped, and would probably never fill out, her hands were coarsened with work, her dress was unbecoming. Masses of dark hair fell untidily round neck and forehead, her soiled sunbonnet hanging half-way down her back. Her mouth was too hard for her years, her eyes too brooding. She seemed to be one whom the world could scarcely be said to have disappointed, for it had obviously made no promises. Her attitude, as she sat there, staring unemotionally forward, might have been taken as a symbol of her outlook on Life.

Ridley, beneath his cynicism, had good natural sympathies, and when these moved him he recognised them as such, and gave them full play. He knew now that he was sorry for the girl, quite apart from the fact of her being another victim of his own enemy. He determined to rouse her. To address her outright would probably have no effect. At most, it might awaken that suspicion, never very deep down in an untrained mind, that she was an object of ridicule. Ridley therefore spoke, but not to her, or to anyone in particular, though a few loiterers paused to listen before he had done.

In an even pleasant voice, too monotonous to suggest religious fervour, too calm to be irreverent, he recited the Hundred and Nineteenth Psalm. At the end of it they were left alone. But the girl had not moved. He straightened his back wearily, and started off again. This time it was the curse from *Manfred*, with much dramatic feeling thrown into it, and he had the gratification of seeing her shiver.

She turned her head slowly, lifting a pair of brooding eyes with conscious effort.

" Don't 'ee," she said.

Ridley smiled at her—a smile which had nothing behind it.

" I'm sorry you're here," he said.

" Why ? " she asked, half a minute after he had spoken.

" Because it's no fit place for a woman."

" What about you, then ? " she asked.

He shrugged his shoulders.

" You're different," the girl went on. " You're quality. You didn't ought to be here neither."

" Well, if that's so," said Ridley, " since we're both here,
all we can do is to make the best of it for each other's
sake."

" If you like," she said vaguely.

She was countrified without a doubt, untaught, un-
polished. Yet her accent was smoother than might have
been looked for, and intelligence lurked plainly behind her
listless manner. With her brooding eyes, and odd passivity,
it was no wonder that her neighbours called her *wise*.
Had her unattractiveness been of a more pronounced order,
possibly she would have been shunned as an evil thing.
As it was, popular prejudice exalted her peculiarities into a
reputation for knowledge of the more beneficent kind.

" Why won't you look at me, Sophy ? " asked Ridley,
after another attempt to ease his cramped body from the
tension. " I looked at you on Saturday. You gave good
fortunes to the other girls, and couldn't mend your own."

" That be the way of things."

" Poor Sophy ! I wish you'd promised Dolly Pouncey a
miserly sot for a husband, and sent her off crying. It might
have helped the hussy to mind her own business."

" I'd not wish any of the maids that ! " said Sophy, with
vehemence.

Ridley bit his lip. For the moment, he had forgotten
Amos Hoddinott, drink-sodden and doddering.

" Poor Sophy ! " he said again, and resolved to double
the old sinner's pension for her sake.

" I don't see why you should care ! " she burst out.

" You're not very friendly," he laughed.

" You're a gentleman. I thought all the gentry hated the
poor."

" I don't think I do," he said. " Come ! You've no
quarrel with me."

He reached out his hand, and caught hold of hers. She
tried to pull it away, but presently yielded to the soft warm
pressure of his fingers, and let hers lie in his clasp quite
passively. The sensation was novel. She had never touched,
scarcely even seen a hand so smooth and yet so firm before.
She took it between her palms, and examined it with an
absence of self-consciousness that reacted on her companion.
Ridley was no more embarrassed than he would have been
if a child had played with the seals on his watch-ribbon.
The girl passed her fingers over the smooth skin with a
sense of luxury, noting the fine texture of it, the carefully

trimmed nails, the shapeliness of each finger, the narrowness
of the wrist. She knew that it was a finer thing than she
had ever handled in her life, and she prolonged the moment
caressingly, until some sense of race-antagonism stirred her
empty heart, and she flung his hand away.

" Thank you," said Ridley. " Did you see anything
particular in it ? "

" 'Tis a gentlefolk's hand," muttered the girl. " I reckon
'tis no good."

" At least," said Ridley, " I've kept it clean."

But Sophy did not understand. She flushed, and glanced
at her own.

" 'Tisn't dirt," she said. " 'Tis the colour."

" I know that," he said.

Their eyes met. The flush, instead of dying away, continued to stain her cheek. When her glance fell, she had
grown apologetic and humble.

" I'm sorry I was rude," she said.

" Don't mention it ! " cried Ridley.

Presently he looked at his watch.

" Your time's nearly up," he told her. " Twenty minutes
more ! Then you'll be free. Are you tired, child ? "

" 'Twill be raining long afore I get home," she said. " I'll
be wet through."

She cast her weather-wise eyes up at the sky. The day
had been dull and lowering. Thunder was about. Ridley
himself had been watching the masses of leaden cloud banking
up in the south-west.

" One needn't be among the prophets to see that," he
remarked. " But I suppose you're a good judge of the
weather, Sophy ? "

The girl seemed pleased at this careless praise, though she
answered him evasively.

" The good God writes His signs plain enough," she said,
" only the fools can't read 'em."

" You live out Corfe way, don't you ? "

" Ay."

" What are you looking at ? Who are those people ? "

Two figures were approaching. The girl had her eyes
fixed on them. Glancing from them to her, Ridley was
surprised at the eager vindictiveness of her expression. For
the moment, her face was almost repulsive. She gave no
answer to his question, and the two pedestrians came nearer.
The one was a stout elderly man in livery, the other a sickly

looking youth of about fifteen, who went with a limp, and leant on the servant's arm. Abreast of the disgraced pair, he forced his companion to halt, and looked at Ridley with a half-smile, betokening, not recognition, but amusement. It was perhaps the hardest moment that the young lawyer had encountered that day. But he met it bravely, and bared his head with a courteous salute. The lad instantly coloured, and turned towards the other victim, who spat suddenly at him, and cried out an ill wish. The man immediately led the boy away.

"Why did you do that?" asked Ridley. "He seems a nice lad. And I think he was sorry for you."

"He laughed at you," said Sophy. "I hate him—ugly lame brat!"

"Who is he?" Ridley asked, though he had already guessed.

"Her brother."

"Miss Chideock's?"

"Ay."

"Fond of him, isn't she?"

"She'd sell her soul for him, they say."

Ridley thought this over. Then he said aloud:

"Seems hard to fancy her being fond of anyone."

Sophy darted a glance at him—a glance so shrewd, yet at the same time so elusive, that it set him wondering. He had never pretended to understand women, so he found no solution to it, but an odd sense of discomposure followed, and he was relieved to be able to start a fresh topic.

"Here's the rain!" he said.

Sophy drew her shoulders together with a word of dismay. Already the great thundery drops were spreading in patches on her flimsy cotton gown. Ridley remembered that she had some few miles to walk to reach her home, and that possibly the townsfolk might refuse assistance and shelter to one who lay under their great lady's displeasure. With some difficulty, he stripped himself of his outer coat, and handed it over to her.

"Put it on," he said.

She hesitated, staring.

"Put it on," he repeated. "Over your head and all. Do as I tell you, child!"

"But—you?" she stammered. Yet already she was obeying him, not eagerly, not in a frightened way, but as if he were forcing her to it.

" I'm well protected," he said curtly.

She pulled the coat over her head and shoulders, and sat enveloped in it, even down to her imprisoned ankles. Silent she sat. There was no word of thanks, no sign of gratitude. The immensity of the consideration overwhelmed her. She felt almost ashamed.

The rain descended on the pair in torrents. The flash and roar of the storm were elsewhere. Here were floods of water, sweeping the townsfolk indoors, and driving the less fortunate ones afield to the poor shelter of tree and hedgerow. Ridley bent his head under the deluge. The rain poured on to neck and shoulders, so that in a very few minutes he felt himself wet to the skin. He knew that a sensitive throat would pay for this day's adventure, and the prospect, in his present mood, had the power to augment existing misery. Yet, with it all, his obstinacy increased, and his spirit was far from being broken.

When the rain, after ten minutes' downpour, abated some-what, he raised his head, shook out the water that had collected round the brim of his hat, and sat up. Sophy's hour of detention had been exceeded by five minutes on account of the storm, but the girl was warm and dry, and Hutchins was at that moment coming towards them. Ridley touched her arm.

" All over for this time ! " he said, with a great show of cheerfulness. " And for God's sake, don't let it happen again ! "

Her grave eyes peered at him from beneath the hood she had made of the coat. Hutchins was close at hand.

" How about you ? " she asked.

" Oh, I've got another hour of it ! " he said.

" Another hour ? "

" About that."

" Miss Chideock must hate you a lot," said Sophy, musing.

" I wonder ! " he said.

Then the constable came up, and set the girl free. She had been sitting at the unhinged end of the stocks, and, after stretching her limbs in the rain, she moved slowly round and stood at Ridley's side. He smiled at her, holding out his hand. Hutchins waited a little impatiently.

" Good-bye, Sophy," said Ridley.

She did not take his hand, though at first her own had fluttered towards it.

" I wish you was coming too," she said.

" Come on, maidy ! " cried Hutchins, whose duty it was to see her out of the town.

She began to take off the coat. Ridley protested at once. The rain was not yet over, the girl had some distance to go, and he himself could hardly get any wetter than he was already.

" Keep it," he urged. " Go home in it. Give it to the old man ; make yourself a pelisse out of it. I don't want it back."

" You mean you won't wear it again after me."

" Silly child ! There—take it and go ! I really want you to have it."

She wrapped it round her ; it covered her from head to heel, the skirts dragging a little round her feet. Seeing this, she pulled it quickly up, and came a step nearer.

" Nobody never gave me anything afore," she whispered. " You're good to me."

" Good-bye," he answered, in a matter-of-fact tone. " Don't keep our friend here waiting."

She moved away, suddenly came back, then caught his hand, and kissed it once. There were tears, he saw, in her eyes.

" Nonsense, child ! " he said, and pushed her away.

The next hour passed slowly. He missed his homely companion, and had more time to think of himself. His cramped position was becoming a positive pain, and his mouth grew a little grim as he thought of the injustice. Running his mind back over the incidents which had led to his present distress, he came at length to the important discovery that he had allowed Sophy Hoddinott to carry away the Chideock locket and chain.

At first he was undeniably vexed. But a moment's thought convinced him that no great harm was done. The girl would know that he had never intended the ornament to go with the coat, even though it lay in the deepest pocket. And she was honest. He would swear that she was honest. She would bring it in to Dorchester next market-day, and he would give her a couple of guineas for her trouble. If the truth came out in the meanwhile, and Quenride Chideock demanded her property, he would have it ready for her by the time that she cared to come. And if Dolly had said nothing, he would approach the owner himself as soon as the chain was restored. Assuredly no harm was done.

After a long time—or so it seemed—Hutchins again
appeared, his red face shining cheerfully through the rain,
which had now turned to a steady drizzle. He carried the
key of the stocks in his hand, and seemed genuinely pleased
at the duty before him. Ridley sat up, alert.

" Glad as yourself the moment hev come, sir," said the
constable.

" Let's have a look," said Ridley.

Hutchins handed him the key in some surprise, an
emotion which deepened to sheer astonishment when
he saw the prisoner thrust it into his breeches pocket, with
a decidedly defiant air. He gaped expostulation from eyes
and mouth.

" If Miss Chideock wants to get rid of me," said Ridley,
" she must come and turn the key. I'll give it up to
no one else, and I don't think you'll take it from me in a
hurry."

" But—why, sir ? " stammered the constable, staggered
at such unusual conduct.

" Why ? Because she put me here, and she must let me
out."

" So she do—in a way o' speakin'."

" It's not enough," said Ridley.

" Such folly I never did hear o' ! Come, sir, give me the
key, an' ye be a free man once more."

" No."

" But 'tis rainin' hard ! You can't expect a lady, gentle-
bred, to step along in the wet."

" She can wait till it clears. But she must come."

" An' ye be skin-drenched yourself."

" Probably. All the more reason for you making
haste."

" 'Tis the wildest folly ! " cried the exasperated constable.
" She'll hold me to blame, that she will."

" I can't help that. You shouldn't have been a fool."

Hutchins went off at last, angry and fearful. His mission
met with the failure he had anticipated. Miss Chideock,
bright-eyed and red of cheek, declined to wet her feet in order
to humour an unruly culprit. If the man refused to leave the
stocks, he must stay there until he was more reasonable.
The punishment, it was apparent, had not been excessive,
though she had heard whispers that it was.

Thinking it wise to allow the prisoner fair time for reflection, Hutchins left him alone for another hour. He found

him then looking slightly worn, but as obstinate as ever. He reluctantly returned to the lady, who showed a spirit as yet equal to Ridley's own, and forbade Hutchins to trouble her again.

As the afternoon wore on, the news of the culprit's contumacy spread abroad. As the rain lightened, the idle and curious came to stare at so remarkable a man. Hutchins also appeared at irregular intervals, expostulating and persuading, meditating force, but always deterred by the look in Ridley's eyes. At length, grown desperate, by reason of his own responsibilities, he summoned courage for a last appeal to Quenride.

She came to him after a short delay. But now the fire seemed to have gone out of her. She was pale and nervous.

" I thought he had gone hours ago ! " she exclaimed, on hearing the man's story.

" 'Twill be dark in no time," said Hutchins deferentially. " And he've sat there since eleven, ma'am. Beggin' pardon humbly, but 'tis well-nigh unhuman to keep him there longer."

" I have not kept him," she said.

" It do seem to come to the same thing," observed Hutchins sagely.

" You are greatly to blame ! " cried Quenride, with a sudden flash.

" They be cryin' out on ye a'ready, ma'am," he muttered, to avert catastrophe. " If a' was a common rogue, it 'ouldn't matter a groat. But bein' a gen'leman, an' in the law too—— Maybe, 'tis scarce wise."

Quenride bit her lip. She would not have suffered this dictation had not her own reason already told her the same.

" Did he send any message ? " she asked.

" He said, ' Tell Miss Chideock that she is making the impossible more impossible still.' "

" Insolent ! " she cried, with an angry flush.

She remembered the phrase in his letter of yesterday, and to what it referred. Now, he threatened her. Or was it a promise ? If she would bend her pride in this matter, would he be satisfied with that humiliation, and give her her letter back ? She sprang at the chance. At any rate, she was weary of the whole affair, anxious to set as many miles as possible between him and herself, panting to be out of reach of his shrewd mocking tongue. For this, and other reasons, it seemed good to yield.

"Bring me a cloak!" she called, aloud. And when it was brought, she turned to Hutchins, and said curtly, "I will come."

It was close on six o'clock when she arrived at the place of detention. By this time, had his sufferings been less voluntary, Ridley would have deserved some pity. His face showed white and drawn. His back, from neck to loins, was one intolerable ache ; his legs appeared to belong to another man. Moreover, his last meal had been a light breakfast at seven o'clock that morning, and long ago his healthy young body had cried out for food.

Quenride came forward steadily, making of the act a condescension, when it was in truth a humiliation, and one which they both appreciated. The little cluster of her townspeople gave way before her, and stood back to see what would happen. An odd stillness prevailed. Hutchins watched in the background, stolid, yet self-satisfied.

Ridley bowed a little stiffly, but with no apparent ill-will. He drew out the key, and handed it to her with what seemed to the onlookers to be a pleasant smile. Quenride took it with fingers less steady than his own. She bent down, and thrust the key angrily into the lock. The next moment, Hutchins was helping Ridley to his feet. He stood there, swaying slightly, evidently expecting her to speak.

"You are now free, sir," she said, since he forced her to break silence. "You will put it about, I suppose, that I kept you imprisoned here for seven hours ? "

"Do you think, madam," he said, "that I am so proud of my appearance in your town that I shall wish to brag about it to my friends ? "

"You may say what you like," she retorted, with quick breathing, "if only——"

"If only, madam——? "

Her eyes shot up to his, wavered and fell. She hated herself for yielding to the mastery that was in him, yet yield she did, none the less. She dared not ask him for her letter— would not have dared, had the rest been a score of yards away. She threw out her hands with a little helpless gesture, and turned from him.

"Nothing," she said. "I have nothing more to say. You will forget all this, for it is merely the record of a fool."

"Yet even fools have memories," he answered. "Shall I see you again, madam ? "

"I do not know. Perhaps. I cannot say."

She had moved away, as if to throw off the fascination of his presence. The ground was rising under his feet, and he would not risk following her.

" To our next merry meeting, then, madam ! " he cried after her. And stood so, hat in hand, until she was out of sight.

CHAPTER X

A BRANCH OF THE CHIDEOCKS

QUENRIDE CHIDEOCK had not been alone when summoned out to see the constable for the last time. A visitor had arrived during the day, and chanced to be in the room with her when Hutchins sent in his final appeal. He saw her leave the house with the man a minute or so later, protected only by a hastily donned cloak, and his interest was aroused. He rang the bell, and asked where she had gone. Some of the facts came out, and he listened with evident amusement.

" What had the man done ? " he asked.

No one was very sure, so all were eager to tell what they did know. Ridley's extraordinary behaviour was described at full length.

" So Master Lawyer got the better of my fair cousin at last," he said, when the story had been embellished to a finish. " Ha ha ! 'Tis a good tale ! "

Few echoed his laugh, for this man, Alaric Mohun, was not liked in this household. It was rumoured, and very generally believed, that in the days of old Mr. Chideock's activity he had been forbidden the house. That he now paid short visits at irregular intervals was only one instance, they said, of his defiance of his cousin's wishes. Many wondered why a lady so imperious by nature and habit should put up with it.

He was not the sort of man to be popular with his inferiors. He was known to be comparatively poor, but that was held as no excuse for a close-fisted disregard of his obligations. He demanded service arrogantly, and refused even the small change of courtesy in return. When he was put out, he was unjust in a mean calculating way that lacked the warmth of Quenride's impetuous deviations from absolute fairness. On many points, he was a travesty of her. The imperious blood that ran in both of them had thinned and soured in the man, turning into a mere desire for personal gain what still remained as a hereditary instinct for authority in the woman. In the same way, the pride which such perceptions naturally engendered became in Mohun little more than a dictatorial habit of speech and thought. Where she was dignified, he was merely stiff, tact in her was dissimulation in him, her cleverness was his cunning. All through the distemper ran. It was even apparent in his distorted resemblance of feature, where her rich colouring and delicacy of outline reappeared as a healthy floridness spread over sharp-cut lineaments and the high narrow forehead of a calculating man. The effect of the two seen together was much as though one should look at a miniature by a master hand and then compare it with a copy, which, while striving to preserve a few characteristics, misses the refinement of the whole, reducing it to the level of the commonplace.

Finding his mirth unappreciated, Mohun dismissed the servants, and stood awhile at the window, tapping his chin with his finger-tips in deep thought. At all times he had a curious secretive air, but it was seldom more marked than when there were no observers by to notice it. It was strong upon him now, as he crossed the room softly, and stood listening at the door.

The house was always a quiet one. That was to be expected of it, when one out of the three young people in it limped about the place, or lay peevish on a sofa, and an old man was said to be slowly dying overhead. Mohun crept into the hall, and made his way up the stairs, coming to a halt before a closed door on the first landing. He slid his hand up and tried the fastening. The handle turned, but the door remained firm. A little oath of surprised annoyance broke from Mohun. Bending down, he called aloud in a low voice, rattling the door gently as he did so.

"Sir! It is I—Alaric Mohun. Can I come in? Are you alone?"

There was no reply. The visitor was scarcely disappointed. He had no reason for expecting a cordial welcome from his relative, who had quarrelled with him bitterly, and, as it seemed, finally, some eighteen months ago. Soon afterwards the old man had taken to his bed, and the two had had no more interviews.

Mohun bent his ear to listen again. Footsteps shuffled across the carpet, and a thick voice breathed reproval.

"Hush'ee, master, the poor gentleman be asleep. Miss Quen will never forgive me if you do wake him up."

" I'd like to see him," said Mohun, in his peremptory way.
" Let me in ! "

" It can't be done, sir ; indeed, it can't."

" And why not ? "

" Miss Quen——"

" Hang Miss Quen ! Am I not to have a say in my grandfather's house ? What right has your mistress to keep me
away from him ? "

" 'Tis his own desire, sir."

Mohun stamped irascibly.

" I'll come in," he threatened, " if I break the door down.
Unlock it this instant."

There was a moment's pause, during which Mohun
listened intently. But he did not break forcibly into the
room that day, for into the silence came a new sound, and
his attention was caught afresh. Light footsteps were
pattering down from an upper floor, and he raised his eyes
appreciatively as Dolly Pouncey came into view.

Dolly was in a chastened mood. Quenride's notice to
quit had not been withdrawn, and there were several reasons
why the girl disliked the thought of returning home. The
Chideock establishment was quiet—intolerably dull, she
called it at times—but at least it had the elegance and refinement which were hoped for in vain at Medley's Croft. Some
eighteen months at a finishing-school at Weymouth had
spoilt the farmer's daughter for a purely rustic life. A
kitchen existence was abhorrent to her aroused sense of
gentility, while to sit alone in the cheerless and solemn keeping-
room would have been less desirable still. Quenride's tongue
was sharp at times—but Mrs. Pouncey's lapsed into the
vernacular in her ordinary life. Young Mr. Gilbert was
often exacting and impatient, but he did not make undue
use of a knife at table, nor sit down to it perspiring, in soiled
shirt-sleeves. Moreover, what matrimonial prospects could
be looked for, in a place where only neighbouring farmers
and their loutish offspring paid occasional visits — where
even Robin Fiander borrowed a note of gentility from contrast with the rest ? Wareham offered little enough in this
respect, Dolly admitted. But an interesting stranger might
put in an appearance at any moment—as yesterday, on the
bridge.

Concerning that same interesting stranger, Dolly's compunction had been considerably thinned by reason of her own
misfortunes. As his generosity towards her had not brought

the sense of security which he had intended, she was scarcely conscious of gratitude. Her innocent flirtation with him had ended disastrously, but she was more inclined to blame his good looks than her own flightiness. And she was quite ready to begin again.

"Well, here you are!" cried Mohun, with a familiarity which spoke of some degree of intimacy. He held out his hand. Dolly let hers fall into it as if by accident, then pulled it hastily away.

"I wondered where you were," continued Mohun. "I'm afraid my cousin works you too hard."

"She's not going to, in future," said Dolly viciously.

"No?"

"I'm packing up—to go," she explained.

"To leave?"

"Yes—Miss Quenride's sending me away."

"Tired of you, eh?"

Dolly hesitated, considering which card to play. Mohun looked at her inquiringly. He was not in love with her, but she amused him by her apparent desire to trick herself—and perhaps him also—into believing that he was.

"She's angry with me," she said, at length. And said it pathetically enough to arouse his interest, if not his sympathy.

"H'm! Seems to me she's angry with a good many people," said Mohun.

"Is she?" said Dolly, with a pretty deprecating look.

"What's this story about her setting the lawyer in the stocks?" Mohun demanded. He had apparently relinquished his design of breaking into the room, and with the girl at his side was moving towards the staircase.

"I'm afraid," said Dolly, "that 'tis partly my fault."

"That's nonsense, I suspect. Must be. How can it concern you, my dear child?"

"I spoke to the gentleman—that is, of course, he spoke to me. And Miss Quenride got angry with both of us."

"A very Tartar! Why shouldn't you speak to anyone you choose?"

"That wasn't quite all," said Dolly, after an effective pause.

"No?"

"I think," said she, "that your cousin was chiefly angry because—well, because—he kissed me!"

"The devil she was! And why? Did she want him to kiss her?"

" I don't know," said Dolly, and thought it over for a moment. Mohun had suggested a point of view which she had not arrived at by herself. But since it was flattering to suppose her own lips favoured by those which Quenride Chideock desired in vain, Dolly adopted the idea without much difficulty. " Very likely you're right, Mr. Mohun," she said. " I really think you must be. I know she was dreadfully angry with him on Saturday night. And, of course, he's quite young for a lawyer, and rather handsome——"

" Stop a moment ! " cried Mohun, and Dolly stopped, for he was frowning at her. " Who is the fellow ? "

" His name is Ridley," she told him. " He comes from Dorchester, they say."

Her companion struck his fist on his cousin's work-table.

" Ridley of Dorchester ! " he exclaimed. " Of course. What a fool I am ! Go on, my dear. What were you saying about Saturday ? Was the man here then ? "

" What do you mean by *here* ? " asked Dolly, with a little hesitancy.

" In this house. In Wareham."

" He was in Wareham," murmured the girl. " Not in this house."

" Oh ! But my cousin saw him ? "

" I don't think she did ! " cried Dolly, with a smile.

" How do you know that she was angry with him ? " persisted the man.

" By the things she said."

Mohun looked thoughtful for a moment. When he spoke again, it was to throw out a remark in a haphazard way that covered real persuasiveness.

" Then she'd had a letter from this Mr. Ridley, I conclude."

Dolly fell into the trap.

" I dare say," she said. " She seemed to be expecting him."

" To call ? "

" No—we went to meet him."

" An appointment, then ? "

Mohun was off his guard for a moment, and allowed something to creep into his eyes—something sinister of which the girl became suddenly aware, for she roused up to a sense of danger, growing nervous and apprehensive.

" It may have been, Mr. Mohun. I really can't tell you anything. Miss Quenride sent me away directly he came up. And she didn't want me to say as much as I have. Indeed, I promised not to tell; and I wouldn't have said a word, only it can't matter, as I'm going away."

Mohun failed to understand her logic, which it was evident she believed in. But since it was advisable to allay signs of uneasiness, he affected to agree with her.

"No, it can't matter now, of course," he said. "And, in any case, no harm would be done, for I shan't mention anything about what you've told me to my cousin. If she wants her talk with the lawyer kept private, 'tis no concern of mine, naturally. After all, why shouldn't she see him? He's the family's man of business now, I suppose. Where did you say they met, Miss Dolly?"

"Out on the walls; yes, it was dark. But she and I could walk there blindfold, I believe."

Mohun turned to the window. The plain façade of the house, set a little distance back from the road, did not allow of an extensive view of the village street, but as far as it went his cousin was not yet in sight. There was time therefore to say a few more words to Dolly. He picked up the thread of the discourse in a casual way.

"And so—the lawyer didn't kiss her!"

"I'm afraid not," said the girl a little self-consciously.

"And he did kiss you. Therefore—you're to go! Rather hard, isn't it, Dolly?"

"I was thinking so, too!"

"Don't you want to go?"

"No. Home is so——"

"Dull?"

"I didn't mean quite that."

"No one to kiss you there, except Papa and Mamma, eh?"

"I didn't mean that, certainly."

Mohun shot another quick glance into the street. His cousin was returning to the house. He turned hastily to Dolly.

"Do you like kisses?" he asked, with a soft tongue.

"That depends," she said.

He gave her one and drew back, laughing.

"You're a good girl, and a charming girl, Dolly," he said. "And I like you. So, if you want to stay on here, you shall!"

Thus the pretty, weak-natured minx was kissed diplomatically twice, in as many days, and was very little the worse for it, the second salute setting right, as it were, the harm done by the first. The next instant, Quenride came into the room. She sent Dolly away with the damp cloak, and sat down without a word.

"Miss Pouncey tells me that she is leaving," Mohun began, after a quiet scrutiny of his cousin's face.

"Yes," said Quenride, listless after her recent encounter with Ridley.

"Why are you sending her away?"

Quenride made no answer. It was difficult to find a reply at once convincing and accurate. Impulse had entered very largely into her action—a vehement revulsion of feeling that moved against herself as much as against the girl, whose triviality had appeared the possible reflex of her own conduct as the young lawyer saw it. Mortified and angry, she could tell nothing of this, and so kept silent.

"You're making a mistake, I fancy," said Mohun, watching her.

"Dolly Pouncey does not suit my tastes—or my moods," she said, at length.

"Hang it all, my dear coz, who could hope to fulfil all your airy whims? The girl's company for you. You'll get less sweet than ever with only that miserable Gilbert to talk to. Let the girl stay."

"Why should I? I have told her to go."

"Why? Because, my dear Quen, I wish it."

"You?" Her eyes grew hard. "Is this your house, then? Am I to take my orders from you?"

Mohun looked at her in silence.

"In any case, what does it matter to you?" she asked, presently.

"Nothing, of course," he answered. "The girl wishes to stay, and I promised to persuade you."

"I cannot see why you should interest yourself on her behalf," Quenride said coldly. "I am afraid she must go."

"It strikes me, my amiable cousin," returned Mohun, "that you're a deal too fond of your own way. If our worthy grandfather's illness does prevent his being master in his own house, there's no reason why you should be absolute mistress. This is a whim of mine. It's a long time since you did anything to please me, and I say that the girl is to stay."

"And if I refuse?"

" I shall appeal to the old gentleman upstairs."

Quenride stiffened.

" I can't have him disturbed," she said. " The least excitement may be fatal. You know that."

" I do know it, Quenny. That's precisely why I use the argument. You don't want the old man to die just yet. Very well—you keep him deuced close, but devil take me if I don't find some way of getting in, unless——"

" Oh, have it your own way ! " cried Quenride wearily. " I've no wish to quarrel with you."

" The girl shall stay ? "

" If she wants to, she can."

Mohun smiled behind his cousin's back. Dolly Pouncey, the pretty little rogue, might have more stories to tell him of her lady's goings-on. The thought naturally took him back to Ridley. He turned to Quenride again.

" Speaking of quarrelling," he remarked, " it is generally a mistake. What's this I hear about you and the lawyer ? "

" I don't know what you have heard," she said, and only an ear listening for it could have caught the tremor in her voice.

" Rather an unusual thing—isn't it ?—to clap one's family lawyer in the stocks ? "

" If a man is brought up before me, on a charge of behaving disreputably on a Sunday, it is my duty, surely, to see that justice is done, irrespective of persons."

" Still—I know something of the man——"

" So do I ! " she struck in, off her guard for a moment.

" What ? "

" He is insulting and unbearable to a degree," she said. " He respects no one—one of those inflammatory creatures who would turn Society upside down. He deserved all he got, and more ! The girl perhaps suffered more than she should. At all events, I sent to Hutchins to release her directly the rain came on, and it was not my fault if he was too afraid of the wet to obey. But the man—it will teach him a lesson, I hope, and Heaven knows he needed one ! He mocked my authority in court to-day in the most brazen manner ! "

Mohun listened with a half-smile. The room was growing dark, but he could fancy a flush on his cousin's face, and wondered what lay behind the vehement words. She, for her part, gave rein to her indignation, with all the eagerness of insincerity. She knew well enough that Ridley had been punished, not for his own conduct, but for his manner of regarding hers.

"Was it quite judicious, I wonder ? " suggested Mohun, presently. "Lawyers are the wrong sort of people to fall foul of, my dear. And, after all, I doubt whether the stocks were intended for a man of his degree."

Quenride gave an angry laugh. Her cheek was burning very brightly now, though he could not see it.

"His degree ! " she cried. "And what is his degree ? An obscure country attorney, without a hundred pounds to his name, who ought to feel honoured by having the Chideocks among his clients ! Why should I care for a man like that ? As soon would I be afraid of—of——"

"Of—me, Quenny dear," suggested Mohun, with a bow to her across the table.

"Yes "—she sat up and looked at him —" of course, of you."

PART II

THE SENTENCE

" It is my turn now to call the tune, and on my soul, madam, you shall dance to what air I please ! "

CHAPTER XI

THE LAWYER AT HOME

THERE was no sound in the room save the stealthy crunching of Gibraltar rock by Robin Fiander, and the scraping of his quill. There was a day's work to be made up, owing to his employer's absence the preceding day, and for once the gentle-natured youth needed no spur to his application.

Ridley himself sat at his own table, more than usually taciturn and reserved. He was always a quiet worker, but to-day he scarcely seemed to move. Only at regular intervals, as it appeared to Fiander, watching him from askant watery blue eyes, did he raise a finger to turn over the sheets of a document which he was studying. Either it was a stiff task for even his astute brains, or his mind was perpetually glancing off elsewhere, for Fiander noticed that a page took a long time to read down.

Presently Ridley leant his head on his hand, and coughed slightly. The symptoms of a heavy cold were already upon him. He had come into the office that morning with his throat swathed in flannel, and had a good reason for being laconic—since speech was painful. The story of his disgrace was all over the town. He was aware of that. The news had somehow arrived in advance of himself, although he had lost no time in getting away from the scene of his adventure, travelling post-haste without rest or refreshment. The scandal would have to be lived down, and he proposed, after a night's reflection, to do this by behaving as if it had never arisen. The truth was, yesterday's episode—humiliating though it had been, to a degree which he now hardly cared to dwell upon—had not left any uncomfortable sense of dishonour behind it. If he had been shamed by the punishment, he was not ashamed of the offence, though he regarded the aggressor with no more favour because of the distinction.

A clock on the wall struck one. Fiander laid down his

pen, and glanced at his employer. Ridley roused himself, and nodded his head.

"Dinner-time already?" he said. "You can go. Wait a moment! What's that?"

The sound of light wheels coming down the street had suddenly ceased. Fiander went to the window. A hooded chaise, evidently a hired vehicle, stood outside the house. He reported the matter aloud.

"See who it is before you go," said Ridley. "And unless it is important, say I can attend to no one just now."

It was against his taste to allow himself to be at the beck and call of captious clients at whatever inconvenient hour they chose to interrupt him. His annoyance was genuine when Fiander returned with a tell-tale apologetic expression.

"No name, sir. Very important business."

"What kind of person?"

"A young gentleman, sir."

"Oh, Lord! Show him in."

A moment later, Gilbert Chideock limped into the room.

Ridley's face hardened slightly, and his bow, though courteous, was distinctly cold. Was he not done with this interesting family yet?

The boy came in alone, and was using a light crutch in default of the sturdy arm which had supported him yesterday. Ridley pulled forward a chair.

"This is an honour which I did not expect," he said. "I think we have met before. Pray be seated."

The boy rested his weight on the back of the chair, but remained standing.

"You wished to see me?" asked Ridley, more gently. The incongruous helplessness of the young figure appealed to his own youthful vitality. He had, he remembered, no quarrel with this lad.

"I have come," said Gilbert Chideock, in a high-pitched voice, "to apologise."

"Have you?" Ridley still spoke a little drily. "I am always ready, I hope, to hear an apology."

"And to accept it, too, I trust," said the boy.

"If it is genuine—yes. I don't think I am an unforgiving man in the main."

"Then perhaps you will forgive me," said Gilbert.

Ridley was checked. He had been foolish enough to suspect that either Quenride Chideock had repented of her

injustice or that the lad was blushing on his sister's
account.

"Yes ? " he said, in his level-headed way. " What have
you done ? "

" I was rude enough to laugh at you yesterday," explained
Gilbert, " at a time when it must have been particularly
annoying. I ask your pardon. I didn't mean to
hurt you, or to be unmannerly. But I thought it amusing
to see you in such a ridiculous position, and it was only
afterwards that I understood how much more undignified I
had been."

" H'm ! " said Ridley, looking at him carefully. " You're
very frank."

" Will you accept my apologies, sir ? Will you shake
hands ? "

" With all my heart," said the young lawyer, and the
two palms met. " You have made rather too much of the
affair, but I like anyone who's not too proud to own himself
wrong."

The boy—who was an odd personality, combining the
simplicity of a youth with the speech of an adult—drew
himself up and bowed.

" If we Chideocks were not proud," he said, " I should
not have come. The thought of it hurt me, you see. I
wanted to clear my honour."

" It was your own idea, then ? " asked Ridley carelessly.

" Of course ! Who should send me ? "

" Ah ! Quite so ! Who should ? Well, my boy, I think
all the more of you for coming, though I don't expect my
opinion is of much account to you."

" I don't know that," said Gilbert. " I think I like you.
I shall tell Quenny she was wrong."

" Does your sister know you are here ? " asked Ridley
quickly.

" Oh, no. I didn't tell. She mightn't have let me
come."

Ridley thought this extremely probable. But he
refrained from following the subject. He was too generous himself to seek to gain information about his fair
enemy out of her brother's frank simplicity. As soon
would he have rejected the boy because of her untoward
attitude.

It was therefore out of pure friendship that he spoke
next. Gilbert Chideock's complexity of manner made him

hesitate between offering the visitor a glass of Madeira and placing Fiander's bag of sweetstuff at his disposal. A compromise now suggested itself.

" Dinner will be served in a few minutes," he said. " May I ask you to join me ? "

Obviously, Gilbert was pleased. He accepted at once, and allowed the young man to help him into the living-room. Here Ridley played the host, with a freedom from embarrassment somewhat remarkable in the circumstances. It was not often that he consciously troubled to entertain others, being usually more engaged in probing their foibles and weaknesses. Society, such as was within his reach, had small attraction for him, and he was not sought after. The better class of tradesfolk and the few professional men of the town, were shy of adding the young attorney's caustic tongue to their card-parties. Euphemistic satire was scarcely likely to be appreciated in an unimportant country centre, where the weather and the state of the corn market formed staple topics of interest. The only man who had ever tasted Ridley's quality was his friend the Governor, and that elderly official could have praised him as an original thinker, and a fascinating companion in the sunnier paths of conversation. To the lad Gilbert, he proved himself the most entertaining talker who had yet penetrated that narrow experience.

Ridley continued to speak only on general subjects, and consequently learnt little concerning the boy's household beyond what he had gathered already. Among these facts, the deep affection of brother and sister stood out plainly. In spite of himself, Ridley was impressed by it. He sat silent, trying to reconcile this side of Quenride's character with what he knew of it.

Gilbert laughed.

" I know what you're thinking, sir," he said. " That I shall miss my sister when she marries."

" Why, yes——" said Ridley. " I suppose you will. Though I hadn't realised that."

" But Quen isn't likely to marry," the boy went on, contentedly. " She hates all men."

" That's a hard saying, too ! "

" She said it herself—only last Sunday night."

Ridley maintained the silence of complete comprehension.

" She might have married half a dozen," Gilbert ran

on. " Last year Cousin Alaric was wild about her—always hanging round the house, although he didn't dare come in, because of gran'dad. It's different, I'm sorry to say, now that my grandfather is always upstairs. Cousin Alaric just comes and goes as he likes. My sister hates it, but she doesn't seem able to stop it, unfortunately. Just think, sir, my cousin asked me the other day how I would like to go and live with him ! Quen looked as if she could kill him, and he laughed at her—oh, so horribly !—and said it might come to it yet. I hope and pray not ! "

The boy was speaking with an excitement which betrayed a delicately poised temperament, and Ridley, looking at his narrow flushed face, understood the disastrous effect which any undesired change might have on a physique so little able to bear it.

" It's not likely to happen, is it ? " he said, to soothe the lad. " Your sister, surely, will look after that."

" Quen ? Oh, she's gold all through ! Gold and fire—like her hair, I tell her. Ah, I was forgetting. You're not friends. I'm rather sorry for that. It was a pity you kissed Dolly Pouncey—though you might have done worse."

" A great deal," assented Ridley, with a quiet smile. " I might have kissed your sister."

" Oh, Lord ! " cried Gilbert. " I think Quenny would have had you whipped for that."

" A good thing, then, that I didn't attempt it."

" But as to Dolly Pouncey—well, I candidly own that I don't exactly blame you. Once, when I was feeling worse than usual—that is, when she thought I was, of course—she came and kissed me. I thought it rather pleasant. She's not a bad little thing," continued Gilbert, in his old-fashioned way, " but flighty, very flighty."

Soon afterwards they left the table, and returned to the office, where, as Ridley was helping the boy on with his greatcoat, he asked casually if there was any likelihood of his being permitted to see Mr. Benjamin Chideock, if he called.

" He's my client, you see," he said. " I ought to have paid my respects before this."

But Gilbert shook his head," he invited, " though I can't promise that you shall see gran'dad. I haven't seen him myself for months. He always seems to be a little better just when I'm worse."

"How long has he been laid up ? " asked Ridley. "Since my uncle's death ? That was in February. He was found dead in this room, you know, and I came over from Bath to carry on his practice."

"Gran'dad and Quen went to Leicester in February," said Gilbert. "I was down at Weymouth for the winter, and my sister was spending some time with me. Then she left me, and I heard from home that my grandfather had set out to see about some property in the North. He'd only taken our old nurse with him, and my sister was mortally afraid he'd come to harm. He really was in a bad state then, and had to be kept very quiet. Quen went after him, but he got worse, and when she brought him back he took to his room, and has kept there ever since. He sees no one but Quen and Hannah."

"That's unfortunate," said Ridley. "I must think it over. I suppose if he'd wanted me, he'd have sent for me. He hasn't changed his man of business—I mean, taken a new one, since my uncle's death ? "

"I don't think so," answered the boy. "But my sister attends to all that sort of thing now. She even pays the bills out of her own money, for to tell the truth gran'dad was always a bit—— Hulloa! that's odd too ! "

They were at the front door by this ; the chaise had been brought round, and the boy's attendant was waiting to help him into it. But Gilbert's attention was elsewhere. Following the direction of his gaze, Ridley saw a florid-faced man riding up the street.

"If it's not Cousin Alaric himself ! " cried Gilbert, with more surprise than pleasure in his tone. "Upon my soul ! he'll wonder what I'm doing here, won't he, sir ? "

Ridley made no answer, but looked with some interest at this unfamiliar member of the family with which he had got himself involved. The man was coming on at a brisk trot, but before he was abreast of the lawyer's office Ridley felt sympathy with Gilbert Chideock's evident repugnance to his relative. Such prejudices were not uncommon with the young man, and were none the less keen because he never allowed them openly to bias him in the early stage of an acquaintanceship. But they were invariably based upon scientific, as opposed to emotional theories, which is to say, that with any given antipathy he could have named without hesitation the precise cause, physical or moral, of his dislike. In this case, he would have said that the new-comer's eyes were too small and too closely set together to belong to a large-souled man.

Mohun drew rein, and ignoring Ridley greeted Gilbert with a sour look.

" Who the deuce expected to see you here ? " he demanded roughly.

" Is it so very strange ? " replied the boy, with a smile. " I mean — any stranger than to find you in Dorchester ? "

" A good deal, you young idiot ! One doesn't expect to find cripples so far from home. You'd better make haste back, or you'll be whining on the sofa the rest of the week, and making the house unbearable."

Gilbert, wincing perceptibly at the brutal sally, turned his crimsoned face to Ridley.

" Good day, sir," he said, in a low voice, " and thank you for all your kindness. I hope your throat will soon be well. Oh, thank you. Good-bye ! "

Ridley, ignoring in his turn the unamiable scion of the Chideocks, helped Gilbert into the chaise, made him com-fortable there, shook hands cordially, and waited at the door until the vehicle had driven away. Then he looked up very sharply, and surprised a look of unmistakable hatred in his companion's eyes. That the expression had reference to the departing Gilbert, and was not fixed directly on himself, only made it a little less interesting. He turned, and stepped back into the house.

" Hi, you there, sir ! " called Mohun, withdrawing his vindictive gaze from the retreating carriage. " A word with you, if you please ! "

Ridley looked back. Mohun dismounted, hitched the reins over the railings, and came forward. It takes even a clever man a few moments to wash from his eyes such a look as Mohun's had just been indulging in, and his smile of introduction was therefore less convincing than he in-tended. He thrust out a hand, which Ridley did not accept. He stood quietly waiting. From his face all emotion was carefully excluded. It was like a well-moulded mask, needing a touch here and there to quicken it into life. The prejudice against this man was strong upon him in these first moments, but he was keeping it under until it should be openly justified. Meanwhile, he bowed, and said never a word.

"Mr. Ridley, I presume?" said the visitor, with a glance at the brass plate on the door.

"The same," was the quiet reply.

"I'm glad," continued Mohun, with a feeble attempt at facetiousness, "to find you ready to admit so much. You lawyers are such devilish reticent fellows as a rule—ha, ha!"

"We're always ready to admit the obvious," said Ridley, in his dry way.

"Yes—yes; quite so. I have heard of you, of course. Your name is fairly well known."

"If," said Ridley, without turning a hair, "you mean since yesterday, no doubt you are right."

Mohun stared at him, a little nonplussed, like the majority of those who met old Thomas Ridley's successor for the first time.

"No," he said awkwardly, "I didn't mean that."

"Then I'm afraid you've too high an opinion of my reputation, sir," answered Ridley. "It probably goes no further than your own."

Mohun flushed, thinking the insolence too gratuitous, for all its delicacy. But the young lawyer had not spoken unadvisedly, and the remark was intended to do more than merely irritate its hearer.

After uttering it, Ridley again turned, as though expecting the interview to terminate at that moment. And again Mohun, choking down his wrath, called him back.

"Can you grant me the favour of a few words, sir?" he asked.

"Certainly," said Ridley, with no show of the interest which he felt in a man who had swallowed a deliberate slight, and immediately asked for a favour. He was assured now of his visitor's earnestness, be his object what it might.

"Within doors?" asked Mohun. "Can we talk privately there?"

"If you wish it. My clerk needn't come in."

A small room at the back of the house served on occasion as a sort of outer office, and to this Fiander was relegated on his return, which coincided with Mohun's introduction into the house. Ridley, weary in body, and with his throat painfully strained by its recent exertions on Gilbert's behalf, but alert enough in mind, and greatly interested, led the way to the front room. Once there, Mohun suddenly held out his hand.

" I hope we are going to be friends ! " he cried.

Ridley did not move a muscle.

" You must excuse me, sir," he said. " We lawyers are cold-blooded fish. Friendship has very llttle to do with our profession, I fear. Pray sit down."

And he indicated a chair facing the window.

CHAPTER XII

A DELICATE PROPOSAL

"I OWN that I am a little disappointed, though I am scarcely surprised at your attitude," said Mohun, as he seated himself. "After what occurred yesterday, I suppose I had no right to expect much geniality from you."

"What occurred yesterday," replied Ridley, "was, I imagine, none of your doing, sir."

"Certainly not!" Mohun assured him a little too eagerly.

"Then suppose we ignore it as an unpleasant episode, which concerns only one of us."

But Mohun shook his head with apparent regret.

"As a member of the family which has insulted, I may even say outraged you, Mr. Ridley——" he began.

But the other struck in.

"Have I complained of outrage or insult?" he asked quietly.

He had seated himself at his desk, and was engaged in cutting a quill, only glancing at his companion from time to time.

Mohun replied :

"I can't say that you have—but you have probably been swearing over the incident to yourself."

"Ah!" said Ridley, in a tone which told nothing.

Mohun was forced to go on. He assumed a more confidential air.

"You may choose to make light of the matter, Mr. Ridley," he said. "You may even be magnanimous enough——"

"You flatter me again, sir. I fear I cannot claim that virtue."

Thrown back upon himself at every turn, Mohun now exhibited a little impatience.

"Well, well, be that as it may!" he cried. "If you are annoyed with us, I really cannot blame you."

" With us ? " repeated Ridley.

" With my cousin, then, though I would naturally have preferred to keep a lady's name out of this."

" Perhaps," said Ridley, after a tantalising pause, during which he finished off the pen to a nicety, " it would put things on a better business footing if you formally introduced yourself."

" This," objected the visitor, " is hardly business."

" I'm inclined to agree with you, sir. That is why I spoke."

Mohun reddened, and endeavoured to cover a momentary discomfiture by replying quickly to the implied question.

" My name is Mohun," said he. " The Mohuns, of Bridport, who intermarried with the Chideocks a generation back. I beg pardon for not telling you so before, but seeing that youngster with you as I rode up I naturally took it for granted that he had mentioned the fact."

" It's a bad plan to take things for granted," Ridley told him, " worse still, to admit it. It makes people wonder whether you are not taking other things for granted too. So you are Mr. Mohun, of Bridport. I have heard of you."

" Nothing to my discredit, I hope ? " asked the visitor, hiding resentment under a show of jocularity.

" Indiscreet again, Mr. Mohun ! You might embarrass me."

" I'm afraid," said the other, a trifle sourly, " that I can't hope to attain to your balance. You are making my errand rather a difficult one to perform."

" I beg pardon. You had not said that you had—an errand."

" Nonsense, sir ! Should I be taking up your time unless I had ? "

Ridley merely waited. He had swung round in his chair, and was watching his companion more openly now.

" I came," said Mohun not without dignity, " to apologise."

" The devil ! " cried Ridley, with a hoarse laugh. " 'Tis in the family ! "

Mohun questioned him silently. Just as silently Ridley waived the point aside for the moment, and the other continued :

" My cousin wronged you, sir, both personally and professionally, in subjecting you to an indignity which no gentleman should be called upon to suffer."

"I'm not a gentleman, according to the popular notion. I'm only a poor devil of a lawyer, with my living to get."

"Still, I maintain that she exceeded her privilege ; and as to that grinning young rascal of a brother of hers, I'd have thrashed him for his impudence if he wasn't such a miserable weakling."

"Thankye," said Ridley. "Very disinterested of you, I'm sure. But, when I want a boy thrashed, I'll do it myself."

"You're a generous young man, I perceive," remarked Mohun, at a loss, and showing it.

"The lad has made a very ample apology," Ridley explained. "And I have accepted it. That is all."

Mohun endeavoured to cover his surprise—possibly his chagrin also, Ridley thought—by a slight sneer.

"His sister's influence, perhaps ! " he remarked.

"Whether or no," said Ridley easily, "I've accepted it, and so there's no more to be said."

"I am in hopes," pursued Mohun, recovering himself, "that you will also accept mine."

"On Miss Chideock's behalf ? "

"Assuredly."

"Her—influence, perhaps ? " suggested Ridley.

Mohun made answer slowly.

"No, I'm a truthful man, and greatly as I should prefer to tell you that the lady has repented of her high-handed ways, I am compelled to admit that I am not her envoy."

"Ah," said Ridley, convinced that there was a lie somewhere, though at present it was not easy to fix it, "I suppose you can see, sir, that that makes a deal of difference ? "

"In what way ? "

"I can't very well accept an apology from one who hasn't to my knowledge done me any harm, on behalf of one who has, but who refuses to ask pardon. Now, can I ? "

"Perhaps not, as you put it like that. But at least you'll do me the credit to admit that I desire to be friendly."

"Oh ! " said Ridley very drily. "Yes, I'll admit that. Can I be of any other service to you, sir, or——"

He stretched out a tentative hand towards the bell-rope. Mohun checked him with a quick gesture.

"Not so fast ! " he cried pleasantly. "A moment more, if you please ! "

The young lawyer settled himself back in his chair, and waited. The other seemed, after all, in no hurry to begin.

It was the lawyer himself who opened the second part of
the interview, and he did it in a characteristically odd
way.

"Are you quite comfortable there, Mr. Mohun?" he
asked.

The words might have been satirical, and the visitor
glanced quickly at him to see if they were. Apparently they
were not.

"I have seldom been in a better furnished office," declared
Mohun, wondering a little.

"Ah, I made a few changes when I came on the scene,"
said the owner of the room. "There's no reason why a place
should be uncomfortable because work's done in it. My
uncle, now, only had one decent chair in the office—his own.
The one you're sitting in. He died in it. A fact!"

Mohun assumed a casual interest, but otherwise was un-
affected by the gloomy tradition.

"Ah, you're not sensitive, I see," Ridley went on. "I
guessed you weren't. Now, I never felt quite at ease in that
chair. So I gave it up to the clients, and put it so. I like to
get a full view of their faces while they talk. Then I can
give a good guess as to whether they're concealing anything
or not. No, it's fixed, you can't move it."

Mohun's hands dropped quickly from the arms of the
chair. He said nothing, but if looks, in truth, could be trusted,
he was inwardly cursing the adroit naturalness with which the
other had led up to the disquieting statement—a method,
moreover, which had induced him to leave small room for his
own escape without going back on himself.

Ridley, guessing all this, smiled provokingly. Mohun
sprang up.

"Damn it all!" he cried irritably, "I think I do object
to dead men's chairs, after all. I'll—I'll stand."

The only other seat besides Ridley's own being Fiander's
high stool, this was a necessary conclusion, and one which
Ridley acquiesced in without compunction.

"And now," said Mohun, "let's get to business."

"Oh, there is a matter of business, then?"

"Certainly."

"I understood from your words that it was a mere friendly
call. But that's my fault, perhaps. Anyhow, sir, I'm
entirely at your service. Well?"

"My grandfather, Mr. Benjamin Chideock, is a client of
yours."

" I believe so. But I have had no personal transactions with the gentleman."

" You'll find him a deuced odd old blade when you do ! However, you don't surprise me. He sees no one now. That is why I am here."

" Faith," said Ridley, " you're an economical man, Mr. Mohun. You make one journey serve two purposes, eh ? "

" Now," the other went on, not heeding the innuendo otherwise than to flush at it, " my grandfather being, as I say, rather an eccentric old patriarch, he has lately taken a curious whim into his head."

" Not at all unusual," commented Ridley. " Eccentricity forms the groundwork of many interesting cases."

" Just so ! But you are not asked to deal with a case at present, Mr. Ridley," said Mohun, with a touch of asperity. " Only with an invalid old man's desire."

" For what—may I ask ? "

" To hold in his own possession a certain legal document now in yours."

" That sounds simple," said Ridley. " What particular document is it ? "

" His Last Will and Testament, executed this year."

" By my late uncle, I suppose ? "

" Exactly."

Ridley sat silent. Mohun watched him with an anxiety which should have won him credit.

" The terms of the will are, I presume, known to you ? " he said, then.

Ridley roused himself, and shook his head.

" I'm bound to admit that they are not, Mr. Mohun," he said. " You must remember that I have been settled here less than a year, and have had no intercourse with Mr. Chideock. There are many wills in my possession. I am chiefly concerned, not with their contents, but with their safe custody, sir."

" Well, well, there's no secret about it, as far as I'm concerned, and I only alluded to the details because your knowledge of them tends to give me a better standing in your eyes. The fact is, with the exception of a few trifling legacies, and the entailed property—not of much value—I am my grandfather's sole heir."

Ridley sat amazed at what he could only regard as the man's audacious lying, which seemed only equalled by the stupidity which uttered a statement so easily disproved. But to the man himself he merely said very coldly :

" I don't see what difference that makes, sir."

Mohun laughed a little uneasily.

" I should have thought that it would make a great deal ! " he said. " A man can surely be trusted to carry a will under which he benefits to a pretty tune."

" Am I to understand, then, that Mr. Chideock wishes me to entrust the will to you personally ? "

" That is it," agreed Mohun, with a perceptible air of relief. " There is no difficulty, I suppose ? "

" If I am so instructed by my client," said Ridley, " I have no reason for refusing, though, as a professional man, I should prefer a more legitimate mode of transit. Let me see the letter of advice, if you please, sir."

He held out his hand. Mohun went red again, drawing back with a frown.

" I've not got one ! " he blurted out roughly.

This time the lawyer was not in any degree surprised ; he again concealed his real sentiments.

" No word authorising me to hand over the will to you ? " he exclaimed, balancing himself back in his chair to stare up at his visitor. " No line of writing ? "

" No. The fact is, the old gentleman has got rather beyond that. He can't hold a pen. I suppose he thought it would be all right. At any rate, he entrusted the errand to me, and he'll be woefully upset if I don't take the will to him."

" He need not be disappointed," said Ridley, the lines of his face settling inflexibly. " I'll bring it over myself to-morrow."

" You're damned cautious," said Mohun, with something like a snarl.

" Yes ; I am. A lawyer has to be damned cautious, sir."

Mohun made an effort to recover himself. There was a look in the other's eyes, a tone in that hoarse voice of his, which he did not like. It occurred to him that a man who had sat wet and hungry in the stocks all day, out of sheer unprofitable obstinacy, might prove a tougher individual to convince than he had expected. He determined to force his companion's hand.

" Don't you trust me ? " he asked.

" Pray don't make a personal matter of it, Mr. Mohun," Ridley responded lightly. " You must take it as a business affair. I should say the same to anyone."

Which was true enough, for the young lawyer had brought into the office a new conscientiousness, little likely, it seemed, to be appreciated in the present case. Some such contrast between the past and the existent struck Mohun at this moment.

" Your uncle would not have been so particular," he said unpleasantly.

" Probably not. I'm afraid that he did many irregular things which I'd be sorry to repeat, sir."

" I tell you my grandfather is anxious to have it. In his present precarious state——"

" Not worth worrying about, Mr. Mohun, since you can assure him that he shall have the will without fail before noon to-morrow."

Mohun swore under his breath. He took a turn round the room, and came back to his former place.

" You know well enough that my cousin won't admit you," he said, sneering.

Ridley kept his composure.

" That's my business," he said.

" You'd not have the face, after yesterday, to show yourself in the town."

" I've plenty of assurance when it's necessary," said the other.

Mohun's hand twitched to strike the obstinate young mouth. He stood there frowning. The truth was, that while Ridley was certain of his duplicity Mohun was as yet only half convinced of Ridley's honesty, hugging to himself the thought of his possible corruptibility as long as a chance remained.

" I'm afraid, Mr. Ridley," he said, after a savage scrutiny, " that you're too scrupulous for your trade, as you're certainly too young and well-favoured. You'll come to grief."

" My youth will mend, though I'm not so young— twenty-nine, if you want to know ! My looks I can't help, and my scruples I can. As to my fortune—that's gone already, as no doubt you're aware."

" Yes," said Mohun, looking at him steadily. " I am."

" Good God ! " cried Ridley, springing to his feet. " What do you mean ? "

" This ! " said the other, flinging aside all pretence, and thinking that it was time to prove his man to the uttermost. " You're in want of money ; you must be ; you are. I've made you a proposal which you've refused with a per-

sistency that may be conscience or may be avarice. If it's
the first, and your knowledge is less than it may be, I'd like
to point out that I'm offering you a fine opportunity of
paying off a recent score. If it's the latter, I'm ready to
meet you to the extent of an appreciable advance on any
sum that you may name. As much as I can conveniently
manage at present, and the rest when I inherit the estate.
I don't suppose you'd have to wait long. Now, sir, shall we
talk business ?   Is it a deal ? "

" I rather think it is," said Ridley, relaxing his lips at
last.

And the next moment Mohun was on the floor, receiving
the soundest kicking he had ever tasted in his life. When he
had finished, the lawyer drew back, panting, and pointed to
the door.

" Get out ! " he ordered, and there was that in his gleam-
ing eyes which the bruised and battered Mohun did not try
to defy. He crawled to his feet, and staggered across to the
door, flinging a bloodshot glare over his shoulder as he went.

" If you don't repent this," he gasped, from the threshold,
" I'm no match for you ! "

Ridley sat down to recover his own breath.

" Oh, these Chideocks, these Chideocks, with their insufferable insults and enigmatic ways ! " he cried.   " Which
one of the family shall I have to trounce next ? "

CHAPTER XIII

PARCHMENT AND PAPER

AMONG the other changes which Ridley had made on his late uncle's premises, was the conversion of one of the cellars into a strong-room. He had spoken truly enough when he discountenanced the old lawyer's methods as reprehensibly careless. Economy had always been the keynote of all the elder man's arrangements, and in his later years a disinclination to anything that savoured of unnecessary trouble took a firm hold of him. His nephew's business capacity, and its expression in details, would probably have shocked him far more than his lax rules did the younger Ridley, who lost no time in collecting all the more important documents belonging to the firm, and transporting them to a place of greater security. A cellar being the most inaccessible repository to outsiders, hither he carried the valuable bundles, and laid them, carefully docketed and numbered, in a metal-lined chest, clamped to the floor, and secured by a lock of a peculiarly intricate design. The key of this chest hung round Ridley's neck in the daytime, and lay at night beneath his pillow. Further precaution was supplied by a heavy padlock fastening the cellar door, this key being safely hidden in a secret drawer of the writing-table upstairs. Ridley's carefulness was justified by the fact that jewels and other articles of value were frequently entrusted to the family lawyer by old-fashioned folk who had small faith in more modern modes of securing their property.

The cellar itself was not a cheerful place. Beyond making it as impregnable as possible, Ridley had not troubled much about it. It was dry, but dingy, as such places are apt to be. It had a roughly paved floor, and walls which had been white-washed at some remote period, but which now showed patches of stone through the crumbling covering. An immense amount of litter had been cleared to one side, but little more

than free access to the chest had been as yet attempted.   A
bench and a small table occupied part of the recovered
space.   Though the place was fairly high in the ceiling, there
was no contrivance for lighting it from outside, and as no
fresh air ever came into it its atmosphere struck rank and
chill, and gave an impression of general mouldiness, though
no such condition lurked there.

On this same evening Ridley descended to the cellar,
after office hours, his errand having so much of private
gratification in it as to demand postponement until a time of
leisure.   From naming his entanglement with this especial
family the Chideock Affair, he had come to regard it as
the Chideock Mystery.   And it was in order to investigate
this mystery, as far as he could, that he chose to spend an
hour or so in a dreary cellar at a time when he would have
been better in bed.

First placing a heavy bar across the door, he set down his
light, and pulled out the key of the chest.   Inside lay sheaves
of documents in orderly arrangement, the name of the family
to which each referred being exposed on the outer covering.
The Chideock bundle was a thin one—merely some dozen
various papers of odd sizes.   Apparently the parsimonious
Benjamin Chideock had not wasted much of his substance
on lawyers.   Ridley's humour found amusement in the
mental conjuring up of such scenes as must often have
occurred in his uncle's lifetime—the client beating down the
lawyer's fee, and the lawyer grossly overcharging his client.

He carried the packet to the table, and quickly untied it.
The document he was interested in fell uppermost:
the Last Will and Testament of Benjamin Chideock, of
Chideock House in the County of Dorset and Stapleton
Manor in the County of Leicester, Esquire—so inscribed in
old Amos Hoddinott's writing.   For a wealthy man, the
testator had disposed of his estate very compactly, for the
will consisted of a single sheet.   Ridley read it through
quickly.   When he had finished, he sat back, and wondered.

If Alaric Mohun's audacious statement had made him
gasp, the will itself was even more astonishing.   There was
no getting away from the fact, now staring up at him from
the parchment, that the old man had named this ill-con-
ditioned grandson of his as his sole heir.   As a rule, Ridley
accepted professional facts without much comment, attri-
buting the unusual to either eccentricity or foolishness.   But
here was something which out-distanced all previous experi-

ence—something, moreover, which went deeper than a mere business detail, and engendered an interest which was as warm as it was keen. As a matter of fact, he was not called professionally to take any notice of the circumstance at all. To all intents and purposes, he had finished with Alaric Mohun when he kicked him out of the office. But the singularity, the amazingness of the thing held his imagination, and filled his mind exclusively.

There were facts—plenty of them—to be rehearsed and set in order, each presenting its own little problem of *how* and *why*. But dismissing these for the moment, Ridley gave himself up to a careful, even a critical examination of the document in front of him.

It had been written out by his uncle's hand—Hoddinott, at the time of its execution, being presumably past such continuous effort. The date was recent, January 16 of this same year. There was no mention of the revoking of any previous testament. The whole was carefully worded, and was in effect precisely what Mohun had claimed it to be. Various small legacies were left to servants and acquaintances, the residue of the estate was to pass to " my eldest grandson, Alaric Mohun, of Sidcombe Place, Bridport, in recognition of the generous spirit which he has shown throughout our late unhappy disagreements, and in token of my full forgiveness of those matters wherein he has previously offended me. And furthermore, as I desire to show my confidence in the said Alaric Mohun, I do herewith appoint him sole Guardian of my younger grandson, Gilbert John Chideock, until he attains his majority, the cost of the said Gilbert John Chideock's education and other necessary charges to be defrayed by the said Alaric Mohun during the same period. And to this I set my hand and seal——''

Then followed the signature—that of a man already stricken by a mortal disease, and those of the witnesses, in coarse, sprawling penmanship, names utterly unknown to Ridley, though of true Dorset flavour. Their signatures interested him less than did that of the old man himself. Looking at the thin wavering lines, he imagined the probable scene—the miserly old testator, propped up in an arm-chair, and bending cramped fingers to perform what must have been the most distasteful task of his life. But the picture held him for only a brief space, since there were more interesting things to think about.

Nowhere in the will was the beautiful Quenride mentioned,

she who seemed to be most intimately associated with her grandfather, she who acted as the mistress of his household, and manager of his affairs, she who, out of all his relatives, had access to his sick-room. The point was curious, though it might be that her fortune from other sources was already large enough for her needs, whereas Mohun was admittedly poor. Ridley remembered that, in her first letter, she had represented herself as a woman of considerable wealth.

The fact of the guardianship was even more striking, though it seemed to explain the look of hatred which Ridley had surprised on Mohun's face as Gilbert Chideock drove away. He was precisely the sort of man to regard the responsibility as a miserable encumbrance, even though, on the lad's showing, he was capable of taunting both brother and sister with the fact. This reflection raised another in Ridley's mind. Mohun was aware of the contents of the will. Had it been drawn up under his influence in the first moments of reconciliation ? And, if so, did Quenride know of this ? Was she seeking, by keeping the two apart, to undermine that influence, and induce a settlement more favourable to her own and to her brother's interests ? Or was she fostering an apparent estrangement in ignorance of the truth ?

It was natural that Ridley should think of her. Throughout the perplexities with which the whole situation bristled, her face kept rising before him, with its tender mouth still claiming that sympathy which her eyes refused to accept.

" Confound the vixen ! " thought Ridley, at length. " I dare say the old gentleman has a good reason for keeping her out of it. Angry perhaps that she won't wed the amiable Alaric ! Odd, though, as he and the grandfather have been reconciled since January, that the people don't seem to be aware of it ! "

But the most extraordinary point of all was Mohun's visit itself. Why, Ridley wondered, should a man itch to get hold of a will drawn up in his own favour—desiring it to the extent of offering a heavy bribe to its legitimate legal guardian in order to obtain it ?

He thrust his hands into his pockets, and leant back against the table, tapping his heels on the dusty floor. This interesting point held him in thought for some minutes. Presently he rose, with a serious face, and rummaged again in the chest. When he came back to the table he had in his hand a small bound volume.

It had come to him while he thought the affair over that his uncle, punctilious in some matters, had made a point of recording each day's happenings at some length, the book in which they were set down forming a kind of business diary. It was this which the young man now carried to the light.

Turning up the date January 16, he was surprised to find no mention of Mr. Benjamin Chideock's will, but on running his eye down the page he came upon the explanation of the omission. He read :

"*Jany.* 19.—*Bitter cold day. Wind N.E.E. Slight fall of snow towards evening. Waited upon early in the day by Mr. Alaric Mohun, who brought the will (Mr. B. Chideock, of Wareham) as arranged. Signed, sealed, and witnessed. All correct. Placed it among the other Chideock papers. Examining evidence in the Horner case. Hoddinott drunk as usual.*"

Ridley turned the pages back, and found another entry :

"*Jany.* 10.—*Frost 10°. Mr. Alaric Mohun brought details of Mr. B. Chideock's will. Set it out in order ready for his signature. Hoddinott incapable of doing more than title-sheet. Mr. M. called for it in eveng. Congratulated him on his reconciliation with his Grandfather. He blames his Cousin for the estrangement, and states that she is at present at Weymouth.*"

And again :

"*Jany.* 6.—*Too ill to attend to business. Heard that Mr. Mohun of Bridport called. Left no message.*"

So much, and no more. Apparently then, Alaric Mohun had acted throughout as negotiator in the transaction, and had himself deposited with the old lawyer the very will which he was now anxious to purloin. The whole affair offended Ridley's business sense by its slight irregularity, which distinctly encouraged his former conjecture of undue influence on Mohun's part—an influence apparently exercised during his cousin's absence from home. One thing was clear, at any rate—there was no longer need to wonder how Mohun had obtained his information regarding the contents of the will. For the rest, nothing seemed certain, save that Quenride would litigate as soon as it was produced.

" I wonder whether she'll retain me to prepare her suit ! "
said Ridley to himself, with a reminiscent smile.

And again a red mouth, soft and kissable, under scornful
eyes, rose up before his inner vision with a distinctness that
surprised himself.

He stayed there yet awhile, letting his mind play round
the matter, finding no fresh theories, but fitting and refitting
his previous ones to the case. The only other entry which
might possibly bear upon the transaction was one relating
to the very beginning of the year, under date January 3.
It ran :

" . . . *To Mr. B. Chideock's—having other business near
by. Discussed the sale of the land at Warminster, and divers
other concerns. . . .*"

It might have been during this visit that the old gentleman
had mentioned the making of his will, and some such arrangement as that subsequently carried out might have been
suggested or agreed upon. There was no other memorandum
calculated to interest the old lawyer's successor until he turned
over to the page whereon the last words were written. Then
again his attention revived, and he called to mind a gloomy
circumstance which he had forgotten until now. The book
which he was studying for its outside interest had one of its
own—and the last entry combined the two. It was dated
February 20—the day of Thomas Ridley's death—and in
penning these lines he was writing the one awful word " Finis "
across his life.

" *Feb.* 20.—*Very unwell. Should have been at Mr. B.
Chideock's, who sent for me. Deputed Hoddinott (sober for
once, being his annual holiday) to ascertain the message for
me, and to return at once if necessary. Bridge being repaired,
I hear—so warned him. . . .*"

No more. The old lawyer's own warning had come, and
a more important message than that of Quenride's grandfather had summoned him across a longer Bridge than any
Amos Hoddinott might stumble over with mortal feet. He
had been found dead at his table, the book in front of him,
while the drop of ink which was to have finished the record
had dried upon the pen some hours before. His nephew
remembered that they had shown him the book on his arrival,

but that, in the multifarious duties claiming his attention, he had scarcely glanced at it. He realised now that he should have done so, while the matter was still fresh in the old clerk's mind, for at this time of day it was impossible, without direct application to the client, to ascertain what the business had been about.

" Though," reflected Ridley, " since Mr. Chideock has said no more about it, I suppose it's not important."

The other allusions in the entry were clear enough, after a moment's thought. Hoddinott was apparently allowed a short holiday. He would naturally visit his only relative in the district, his grand-niece Sophy, and to reach her after his business at Wareham he would have to pass over the lower bridge from that town. The bridge being under repair would present a possible danger to unsteady feet—hence the timely warning from his employer.

Affection, even an appreciable amount of respect, it was scarcely possible to entertain for old Thomas Ridley, but his representative closed the diary with a diluted kind of sentiment because the tragic end somehow redeemed the sordid life.

The cellar was growing cold to his chilled blood. He rose with a shiver, retied the Chideock papers, and placed them back in the chest. He laid the memorandum book by the side, swung down the heavy lid, and secured it with his key. But the thought of the will still troubled him.

He was thinking of the boy Gilbert, allowing sentiment to interfere with his professional code. It was no part of his business to consider what causes had led to the drawing up of any particular document—that is, not unless the matter came before him to be sifted legally. But he could not blind himself to the knowledge that a man like Mohun could make life a hell to the delicately organised lad, and that, if left in sole guardianship, he was just the brute to do it. At some cost to himself, Ridley resolved to go over to Wareham, and make an attempt, at least, to interview his client, and to suggest the imprudence of such a nomination. It was apparently all that he could do to help his young friend.

" I'll take 'em by surprise," he thought, as he padlocked the cellar door, and mounted the stairs to the floor above. " I'll go to-morrow, if this confounded cold isn't any worse. It won't be pleasant ; but he's a nice lad—and worth it."

But when the next day came, he was forced to modify his plans. He was too unwell to leave the house, and decided to forego the pleasure of presenting himself unexpectedly before Quenride Chideock. He sent a letter instead, addressed to his client, in which he desired the favour of an interview with Mr. Chideock, on a matter which he believed greatly concerned the happiness and well-being of his grandson, Mr. Gilbert Chideock. He instructed his messenger to wait for an answer, which he could not expect to receive until the afternoon.

In the meantime, the mail-coach came in, and brought Ridley a budget of letters, which he sorted into two piles—private and professional—and examined at his leisure, taking the business communications first. And among these he came upon one which might reasonably have been assigned to the other lot, though it bore the signatures of two members of his own profession. It ran:

" SIR,—We are instructed by a Client who desires to remain unknown to yourself, to inform you that the sum of Six Thousand Pounds (£6000) has this day, the ninth of September, one thousand eight hundred and twenty-eight, been placed to your credit at the County Bank of Dorset. We have pleasure in adding that the amount has been placed unconditionally at your service. We have the honour to be, Sir, your obedient Servants,

" REEVES & FRAMPTON."

Coming at once to a natural conclusion, Ridley was touched, but scarcely surprised by the letter. He called to mind the Governor's generous permission to draw upon him to any amount—permission of which the younger man had declined to avail himself. He now applauded the tact and kindliness which again insinuated the gift towards him with so much delicacy. Affectionate gratitude filled his heart, even though in spirit he still refused the help.

The letter had lain at the bottom of the pile, and turning immediately after its perusal to the other assortment Ridley took up an envelope which he had hitherto overlooked. He recognised the handwriting of the man of whom he was thinking. Tearing the cover open, he read the note with a sense of shock, and laid it down to think. The Governor had written:

" H.M. PRISON OF DORCHESTER,
" September 9, 1828.
" MY DEAR KENELM,—I think it would be better for you

not to present yourself at my table on Saturday next as arranged, as I am expecting guests to whom every consideration is due.

" I should also greatly prefer that you should refrain from intruding upon me until a certain unhappy episode is less painfully present to my mind. I might, I fear, say things which we should both regret. Trusting that you will respect my wishes. . . ."

Ridley bit his lip, and read no more. When the first shock of surprise was over, anger took him. When that had passed, a deep sense of pain was left. The shame which Quenride Chideock had laid upon him had never bitten so sharply into him as in these moments when it seemed likely to prejudice his best friend. That he had been humiliated unjustly, and had deliberately made no attempt to clear himself, were points which he could hardly explain to a third person. In a momentary revulsion of feeling he caught himself almost agreeing with the Governor that a young man who had recently been put to the ignominy of a public punishment was assuredly not fit company for the guests of a high Government official.

The mood did not hold for long. Within the hour he was ready to lift up his head, with his usual self-confidence, strong in his own private knowledge of the affair. Having thus come back to his former attitude of mind, he read the letters through again, saw no discrepancy in the supposition that they had both emanated from the same brain, and sent a formally courteous reply to each. He avoided any reference to the six thousand pounds in his letter to the Governor, and informed the lawyers that the money would not be touched.

The afternoon brought his messenger back from Wareham. He presented a letter in Quenride's well-remembered hand. She begged to thank Mr. Ridley for his thoughtfulness on her brother's behalf, but regretted to inform him that her grandfather was, at present, in no condition to receive strangers. Should his health improve, she would, however, lay Mr. Ridley's request before him.

To this, Ridley, in no mood to answer her gently, sent back a sharp reply. He informed her that, if Mr. Chideock's condition were so precarious as she implied, there was no time to be lost, as the matter referred to related to a clause in that gentleman's will, which had recently come under his own notice.

The next day brought him a few icy lines from the lady.

" Sir,—Your interest in my family is flattering, but mis-
placed.   I am aware of the clause to which you refer, and
regret it as deeply as yourself.   But I fear we have no alternative but to submit.   If I should see reason to think otherwise, I shall not fail in an obvious duty.   Until then I desire
that this correspondence may cease.

" QUENRIDE CHIDEOCK."

" So," thought Ridley, " she knows that much, does
she ?   The chances are, she knows a little more.   Now—has
she given herself away inadvertently, or is she playing a
deeper game than, at the present moment, I've any idea of ? "

CHAPTER XIV

HER KINGDOM

SOPHY HODDINOTT'S outlook had hitherto been as limited as her experience. Here was something to minister to content; for while to know usually means to suffer in some sort, to look and to long ineffectually brings the hopeless misery that finds no counter-irritant in sharper pain. Heart and brain alike had existed in an unconscious stagnation, vaguely aware that better things were to be found, but scarcely desiring, since the creed of her forefathers had been learnt in infancy, and adhered to with a fixity denied to any religious one. She was one of the poor folk, she would have said, and would have deemed all further exposition of herself superfluous.

She had very few possessions. The cottage which she shared with her grand-uncle had been tenanted by Hoddinotts for over a century, but Amos represented the last life in the tenure. When he died, Sophy would have to seek shelter elsewhere. It was a poor enough place, long since fallen into disrepair—situated on the road between Wareham and Corfe—built of roughly piled blocks of Purbeck stone, and roofed with slabs of the same. As is sometimes found in these parts of the country, it stood immediately on the road, with no daintiness of wooden palings and bowery front garden to indicate a rural demesne. Only a narrow strip of soil intervened between the highway and its multi-coloured walls. But in the rear there was a considerable length of cultivated land, enclosed between low walls contrived of slabs of stone placed with irregular exactitude and unbound by mortar. Here were found tokens of Sophy's more legitimate modes of livelihood. A dilapidated cowshed leant against the end of the cottage, and stabled a couple of beasts. By the side of the path stood a row of beehives, and at the end of the garden was a small orchard. These slender industries, together with the trifles the girl earned by

her reputation as a white witch, formed a slight addition
to the pension allowed by Ridley to the old man, and the
whole enabled the pair to live.   Their wants were few,
their tastes simple, and though they were poor they were not
apprehensively so.   The cottage standing at some distance
from both Corfe and Wareham, Sophy had less difficulty in
curbing her relative's besetting vice than she might otherwise
have experienced.   By keeping a tight hold upon the coins
that came their way, she could ensure sobriety if not soundness of mind, since inns and taverns were too far distant for
the chance of a stray invitation to be feared.   For the rest,
the girl left the old man very much to himself, neither feeling
affection nor making any pretence of doing so.   Had Amos
Hoddinott been in his full mental vigour, such a life would
have been irksome to him.   Considered the smart one of
the family, some effort had been made to fit him for something better than had contented his forebears.   Hence, he had
lived the greater part of his life in towns, and among educated
men, gravitating toward the end of it to his native scenes,
and coming back to die in the cottage where he had been
born.   The trifling element of refinement which Ridley had
noticed in Sophy had been imbibed from Amos, but unconsciously, and without awakening resentment or desire
within her breast.

In spite of her sex, the girl had suffered far less, both
spiritually and physically, from Quenride Chideock's notions
of justice than had the young lawyer himself.   A disgrace
which leaves the body whole, and evokes no jeering comments
—since no one is at hand to jeer—is easy to forget, to an
uncultivated nature.   Sophy, whose passions, when they succeeded in penetrating her apathy, were strong and unbridled,
would have hated the Chideocks, stock and branch, for
interfering with her, but without much sense of humiliation.
Then the incident itself would have shrunk to a trivial detail
of that interference, though the hate would have remained, in
accordance with her belief that the rich were the natural
enemies of the poor.   All this, if she had suffered alone.
But she had not suffered alone.   She had a companion in
her misfortune, and because of that companion the episode
was unforgettable.

She was absolute mistress of but one spot in the world—
and that a poor enough place—but here at least her will
was law, since she alone ever entered it.   It was no more
than a garret thrust in under the high-pitched roof of the

5

cottage, and bearing in its ceiling an unswerving conformity to the elevation without. Hence, it was impossible
to stand erect save in the exact centre of the floor. At
one end was the door, at the other a tiny window,
opening outward on a hinge. Under one of the shelving
sides was placed the bed, beneath the other a wooden
box tied with a cord. A backless chair stood beneath
the window. The ceiling was beamed, and consisted of
the under sides of the slabs forming the roof. Here and
there these had become broken or displaced, and Sophy,
lying in bed, could see a star or two, or count the slow dripping
of the raindrops as they struck upon the beams beneath.
The fragile door, opening sheer on to the staircase, had
once been secured by a bolt, but now only the empty sockets
remained. A barren and dreary place for the delicacies
of a young girl's fancy to flourish in. Yet, to Sophy
Hoddinott's awakened imagination, it had become a revered,
almost a sacred place, for here, and only here, in all the
world, could she open out her heart to herself, in the full
confidence of utter solitude. More still—the room held
the two things which had come to constitute the material
evidence of her newly arisen emotion.

Down at the bottom of the box, which held all that she
could call her own, she had placed the coat which Ridley
had given to her. A piece of clean calico prevented its
contact with her own shabby garments. At irregular intervals, occasionally three or four times in one day, Sophy
would lift the coat out, and smooth its folds caressingly. Her
thoughts, wild untutored things, played, with an ever-
increasing sentiment of tenderness, round the remembrance
of the man who had once worn it. When the late afternoon
sunshine yellowed the bare walls, she loved to spread the
good broadcloth in its beams, and smiled to see how each
tiny hair glistened in the light, until the inky blackness
itself seemed to throw out a lustre of its own. The coat
had collar and lapels of velvet, and even better than making
it shimmer in the sun was it to lay her cheek against that
inexpressible smoothness and match it with the feel of the
hand which she had derided, in conformity with her peasant
creed. In the first days of her possession she drew the coat
on to her own slight body, and, glancing down, saw her torn
skirt showing through where the coat flapped open over
her feet. Before long, she had mended the skirt, and begun
a scrutiny of the other articles of her poor wardrobe. In

a few days, anyone who had known Sophy Hoddinott since she had grown into young womanhood would have found her more neatly attired than hitherto. But no one was at hand to comment on the fact, save old Amos, and his bleared eyes noticed little.

She took to regarding her hands attentively. Fine ladies, she had somewhere heard, slept in gloves to keep their hands white and soft. Sophy had no gloves ; and, other emollients being beyond her, frequent washings had to serve as a not unhealthy substitute. From her hands her thoughts passed naturally to her face. It was long since she had seen it. Not since she had thrown her uncle's fragment of looking-glass and razor down the well, lest he should do himself a fatal injury while shaving, and pension and roof-tree be lost. Now, striving to arrange her long strands of hair, she regretted such prodigality, and sought means to replace the loss. The next applicant for the benefit of her healing arts was required to secrete a mirror in a certain place, by the light of the moon, the working of the charm depending on the subsequent removal of the article by an unknown hand. The white witch took her fee, with no blush for her duplicity, and the dark hair lay more smoothly over her forehead.

But withal, Sophy was not mercenary, though this lack of a vice was, in her, no more of a virtue than was her apparent content. Both originated in the limitation of her ideas. But, being so, it fell out that several days had elapsed before she dipped casual fingers into the pockets of the coat, and found Quenride Chideock's locket and chain.

At first the unaccustomed beauty and value of the thing drew her mind from all other considerations, but at length various significances became apparent. She sat holding the lovely wonder in her hand, and thought. To begin with, it was certain that the donor of the coat had forgotten this treasure in his generosity. Sophy, apart from her white-magic practices, was an honest girl. The trinket was not intended for her, and must therefore be returned Her cheek glowed at the reasonableness of such an excuse for journeying to Dorchester and asking to see the man whose kind tones and friendly eyes had penetrated down to her deeply hidden heart, and given her a glimpse of a woman's kingdom. The anticipation was so keen that it carried a warning in it. The trembling joy of it all would so soon be over, and what would be left ? It was characteristic of human nature that Sophy did not remind herself that at least she would be no worse off than before she had made the discovery. She decided not to squander a pleasure that could not return. Presently she would take the locket back—presently. She turned it over, catching the sun-rays on its edges, and examining the intricacies of the monogram, which she did not understand as such. It was made to open ; she soon found that out, and pressed the spring repeatedly, gently at first, then more heavily, but it did not yield. Some injury to the mechanism had been received in its fall from Quenride's breast, and the catch would not act.

Curiosity arose in the girl. She longed to see what was hidden within, but, since she intended to restore the locket, dared not force the lid open for dread of inflicting damage to which she would have to own. Imagining that there was some legitimate way of causing the spring to act, she found here an additional inducement to delay. It would, she felt, be impossible to part with the locket until she had seen what lay within. A double reason is frequently the cause of a prescribed course of action, and is usually an unanswerable argument to the reasoner, though lacking the dramatic quality of a single-hearted one.

That such a dainty ornament should be found in the pocket of a man's coat was a significant fact even to this unsophisticated maiden. She knew only the superficial difference between the attire of a man of the better class and that of one of her own. But the feminine instinct in her claimed the locket and chain as belonging to her own sex. And in guessing at the why and wherefore, she hit upon the rightful owner without going near the truth of its recent possession.

The suggestion disturbed her for a few hours, not because her infatuation for the only man who had appeared other than an ordinary mortal had as yet grown out of reason, but because a third figure—and that, moreover, of a woman whom she already hated—had obtruded into her dreams. Then uncertainty swayed a heart very willing to reassure itself. She found a dozen different reasons for Ridley's possession of the ornament, even granting that it had originally belonged to Miss Chideock, and, thrusting aside the more distasteful persuasions, continued her hero-worship with the added joy of knowing that she was the custodian of one of his treasures. When she could open the locket, she fancied that one point at least would be decided. Surely there lay hidden inside some clue as to its previous possessor. And not until she had learnt the truth would she relinquish her guardianship.

So she wrapped the locket and chain in a handkerchief, and laid it at the bottom of the box, taking it out at times and endeavouring to make it disclose its secret, which was still labour in vain.

To this point had Sophy's emotional experiences moved, when an event occurred to further their development.

It was a Sunday—the third one since Wareham Fair, the second since her parting with Ridley. The day was fine, one of those warm periods of mellow sun and soft airs that in these latitudes frequently compensate in the month of September for the ungenial sullenness of earlier skies. Sophy, who kept no Sabbath, took a basket, and went out blackberrying at some distance from her home.

It was an occupation which, being restricted to a brief period of the year, carried with it some of the elements of a holiday. Of merry-makings pure and simple, Sophy had no experience as a participator. Fairs, maypolings, gipsyings—these she attended regularly, but brought home no fairings from the one, neither danced at the others. They were to her only the gatherings where pence might be earned more easily than at other times. But a blackberrying usually meant a day's outing under blue skies, and in her way she drew pleasure from it.

The berries were ripe and plentiful. Sophy knew better than any where to look for them. By noon the basket was nearly full, but she was in no hurry to return. She sat down in a field that bordered the road, and took out her dinner of bread and cheese. When she had finished her meal, she went to lean over the gate and to turn her mournful eyes up the road. It led to Wareham—the place of strange adventures. Beyond lay Dorchester, already, to the love-smitten girl, a town of romantic dreams.

The sound of approaching horse-hoofs made her raise her languid head, and, straining forward idly, the blood sprang to her forehead as she recognised Ridley himself coming towards her at a quick trot. At the sight, the complexity of love worked within her. She wanted him to stop ; she longed for him to pass by. She hoped that he would not see her ; she yearned for him to look and recognise. And with it all, she did nothing. Dolly Pouncey would have turned the moment to ingenious advantage. A coarser-moulded mind would have ensured acknowledgment. This girl merely waited, her attitude unchanged, her colour returned to its normal insignificance, until the rider came up.

He all but passed her, so drab and unnoticeable a figure was she, so much akin, it seemed, to others of her age and rank. But a casual glance, given in the very act of riding by, brought him to a halt with her name upon his lips.

"Why, Sophy!" he cried. "This is odd! I was coming to find you."

"To find me?" she repeated, looking up at him.

"Yes, I wanted to speak to you—and to your grand-uncle," he added.

"You won't get no sense out o' he," she said.

"Ah, so I'm told. Is he so bad?"

"He be a girt trouble," she said viciously. "Just a silly wold man—good for naught at all!"

"Still," said Ridley, after a moment's thought, "I'd like to see him."

"Oh," said Sophy, "you can see him if you want to."

"Is he with you?"

"He's at home," she said.

"Is that far?"

"About three miles."

"Can I find the place easily?"

He could, from its situation, hardly have missed it. Sophy knew that, but her wits were recovering from the initial glamour of his presence, and an idea came to her.

"If you could wait till I be rested," she said, "I'd show 'ee the way."

"Very well," agreed Ridley, seeing here an opportunity of speaking to the girl of the matter which concerned herself.

He dismounted, drew the reins over his arm, and leant over the gate from the other side. Sophy sat down again, breathing a little quickly. The brambles ran right up to the gate-post, and waved over Ridley's head. He stretched out an idle hand and picked the ripest berries. While he ate them his eyes grew retrospectively amused. Sophy saw that he had practically forgotten her.

"Don't ! " she whispered, starting up. "Have some of these ! They'll stain your gloves—you can't think ! "

But he declined her basket, and continued to help himself to berries in his own way. He was in a complacent mood. His health had returned, the ride had done him good, and he had managed to skirt Wareham unobserved.

"Why did you want to see me ? " asked Sophy, looking up at him.

Ridley hesitated. The matter was the locket. He had expected her to come in to Dorchester before this ; when she had failed to do this, he had tried to believe that she had not discovered it. There was nothing in her manner now to suggest anything.

"When I gave you the coat for your uncle the other day," he began, delicately, "I forgot that I'd left something in the pocket. Something of value. Did you find it ? "

"Yes," said Sophy, without thinking.

Ridley was glad, relieved at the recovery implied in her answer, and pleased that his first estimate of her seemed justified.

"That's good ! " he said. "I must have it back, though you shan't lose by taking care of it for me. I'll come with you, and you can give it to me."

Sophy was silent, sitting downcast amid the wreck of her dreams. Realisation of meeting him had come too soon. In an hour or so it would all be over. He would have ridden away for ever. The chill, the disappointment, almost frightened her. She could not bear to end it yet—and never learn the secret of the locket at all. The misery of such anticipation goaded her to her next words. She spoke without looking at him.

"I can't," she said.

"Can't ? " cried he. "Why not ? "

"I've a-lost it ! "

"Good God ! " cried Ridley, frowning. "How could you do a thing like that ? "

"I—I didn't mean to ! " she whimpered, the lie still hot in her mouth. "'Twasn't my fault ! "

"I mean the locket and chain," he explained anxiously.

"Ay," said Sophy.

Ridley's foot was tapping the ground in his vexation.

"I'll tell you," he said. "If the thing had been just my own, I wouldn't have cared. But it belongs rightly to some one else—to Miss Chideock, in fact. You see what you've done by your carelessness."

Sophy's hands were clenched in the long grass. To her raw perceptions, the thing which she dreaded actually did exist. The locket was valuable only because it had belonged to the great and beautiful Miss Chideock. This, to Sophy, meant only one thing. This man, with the kind eyes suddenly gone hard and stern, with the pleasant voice grown cold and harsh, loved the lady who had used him so ill, and treasured a gift which she had given him in sunnier mood. A miserable rage racked the girl's heart, yet because the retention of the locket was her one poor chance of seeing Ridley again she would not confess the lie.

" Maybe—maybe I'll find it, if you give me time," she faltered. " If—if you come again."

" How can you hope to find it ? " he asked sharply.

" I think I know where 'twas lost," she muttered. " I'll look again."

" Then, in heaven's name, do ! " he cried. " And bring it to me at once ! You've done me a good deal of harm by this, Sophy. I thought I could trust you."

" I'm sorry," she said, her gaze on the ground.

There was a strange dejection in her manner which struck her companion. Knowing nothing of the facts, he attributed it to contrition ; whereas the girl was tasting the gall of an unreasonable jealousy. Ridley's anger was spoiling the pleasure of the present moments, but in a lesser degree than her supposed discovery of his attachment to Miss Chideock. It was a trouble which she could herself remove at their next meeting, so that the smart of his displeasure was not so keen as it might have been. She offered neither explanation nor excuse, but brooding over the deeper matter pleaded her own cause in the case as he knew it, by breaking into tears, while he looked at her.

Ridley checked a continuance of reproof, and putting his hand over the gate touched her shoulder. It was true that she had done him a bad turn. There would be nothing for it but a letter of explanation to Quenride Chideock, and an offer of compensation for the value of the ornament, which offer he fully expected she would refuse, thus leaving him with a distasteful sense of obligation to her. But he was fair-minded enough to admit his own share of blame in the matter—both for his holding back of the locket after its discovery and for the thoughtlessness which had allowed it to pass into Sophy's hands. It had been an unpleasant business from the beginning, but there was no sense in scolding the girl any more.

"Don't cry!" he said—not gently, but less harshly than before. "It can't be helped now. I must make the best of it. If you can find the thing, I'll be glad, but I'm afraid you won't. Tell me how you lost it."

Between her sobs she fabricated a plausible story. When both tears and account had come to an end, silence fell between them. Glancing up timidly, she saw that he had resumed his occupation of picking off the ripe berries and eating them. But his action was more mechanical now, and his eyes were thoughtful under a frowning brow. Again, he seemed to have forgotten the girl at his feet.

"He's thinking of—her!" she told herself, and her softer mood gave place to one more resolute. After all, for these brief moments, she had him to herself. She hugged the consolation deliberately—and even drew cheerfulness from it. Why should he think of Miss Chideock?

"Did you ever go blackberrying?" she asked suddenly.

"Often and often," he told her, not sorry for the change of subject.

"Well—and what did you find?"

"Generally the schoolmaster waiting for me the next day. It wasn't part of his curriculum."

"Did he hurt you much?" she asked, with retrospective sympathy.

Ridley laughed.

"Very likely! I didn't care. I had blackberry pudding for dinner."

"Don't you mind pain?" she asked, wondering.

"Not much—so long as I get what I want."

"It vexed your mother, I reckon."

"I lost my mother early, Sophy."

"Your father then?"

"I can't think that it would have worried him!"

"Oh," she cried, "wasn't there anyone as cared?'

"I had a jewel of an old nurse. But I didn't tell her. There's no sense in making people miserable when they can be happy."

He said those words to the girl kneeling before him, looked into her tragic eyes—and read nothing there.

"Girt-uncle used to beat me when he were drinky," she

said. " I hated him, and paid him out when I could. Didn't you hate the master ? "

" The good church books tell us to forgive our enemies, don't they, Sophy ? "

" I don't know. I can't read. And I don't go to church."

" That's a pity. You ought to do both."

" Do you ?—go to the church, I mean."

" Oh, yes. I'm no pagan. I don't believe that man's highest aim is happiness—sensual happiness, that is. For it's quite possible to be happy even while you're miserable ; and that's a much better state than being miserable while you're happy."

She understood nothing of it, but asked :

" Why ? "

" Because to be happy while miserable usually means that you're helping some one else to happiness. And to be miserable while you're happy means as a rule that you're making somebody suffer."

She was listening with an earnestness which might have surprised him.

" Is that what makes you wish it done ? " she asked.

For the moment Ridley was at a loss.

" You said it, that day," she told him. " The sun, it were. How can anyone hate the sun ? 'Tis silly talk, I reckon. But you said it—an' I keep thinking of them words. What do they mean ? "

Ridley remembered and laughed. He repeated the lines :

> " ' *In the wind there is a voice*
> *Shall forbid thee to rejoice ;*
> *And to thee shall Night deny*
> *All the quiet of her sky ;*
> *And the Day shall have a sun*
> *Which shall make thee wish it done.'*

Yes ; it means what I'm saying. It's a curse, and—well, we make our own curses more often than not ! You don't understand ? Well, Heaven keep such tragic experiences from you, Sophy ! What did you mean about the blackberrying ? "

" Oh, just this. Didn't you find as the ripest and sweetest of 'em were the ones quite low down an' ready to fall into your hand ? "

" I cared nothing for those," he said. " I prized far more the ones I had to scramble and tear my fingers for."

Sophy looked depressed again, then spoke with sudden vehemence.

"After all," she cried, "I'm glad the master was waiting for you ! I hope he hurt you a great deal ! "

"The puddings were good," said Ridley. "I never get them now."

"How's that ? "

"Upon my soul, I hardly know. I suppose I forget to ask."

Sophy cooled again, and looked at him shyly.

"I'll make 'ee one, if you'll come back wi' me," she said.

"That's good of you ! How long will it take ? "

"An hour or so," said Sophy, with deliberate vagueness.

"Well, if I'm home by dusk, that will do," said Ridley. "Thank you ; I'll accept your pudding, Sophy. And now, are you rested, do you think ? "

But the girl's plans had been rearranged. The nearness of his presence oppressed her—it was, in her excited, complex mood, more than she could bear. She must be alone, to collect her thoughts. Since his friendliness had returned, she was growing ashamed of her duplicity, and the walk home at his side would have been more of an ordeal than a pleasure.

She therefore sent him to the cottage by way of the road, and herself raced home across the fields, reaching it slightly in advance of the leisurely rider.

By the time that Ridley arrived, Sophy was as quiet as usual, and not much more talkative. She brought him into the garden, showed him the stable, and helped him to put up the horse. Then she pointed to the orchard.

"Girt-uncle's down there," she said, and went back to her berries.

Ridley found the old man sitting half-asleep in the sun. He looked at the withered face and bleary eyes, and any hope which he had had of finding out from Amos Hoddinott the reason of his last visit to Mr. Benjamin Chideock died on the spot.

The bloodshot eyes winked at him without the least recognition. Ridley sat down on the bench beside him, and spoke.

"Don't you remember me ? " he asked.

For a long time there was no answer. The old man seemed so abject a thing sitting there under the fair yield of the orchard, wrapped round by the autumn sunshine, that the young lawyer pitied him much as he had pitied Gilbert

Chideock. He was about to repeat the question, his voice softened to the persuasive tones suitable to such weakness, when the old man suddenly began to beat the bench with his hands, and spoke.

"I can't find it! I can't find it!" he wailed.

"Lord!" said Ridley; "your family's good at losing things, it seems. What can't you find, Amos?"

There was no reply. The old man was fumbling in his pockets, and shaking his head.

"Do you remember Mr. Thomas Ridley?" asked the other. "You were his clerk for a number of years. Ridley! Look at me, Amos!"

The grey head came round slowly, but no intelligence brightened the dull gaze.

"Can you recall this name?" asked Ridley. "Chideock, Mr. Benjamin Chideock, of Wareham."

Amos shuffled along the bench, and looked at him with a faint gleam of comprehension. Ridley's hopes rose again.

"Chideock!" he repeated. "You remember that?"

But the light had gone, and the shadow of imbecility fell as darkly as before.

"I can't find it," he said, "I can't find it."

"What?" asked the young man, but with small hope of an intelligent reply.

Instead of replying, Amos, the poor besotted wreck, got up and shambled away. Ridley did not follow. The matter of that last visit seemed likely to remain a secret, unless Mr. Chideock should reveal it in his own good time. Ridley leaned back against an apple-tree and hoped that it was not important.

Later on, Sophy came out to him. She had on a clean print dress, and her hair was neatly braided. Her mouth was almost smiling as she told him that dinner was ready. She had given herself up to the pleasure of the moment, and had thrust the hated figure of Miss Chideock into the background of her mind. Ridley, who had been thinking for the past hour of the same young lady, followed Sophy into the stone-flagged kitchen, and sat down to a meal that was a novelty.

It might have been called by any name. Sophy had brought out of her store lavishly, but indiscriminately. In addition to the promised pudding, home-made bread was there, cheese of her own pressing, butter from her churn, newly-run honey, cold bacon, golden pippins, eggs and milk. A feast for a hungry man. Amos shuffled in after them, and

ordered into silence by the girl, took his meal in apparent
indifference both to the unusual hour and the quality of it.

" I owe you thanks, Sophy," said the visitor, when, at the
end, Amos had been sent to saddle the horse and take him
round into the road. " When you're next in Dorchester you
must dine at my house. Mrs. Channing will make you very
welcome."

She flushed with pleasure, scarcely understanding the
implied reservation.

" And you—you'll come again, won't 'ee ? " she asked,
in a low voice.

" No," said Ridley. " No. I can't do that."

" Why can't 'ee ? "

The horse, led by Amos, passed the window.

" That's not for me to explain," said Ridley. " But, no.
It couldn't be."

She wondered over his words, missing their true meaning.
Then she sighed impatiently, and saw that he was holding out
his ungloved hand. Very timidly she took it in her own, and
held it for a moment. She would have given much to kiss it
as she had done before. But with a realisation of the emotion
which he had unwittingly awakened in her had come self-
consciousness—and she could not.

" Good-bye," he said. " And find the locket, if by any
means you can."

She followed him to the door, and watched him ride away.
He turned to wave his hand before he got out of sight, but
by that time tears were raining down Sophy's face.

" 'Tis her ! " she muttered. " That's why he'll come no
more. Oh, I hate her—the proud cruel thing ! "

With sudden desperate misery, she turned and ran upstairs.
Down by the box under the shelving roof she knelt, and
pulled out the coat less gently than usual. She found the
locket and chain lying underneath, and snatching them up
carried them to the window.

Without a moment for reflection, she inserted her strong
thumb-nails between the lid and the body of the locket, and
wrenched at them until, at the sixth attempt, they fell apart,
and a lovely face smiled up at her.

" 'Tis her ! " she whispered. " Now I'm sure. 'Tis
her."

But she was wrong. The miniature was not of Quenride,
but of Quenride's mother—idealised by the artist into a close
resemblance to her fairer-featured daughter. Not guessing

this, Sophy hung over the picture, though every line of it mocked her cruelly, and when she laid it down it was only that she might fetch the mirror from the box, and learn to hate her own face.

In rising, she happened to glance towards the door. In her impetuosity she had forgotten to secure it. It stood partly open, and there, on a level with the threshold, appeared Amos's head, his body out of sight against the ladder-like stairs. He was watching his grand-niece with more expression in his eyes than she had seen for many a day.

She sprang up, stamping and shrieking at him.

" Go away ! " she screamed. " Go away—bad wold man ! I'll throw 'ee downstairs ! I'll break your neck ! How dare 'ee come spying on me ?   How dare 'ee ? I say ! "

He fled at her first words. But that he had seen was unmistakable, and Sophy, flushed and panting, cast round to find a securer place in which to secrete her treasure.

CHAPTER XV

A GAME OF SHUTTLECOCK

IT was one of Gilbert Chideock's bad days. He lay on a sofa, his face puckered peevishly, and made shift to quarrel with every one. Dolly Pouncey, who was warm-hearted and absolutely natural with a youth of his age, had vainly tried to win him to a better humour. But he drove her away at length in a mood that was but little pleasanter than his own, and Quenride took her place.

Dolly would have said that it was one of the young lady's bad days also. The girl had already incurred sharp words for being noisy about the house. She was a careless little creature, and doors had a trick of slipping out of her fingers. When the last crash had reverberated through the house, Quenride showed signs of being in what Dolly considered an unladylike temper ; none the less so because the girl was reasonably apologetic before a word had been uttered.

" I'm sorry ! " said Dolly. " I forgot your grandfather. But perhaps he doesn't mind."

" You never remember anything ! " cried Quenride. " How dare you say such things ! "

And Dolly was rated sharply for her ways. She became a little obstinate and stuck to her point. In truth, she found it difficult to sympathise much with an invalid whom she had never seen.

" I really think," she declared, " that a little noise like that can't harm him much. Perhaps he fancies he's worse than he is — and if so, he can't be as delicate as he pretends to be."

" What do you know about my grandfather's ailments ? " cried Quenride, in the high-pitched tones that sounded like Gilbert's, and would have spoken, to more discriminating ears, of nerves stretched almost to breaking-point.

" Only this," said Dolly a little disrespectfully, " if he

were as bad as he makes himself out to be, you'd call in a doctor sometimes."

"How do you know that it is not his own wish to be let alone?" asked the other. "Have you never heard of maladies which doctors can neither cure nor alleviate? Do you mean that I am neglecting him?"

"People might say so," muttered Dolly perversely.

Quenride gave her a look.

"And do you think," she said, "that I care so very much what people say, as long as the family physician is satisfied with my conduct? It is a very poor sort of mind, Dolly, that allows the opinions of inferior people to turn it from its own way."

And with that rebuke, characteristic both in its utterance and in its reception—for Dolly immediately adopted it as a tenet of the upper classes—Quenride walked down the stairs with a mien which suggested that whisperings and slanders were nothing to her.

The letter-bag had been left in the hall. She carried it with her into the room where her brother lay. Gilbert watched her with an unusual interest which would have aroused her own, had she been less absorbed. As it was, she greeted him with forced cheerfulness, and proceeded to open the bag in a leisurely way. As she looked over the letters, she told him to whom they were addressed, and continued to give him information as she broke the seals of her own. Presently, she opened one, and remained silent over its contents so long that the boy grew impatient.

"What is it, Quen? How grave you look! Are you angry at something?"

She appeared to be reading the letter a second time, and gave no reply.

"Whom is it from? Why don't you tell?" persisted Gilbert.

After a full minute she raised her eyes. They were very bright; excited in their animation, filled with some emotion which the boy could not comprehend. It was, in truth, the look of a woman wrought up to the pitch of daring greatly for a great gain or loss. Such a look as a gambler may be supposed to wear when he throws down his last coin, and salvation or ruin will claim him in a moment's time.

"Well," said the boy, "what is it? How strange you look, Quen!"

" You wouldn't be interested, Gilbert," she said slowly.
" It is only a business letter."

" So were some of the others! Why won't you tell me
about that one? It appears to interest you."

" How curious you are! " she said, the natural harshness
of the rebuke softened almost to an endearment. Her eyes
had not altogether lost their luminous look, but they dwelt
on him tenderly. " If you must know, it is from the lawyer
at Dorchester. Now, ask me no more, or I shan't love
you."

But Gilbert was already questioning her with some eagerness.

" From Mr. Ridley? I thought as much! I mean—
I hoped it! Is he coming here? Oh, Quenny, don't say
that he shan't! "

Quenride had folded the letter, and replaced it in its
envelope. Gilbert was holding out his hand for it. She did
not give it to him. Instead, she leant her chin on her palm,
elbow on raised knee, and looked at him thoughtfully across
the room.

" Why do you want the lawyer to come here? " she asked.

" Because he's my friend."

" Nonsense! " Quenride frowned at him. " How could
you make a friend of a man of his degree? "

" What's the matter with him? " demanded Gilbert, in the
tone of a partisan.

" He's not a gentleman," she said. " There's enough for
you! "

" He's a deal more of a gentleman than some of the county
men! " declared the lad hotly. " Look at old Sir Georgius!
I can remember grandfather's dinner-parties. Sir Georgius
always got drunk and insulted everybody. Kissed you once,
didn't he? And you slapped his red old face, and there
was a deuce of a row. I remember. And there's Cousin
Alaric. He's ' county '; he's a Mohun. Do you call him a
gentleman? "

" He has birth," said Quenride, in no very convinced tone.
" I never heard that Lawyer Ridley was a man of family."

Gilbert writhed restlessly on his sofa.

" I don't care for that! " he said. " Mr. Ridley's the most
interesting and the pleasantest man I know. He's very
kind, and his manners are perfect. Quen, you are all wrong!
You made me think that every one who did anything for a
living was a regular chaw-bacon, who didn't know even how

to sit at table. Why, Mr. Ridley makes a perfect host! I
know because I've dined with him."

"You never told me that before!" cried Quenride
quickly. "When was it?"

"The day I called. He asked me to, and I didn't see
why I shouldn't. Yes. I knew you'd disapprove."

"I do," she said, "strongly. Gilbert, you have acted
very ill. You must never do such a thing again."

But the lad, made fretful by indisposition, and anticipating
the disappointment of his desire to see the lawyer again, had
fallen into a rebellious mood.

"I shall not promise," he said, with his old-fashioned
dignity. "I can't always be doing just as you like.
Especially when I know you're wrong."

Quenride clasped her hands on her knee.

"Oh," she said, in her softened anger, "that man
has influenced you already! He has led you on to this.
You never defied me before. He has taught you how to
do it!"

Gilbert laughed in a superior way.

"How strange you are to-day, Quen!" he said. "Do
you think Mr. Ridley and I hadn't anything more interesting
to talk about than you?"

"Didn't he speak of me?" she cried.

"Not much—and then only when I did. You're really
most unfair. And if you do prevent his coming here you
can't stop my liking him."

She continued to regard the boy with unwavering eyes,
in which, nevertheless, emotions rose and gathered force,
finally deepening to a fixity of sorrow that must needs have
its generation in other eventualities than those under discussion—so intense and brooding was it. Yet when she
spoke, she followed her brother's argument, as though it was
not discordant with her own thoughts.

"No," she said. "I cannot hinder that. And if he
teaches you to despise me—Oh, Gilbert, may you never
know what it is to be despised by one you love!"

The lad raised himself to look at her. This mood was
so new to his experience of his high-spirited sister that
he could scarcely take it seriously. Again he laughed—and
laughing lay down once more.

"I don't despise you, and I do love you, Quen," he said,
adding with boyish candour, "Don't be a fool. You're
making yourself very disagreeable over nothing. I haven't

got so lively a time of it that you need make things worse.
May Mr. Ridley come to see me ? "

" Gilbert, don't tease me any more. You shall have
whatever else you like. But I cannot let that man visit
here."

" Why not ? "

" For many reasons."

" Because he's not what you call a gentleman ? "

" If you like," she said wearily.

Gilbert turned to the wall, and sulked.

" Then you are disagreeable ! " he said. " Here I am,
cooped up with a lot of women, and you deny me a man's
friendship. Yet you say you're fond of me ! "

" Gilbert—Gilbert—do you turn against me ? You ? "
she cried, with heaving breast and brimming eyes.

He flung back his answer crossly.

" It's your own fault ! " he said.

" He shan't come here ! he shan't ! he shan't ! " she cried.
But her voice shook, and looking round sullenly a minute
later Gilbert saw her head abased on her arms, which were
spread across the table in the carelessness of grief. She was
sobbing ; it was the sound which had brought his gaze round
to her.

The sight was sufficiently unusual to turn the drift of
his own mood. He was at a somewhat impercipient age,
but could realise clearly enough that his sister could scarcely
be weeping her heart out because he had chosen a friend of
whom she did not approve. In spite of his perverse humour,
Quenride's obvious grief troubled him. By degrees, he
left the sofa, and managed to reach her side. She started
when he touched her, as though she had forgotten him.
The boy said nothing, but stood there, leaning on her shoulder.
She reached up her arm and encircled his frail body.

" Gilbert ! " she said very tenderly.

He stooped, and kissed her. She caught his face, and
held it near her own. There was again a look about her
which he could not understand.

" If all the world turned against me, you would remain,
would you not, Gilbert ? " she said.

" Of course," he answered, with a boy's readiness. " But
how should the world dare ? "

She dried her eyes, and put him from her, with a faintly
proud smile.

" There is always one's own heart," she said.

" For what, Quen ? "

" For courage," she replied.

She led him back to the sofa, and then left the room.

Sitting down alone, she reopened Ridley's letter. It was not, as Gilbert had supposed, one containing a proposal to come to Wareham—the boy was happily unaware that such a suggestion had already been made, and prevented from being carried out—but that the matter of this last communication was interesting, even suggestive, Quenride had already shown. Now she read it again. It ran :

" MADAM,—I feel it my duty to acquaint you with a circumstance which, I fear, cannot but lead to your very serious annoyance, and to my own just blame. I am referring to a loss of which you are doubtless aware. When I say that the article of which my culpable carelessness has deprived you is a gold locket and chain, there will be no need for me to indicate either its loss or its subsequent discovery by myself. It was my intention to communicate with you on the matter, but pending a suitable opportunity I regret to say that I was remiss enough to allow the ornament to pass into the possession of another. The lack of evil intention is my only excuse for so doing. An insufficient one, I fear, for, to my genuine annoyance and deep regret, I am obliged to inform you that your property has been lost for a second time. I dare not hold out any distinct hope of its recovery. But should such a circumstance come to my knowledge, I will immediately advise you of the same. In the meanwhile, since the blame rests entirely with me, I request permission to restore the monetary value of the ornament, trusting that you will allow me to ease my conscience thus far. If you should wish to see me personally on this matter, I shall be at your service any day except to-morrow (Friday), when I shall be away from home until evening.—I beg to remain, Madam, your humble servant,

" K. RIDLEY."

The indignation and regret which the letter had naturally at first aroused was left behind. She no longer winced at the suggestion of a personal interview, or asked herself whether he had proposed it out of sheer malice, or merely as a ruse to get a footing in the house. As a matter of fact, it was neither, Ridley being perfectly sincere in his expression of regret, and paying her the compliment of allowing that, in the present instance, she had a decided advantage over himself. He was not one to condone his own faults, when once persuaded of their existence. He now admitted that in his original retention of her property he had pressed the case somewhat too hardly against her.

But Quenride had no thought to spare for his culpability. She had even lost sight of the mischief which his action had caused. In truth, her loss was hardly so disastrous as Ridley might have supposed. The miniature was not the only one of her mother which she possessed ; the trinket itself was her own, and she had other more valuable ornaments. That side of the affair, therefore, made less impression on her than Ridley had conjectured. The real effect of his letter would have surprised him.

She put the sheet of paper back into its envelope, and locked it away. Then she went to look for Dolly Pouncey.

Her appearance slightly astonished the girl, considering that they had parted out of humour with each other. For Quenride was not the one, on such occasions, to make the first advance, and now she addressed her companion with apparent friendliness.

" Haven't I heard you speak," she asked, " of Mr. Ridley's clerk ? The lawyer at Dorchester, I mean."

" I'm sure you never heard me mention him in your life, ma'am," asserted the girl.

" 'Twas your mother, then."

" Very likely," said Dolly, trying to look embarrassed.

" Yes ; it was. I remember now. When she was here on fair-day."

" Oh, indeed ! "

" You know the young man, I understand ? "

" I wouldn't go so far as that," murmured the other.

" Do you, or do you not know him ? " asked Quenride, with a little frown.

" Yes," said Dolly suddenly.

" What sort of a young man is he ? "

" Well," said the girl, after consideration, " he's not so bad looking, as young men go nowadays. Though I don't care much for fair-haired men——"

" That's not what I mean ! How your silly head runs on exteriors ! What is he like in himself ? "

" He's countrified," said Dolly, rather offended. " Of course, he's only humble connections. His mother——"

" That's enough of that ! I don't want to know his

family history. Is he a clever, far-seeing sort of young fellow ? "

" I shouldn't think it," said Dolly, at once.

" Still, he can't be quite a fool, or Mr. Ridley wouldn't put up with him," said Quenride. " But, on the other hand, he can't be quite remarkable, or he wouldn't put up with Mr. Ridley."

" He hasn't got too much spirit," said Dolly. " To speak plainly, though I don't want to make you think poorly of him, he's a bit too soft a creature for any maid to think seriously of."

Quenride pondered the words.

" A good-natured, weak-headed sort of youth. Is that it ? " she asked.

Dolly appeared to consider this an excellent description of her admirer.

" Fond of you, I think your mother said ? "

" I—I believe so," admitted the girl.

" Against your father's inclination ? "

" Well, in a way, father is quite right. For though Robin is pleasant enough, there's no denying that father has a claim to expect more than that from me."

" That will do," said Quenride, rising. " Now dress yourself to come out driving with me. Order the gig to be round in ten minutes. I am going into Dorchester on business."

It was late afternoon when they reached the town. On the way Quenride had kept silent as to her destination, maintaining a preoccupied air, for, in truth, her thoughts dwelt largely upon the circumstances of her last journey along that road. She experienced an almost morbid anxiety to see again the spot where she had waited for her servant to bring back the lawyer's answer—yet, when she reached it, she urged her horse on still more rapidly, so poignant was the remembrance of what she had subsequently endured. Her cheek was scarcely cool by the time that the gig rattled into the town, and her hand shook slightly on the reins as she brought the vehicle to a standstill before Ridley's door. Dolly, in some flutter of excitement herself, prepared to get down, for her mistress, contrary to her usual habit, had brought no groom with her.

Quenride stayed her, put the reins into her hand, and, bidding her wait, herself alighted, and passed into the portico.

Her summons brought the housekeeper, who gave the information that the lawyer was not at home.

" I will wait," said Quenride, preparing to enter.

" He'll not be in, ma'am, till ten o'clock to-night," said the woman.

Quenride drew back her foot, and was thoughtful.

" I have come some distance," she said, then. " Is there no one else whom I can see ? Surely Mr. Ridley does not leave his business unattended to, in his absence ? "

" There's the lad Fiander, ma'am. Not that he's likely to be of much service to your ladyship."

" Is he so stupid, then ? "

" He ha'n't the headpiece of the master, naturally. Still——"

Quenride happened to glance sideways, and immediately had a view of the headpiece in question, as it appeared over the wire blind in the office window—a shock of tow-coloured hair and wide blue eyes gazing entranced at Dolly Pouncey.

" Perhaps the clerk will serve as well as the lawyer," said Quenride, after one glance. And without further parleying, she entered the house.

Shown into the office, she was received by Fiander in a state of bewilderment verging on distraction. The mere knowledge of the nearness of his beloved one was sufficient to throw his weak wits off their balance, and here, in addition, was the arrival of a very beautiful and gracious lady, who appeared to take the office by storm and dominate it from the moment of her entry. Blushing and confused, he had introduced her into the lawyer's own chair before he realised his error.

" Mr. Ridley is out, I understand ? " began Quenride, calm as a lady should be.

" He'll not be back till late," Fiander told her. " He had business out of the town."

" It is unfortunate," she returned, fixing him with her eloquent eyes.

" You wanted to see him, ma'am ? " asked Fiander, fidgeting under that gaze.

" Why should I else be here ? I have driven some miles."

Fiander expressed regret, and asked if he could convey a message. Quenride appeared to consider.

" I had a letter from Mr. Ridley this morning," she said. " He is looking after a little affair of mine, and seemed to think that an interview might be desirable."

Fiander tried to be as attentive as was consistent with a

longing to throw glances over the blind every five seconds.
Bringing his eyes back from one of these wanderings, he
saw that the visitor was holding a sheet of paper in her hand.

"Oh, yes. A letter, ma'am," he said. "But I wonder
he should have asked you to call this afternoon, as he told
me some time back that he would have to go to Weymouth
to-day. 'Tisn't like him to be so careless, ma'am."

"Don't trouble your brains over that," said Quenride.
"Perhaps I had better explain more fully. Mr. Ridley is
engaged in tracing some lost property of mine. As far as
I can gather, it is likely to be recovered at any moment.
Have you heard him speak of it ? He wrote to me yesterday ;
it had not been discovered then, but since any hour might
bring it forth, there is just a chance—— Mr. Fiander! this is
really a matter which interests me greatly ! Kindly attend !"

"I beg pardon," stammered the young man, and with
an effort of will, he turned his back on the window. "You
were saying—that—that you'd had a letter——"

"Has Mr. Ridley mentioned this matter to you ? "

"I don't remember his doing so."

"Then it is possible that he may have ended the search
successfully without telling you either, and ended it since
his communication to me."

"'Tis—possible," assented Fiander a little doubtfully.
"Not very likely, perhaps."

Quenride glanced sharply at him.

"You must allow me to be the best judge of that," she
said, with a touch of hauteur that instantly reduced him to
humility. "At all events, perhaps you will not object to
ascertain for me whether it is so or not."

Fiander stared at her, but finding that her ripe beauty
still further bewildered him he dropped his eyes to the floor,
and muttered that he did not understand what she wished
him to do.

"Surely it doesn't need much explaining," she said. "If
Mr. Ridley has my property, he is not likely to have left it
lying about, since it is an article of some value. Neither, I
suppose, would he put it among his own belongings. In all
probability he would regard it as property left in his care,
and treat it as such. I dare say you know his custom in these
cases. What does he generally do ? "

"Everything of value is kept downstairs," said Fiander.

"Jewels, plate, and documents all together ? "

"Yes, ma'am, in a large strong chest, in the cellar."

"What an odd arrangement! It doesn't sound very safe."

Robin Fiander laughed.

"Oh, I assure you, it is. Mr. Ridley sees to that. He's very particular."

"I'm sure I hope so—if he's got my property! But a mere chest, in a cellar!"

The youth grew warm. It was unseemly to contradict a grand lady, but his employer must be defended at all costs.

"But really, ma'am, 'tis quite safe," he protested. "The chest's fastened to the floor with iron clamps, and the door's locked with a large padlock; and the key of that's kept here."

He laid his hand on the writing-table as he spoke, with an almost defiant air. Quenride regarded him languidly.

"Well," she said, "since you seem to know all about it, we'll get back to what I was saying. Can you oblige me by going down to this cellar of yours, and ascertaining whether my property is there or not? Since I've come so far, it seems a pity to learn no more than if I had stayed at home."

"It certainly does," said Fiander, with a perplexed look. "But—'tis very awkward, ma'am, if you don't mind my saying so."

"Why? I am not asking much."

"Not at all! Only—I don't know what Mr. Ridley would say."

"I can't see your objection. You're here in authority. You're his representative in his absence."

"Am I?" This aspect of his position seemed a novel one to the young clerk. On the whole, he found that he rather liked it. He smiled, drawing a similar response from Quenride herself. He tried to assume a manly air.

"Still, though indeed you're quite right, ma'am," he said, "I'm not supposed to open the chest unless by Mr. Ridley's orders."

"And if he were here sitting in this chair at this moment, and knew my packet was in the chest, what do you think he would say?"

Put like that, the argument seemed sound. Fiander reviewed the situation anew.

"I daresay," he told her, "he'd open his secret drawer, give me the keys, and tell me to fetch the article."

" Well ? "

" But, you see, I'm not supposed to know where he keeps the keys ! "

" It seems that you do."

" By accident, as you may say ! He opened the drawer to put a letter inside, and didn't know that I was in the room."

" Can you open it yourself ? " Quenride asked, looking with interest at the table.

" I never have. I—I—daresay I could."

" Your hesitation to oblige me doesn't say much for your master's temper," remarked she. " I wonder a lad of spirit stays with such a man."

" He's the best master in the world ! " cried Fiander distractedly. " And if anyone says he's not——"

" Oh, I daresay. Yet you seem to dread his anger very much."

" No, I don't ! Only—— Well, ma'am, to oblige ye I'll do it."

He turned towards the table, with a desperate energy. Quenride swung round to watch. After two or three attempts, he succeeded in giving the right degree of pressure to the spring, and a small drawer leapt into evidence from an unsuspected quarter. Two pairs of eyes glanced quickly into it, then turned towards each other. Fiander's were rather blank.

" I'm sorry ! " he exclaimed.

The drawer contained only the large key of the padlock, and a letter which Quenride recognised.

" I thought the little key would be there too—the key of the chest," Fiander went on.

The letter seemed to dazzle Quenride's eyes. She clasped her hands very tightly on her lap ; little bursts of strange hysterical laughter came from her. She would have snatched it to her had she dared.

" Shut it up ! Oh, shut it up ! " she cried, at length. " It doesn't matter. It is not your fault. I must come again."

Fiander allowed the drawer to spring back into its place. He then withdrew several paces, evidently expecting the visitor to take her departure. Quenride looked up at him.

" It might be as well for me to leave a written message for Mr. Ridley," said she. " If you will give me pen and paper——"

He placed them before her. She dipped the quill, and again looked at him.

"Miss Dolly Pouncey is outside," she remarked. "I believe she is a friend of yours."

He admitted the fact—red and stammering.

"Perhaps you would like to say a few words to her. You might offer her a cup of tea."

The young man vanished on flying feet, and a minute or so later carried the refreshment out to the gig. Dolly accepted it with an air of great surprise.

"Upon my word, I didn't expect to see you, Mr. Fiander," she said. "Do you live here?"

He explained his position timidly.

"I see," said Dolly. "Then I suppose Miss Chideock's talking to your—master?"

Fiander explained again, looking mute admiration at his pretty companion.

"I do wonder that you'd the heart to leave her alone!" said Dolly.

"She said I might come to speak to you."

"Did she? I wonder why?"

"I suppose she guessed I'd like it."

"She might have considered me."

"Oh, Dolly!"

"I wish you wouldn't address me as if I were a dairy-maid, Mr. Fiander," said the girl.

"You used to let me call you by your name. You used to call me by mine."

"Did I? Well—ever so long ago! Things are quite different now."

"I don't see that."

"You never were very clever at seeing things, were you? I'll try to make you understand. At the time you're talking of, I was at the farm, a bit of a hoyden, I'm afraid. Now, I'm Miss Chideock's companion. There's a very great difference."

Robin stared miserably up the street.

"I suppose," he said awkwardly, "you see a heap of gentlefolk there—gentlemen, I mean."

This was very far from being the case, but the girl was not going to admit it.

"Oh, well——" she returned. "A tolerable few. Miss Chideock's cousin, Mr. Mohun, often comes. He's a great friend of mine."

Robin's face took on a still more doleful expression. He got as near to the gig as he could.

"I suppose," he whispered up, "he—he hasn't said anything?"

"Said anything?" repeated Dolly blankly.

"Yes, made love to you. Hang it all! he doesn't want to marry you, does he?"

From her elevated situation, Dolly had a decided advantage. She looked down at him with a passable imitation of Quenride's coldest manner.

"Really, Mr. Fiander," she cried, "you are very indelicate! How do I know what Mr. Mohun wants? And now I really think you'd better go back to Miss Chideock. She doesn't care about my gossiping in the streets."

"Good-bye," said Robin, not daring to offer her his hand, but contriving to touch Dolly's as he took the cup and saucer from her.

"Good-bye!" she said airily, with a half-glance and a smile.

A dejected young clerk re-entered the house. He found Quenride drawing on her gloves. She spoke at once.

"After all," she said, "I have decided not to trouble Mr. Ridley. On the whole, I think it might be better not to mention my visit at all."

She made the statement calmly, as though expecting him to accept it without demur. But that the lad was too honest to do.

"I'd rather tell him, if you don't mind, ma'am," he said.

"To be frank—I don't wish it," she said. "I acted on impulse in coming at all, and I've reason to believe that Mr. Ridley would not be best pleased at my coming without an express appointment. The fact is, matters are a little strained between us at present. You know who I am—and you must have heard something."

Fiander's looks showed that he had, though her cool business-like attitude had hitherto taught him to forget the fact.

"There is small sense in annoying him unnecessarily," Quenride went on, still in the most confident of tones. "Besides, in this case, there will be no need for you to confess that you tampered with his private drawer in his absence."

Fiander was too worried to notice how hard a way of expressing the fact this statement was, or to remember that she had previously maintained his absolute integrity in doing what she requested. But his mind was not satisfied with her latest proposition, and he entered another protest. Quenride quickly bore him down.

"That's nonsense!" she said. "What harm will be done by forbearing to trouble your employer with a trivial incident which has led to nothing? He'd thank you for your excellent tact, if he understood. Say no more. If you are willing to oblige me in this matter—and you will really place me in a very false position if you mention my visit—I may be willing to oblige you on some future occasion."

Robin said nothing.

"I believe that you have formed an attachment to Miss Pouncey," Quenride continued, in her cool tones, "and that your wooing does not speed as smoothly as lovers wish. I have some influence with the girl herself; certainly, a great deal with her parents."

Fiander was overwhelmed—still smarting under Dolly's recent disdain, madly suspicious of a possible rival in the unknown Mr. Mohun, and utterly dazzled by the thought of what a splendid ally this great lady would be. He began to see that the disloyalty to Ridley would not be so dire a treachery after all. He promised her that he would not trouble his employer by mentioning the affair.

But what he did not see was that he had that afternoon fulfilled the noble office of a shuttlecock.

CHAPTER XVI

THE END OF HER TRUST

ALL day the old man had been strange in his manner ; strange with an oddness which, by eclipsing his habitual distractions, made them seem almost sanity to one who watched them daily. He moved about secretively, and finding his niece's contemptuous eyes fixed upon him he seemed to shrink into himself, with a cunning leer on his lips—ghastly, because it was apparently meaningless. At such times the girl was filled with something like loathing, and made the sign of the Cross, for though she knew well enough the value of her own incantations she was superstitious in her degree.

She kept a narrow watch over him without appearing to do so. In truth, she had scarcely let him out of her sight since the day, now nearly three weeks ago, when she had become aware that he had possessed himself of Miss Chideock's locket and chain.

The discovery had hardly surprised her, though the realisation of what had been an unlucky possibility had come with a shock. On the evening when she had lifted her eyes from the trinket to encounter Hoddinott's, she had read a covetous desire in his, and knew that his wildered wits would retain the memory of what he had seen. Immediately after driving him below, she found a fresh hiding-place for her treasure, by thrusting it in between the interstices of the stone slabs which formed her ceiling, and shifting these to cover the aperture. At first, she looked constantly to make certain that the little packet was safe. Then, as she always found it undisturbed, her vigilance was allowed to relax somewhat. The locket itself had lost the interest of mystery, and from its positive association with Miss Chideock had now become a distasteful thing. The sole value which it possessed in Sophy's regard was the opportunity it suggested of seeing Ridley again.

Going somewhat perfunctorily one evening to assure
herself of its safety, her fingers raked across the rough slab,
and found nothing there.   The previous day she had attended a neighbouring market, and presumably the theft
had been committed during her absence.   How Amos had
discovered the hiding-place was a matter of small importance
now. Sophy, who had a primitive instinct for essentials,
dismissed that conjecture, and turned her attention to the
question of what he had done with his find.

Here she was more or less nonplussed, having no precedent to guide her.   Amos had no possessions.   He had
never saved money.   There was no hole or cranny that she
knew of dedicated to his secretive use for treasure-trove.
Moreover, she had never missed anything before.   Even
the sooty corner where she hid the household money had
never been spied out to her loss.   His behaviour in the
present instance had been unique ; consequently, his subsequent procedure must be unique too.

She considered long and earnestly how to meet the case.
Her first impulse, to frighten the old man into confession,
was rejected as a method likely to defeat itself.   Once let
Amos become assured in his doitered old brain that his
new plaything was coveted by another, cupidity would
lend him courage, and a sense of possession teach him to
defy her strongest threats.   So it seemed to the girl, called
upon to deal with a new situation without any appreciable
forewarning.

There remained the possibility of a chance recovery.
This she did not expect to achieve through her own effort,
since Amos seldom left the cottage and would soon divine
what she was after.   A false start would inevitably augment
her difficulties—his alarmed wits choosing a still more cunning
hiding-place.   There was nothing rational to be done, Sophy
decided, but to wait and watch.   Sooner or later, the old
man was certain to betray himself.

So she waited and watched stealthily for nearly three
weeks.

Until this particular day all her vigilance had gone for
nothing.   Amos had behaved himself much as usual, and had
shown no predilection for any special corner, either within
doors or out.   But at length there came a change.   He
grew talkative, speaking with more sense and relevancy
than he had exhibited since his retirement, and recalling,
with some fluency, various minor incidents connected with

the days of desk and stool in Thomas Ridley's office. In all these anecdotes, the Chideock family had a large share, that name being oftener upon his lips than any other. Sophy listened, with a dark frown. Had the pictured face of a fair member of that household raised these reminiscences, she wondered.

The sun went down that evening in flame-coloured mist. Grey masses of cloud, heavy with rain, bulked themselves in the south-west. The wind raised its voice, and though the cottage was a few miles inland had a tang of saltness in it. As dusk fell, a gull or two sailed overhead, their wings immaculately white against the sombre sky. The time was mid-October, marked by a desolating fall of leaves, when trees, half-stripped, stand transitionally between the glory of summer's full leafage and the austerer beauty of winter's nakedness. Late blooming shrubs and lingering flowers had a dank over-bedewed look, and a certain untidy rankness was rife in the trim garden. Sophy's hollyhocks on either side the door were rotting to their fall. The pansies ran wild ; the jessamine showered its stars over the path ; the clumps of Aaron's rod and Michaelmas daisies had been beaten down by recent rains. Brushing too closely to them, the girl's gown became drenched.

When she went indoors, there was but little light left outside, and a still deeper gloom had penetrated to the interior of the cottage. Only a faint radiance came from the hearth, where burnt a small fire of the fuel obtained locally, and known as Kimmeridge coal. From the day when Sophy's great-grandfather had first lit a brand on that hearth, it had never, for an instant, lacked a fire. Hands that had once tended it had grown cold long ago ; fresh hands had been stretched out to its warmth, and in turn had been withdrawn, the hearth knowing them no more. The everlasting trilogy of Birth and Growth and Decay had been enacted a full score of times by its light. The fire which cheered the christening party in the process of years lent its pale glow to animate the shadows into a dance of Death. By its long continuity it had made such a friend of Time that it had gathered to itself some of the attributes of Eternity, cheating the imagination into a belief that in the confusion of a disintegrated planet it would still be found as the one stable thing left in an overthrown universe. To the gloomy-minded, self-centred girl, it was a companion whose moods took colour from her own. In her hours of dull complacency, it was a friend on whose continuance it pleased her to speculate ; when depression made the burden of life a well-nigh hateful thing, the thought of its transhuman existence fascinated her with a feeling akin to horror.   It was mainly so that she had regarded it since her parting with Ridley.   But as yet she would no more have thought of extinguishing it than of taking her own life.

To-night, as she came in, her eyes went towards it naturally.   Irregularly outlined against its faint glow, was the crouching form of her uncle.   He knelt upon the hearth-stone, raised a few inches above the floor, and leant forward over the peats at such an angle as would have alarmed the girl at another time.   But, to her excited imagination, his present attitude merely suggested the close inspection of some object held thus to the light.   Closing the door noiselessly, she slid across the floor, and looked down over his shoulder. The locket, with the broken chain dangling, was clutched in his fingers.   Sophy involuntarily raised her hand.

At the same moment, Amos looked up.   Their eyes met. With a hoarse scream the old man thrust the trinket away inside his shirt, and stooping, with an incredibly rapid movement, seized a peat from the hearth, and swung the glowing end into the girl's face.   Half-blinded and stifled, she flung herself upon him, clutching at his breast.   No word was spoken, but for a minute or more the two strove together, swaying about before the hearth, Sophy careless of defending herself, and only bent on recovering Ridley's property.   It was not until she found that Amos was gradually forcing her nearer to the fire that she was conscious of any danger. Reluctantly, she relaxed her hold on his shirt, and adopted a more defensive attitude.   A moment later, her heel struck against the hearth-stone, and her slight body bent backwards under the abnormal pressure which the old man was using. His crooked fingers were at her throat.   His breath burnt her like a flame.

" You hell-cat ! " he hissed, looking at her with mad eyes.   " Still at your tricks, are you ?   But it's safe—safe— safe now !   It shall go where you shan't find it.   And the master shan't call me careless again !   Ah !—would you ? Then choke—choke, witch—choke and burn ! "

Matching her rage against the strength of his madness, Sophy wrenched herself free, and dropped, gasping and fainting, to the floor.   When she looked up, Amos had disappeared.

6

She brushed her loosened hair away from her eyes, and sat up.

"I was a fool!" she muttered. "I ought to have known! 'Tis lost for ever now."

Realising her mistake in allowing Amos to know that she had seen the locket in his hand, she suffered the full torment of the wisdom that comes too late. Trouble never softened her; her eyes grew hard as she thought of her own disappointment, and her protest rose up to Heaven.

"Why don't the wold man die?" she complained, as she got to her feet. "Why don't he die, an' leave me alone?"

Opening the outer door, she peered into the dusk. At a little distance, she could hear her uncle creeping about the garden. In moody anger she went back to the fire, and sat there awhile, brooding. Presently Amos lifted the latch and came in. With her curious acceptance of facts, Sophy rose as if the events of the last hour had not happened, and lit a rushlight. Then she set about preparing supper by placing a few potatoes in a tin. These were covered with an iron pan, and the whole laid on the hearth underneath the embers, in the same way as she baked bread. While the food was cooking she stared into the fire in silence.

The old man's paroxysm of fury had passed, even the recollection of it being swept, apparently, from his mind. He regarded Sophy with neither hatred nor fear, and waited, with his customary docility, until she called him to supper. During the meal, she watched him suspiciously.

There was nothing in his manner to guide her to what she wanted to know. She was still wondering, as she cleared away the platters, whether he had hidden the locket in some secret place, or had it yet concealed upon him. While the night was still young she drew the bolts of the doors, and turned to feed the fire that it might last until dawn.

Amos slept in the kitchen, a corner being roughly curtained off to accommodate his mattress. But to-night he showed no immediate inclination for his bed, and Sophy left him sitting by the fire, senile, and apparently harmless.

In the dark, she went up to her own room.

Here a little pale radiance made contrast with the blackness of the staircase, and promised full moonlight later on. Sophy was satisfied. She thrust the door to, and entered into her kingdom.

This girl knew no prayers. But her irreligion was due more to circumstances than to temperament. She saw the finger of God in Nature, since here was something she could understand and sympathise with. The eternal growth of things spoke of power, and overawed her mind into some sort of reverence. The problems of life she left alone, her intellectual limitations being soon reached. She did not consciously worship Divinity, but that such capacity existed was shown by her attitude towards the one human being who had touched her imagination, and stirred her deep-lying emotions.

She loosened her long black hair, and crept on her knees to where her treasure lay. When she had taken out the coat, she sat back on the floor, and spread its folds over her lap. Instantly, she became swept away into a world of essences more refined, more pervading, infinitely more uplifting than the ordinary experiences of the everyday world. In truth, that world itself was in a sense a far better thing, since in it lived and moved the man of flesh and blood, warm, palpable, breathing and speaking before her. But here, in this dream kingdom, there was time to estimate better the glory of his physical nearness ; to live over again the intense moments of his actual presence, recalling every look and tone ; to anticipate another meeting ; to pour out her poor devotion unreservedly.

When the first clear rays of moonlight struck into the room, the girl was still kneeling there. She caught sight of the gleam falling across her shoulder, shivered, and roused herself. It was time to hide the coat away again, replacing the sprigs of lavender and rosemary which her fancy had laid with it. Very carefully this was done. Then Sophy suddenly leapt to her feet, and stood listening.

The silence of the night had been broken by a noise. In this primitive household, such an occurrence was in itself unusual. When a second sound, following immediately, determined the nature of the first, Sophy stepped eagerly enough into the world of actuality once more. The old man below was stirring ; he had withdrawn the bolt of the door leading into the road—and now he was opening it.

Sophy flew to her window, and pushed it outwards on its hinge. The door being immediately below, there was the certainty of obtaining a sight of Amos if he passed outside. This he did not do until a few seconds had elapsed. Then he emerged, pulling the door to after him. Sophy's interest was now firmly compelled, for Amos was carrying a lanthorn, the lighting of which had presumably occupied the time between the second sound and his appearance in the roadway.

" Cunning wold toad ! " muttered Sophy. " He feared I'd hear him, so he opened the door first thing, ready to get away if I came down an' caught him fiddlin' wi' the lanthorn ! "

She stumbled downstairs, and across the kitchen. Then she pulled the outer door back, and looked out. The road lay white in the moonlight. A hundred yards ahead moved Amos Hoddinott, his lanthorn dangling like a yellow star by his side.

Sophy latched the door behind her, and followed in his tracks.

CHAPTER XVII

A WHITE STONE

THE night air was chilly, but Sophy felt nothing of it as she crept forward after her grand-uncle. Her loosened hair hung warm and heavy round her neck, and she had removed none of her clothing when the sounds below had drawn her downstairs again. In any case, she would have gone on. That the old man's unusual movements formed the climax to his eccentricities of the day, and that both, in some way, had a bearing upon the locket which he had stolen from her, the girl had no doubt. The episode of a few hours ago had taught her caution, if not cunning, and though she might easily have overtaken his shambling steps she dared not risk a second struggle. Moreover, curiosity induced patience. What new place of safety had he hit upon? Or what fresh thought was stirring in his crazy brain?

Amos had set his face towards Wareham; a fact not without significance in Sophy's eyes, since throughout the preceeding day his mind had obviously turned upon the Chideock family, and the time when he had acted as Thomas Ridley's messenger to his most important client. If he should mean to restore the ornament to the young lady herself, Sophy would not quarrel with his fancy. Her newly roused intuition told her that so imperious a temper as Quenride's could not fail to feel affronted at the carelessness of a lover who had allowed his lady's token to pass out of his hands. In her ignorance of the real relations between the two, Sophy had come to believe that past encouragements had been temporarily overshadowed by some quarrel or coldness. She would not have risked drawing down Ridley's wrath on her own head by herself restoring the locket to Quenride, but if Amos's action widened the breach between the young lawyer and the lady Sophy would breathe satisfaction.

At times, Amos paused in his shuffling gait, and glanced

over his shoulder. Ever on the watch for such sudden lapses, the girl was ready to drop to her knees in any covering shadow that happened to be at hand. When there was none, she lay forward on her face at full length, trusting to the dimness of his vision to escape detection. Once he waited a full minute, peering behind him and listening. She watched with tense muscles. When he came a few steps in her direction, she almost betrayed herself by springing to her feet. But his impulse died out, and after another short pause he went on as before.

Mile after mile was put between them and the cottage, and Sophy was sure now that Amos would not finish his task until he had reached the town itself. At one point of the journey the lanthorn went out, a contingency which the old man had evidently foreseen, and provided against. To the crouching girl came the sound of flint and steel, carried sharp and clear to her in the still air. When another candle had been kindled and placed in the socket, the stealthy walk was continued by both.

No other traveller either overtook or encountered them. Being little more than a coast road, it was lonely at all times. Now and then, it was raked by a gang of smugglers from the adjacent coves, or echoed to the tread of the Preventive men bound on a midnight expedition, but Sophy and Amos passed along it unhindered and unobserved. The distant roar of the sea, the flutter of a bat across their path, the crisp rustle of a dead leaf—such incidents alone broke into irregular periods the quiet monotony of that strange walk.

Presently—but not until the end of the journey was nearly reached—the sky became obscured in a partial degree, by the clouds which had collected when the sun went down. The moonlight was rendered fitful, and an altogether unsatisfactory medium for the girl's purpose. It became necessary to follow Amos at closer range if she was to keep him in sight at all. And although, on the road itself, there was little likelihood of his turning aside, she knew that the town, now near at hand, would offer various opportunities.

But the town, as it happened, was not entered by the two at this particular time. Amos Hoddinott travelled no farther than the bridge at the lower end. He did not even cross the bridge to its opposite extremity.

At the time of his arrival at the spot, the moon was blackened out by a heavy belt of cloud, and Sophy, tireless in her vigilance, was forced to follow by sound instead of sight. This was no difficult matter, for the hour being now close on midnight the little town was as quiet as the surrounding country. Listening intently, Sophy, with some quickening of the pulse, heard the old man pause, when, as she judged, he was half-way across the bridge. He had gone on so steadily, save for the incident of relighting the lanthorn, that any variation would have given rise to speculation on her part. While she hesitated, the light which he had carried, concealed for the most part beneath the skirts of his coat, flashed out. Its rays fell upon the rough wall of the bridge. Then the old man began to move forward very slowly.

Sophy ran onwards noiselessly, approaching as closely as she dared, and being careful to remain on the opposite side of the bridge. A chance swing of the lanthorn would otherwise have betrayed her at once. She could hear his feet scuffing amongst the loose stones in the roadway.

The darkness round her lifted as she waited, watching that thin ray of light travelling across the wall, and the moon broke forth once more. She was now able to play the spy at greater advantage, but with less security. After a moment's eager straining forward, she reluctantly drew back a few yards, crouching beneath the wall on her side.

Amos stood the lanthorn down on the coping of the bridge, and raised himself from his own somewhat cramped attitude. Then he began fumbling beneath his coat, and presently laid something beside the lanthorn. As to what the article was, the girl had no doubt. With more anxiety than she had yet felt, she ventured to creep a little nearer again. Once more, the moonlight decreased, and the obscurity was such that it became impossible for her to follow Amos's movements with any certainty. She saw him move forward, close to the wall, and almost on her knees she followed him. Suddenly, a low moaning cry quivered out from him. It scared Sophy to her feet, one hand on the head of her wall, the other laid across her breast. Amos flung his arms into the air, and wailed anew.

Sophy recovered from her alarm, and frowned. Had she been led such a dance for nothing? Had the old man unconsciously fooled her into watching nothing more than a silly caprice born of crazy wits, and leading to no advantage? Yet undoubtedly, the locket lay on the opposite wall. A rapid step or two, and she might regain possession, and dart off into the surrounding darkness unmolested. She poised her lithe body for the attempt, ran quickly aslant over the

roadway, struck her foot against an unsuspected stone, and
stumbled heavily. Uttering a yell of fear, Amos turned,
with wild arms spread abroad, flung himself upon the
top of the wall, and hung there, mumbling in a low voice.
In doubt and vexation, Sophy raised herself. But while she
did so, a sudden splash came up from the river at a point
almost immediately below her ear, followed, the fraction of
a moment later, by a fainter and less appreciable concussion
from the same quarter. She remained as she was, half-risen,
half-crouching, setting her mind to grasp this new calamity.
Without a doubt, both lanthorn and locket had been pushed
over into the river.

When the personal instinct came back to her, after its
momentary abeyance, she stood up and found Amos lying
huddled across the coping, motionless and silent. Whether
the loss of the trinket had been caused by accident or of
set purpose, whether this had been the intention working
waveringly in the dim recesses of that doitered brain, throughout the night, were questions which held the girl motionless
for some minutes before she cast about in her mind for a way
to terminate this series of strange happenings. Initiative
being still an only partially developed quality in her, she
waited in moody anger to see what Amos would do next.
Although she was now barely a couple of yards away, he
still seemed unconscious of her presence. With the remembrance of the fierceness of their former struggle in her mind,
Sophy had no desire to risk calling his attention to herself,
in the present lonely and dangerous place. She neither
advanced nor retreated, but remained alert and watchful,
ready to flee at his first movement, should her safety require
flight. She might, even now, it seemed, have crept away
unmolested, but some tie of blood, some convention, vaguely
felt, and scarcely understood, held her there, weighing the
probability of the old man's attempting some injury upon
himself.

At the end of a quarter of an hour, the need for such
precaution had apparently passed by. Amos lifted his head
from his arms, and drew his coat about him with a shivering
sigh. With a rapid movement, the girl darted back to the
other side of the bridge, reached it safely and remained concealed in the gloom which again rendered discovery unlikely
at a short distance. In another moment, she heard once
more his shuffling tread, now in retreat from the town. He
had turned back the way he had come. In a short time,

the sound had been swallowed up by the distance. The girl was alone, with only herself to think of—since there was no reason to imagine that her uncle would not reach the cottage in safety.

The obvious course—to return herself to her home—was one which offered no great attraction to Sophy. In truth, there was difficulty. She had allowed Amos to get the start of her, and access to the cottage now depended upon her being able to pass him unobserved, since he would bolt the door on his arrival home. Should he see her on the road, he might recognise her, and know that he had been followed. Sophy's throat still ached from the grip of his mad fingers, and she wanted to give him no second cause for a quarrel.

Above all—and though she listened to these more practical arguments, she did not hide from herself the persuasiveness of this one—Dorchester called to her. Across the intervening miles, and through the darkness of this mid-October night, the personality of the unconscious Ridley drew her to his side. Since he would not come again to her, she must needs go to him. She had the wild creature's instinct for locality, and now set her face in a direct line towards the larger town, and stared out with all her poor primitive soul in her eyes, while her heart throbbed and ached with longing. Away there, separated from her by distance and a score of more insurmountable circumstances, lay the man who had, with a look and a word, called her love into being, and all unwittingly given her a cup of heavenly bittersweet to drink. The gall might be bearable—if only she could have the honey as well. Why not? Here was reason enough for her going. Were others to see his face, hear his voice, touch that smooth hand of his, and she— never? Rebellion stirred her to decision. He would not come to her; she would go to him. How could she keep away, when his presence was so dear and real a thing to her, even now, when he lay asleep, and dreaming of another woman, so many miles distant? Surely he would not look blackly at her, when he learnt that she had journeyed so quickly to tell him the truth? And the truth, in Sophy's argument, meant just so much of it as she chose to speak.

So her decision was made. The carrying out of it was not likely to be difficult. The day which had already turned was market-day in Dorchester, and to it flocked the carriers and farmers from the outlying towns and villages. To obtain a lift from such a one going thither from Wareham was simple enough. Sophy's peculiar reputation made her neighbours anxious to stand well with her. In the same way, food was assured to her as soon as daylight brought the market-folk from their beds. Earlier in the night, she might have counted on shelter as well. But this was a matter which gave her no moment's pause. Exposure was less to her than to other girls of her own class. She had often trudged all night to a distant fair, in order to secure a prominent site for the practice of her supposed arts.

So she found a corner out of the wind, at the back of the church of Lady St. Mary—and crouched there contentedly until morning broke. A somewhat boisterous day it proved to be, yet with broad gleams of sunlight to turn to gold the russet leaves that dangled delicately from the thinned branches.

As soon as the first wheel had turned in the street, Sophy betook herself to the cottage of the many-officed man, Timothy Hutchins. That kindly disposed individual welcomed her timidly, but provided a breakfast despite his wife's scowls. He promised to get the girl a lift to Dorchester in the cart of a dairyman bound for the market.

It was still early when the pair set out, though the long, straggling street was astir with other vehicles besides theirs. Half-way out of the town there came a lull in the noisy traffic. Looking down into the road, Sophy saw that it was strewn from side to side with straw. The yellow patch extended for some yards on either side of the Chideocks' house.

" Is the wold man dead ? " asked Sophy, as they got on to the road again.

" No, my dear. 'Tis young Measter Gilbert ha' been took bad. Miss Quenride had that straw put down."

" I reckon it wouldn't so much matter, if he were taken altogether," said Sophy callously. " A slack-twisted half-made lad like him."

" But, my maidy," remonstrated the dairyman, " Miss Quenride fair worships he."

Sophy made no reply. It was a long time before she spoke again. Then she asked a question which had been burning on her lips ever since they had set out.

" Does Mr. Ridley often go to see her ? "

" Who, my dear ? Oh! tew be sure—our young lady yonder. Why, no, my dear. Ha'n't ye heard ? Lar', I thought all the warld knew ! "

" What ? " asked the girl, defiance in her eyes.

" Well, you see, he were brought up afore her t'other week, and Miss Chideock——"

" I know ! " cried Sophy, the blood in her sun-tanned cheek. " I know ! The spiteful she ! "

" Though," her companion went on reflectively, " 'tis said the lady have repented o' her high-and-mighty ways, and have made it up wi' Master Lawyer."

" What makes them say that ? " demanded Sophy quickly.

" Well, I speaks as I hears—an' says no more. But Farmer Pouncey's darter, as bides wi' she, do say as how Miss Quenride drove in to see the young man t'other day."

" I don't believe it ! " said Sophy, with vehement untruthfulness.

" Well, there a' be ! I reckon he do wish 'twere so, if 'tisn't. A rare rollickin' figure o' fun have he cut since it happened. All his fine friends a-sniggering at him. Why, maidy, they do say as the Governor o'| the gaol—the biggest man in Darchester he be—and treated the young man like his own son. An' now, lookye, he've forbid him to show his face within a mile o' he ! Oh ! ay—Master Lawyer's ears must tingle pretty smartly as he do walk down street nowadays."

Sophy would hear no more. The words hurt her, bringing home even to her crude perceptions the fact that a man of Ridley's refinement must have suffered considerably from Quenride Chideock's high-handed action. The girl's fingers crooked viciously, as she realised it all.

" Dear God ! " she burst out, presently, " I'd like to claw her face."

The dairyman was honestly shocked.

" Nay, nay," he said. " 'Twas Miss Quenride."

" D'ye think I care ? " cried Sophy. Then, later on, " And they've a-made it up, you say ? "

" So we do hear ; but 'tis naught to I."

Sophy fell into silence, and maintained it for the rest of the way. She was glad that the locket was lost. Surely Miss Chideock would find this new offence of his unpardonable. And surely also, she must needs learn of it sooner or later.

" An' where med I set ye down, maidy ? " asked the dairyman, some time afterwards.

And Sophy, raising her heavy eyes, found that they were already among the outskirts of the town.

"I've to see a woman at the *White Hart*," she said, naming an inn which stood at the opposite end of the long street in which the lawyer's house was situated. And the man drove her to the place, with a promise to pick her up before starting for home.

Sophy watched him out of sight. Then she walked rapidly up the street, sure of her ground, because Ridley himself, anticipating such an errand, had directed her where to find his house, at their last meeting. The street, although she did not touch the market, was full of small farmers and drovers with their herds, and already a long line of covered waggons and open carts was drawn up at the edge of the road. Sophy, not wishing for recognition, hurried past all these, and reached the residential end of the town. Here all was quiet. The traffic of the lower-lying streets did not trouble the better class of inhabitants.

Sophy found the house, with its flat front and high roof, and approached with some new kind of emotion. In truth, the exterior told no more of the man who lived therein than did that man's face tell to strangers of his inmost thoughts and experiences. It was plain and solid, with a slightly professional air, borrowed obviously from the brass plate and the wire blinds in the lower windows. Otherwise, it might as well have belonged to an elderly widow as to a noticeable young bachelor, with a caustic tongue, and the law at his fingers' ends.

Sophy's timid knock had to be repeated before the door was opened. Her voice, never until now at a loss, dried up in her throat. Mrs. Channing looked at her critically. Had there been a back entrance, the girl would probably have been bidden to make her application there.

"The master's busy," she was told, when at length she had partly conquered her emotions. "I doubt if he can see you. What do you want him for?"

"Tell him," said Sophy, with desperate fear in her heart, "'tis Sophy Hoddinott. He'll know. Say I've come to him about—about what he wants to hear of."

"Eh, and are you old Amos Hoddinott's niece? How is the old man?"

And Sophy's vague message was taken in.

Ridley happened to be working alone that day. Mrs. Fiander had fallen sick, and demanded to have the apple of her eye in close attendance. Ridley had accordingly set Fiander at liberty for the necessary time.

"Bring her in, please," he said, when told of his visitor, and there was anticipation in his look as Sophy was shown into the office.

He gave her a chair, and stood waiting to hear what she had to say. Her embarrassment was noticeable, but he set it down to bewilderment at her unaccustomed surroundings. She, for her part, was miserably conscious, on a sudden, that she was clad in her poorest gown, and was wearing one of Mrs. Hutchins's cast-off sunbonnets—a size or so too large.

When at length she dared to raise her head, she found nothing to alarm her in Ridley's attitude. He was smiling down at her in his pleasantest way. He had lightened his mourning since she had last seen him, and now wore a suit of grey, with touches of dull purple at the neck and wrists.

"Well, Sophy," he said, "you've come to tell me something. What is it? Have you found the locket?"

"I'd not lost it after all," she said.

"That's good!" cried Ridley. "Have you got it with you?"

"I'd not lost it," she repeated. "Girt-uncle had taken it."

"Ah!"

"A cunning thieving wold man!" cried the girl.

"Well, I suppose we mustn't be too hard on him," said Ridley. "And where is it now?"

"In the river. He threw it in—or jerked it over the bridge : I don't know which."

"Oh," said Ridley, "then it is lost, after all?"

"I s'pose so."

She looked at him with a curious shrinking expression.

"'Twasn't my fault!" she cried, suddenly. "I did my best for 'ee—truly I did!"

Ridley concealed the slight disappointment which had given him a moment's gravity, and spoke with a kindliness which fired every drop of the girl's blood. But for the half-told lie, she had no shame. She met his eyes with greater daring now.

"I am sure that you did your best," said Ridley. "Don't fret about that, Sophy. Don't be frightened. I am not going to be angry with you. You've been a good girl all through, and, of course, I don't blame you. Tell me how it happened."

Sophy complied. She gave him a correct and detailed version of the affair. The only dishonesty lay in the fact that she started the story a little farther on than absolute truth required. Ridley was allowed to believe that Amos had already stolen the locket at the time of his own visit to the cottage. She told of the struggle at the hearth-side, and of Amos's midnight journey ; of her following, and of the old man's enigmatical behaviour at the bridge ; of the lanthorn-ray raking the rough stones, and of Amos's apparent despair. Of her own attempt, and the ultimate fate of lanthorn and trinket alike.

Ridley listened quietly, and at the end, found himself facing the distasteful possibility of remaining permanently in Quenride's debt, she having already refused his offer to make good the intrinsic value of the ornament. Whether or not it could be recovered from the bed of the Frome, was a point upon which he could not decide off-hand. But he felt tolerably certain that its owner would neither care to make the attempt herself nor thank him for undertaking it, since publicity must needs go with the endeavour.

But to Sophy, mournful-eyed with a hunger which he did not understand, he spoke comforting words, according to his belief that it was a sense of her own blame-worthiness which distressed the girl.

"Never mind," he said. "I'm only glad to know that Amos didn't injure you. Is it safe for you to stay there alone with him ? "

"I'm not afraid," she answered. "He wasn't ever so afore."

"Still, it doesn't seem right," said Ridley, his eyes on the girl's small figure. "I don't like it, Sophy. Isn't there anyone—some decent woman—who could come and live with you ? "

Sophy met his gaze. Happiness warmed her like wine. It was so wonderful a thing that he should care. But she desired no companionship, and shook her head at his suggestion.

"Then," said Ridley, for the matter hung in his mind, "I'll see if I can't arrange something. I'll make inquiries, and let you know."

Sophy snatched at the chance of further communication with him, and thanked him with a little eagerness which he noticed, and smiled at. In truth, the girl was very happy. Life was a wonderful thing—even a beautiful thing—for these few moments. That the period of such an experience was transient, probably even now half-over, only deepened the fullness of the emotion. She sat there, watching him covertly, while he stood silent, his thoughts harking back to Amos and the locket.

"Sophy," he said, "when I saw your uncle, he seemed troubled over some loss, though I couldn't tell what it was. Perhaps he'd lost the locket for the time being, and it was that which was troubling him."

But again Sophy shook her head.

"Just a silly wold man he be," she said. "I reckon it meant naught! He's been crying out that he's lost some'at ever since he came to bide wi' me."

"Has he?" said Ridley. "Then it probably does mean something; though I don't suppose that we shall ever find out about it." He looked grave for a moment, then laughed lightly and said, "At any rate, I'm glad I didn't keep him on as clerk! He used to work in this room, you know."

The reminiscence had small interest for the girl. She had finished her errand, and knew that she could not prolong the interview much further. She got to her feet reluctantly, but with deliberation. Ridley, who was very busy, owing to Fiander's absence, made no attempt to detain her. The episode of the locket appeared to be now wound up; and the real importance of the interview did not transpire until later.

"You must have some dinner before you go," he said, his kindly tones still pouring the pleasant poison into the girl's heart, so that she might have fallen down on her knees before him. "You've done quite right all through this troublesome business, Sophy, and I'll not forget it."

"And you aren't angry with me?" she asked, not because she any longer dreaded his vexation, but that she might again hear the reassurances which pleased her so well.

He laid his hand on her shoulder.

"Never think it! It was no one's fault but my own."

He dropped his hand before she had grown familiar with the pressure, and moved towards the bell-rope.

Sophy's heart beat a little more quickly. She had not forgotten the assumption which the dairyman had based upon Dolly Pouncey's statement. She must find out the truth from Ridley himself before they parted.

"And—Miss Chideock," she ventured, "she knows?"

"Oh, yes," said Ridley a little drily, "I've told her."

Sophy detected the change in his tones, and proceeded hopefully :

" Did she look very angry ? "

Ridley rang the bell.

" I can't say," he answered. " I wrote to her about it, and I've not seen her since."

" Then—she've given up coming to see 'ee ? "

" Given up coming ? " he repeated. " Why, Sophy, what put that into your head ? Miss Chideock never did come here."

The door opened, and Mrs. Channing, who was particular to answer her master's bell in person, stood waiting for his instructions.

" I heard that she came to see 'ee," murmured Sophy, discomfited and awkward in the presence of a stranger.

" Then," said Ridley, " it's incorrect. Miss Chideock has never set foot in this house since I've been living here."

" Sir,"—it was Mrs. Channing who struck in,—" she called the other week."

Ridley swung round in surprise.

" She did ? Then it's the first I've heard of it ! "

" 'Twas some time back, sir. The day you went to Weymouth. I let her in myself."

" Fiander didn't mention it," said Ridley, displeasure in his tone. " Are you sure 'twas she."

" I don't know the lady myself," said Mrs. Channing in reply, " but Robin told me who it was. He came out to get some tea for 'em."

" Her brother was with her, then ? "

" No, sir. Dolly Pouncey. She waited in the gig. Only Miss Chideock came inside."

Ridley stood silent, perplexity and annoyance gathering in his face. The visit was now three weeks old ; and since then—not a word from his clerk, not a line from the lady herself. Also he remembered he had expressly advised her of his absence from home on that day.

" I must talk to Fiander," he said. And his manner left little doubt as to what the talking would be like.

Then his face relaxed towards Sophy. He asked how she meant to reach her home, thanked her again for bringing her news, confided her to Mrs. Channing's care, and then held out his hand in sign of dismissal.

Sophy crept away, a small insignificant thing, stripped of some subtle dignity, some importance in her own eyes—all of which Ridley's presence had temporarily lent to her. To dine, and listen to the housekeeper's inconsequent gossip, to leave the house with lingering feet and backward glances, to wait at the *White Hart* until the friendly dairyman arrived, and so back the way she had come, to find Amos sitting before the hearth once more, with the memory of last night's happenings wiped out of his mind.

So ended for Sophy the day which, had he but known it, Ridley should have marked with a white stone.

CHAPTER XVIII

BY NIGHT

"HANG Miss Chideock ! " said Ridley, in the middle of the night.

He had had a busy and a worrying day, and had gone to bed with the pleasurable anticipations of a fatigued man, who feels that he has a right to his slumbers. He counted it therefore as a grievance that his brain refused to rest, and as a still greater annoyance that Quenride Chideock was the pivot upon which it mainly turned. Whether he closed his eyes, or lay staring, irritated and wakeful, into the darkness, her face rose again and again before his mental vision. At times, he found himself fitting new expressions to it, expressions of tenderness and compunction such as he had never seen there, and which, in a more professional mood, he would have doubted its capacity for showing. As it was, he grew angry with himself for indulging in such folly. But, nevertheless, her face continued to haunt him, and he not only thought of her persistently, but regarded her from different points of view.

Thus, he tried to picture her as she appeared to the young Gilbert. His sister Quenny : a being to love and admire ; whom to disobey brought a sense of daring ; and whose judgment was a criterion for morals and manners. To the lad, her insufferable pride would be no more than the natural attribute of her race ; her imperiousness, no detriment, save when it irked himself ; her coldness, a thing unseen. In a word, to the boy, she probably seemed a sister whose character surpassed in its fineness the lesser attributes of other women, even as her beauty outshone their slender personal charms.

How did she strike Alaric Mohun ?

Here was an exercise for his wits truly. He had never seen the two together. Quenride herself had not even alluded to her cousin in his presence. It was probable that she habitually disliked him—a sentiment deepening into something stronger when he gibed, with consciousness of power, at the boy. It was difficult, Ridley found, to consider Alaric Mohun as a lover. The most likely assumption was that, in the days of his quarrel with his grandfather, he had courted Quenride, with a keen eye to his own advantage. In which case— and now that he stood to get all that he wanted without her help—it was conceivable that he despised her for her futility as much as he had previously hated her for her lack of compliance.

The truth was, Ridley's thoughts had been turned in this direction by the incidents of the day. The circumstance of Quenride's visit hung in his mind. There were queer points about it which made it impossible to regard it merely as an ill-timed arrival. He had the best of reasons for knowing that Quenride had been aware of his absence on the day chosen for the call. Had she been accompanied by her brother, her visit might have been set down to the boy's whim—persisted in despite her own assurances of the uselessness of the attempt to indulge in it. Then there was Fiander's curious omission to inform his employer of the visit. As a rule, he was irritatingly prolix over trifles, and until this occurrence Ridley had had no reason to suspect his integrity. He was loath to do so now. The lad was a good lad, impressionable, but honest, so Ridley told himself half a dozen times. He was exceedingly reluctant to disbelieve in Fiander. It might be, he argued one moment, that the advent of Dolly Pouncey had thrown Robin's not very stable head off its balance. But, the next instant, his own clear wits were pointing out that that very circumstance must necessarily have fixed the visit in the clerk's mind.

So keen was Ridley's interest in the whole affair that only a sense of decency, aroused by rumours of Mrs. Fiander's condition, prevented his sending for Robin, or at least going to see him after office hours. But the consequent delay and uncertainty tended to give the affair a still greater prominence in his mind.

"I'll get to the bottom of it, if I have to hold Fiander up by the heels and shake the truth out of him!"

Thus Ridley to himself, as he went up to bed. And hence the reason why Quenride Chideock, in her many possible phases, filled his mind and kept sleep away.

But as midnight became a thing of the past physical comfort allured him, though still wakeful, into a more complacent mood. He no longer anathematised her spiritual presence, but let his thoughts run as they would.

" I might be in love with her, from the way my mind hangs round her ! " he said. " Am I in love without knowing it ? " He laughed to himself under the bedclothes—the low chuckling laugh of derisive amusement. " Lord ! one might as well fall in love with a volcano."

Certainly he had no reason to love her. He recalled an incident of the day which had just passed, and in remembering it fell out of his more tolerant humour into one spiced with a little bitterness. That afternoon he had chanced to meet his friend the Governor, who had acknowledged his salute with an acrimonious little bow, and marched on, with no disposition to pause, and with displeasure in his eyes.

One—two—three o'clock. He heard each hour struck, with the whirring and clanging peculiar to old-fashioned caseclocks, by a time-keeper across the road. The street was very quiet. There was no reason why he should not sleep. He grew exasperated at his wakefulness. There was a plenitude of work awaiting him in the morning. Unless he slept soon, he knew by experience that he would rise with a heavy head which would make the day's labour a burden.

Silence. Silence. His mind still worked, but more drowsily at last.

There were fitful moments of perfect mental clearness, when he realised the incoherency of his recent thought. He welcomed the good sign, and forebore to move a finger, lest slumber should take fright. Silence. Silence. At length it seemed that he slept.

He awoke presently with a strong impression that the waking had not come about naturally. Some sound, which he could not define, save that it seemed very loud and close at hand, still rang in his ears. He raised himself on his elbow, and listened. The street, the house, were as quiet as before. He lay down again, and told himself that he had been dreaming. At the same time, he shot an instinctive hand beneath his pillow, and clutched the key which it was his custom to place there for security every night. Then he closed his eyes again. A board in the room creaked, and he drowsily thought that here was the solution of his disturbance.

The next moment he was up again, listening intently. Without a doubt there was a faint sound stirring. It was difficult to locate it—it seemed to come from below the window —but there was no mistake about its actuality. It formed a kind of irregular tapping. Ridley rose, and opened the shutters. The road lay in silence and blackness beneath. The sound had momentarily ceased. He had raised the sash softly, with the intention of calling down to ascertain whether anyone were below, when suddenly he nearly cried out, and bit his tongue sharply as he repressed the exclamation. Very faint, very narrow, a ray of light shot across the darkness, and was blotted out as swiftly as it had appeared. Ridley stood back. The sound had recommenced, but it no longer eluded identification. It was a loose shutter swinging on its newly-oiled hinge, at the window of the room below. And that room was his office.

It was conceivable that he had fastened the latch carelessly, since it was a task usually assigned to Fiander. But it had held firmly enough while he had continued in the room, and he had not quitted it until close on nine o'clock. Moreover, he was positive that he had left no light burning. It was therefore a matter which required looking into.

While these thoughts raced through his mind, Ridley slipped into a few clothes with incredible rapidity, and picking up a loaded pistol from a drawer crept downstairs in his stockinged feet.

Reaching the passage below, he found nothing to arouse suspicion until he came to the entrance to the office, and reaching out a hand nearly fell into the room. The door was unfastened, and he had calculated on finding it closed. He recovered his balance with a keen sense of annoyance, pushed the door wide open, and strode boldly in. Again he was conscious of a shock of surprise. The office was empty.

Not only so, but, at the first glance, everything appeared to be as he had left it, save for the unhasped shutters, and a half-lit candelabrum standing upon his table.

He crossed to the shutters. Then he understood. Behind them, the window stood half-way up, and the draught so caused was responsible for the noise which he had heard upstairs. Turning quickly to fetch one of the candles for a better examination of the catch of the window, he was confronted by another sight. And seeing, he wasted no more time on the question of the means used to force an entrance, for the secret drawer of his writing-table stood open and the key which should have lain inside was gone.

It was Ridley's everlasting self-reproach that, on making the discovery, his mind went at once to Fiander.

But whether Fiander or no, he shut the drawer with a

savage snap, and red with rage turned towards the door. The thief had given him a good clue as to where he might be found.

Running lightly down the stairs, Ridley was brought to a check by the closed door of the cellar. As he put out a wary hand, his foot struck against something which he guessed to be the padlock lying on the ground. The unexpected contact threw him against the wall, and the pistol in his hand struck it with a faint clang. Cursing his clumsiness for the second time that night, he pulled himself together, and noticed, with grim satisfaction, a pale infinitesimal streak of light beneath the ill-fitting door.

He found that it had not been secured by the bolt on the inside, and so yielded to his pressure. It swung back heavily, and Ridley, without stopping to consider what he might meet with on the other side, stepped forward into the cellar.

The eager glance which he threw round showed him very little. A single taper burned on the table. But here also nothing was displaced—no one was to be seen. Ridley continued to advance. And now he spoke aloud, clearly and firmly, although he expected to be attacked from any quarter, and borne to the ground the next moment.

" Who's here ? " he called.

His voice echoed as in a cavern, but no answer was returned. He had scarcely looked for one, and, sparing his breath with an instinctive feeling that it might be wanted, he walked to the table and got possession of the candle. Raising it, he took another look round, having a care to keep himself in a line with the open door. He raked the cellar from side to side as well as he could with the tiny light, and discovered, for his pains, a chisel and mallet lying on the floor. He stared at them with a deep-breathed ejaculation, and kicked them noisily aside. At that moment he saw what he had been waiting for—a slight movement, little more than the fluctuation of the shadows, among the pile of litter at the farther end of the place.

His arm shot out.

" Come forward ! " he ordered. " Or I fire ! "

" Do so—and welcome ! " came the quick reply.

Ridley's hand dropped to his side. Without more than an instant's pause, he marched across the floor, and directed the candle-rays on to the quarter whence the voice had come. A figure in a long horseman's coat shrank away from him against a stack of timber. He gripped it by the shoulder, and compelled it to turn. The dress and form might have been those of a youth, but the voice was a woman's voice, and the face which he now saw was that of Quenride Chideock.

He dragged her out from her hiding-place a little roughly, and, retreating, stood the candlestick back on the table before he spoke. He was amazed, indignant, contemptuous, but also angry, and therefore very cool.

"I admit that I am surprised, madam," he said, in his most biting tones. "May I trouble you to explain the reason of your presence in my house, at this somewhat unseasonable hour?"

She made no reply. She no longer shrank from him, but now stood at her full height, staring at him in the obscurity with wide defiant eyes.

"Come!" he said, tapping the edge of the table with the pistol. "Surely you have put me to enough inconvenience without keeping me here longer than is necessary. I am waiting to hear your account of yourself, Miss Chideock."

"I have only one thing to say!" she broke out with unexpected passion, and she came a step nearer. He could see her eyes, finely luminous, shining above her flaming cheeks.

"Well?" he inquired—and his voice had an edge like thin ice.

"Why didn't you fire?" she cried. "Oh, my God, why didn't you fire?" Again she came nearer, and bending forward a little fixed her eyes on his. It was like a flame playing over an icicle. "Is it too late now?" she asked, in a lower key. "You've your weapon in your hand. A finger-press does it, and even the law would scarcely blame you, I suppose."

Ridley at once laid the pistol down.

"You are talking nonsense, madam," he told her, unmoved. "Will you have the goodness to explain what you are doing here, in this guise, at the dead of night?"

She threw back her head suddenly, with the dignity of desperation. Ridley's next words came still more sharply.

"You will not leave this place, Miss Chideock, until I have heard," he said.

"I have nothing to tell you!" she cried.

"Nothing?" He pointed a contemptuous finger to the mallet and chisel lying on the floor. "Nothing? Is it then a habit for the ladies of your family to put on male attire, and go out housebreaking for recreation in the middle of the night ? Your manner implies that you have done no unusual thing. Perhaps you are not aware that the law, about which you talk rather glibly, has a different point of view. You have committed a crime, Miss Chideock, a very serious one, and in face of your silence I am forced to the conclusion that it does not end there."

" You may conclude what you please, sir," she retorted, in a quivering voice. " But if you are a gentleman——"

Ridley bowed to her across the table.

" Which I am not ! " he said. " It is your own opinion ; you must remember it."

" Sir, I implore you ! Let me pass ! "

" You have heard my conditions," he said, without relaxing a muscle.

She made an attempt to spring past him. He had been expecting this, and forestalled her rush with scarcely a change of position, catching her by the wrist, and tossing her contemptuously back to her former position. Then, though he had used no violence, a cry of pain, low and shuddering, broke from her.

" Did I hurt you ? " The question came from him involuntarily. He took a step forward. She put out a hand to keep him off.

" Hurt me ? " she cried. " Oh, no. You do not hurt. You are kind and considerate to women. You have a man's strength—and you use it most tenderly ! "

Ridley shrugged his shoulders.

" We will not open a discussion on my character, I think, madam," he said. " There is a subject more interesting to both of us. It is the question of your conduct to-night— and its suitable punishment."

At the word, Quenride's dignity fell from her so suddenly that it must needs have been but a poor affectation of her customary manner. She seemed to shrink into herself before him, trembling and alarmed.

" Go on ! " she cried. " Oh, to think that this is the end ! Oh, that I should have fought, and plotted, and lied to my heart's best—and must fail—now—through you ! "

" It is rather ignominious," agreed Ridley, in even tones. " But I am glad to hear you admit so much. Perhaps, in time, you will confess the whole truth."

" Never ! " she answered, with a touch of sullenness.

" Then," he said, " permit me, madam, to make suggestions. If I am wrong on any point, I must remind you

that I am still half in the dark regarding this interesting
affair. This, then, is the case as I read it. Three weeks
ago, you honoured my house with a visit. Unfortunately,
I was from home."

"Who told you of this ? " she cried.

Ridley raised his hand. He went on with his statement
as before. Every sentence, uttered as he uttered it, fell
upon her like the lash of a whip. She dared not look for
mercy ; she was afraid of him. Afraid of his honesty, his
clear perceptions, the cold scorn that showed in every line
of his figure, and withered her soul. His very immobility
froze her into abjectness. If he had bullied and stormed
at her, she could have plucked up courage to give him back
word for word. As it was, she could do no more than throw
in a shivering protest, weak and futile even to herself. He
had cowed her, this man, this obscure provincial lawyer,
with neither origin nor name ; he had raised but his voice—
and her soul was full of wounds. Before him, her lineage
was as nothing, her position of no account. She was no
more than what she actually was—a poor trembling woman
who had done wrong and been found out.

And this man was to be both a faithful witness and the
judge who should pass sentence upon her.

She braced herself up to listen, standing there a little
apart from him, and nursing in her bosom the only possible
weapon with which to wound him, when he had done
wounding her. And this, none the less, because he had
spared her, and, she felt convinced, would spare her the
obvious insult, the vulgar taunt that would have tripped
off the tongue of a coarse-minded man first of all. Ridley
had not reminded her that she had come alone, in the dead
of night, to the house of a single man.

"Are you attending, madam ? " he asked sharply.

"Yes ; oh, yes," she answered, with dry lips.

"You found me out, I say," he continued. "And you
found my clerk here. He was a suitable tool, it seems,
for your honourable purpose, and you set about debauching
him without compunction."

"That is a hard word," she cried. "Do I seem so de-
bauched a person myself ? "

"It is a little difficult to define you precisely, madam,
as yet. I will say that you are merely a fool. However,
you learnt all that you wished to know from my clerk, and
succeeded in inducing him to keep his mouth shut. Am I

right, Miss Chideock ? I am open to correction on any point."

"Go on ! "

"Then you waited for your opportunity.   Three weeks."

Quenride looked at him with a piteous mouth.

"My brother. He has been ill," she faltered.   "I could not leave him—and besides——"

"Well ? " asked Ridley a shade less sternly.

"No matter. Go on."

"To-night you came. And because you must needs enter by my office window, which is protected by high railings, you adopted this—garb. You broke into my house success-fully. You purloined the key of my strong-room from its secret drawer, and you crept down here like a thief in the night. You brought a chisel and mallet with you, pretty playthings for a lady. Shall we say, madam, that you came to look for that locket which I have unfortunately lost ? "

"Say what you please, sir. Only, for God's sake, let me hear the end."

"You did come for a locket," cried Ridley, raising his arm for the first time.   "A locket of gold, with a clasp of red wax, jewelled with legal phrases, and wrapped up in parchment. Can you deny, Miss Chideock, that you came here to steal your grandfather's will ? "

She was twisting a handkerchief in her hands. He saw it falling, strip by strip, to the ground. Yet she said nothing —but only looked at him with eyes which were inscrutable, in spite of their fear.

CHAPTER XIX

RIDLEY CALLS THE TUNE

AS he watched her, she admitting her guilt by silence, revelation came suddenly to Ridley, and he turned on her anew, in a kind of cold fury.

"And it was for this," he cried, "that you desired to marry me! For this—that you might learn my secrets unsuspected—that you might get an established footing in my house, and work your criminal will without hindrance! For your covetous ends you would have sold, not only your own honour, but mine! Mine! The honour of the man whom you would have sworn to love and respect! Madam, in order to obtain the fortune which you dangled as a glittering bait before the eyes of an impoverished man, you would have risked, not only your husband's name, but his life as well. Madam, you have acted with the heartlessness of a devil!"

"Oh!—oh!" she moaned. "You make it seem so terrible. Oh, you are wrong. I did not think—I did not understand."

"Madam," said Ridley harshly, "you did not care."

"No, no! I am not so base as you believe. You should not have suffered through me. As to the fortune—in itself it is nothing to me."

"Yet you risk a great deal to secure it," he reminded her.

"I was driven to it," she murmured. "Spare me, sir. For God's sake, spare me your words! They hurt—oh, heaven! how they hurt. I can bear them no longer!"

She dropped her abased head into her hands, and for the next few moments there was nothing heard in the wide spaces of the cellar but her heavy sobs.

Ridley waited, with tense lips. His duty was plain. He had caught her at night-time in his house, and she had entered it for the commission of a crime. Moreover, as he read it—and it was this that made him so sternly inimical towards her—she had in intent struck at his professional honour, threatening to end with infamy a career which he had kept unquestioned and unsullied. Ridley was not a man unduly elated over his own virtues, but his fair fame was very dear to him, and to have it snatched from him through no fault of his own seemed, at this moment, the very acme of bitterness. Yet, while he so considered what might have been, he was well aware that an attempt to save himself by an exposure of his erring wife would have been an impossibility. He asked no credit for this attitude, though the belief that she had calculated upon it drove him to fresh fury.

But as Quenride Chideock had no such claim upon him, there was no doubt as to what he ought to do.

He explained the point to her when, exhausted with sobbing, she sank down on the bench, and let the candle-light fall upon her disordered hair. He noticed how it shone in the yellow rays with a glory that seemed to brighten all that dismal place.

" Well," she asked, in a weary voice, " what are you going to do ? "

" When I first discovered that my house had been broken into," continued Ridley, with no sign of wavering from some set purpose, " I thought of that unlucky clerk of mine. Now, Miss Chideock, if he had proved to be the culprit, do you know what I should have done ? "

She shook her head almost indifferently.

" No. Whatever you are going to do to me, I suppose."

" Not precisely," said Ridley drily. " I should first have fetched my whip and flogged him until a score of wounds were teaching him due respect for property and the privacy of other men's houses. Then I should have flung him into the road, and forbidden him to come near me again."

Quenride turned her face up to him. For the first time it was wistful and eager.

" Is that all ? " she asked. " Oh, Mr. Ridley, I thought you were a hard man ! "

" Perhaps I am It is a little premature for you to express an opinion on the point. You may, however, thank Heaven that I am neither impulsive nor vindictive. Also for your comfort, I may remind you that we Englishmen are a conventional race, and your sex—however disguised !—protects you from a flogging. But do not build too much upon that leniency. Your offence is too daring, too outrageous, to go unpunished. Yes; it is my turn now to call the tune. And, on my soul, madam, you shall dance to what air I please ! "

" It is a pity," said Quenride. She was sitting quite quietly now, her hands clasped on her knees, and her shining eyes gazing past him into the shadows by the door. " It is all a pity, I suppose. But this, most of all."

For the first time, she had the power to touch him on her own account. There was a subtle pathos in her voice that vexed him—as though she used a weapon to which she had no right. He was irritated into a poor retort.

" A pity, undoubtedly—for yourself," he said.

" No," said Quenride. " For you."

He laughed harshly.

" Your most excellent reason ? " he asked.

She turned her face up to him again.

" It is this," she said, " you are a man who does not know what it is to have a conscience."

" I envy Miss Chideock hers ! " he said at once.

" Don't mistake me, Mr. Ridley," she answered. " There are two classes of men who have no consciences. The very bad, and the others. You are of the others. We have not met often ; but our intercourse has been exceptional, and my knowledge of you has developed very rapidly. You have, as yet, no conscience, because there has been no need for it. You have, as yet, had nothing of your own doing to regret."

" You mean that I shall regret what I am going to do ? "

" You have not told me yet what that is," she answered. " But looking forward I see no chance of a happy ending, and I think that you will probably—regret."

" I will take the risk," said Ridley, with a touch of light cynicism. " And now, Miss Chideock, attend to me. It is time this interview came to an end. There is a great deal more which I have to say to you, but you shall hear it elsewhere."

Quenride rose, and faced him, with the corner of the table between them.

" Where then ? " she asked.

" In the presence of the man whose wishes you would
have criminally transgressed," he told her. " At your
grandfather's bedside."

He saw her face quiver. She failed, it seemed, to recognise
the implied immunity from the penalty which Ridley had
also waived in the supposititious case of Fiander. She
neither showed relief nor thanked him for his leniency.
She merely spoke three words, in a low, agonised voice.

" You are pitiless ! " she said.

Ridley shrugged his shoulders.

" I am not expecting compliments," he told her. " On
the whole, I am letting you off quite lightly. We will not
stay to discuss the point. There are my terms. The only
alternative is to call in the constable. You do not wish for
that, I presume ? "

She winced at the words, which were uttered a little
callously, the truth being that Ridley was more disappointed
than he cared to own at her indifference to his toleration. He had spared her more than she had any right to
expect, and her ingratitude galled him. Fiander, he felt
certain, would have sobbed out his thanks between the
stripes.

" No," she answered, with a long shivering sigh. " Let
me think ! I must have time to think."

" Not now," said Ridley firmly. " Not here. To-
morrow—I mean, when daylight comes—I will ride over,
and we will talk again. Then you shall make your confession
to your grandfather, and I will leave you to be dealt with by
him."

" You forget his health ! " she pleaded, with an eagerness
which Ridley's keen mind fastened upon. " The shock will
kill him."

" I might point out," returned Ridley, " that I should
scarcely be to blame for that." He picked up his weapon
and moved towards the door. Quenride followed him with
lagging feet. " I strongly suspect, Miss Chideock," he went
on, " that you have exaggerated your kinsman's illness for
your own ends. However, in order to avoid risks, I will
bring a medical friend with me who shall judge whether Mr.
Chideock is strong enough to bear startling news."

He pulled open the door, and Quenride passed out. In the
act of doing so, she turned. He was holding the candle,
and had raised it to guide her steps. Each face was plain
to the other's eyes.

" You have the lawyer's narrow mind for details," she said, and her contempt flicked the blood into his cheek.

" Is it quite becoming in you to remind me that I am a lawyer ? " he asked.

Quenride answered him over her shoulder. To his surprise, she gave a short laugh. There was pain in it, and in that dreary place it sounded ghastly enough.

" Oh, I know," she said. " You want to be thanked for your kindness, your consideration, Mr. Ridley."

For the moment, he was furious.

Quenride turned round, and looked down at him as he came up the stairs after securing the cellar door.

" There are six thousand pounds to your credit lying at the County Bank," she said.

" Well ? " asked Ridley, with sudden suspicion.

" I placed it there."

He could do little more than stare at her.

" I did it to place you beyond temptation."

" Of what sort ? " he asked, holding himself in.

" Bribery—by my cousin. One of my plans had just failed."

" You mean, I had just declined to marry you."

" Yes. I had to secure myself against possible risks. I felt certain that sooner or later he would try to get possession of the will. In fact, some incautious words of his own warned me that he would. And I knew that he had visited you. My brother told me."

" I see," said Ridley.

" I thought that you might not have closed with him at once."

" I see," said Ridley, again. His face told her nothing.

" Don't you understand ? " she cried. " You refused a fortune hampered with a wife, but you might have accepted a bribe without such an encumbrance ! "

" I see," said Ridley. " But as it happens, I had already kicked your cousin out of my office for presuming to make the proposal—before the benefit of your money was offered to me."

Quenride leaned down.

" You dared that ? " she asked, with quick breathing. Her eyes shone.

" There was no daring about it. I was in my own house, and a man had insulted me."

" And I ? " she retorted. " Hadn't I insulted you too ? '

"There can't be two opinions about that," said Ridley. "Will you please to go on."

But she neither turned nor stirred.

"I don't mean that day at Wareham," she explained, still dazzling him with her bright eyes. "Surely, placing that money at the bank was an insult. It showed that I had no belief in your incorruptibility."

"Very plainly, madam. Pray go on up the stairs."

This time she obeyed, but when they stood together at the top of the steps she went back persistently to the point.

"Doesn't it hurt you that I should have thought so ill of you ? " she demanded.

But her eagerness pierced through the question, and taught Ridley how to answer her. He raised his shoulders very slightly.

"Miss Chideock." he said, with a snap of the fingers, " your opinion is not worth that to me."

Thus her last shaft fell harmlessly from him. He had even pricked her with the point. In sudden desperation, she thrust it yet more deeply into her own bosom.

"In my heart," she said abruptly, "I did not believe that my cousin could buy you. But it pleased me to think that I had done a thing which might sting you, if you knew. It pleased me no less, because I did not mean that you should ever know. I hated you so much. I hated you even more then than I do to-night."

They had reached the front door by now, and Ridley was unbolting it with caution. In truth, there was small chance of his being overheard, since Mrs. Channing and the maid slept two floors away. The one was slightly deaf ; the other had the reputation of being the heaviest sleeper in the town. Ridley looked up at Quenride, as he stooped over the lower bolt. He had given her the candle to hold, and she was lowering it for his convenience. Their faces were so close together that her breath warmed his cheek.

"You hated me, I suppose," he said, " because I had failed to help on your audacious plan, by marrying you ? "

He saw the rich dye stain her face from brow to chin.

"Partly," she admitted ; then went on, resolutely, "There was another reason. Oh ! you were justified in holding me in light esteem, though I didn't realise that until it was too late. But I had cheapened myself to you, and I saw then what an immodest, wanton creature you must surely deem me. I who had been so proud ! "

"My faith!" said Ridley, with a short hard laugh.
"You had an odd way of trying to win back my respect."

"And now I have lost it for ever," she said, with such a
note of regret in her tones that gentler words fell from the man
than he had meant to utter to her that night.

"I could make nothing of you at the time," he said, as
the last bolt slid back. "But don't distress yourself. You
showed too much arrogance to make the immodesty seem
natural to you, and while I lashed the one I was in reality
striking at the other."

"Thank you," said Quenride, and their faces drew apart.

Ridley swung open the door, and fell back into his
previous manner.

"You have a horse somewhere, I suppose?" he said.

"Yes."

"You can find it alone?"

"Yes. I am not afraid to go by myself. I came
alone."

"Very well, then. As you please." She passed out.
"By daylight, Miss Chideock, we shall meet again. I must
warn you, in the meantime, to build nothing on the hope of
a possible change in my temper."

Her voice came back from the porch.

"I hope for nothing," she said. "If it were worth while,
Mr. Ridley, I could warn you also. I would say—'Keep
out of this; as you value your peace of mind, keep out of
this!'"

He shut his ears, and with them his heart, to the passionate
pleading, the low cry of pain that vibrated in her voice.

"Is that the last you have to say?" he asked, door in
hand.

"No!"

She came back a pace. To his surprise, she touched him
on the breast, laying her palm upon it, and keeping it there
until he moved away.

"Well?"

"You are a just man. Grant me two things, for justice'
sake!"

"What are they? I promise nothing, mind."

"My brother," she pleaded. "You will let me tell him
everything, in my own way?"

"I have no wish to come between you and your brother,"
answered Ridley, and it was then that he stepped away from
her contact, as if he feared it might weaken him for her next

7

petition. He heard her thank him, and he knew, though he could not see, that the tears were running down her face.

"And again," she said, "one thing else. That young fellow—your clerk. Do not let him suffer for my sins. It was all my fault; he was not to blame. He has only a small career before him—don't ruin it at the outset because he was cajoled by a wretched woman."

Ridley's face hardened a little. It was plain that he considered that Quenride was now on more questionable ground.

"Your sentiments do you credit," he said impassively. "You should, however, have considered the young man's career before you jeopardised it. The offence is not one to be disregarded by an employer."

More than that he would not say, and Quenride vanished into the darkness with his cold tones biting at her heart.

Ridley secured the door, and turned slowly into the passage. He carried the light into the nearest room, and ascertained that it was a quarter to five. There could be no question of further sleep. He went into the office, set everything in order, and put fresh tapers into the candelabrum. He went up to his room, and fetched a dressing-gown and shoes. Then, returning, he seated himself at his writing-table, with a sheaf of papers before him. If he was to go over to Wareham later on, there was enough work that must be got through to keep him employed until the end of the morning. After that, he must close the office. The irregularity would have jarred on his professional sense at another time, but now he was in no mood to stick at trifles. He worked resolutely on until the grey light filtered through the shutters, and slowly widening rendered the candles unnecessary. At half-past seven he heard the shaving-water carried to his door, and went upstairs to finish dressing. He breakfasted at eight, and worked again until noon. At that hour, he gathered up his papers, locked the office door, and dined leisurely. There was no hurry in his attitude. Once again, he had made up his mind to be master at the forthcoming interview. As on the previous night, he had himself well in hand; he was angry, but not inflamed; stern, but not vindictive. He was sparing the culprit a good deal. She had outraged his house, and threatened his professional honour. She had deliberately plotted to frustrate the wishes of her helpless relative. In return, she was to pay a forfeit—and an exceedingly light one, compared with what might have been exacted. There was the family name to be considered. She would be protected by that. Her grandfather's displeasure she would have to endure, but at least there would be no publicity, such as Ridley could have obtained for her offence, had he been malicious-minded.

His friend the doctor, whom he had communicated with earlier in the day, arrived while he was finishing his meal, and presently they left the house together.

Thus did the young lawyer, for the second time in his history, set out from home with Wareham as his destination, carrying with him no anticipation of an enlarged experience before he should return. Resolutely, calmly, he started on the journey ; no one could have turned him from his purpose at that moment. But the reckoning lay at the other end — and there a passionate, storm-tossed heart awaited him.

He said little to his friend as they rode along. He had as yet not thoroughly explained the nature of the service he required. From time to time, the doctor glanced at his face, and found that its expression did not induce pleasantries. The gossip about the young man had not died down, and the empty place at the Governor's table was helping to keep it alive. Dr. Homer was not sure that he had acted discreetly in agreeing to ride abroad with young Ridley in the publicity of a high road.

Only at one point did his companion show much interest in the incidents of the ride. This was when, a short distance from the end of their journey, the doctor's nag suddenly shied at a dark object lying at the edge of the road. It proved to be a slouch hat of soft black felt, fresh and uncrushed, a dainty find for a gipsy or a beggar. Ridley, staring at it while his companion struggled with his troublesome beast, had little doubt that some few hours ago it had covered Quenride Chideock's rippling hair as she galloped forth on her desperate errand.

The house, when they reached it, looked blank and sombre as usual. Ridley ran his eyes over it, as he dismounted. In an upper storey a half-drawn blind was pulled aside, and a face showed for an instant. It was Dolly Pouncey, in attendance in Gilbert's room, and unutterably excited by the arrival of two more male visitors, when there was already one in the house.

"We have come by appointment," Ridley announced, when the door was opened. " Miss Chideock, I believe, is expecting us. Will you please to send a man to take the horses."

" Miss Chideock is awaiting you, sir," he was told. " She wishes to speak to Mr. Ridley alone."

The two accordingly separated. Ridley was taken to a room at the back of the house. Quenride, a very shadow of a woman with her white face and pale grey gown, rose up to meet him.

He bowed to her formally. She did not return his salute. In truth, she seemed not to notice it. Yet she was keenly alive to his presence, for her eyes were wide with fear. Looking at her more closely—in those infinitesimal moments that elapse before a conversation is begun on either side—Ridley found that she was not defiant, nor embarrassed, nor scornful. On the other hand, the quality which marked her was an elusive one—fear looked out of her eyes, but her lips and hands were steady. Almost, she might have been said to be resigned.

" You have come," she said. " Yes, I knew you would. Will you sit down ? There was something, I think, that you wanted to say to me."

Ridley remained standing, suspicious of blandishments. This was no pleasant afternoon call, and there was no need to treat it as such.

" There is something, Miss Chideock," he told her, " which I have come to hear you say."

She drew a deep breath, and fell back into her chair.

" My cousin is here," she said, then.

Ridley was annoyed, excessively so. The sole argument in favour of holding his tongue altogether had been the distastefulness of supporting Alaric Mohun.

" That is unfortunate ! " he declared, with warmth. " I don't know that we require a fourth party at our interview."

" You did not send for him, then ? "

" Certainly not."

" I thought that perhaps you had done so."

" No. I meant to spare you that."

" Thank you," she answered. " Though it really matters very little, I suppose."

" I don't see that," said Ridley, the flush of annoyance still on his cheek. " Can't you send him away ? "

Quenride gave a hard little laugh.

" You can try," she said.

She leant back in the chair. It was deep and high. Her

bright hair gleamed against the dull red tapestry, her arms lay along its woodwork. At the ends were carved lions' mouths, fanged and open. Into these, she had thrust her fingers.

"Where is Mr. Mohun ? " asked Ridley, coming back to the point, after he had half unconsciously noted these things.

"He went to the stables. He has a fancy that he is not well served in this house. So he looks after himself."

"That's annoying ! He's certain to see our horses."

"Certain."

"And to ask whose they are ! "

"No doubt."

"Miss Chideock, I came here on a private matter," Ridley announced, standing squarely before her. "My errand concerns you and your grandfather alone."

Quenride turned her face up to him. For the first time, a touch of hauteur lent life to her voice.

"Do you think, sir, that my cousin's visit is a pleasure to me ? "

"Probably not. Still——"

"Still," she interrupted, dropping back into her former listless manner, "since he is here, his presence must be accepted. I sent for you, Mr. Ridley, to speak of something else."

"Yes ? "

"You have brought your friend, I presume ? "

Ridley bowed.

"Then, will you please dismiss him ? "

Ridley stared at her in surprise.

"His services, you can say, will not be required."

"But, madam——"

"His loss of time shall be compensated," Quenride said.

"I did not mean that ! " Ridley cried impatiently. "Am I to understand——? "

"What I say. His services will not be required. Surely that is an easy message to convey ? "

"Before I give it," said Ridley, "I should like to know precisely what it means."

"You spare me very little," she said.

She drew yet more deeply into the chair, and clutched the lions' mouths with her delicate fingers

"You mean," said Ridley slowly, "that Mr. Chideock's state of health has been exaggerated by you of set purpose, and for your own ends ? "

A shiver ran down her from head to foot.

"You have deliberately kept his friends and his man of business from him ? "

She made no reply. But one hand had released its grip, and was now pressed to her bosom. He looked at her for a moment.

"It is in keeping with the rest ! " he said contemptuously. "I will speak to my friend."

As he crossed the hall after dismissing Homer, he came face to face with Alaric Mohun. Two pairs of angry eyes flashed at each other.

"What the devil are you doing here ? " demanded Mohun, his cheek dyed a dull red. "I've a good mind to order you off ! "

"This is not your house, sir," said Ridley. "And my business does not lie with you."

Mohun, puzzled and frowning, blocked his way.

"Not so fast, Master Lawyer ! " he cried. "With whom does your business lie ? May I ask that ? "

"As often as you please ! "

"But you won't answer, you mean ? "

"You take me very accurately, sir."

Mohun scowled. Then he suddenly stepped aside.

"Damme," said he, "but I'll find out ! "

"You'll be a cleverer man than I take you for, then," said Ridley.

"Do you insult me, sir ? "

"I'm not particular, Mr. Mohun."

Ridley's voice had kept to its usual pitch, but Mohun had raised his, and the sound of it brought his cousin into the hall. He turned towards her angrily.

"Quen," he said, "I object to this man's presence in the house. I hold it little better than an intrusion."

"He is not here by my invitation," she told him.

"But you allow him to remain ! "

"The same might be said of yourself. I get as much pleasure from the society of the one as of the other. Yet you both remain."

Ridley was perplexed. The conversation was almost a repetition of that which had passed inside the room. Quenride, whom he had come to humble, had a strange nervous dignity about her. Her fear and her courage were equally matched.

"I am here on business," he said. "Mr. Mohun, a professional man cannot afford to waste time."

"Don't you see," cried Quenride a little uncertainly, "Mr. Ridley is burning to get to work! Don't you admire his—his professional zeal?"

"Madam," said Ridley, "I think that we have trifled enough. Are you ready to take me to Mr. Chideock?"

Mohun swung round on his heel.

"Oho, then! It is the old man, after all. And what is this very pressing business, Quen?"

"Nothing that you have part or lot in, sir."

It was Ridley who spoke. But for once Mohun paid no heed to him. He was looking suspiciously, eagerly, even anxiously, at Quenride. She, for her part, looked at the lawyer, and at no one else.

"I am waiting," he said sharply.

She turned towards the staircase. The two men followed.

"Miss Chideock," said Ridley firmly, "I have already told you that we do not need Mr. Mohun."

"Yes, but—damnation!" cried the other, "this sounds interesting. And, whether you need him or not, Mr. Mohun's coming!"

Ridley halted half-way up the stairs. Quenride, at the top, did the same.

"Mr. Mohun does not accompany us into your grandfather's room," he said, with a resolution which made his attitude seem almost friendly towards her.

"It is you who forbid it," she said, "not I. And the business is as much my affair as yours."

Down below, Mohun gave a laugh of relief.

"Well spoken, Quenny! Keep the knave in his place, my girl o' spirit! Up we go!"

With deepening perplexity, doubt, even an odd sense of resentment, Ridley went on.

"Tread softly, please, gentlemen," Quenride said. "That is my brother's room. And he has been very ill."

A sense of shame deadened Ridley's footfall. The whole affair was so inconceivably different from what he had planned. In some unaccountable way, Quenride, instead of himself, seemed to be taking the lead. He had called the tune, truly; but was she dancing to the right air?

All three stood outside a closed door. It was in a shadowy

corner, and their moods showed only in the tones of their voices. In each case, these were lowered to little more than a whisper. Quenride's was less steady than it had been hitherto, and there was a note of effort in it.

"Mr. Ridley," she said, "you have asked me to take you into that room. I have warned you before. I give you a last chance. Go down those stairs, and you may yet save some part of your peace of mind. Remain where you are—and there will come a day when you shall go into an inner room, to hide yourself."

"You have a pretty talent for melodrama," replied Ridley coldly. "You are putting too romantic a complexion on a rather sordid bit of business. Mr. Mohun, I hope, will see the necessity of retiring when Mr. Chideock, at my suggestion, asks him to do so."

Thus he endeavoured to convey to Quenride his determination that nothing to incriminate her should be spoken in Mohun's presence.

"Egad!" cried the other man, with a thin hilarity. "The devil gets back his own, don't he, Quen? But I'm going to see this business through. Damme! I've not seen the old man since before I went to Paris. How his old pate will wag with delight, to be sure. We patched up our quarrel, sir, but my cousin says he's got a bit nasty-tempered of late, so don't be surprised at my reception."

The others paid no heed to him, although afterwards both knew that each had heard. Quenride had taken a key from her pocket, and was fitting it to the door.

It swung open under her hand. She stood back to let the two men in. Ridley entered first, Mohun at his heels. Just beyond the threshold, both halted.

The room was swept and in order. But, save for themselves, it was empty.

Ridley stared speechless into the other man's eyes. But Mohun, with his wider knowledge, sprang at the truth.

He turned round, foul-mouthed and savage, upon Quenride, who had followed them in.

"You she-devil!" he cried. "This has been your game, then! How long has the old man been dead?"

"Since last March," she answered. And there was a faint show of triumph in her tone—triumph that she had kept her secret so long.

"Damn you!" he snarled, and raised a heavy fist.

Ridley caught it, and sent him spinning across the room.

" Behave yourself ! " he said.   " She's a woman still."

A movement at his elbow drew his eyes back to Quenride. She swayed suddenly, and fell across his feet.

And Ridley, bending over her, saw that proud head abased before him, with its fine eyes closed, and the tender mouth gone white and pinched with misery.

PART III

THE FELON

"Oh, my dear, my dear, do you think that I would love you at no cost to myself?"

CHAPTER XX

RESOLVE

QUENRIDE lay on the bed in her own room, staring with wide eyes at the canopy above. If her fancy coloured the white expanse, she must have seen terrible things there, for she lay trembling. At times, a shudder shook her like a spasm. Her arms were rigid at her sides, with stiffly clenched fingers pressing into the palms. This quiescent mood had followed upon one of extreme excitement, when hysterical bursts of passionate weeping had turned her into a wild and unreasonable creature, whom none might help or serve. But, in all the three hours that had passed since she had been laid there, she had spoken no word to anyone.

It was nearing six o'clock when she broke her silence. The room, the house itself was very quiet. The ticking of a small clock throbbed in the stillness with maddening impassivity. The sound beat in upon her brain and hurt her like a series of blows. The house seemed to be waiting for something. The clock ran through its allotted task with the cruel impartiality of a heedless living thing.

She raised herself and looked between the curtains. The movement brought a woman out of the shadows. It was her nurse—one who held fidelity to her mistress and dislike of Alaric Mohun as ordinances of the Christian faith.

"Feeling better, my dear?" she asked. "There! don't 'ee try to move."

Quenride sat up, and pushed the hair out of her eyes. Her face was pale, and very weary.

"What has happened? How long have I lain here? Who brought me in?"

"The strange gentleman, Miss Quen. Ye've been here nigh on three hours."

" So long ? What have I been doing ? "

" Sobbing, my deary, fit to break your heart."

" Ah ! "

" You was in a swound when the gentleman carried you in, and, dear heart, I thought as I'd never bring 'ee round."

" I wish you hadn't ! But that would have been too great a mercy to such a sinner as I. How quiet the house is ! I hope Gilbert hasn't been alarmed."

" Miss Dolly is with him. They had tea in his room. She've been reading and singing to him."

" That's well," said Quenride. " I will go to him presently. How my head aches ! Give me the sal volatile. Thank you. No. Don't ask me what has happened. You will know soon enough. Oh, yes. I am better now. Nurse, did the gentlemen leave at once ? "

" Mr. Alaric went away very soon, my dear. T'other one —Mr. Ridley, is it ?—is below in the parlour."

" Why ? " asked Quenride, slipping her feet to the floor. Her face had gone hard. " How dare he stay ? "

" He asked permission to wait until he heard that you had recovered, madam."

Another woman, the housekeeper, had entered, and replied to the overheard question.

" He is waiting out of curiosity," said Quenride, looking round at the two. " He thinks that he may possibly see me again—and ask questions in his cold clever way—and find out what he wants to know. Oh," she struck the bed with her closed hand, " I know. I can understand."

" Indeed, madam, I believe you're wrong. He sent his respects, and I was to say how much he regrets your indisposition."

" Regrets ? " cried Quenride harshly.

The two women looked at one another ; then the housekeeper went on, in a matter-of-fact way :

" I have offered Mr. Ridley both a glass of Madeira and a dish of tea. But he would take neither."

" Of course not ! " cried Quenride. " In my house ! Of course not ! " She laughed a little, hysterically. " Oh, he is an iceberg, and no man—and his tongue is like the bitter winds that cut and wither the poor naked flesh. But, indeed, I will bear no more. Tell him to go."

" I think you're a bit hard on the gentleman, my dear," the nurse struck in. " He was very gentle with 'ee, and seemed mightily put about over your swound. ' Keep her quiet,' says he, ' and let me know if I shall ride off for a doctor. I wish,' says he, ' I hadn't sent my friend away.' "

Quenride was pressing her hands to her forehead, trying to recall the incidents which had immediately preceded her faintness.

" Wait ! " she said. " Perhaps you are right. My cousin was going to strike me. I think he would have liked to kill me in that moment. Mr. Ridley interfered, and saved me from the blow. I think that was it. Then I suppose I fainted. At any rate, he is easily tested. Go down and say that I am quite well now, and thank him for his concern. If he be honest, he will take his departure. But I believe that he will make some excuse for remaining."

The housekeeper went downstairs, and going quietly into the parlour found Ridley asleep in his chair—-so soundly asleep, moreover, that she had to clatter the fire-irons to awaken him.

" The fire has gone down, sir," she said discreetly, as he opened his eyes.

" Ah, so I see." He stood up, stretching his limbs. " How is Miss Chideock now ? "

Quenride's message was repeated to him.

He nodded gravely.

" And she will do well now, you think ? " he asked.

" I hope so, sir."

Ridley reached out for his riding-coat, which was lying across a chair.

" Then," he said, " I will intrude upon you no longer. Kindly give my compliments to Miss Chideock, and tell her that I am sincerely glad to hear of her recovery."

" I will, sir."

Ridley walked into the hall, and picked up his hat and gloves.

" Tell her also," he said, " that if she should desire my services I am at her command. As her man of business, I can offer no less."

It was a strange message. It was intended to convey to Quenride that he was ready to hear her explanation of her conduct should she care to give one ; but that, until then, he should remain neutral.

" If I can have my horse, now——" he said. And he waited in the hall.

Into the silence there floated a sweet thin melody :

"Glory to Thee, my God, this night
For all the blessings of the light"—

Upstairs, Dolly Pouncey was singing the Evening Hymn to Gilbert.

A few rooms away, Quenride had asked to have the door opened. She heard Ridley come into the hall.

" He has not gone yet, you see," she said.

The nurse was looking out of the window.

" No, my dear. But he's going. There's his horse being a-brought round."

Quenride walked to the window irresolutely.

Down below, Ridley drew on his gloves. While he waited, he opened the hall door. The draught sent through the house caused the door of Gilbert's room to spring wide. Dolly's voice came down more clearly than before :

"Forgive me, Lord, for Thy dear Son,
The ill that I this day have done,
That with the world, myself, and Thee,
I, ere I sleep, at peace may be."

The words bit into Ridley's mind. They fitted in too well with Quenride's warning to be heard impassively. All the afternoon, he had been telling himself that it was no more than part of her trick—an effective attempt to cajole him into harmlessness—a lie, like the rest of it. It came to him now that he had had to be rather insistent on the point, like a man who argues with a tough adversary.

Quenride's apparent fear still haunted him like an unsolved thing. That she had played a deep game was certain. What he was not sure of, was whether it was not a little deeper than he even now supposed. Her warning ran up and down in his brain. Already, it seemed that his peace of mind had suffered.

After he had placed Quenride in the care of her servants, there had been a brief and rather bitter interview with Mohun. He had demanded, with a touch of savage insolence, to be informed what Ridley was doing in the affair. To which, the lawyer had replied with cold sincerity, that as yet he hardly knew himself. Mohun, looking as though he could say a great deal, then added a few threatening remarks, highly spiced with disrespect towards his cousin. The last epithet brought the fire to Ridley's eyes, and loosened his own tongue. Few men were able to stand against him when he put forth his full strength, and in a few minutes he had Mohun, as it were, under his heel, and wondering how it was possible for a man to express himself so effectively without making use of a single objectionable word. He had cut the interview short with a promise to call at the office the next day.

Ridley recalled all this, and smiled a trifle grimly as he stood at the open door, waiting for his horse to be brought round.

Upstairs, Quenride watched at the window. She was come to the threshold of a resolve, and had not yet stepped over it.

"Asleep?" she said, with disdain on her lips, when she heard of the fact. "In my house! What a liberty! But perhaps he had a disturbed night!" She laughed hysterically. "And he is really going?"

At that moment Ridley came into her view, crossing the pavement to where the groom was holding his stirrup. She leaned forward, wondering whether he would look up. He never turned his head.

A little choking cry burst from her.

She sprang at her resolve, and caught it in mid-flight.

"Stop him!" she cried, suddenly. "Call him back! I want him!"

While they hurried to obey her, a great calm settled down upon Quenride. She was alone in the room.

"I'll see him"—so her resolve ran—"I'll tell him what I've told to no one. The truth, the whole truth, and nothing but the truth, so help me God! If he won't believe, then Heaven help me—and him! And if he does believe and still condemns me, he's not the man I take him for; and the price must be paid. But for Gilbert's sake, I will try."

Ridley was surprised at the sudden summons to return to the house, but he sprang down again at the word, and followed the butler back into the hall. Dolly Pouncey was finishing the hymn. A hiatus had occurred, owing to her stopping to watch him from the window, and to explain matters to the boy.

Passing by the room, Quenride closed the door.

She found Ridley standing before the fire in a room full

of shadows. She entered so quietly that she was at his side before he knew it. She spoke his name.

"I beg your pardon," he cried. "I did not hear you come in."

She smiled sadly.

"Ah," she said, "if only that had happened last night."

Ridley frowned. His manner grew a little colder.

"Perhaps we had better regard that episode as done with, madam," he said.

"No. We cannot."

"I should have thought——" began Ridley.

"That I should like to ignore it?" she said. "You are right. I am not proud of it. I wonder whether you are—still!"

He made no reply, but drew a chair up to the fire for her, and brought a footstool to the rug.

"Thank you," she said, and sat down wearily.

Ridley stood before her, a foot on the fender, an elbow on the mantelshelf. His face was in shadow, hers in the full play of the firelight. Her dress was of some shimmering material, satin or silk, he did not know which, and the flickering of the flames caught it into a hundred points of light.

"I hope you are feeling better," he said.

"Yes. I am sorry that I troubled you. They told me that you were—kind."

Ridley's foot moved impatiently.

"I'm afraid I did nothing to merit such appreciation," he said. And added to the disclaimer, a little brusquely, "I am clumsy—with ladies."

Quenride turned her eyes to the fire.

"Shall I ring for lights, Miss Chideock?" he asked.

"No. Not yet. Afterwards, when I want to see your face—perhaps. Till then, this light will serve. I have something to say to you that no good woman could tell to a man without shame. And, in spite of all, I am still what the world calls—a good woman."

"Miss Chideock," said Ridley more gently than he had spoken yet, "you need not assure me of that. Since I first met you, I never questioned it."

He saw her eyes flash up to his. They were withdrawn slowly, and turned again to the fire.

"What are you going to do?" she asked.

" To do ? "

" Yes. Did my cousin say nothing ? "

" A great deal too much. He proposes calling upon me, to finish, to-morrow."

" To officially report my grandfather's death, I suppose."

" Probably. I concluded as much."

" And to demand the production of his will ? "

" It is a point which Mr. Mohun is not likely to forget."

" You have read the will ? "

" I have. It seemed that I had a right."

" My cousin being sole executor, you will assist him to prove the will ? "

" He may prefer another lawyer. He may need no advice."

" At any rate, you will place the will in his hands ? "

" Miss Chideock, it is useless to pretend that I do not know how that document pains you. I am not justifying what you have done. In fact, both professionally and morally, I strongly condemn it. But I believe that you have not acted solely for your own gain. There is a certain clause in that will which I myself would gladly see swept aside. You will do me the justice to remember that I did make the attempt. Since, however, it is too late to alter it, we must take what steps we can to mitigate the hardship towards your brother later on. If you have reason to suspect undue influence, or any other irregularity, you can contest the will. You know that ? "

" And if I failed to win my case ? " she urged.

" Then, of course, the will would have to stand."

There was a moment's pause. To cover its awkwardness, Ridley stooped down and mended the fire. Then he fell into his old position, as Quenride spoke again.

" You have met my brother, Mr. Ridley ? " she said.

" I have. He is a fine-spirited lad."

" He is a very delicate one. He has, Heaven knows why, taken a fancy to you. He may need a friend presently. I should like to think that I might entrust him to your care."

" If I can ever be of service to him," Ridley answered warmly, " you may rely upon me. But I should think that he would never need a friend while his sister is at hand."

" Ah," said Quenride, " it is that which troubles me."

Ridley stood silent. She still perplexed him, and there was a subtle quality about her which did not tend to reassure his mind. To attribute it to artifice, to set it down to a mere feminine mood, would have been to arm himself against it, or to brush its influence aside. As it was, he could do neither.

In a moment or so, Quenride looked up again.

" Mr. Ridley," she said, " that will must not be produced."

He shook his head at her, not unkindly, but positively.

" I must do my duty. I am sorry," he said. " But there it is."

" It must not be produced," she repeated, in tones that matched his for firmness.

" Unfortunately," he said, " there is no reason why it should not be, Miss Chideock."

" Unfortunately," she answered, " there is."

" A reason why it should be set aside ? " cried Ridley.

She bowed her head. Her fingers were interlacing nervously in her lap.

" Explain yourself, madam! Why cannot the will stand ? "

" Because it is not a genuine document," she told him. " Because it is only a forgery."

" A forgery ! Good God ! " cried Ridley. " You will have to prove your words ! "

" I am ready to do what I can," she answered, and rose up, facing him.

" I cannot believe it," he said. " This is some fresh trick, madam."

" Yes, I was afraid you would think that. But I have spoken, and what I have said to you I will say, if need be, to all the world."

" But," cried Ridley, bewildered and doubting, " if it is as you declare, how do you know this ? "

She looked at him with mournful eyes, but said nothing.

" Who forged it ? " he demanded, then.

" Cannot you guess ? "

" Your cousin ? Mohun ? "

She shook her head.

" Who then ? "

" I did it," she said ; and shrank a little away from him,
like a stricken creature who fears another blow.

" Good God ! " said Ridley.

And his eyes never left her face.

CHAPTER XXI

HER SHADOW

THE next thing of which he was aware, was that she was laughing strangely.

"Yes," she cried, all the pent-up hysteria let loose once more, "that is what I am. A forger! Now you can understand everything, I hope! I ought to be hanged, ought I not? Oh, you legal gentlemen are seldom tender-hearted! There's only yourself to stand between me and the gallows. Oh, you shall have a fine revenge if you wish. The scaffold for the stocks! Did you ever see a woman hanged? They'll do it in your own town, of course. You'll be able to see it done——"

"For God's sake, madam!"

"Don't interrupt—that's unmannerly. But you never were civil to me, were you? You'll be able to come and see it done, I tell you; and you'll say, 'There goes a scheming hussy out of the world. Now I'll go home to breakfast.' Perhaps you'll feel very proud of yourself, Mr. Ridley," she ran on wildly, in spite of his attempt to check her agonised words. "You'll feel glad you had a share in it. And I—oh, I'll not be sorry when the day comes. Can you understand that? Ah, but you haven't lived for months with the shadow over you, and been forced to go on as if you didn't see it always before your eyes. When I plait my hair and hold it out—so!—there's a shadow falls across my throat, so like—*it*!—that I could scream for fear. But I think that I could bear it, if only he wouldn't have to touch me. I saw him once. They pointed him out to me—a little grizzled man with hideous hands. I looked at them, and oh, God, how cold I grew!"

She flung herself down in the chair, and broke into passionate weeping that no man could have calmed. The one before her stood amazed, aghast. In those few moments he had looked into a woman's tortured soul—and his own was full of shame. It was the naked truth that had rolled out from her quivering lips—in one long cry of pain. In those few moments she had revealed to him the hidden suffering of many months. In those few moments he had begun to understand her warning to himself.

Regret stabbed sharply at his heart—and let compassion in.

He stood silent before her, cursing the arrogance which had exalted him unto her accuser and her judge. With what cold-blooded composure had he set forth—to hear this. If harm, in truth, came to her, could he rejoice that he had helped to strike a woman down? He crossed to the window, and stared into the darkening street, and wondered many things.

At the sound of his name he turned, and came slowly back across the room. Quenride was sitting up, her breast still shaken by heavy breathing, but otherwise calm. Her beauty was all disfigured by her weeping, but the shadows softened the defacement, and Ridley, as he fell into his old position before her, thanked God for the mercy of oncoming night.

" You will think me a wild weak creature," said Quenride. " You will say, ' This woman has the courage to commit a crime, but not the courage to suffer for it.' "

" I think," Ridley answered, in a low voice, " that you have suffered much—already."

" Ah, God, I have ! " she said. " And you believe in my guilt, Mr. Ridley ? "

He hesitated.

" I should be glad to think otherwise——" he began.

But she struck in vehemently :

" I do not wish you to think otherwise ! You must believe. You shall. I will prove it, as far as it can be proved. See here ! "

She rose quickly, and went over to a bureau, bringing away from it a pencil and a sheet of paper laid upon a book.

" Write your name in full," she said, thrusting them upon him. " Can you see ? Stir up the fire ! "

" There is light enough," he said, as he took the things from her.

He did as she bade him, kneeling down on the hearth-rug to catch the glow of the fire, and handed the paper back to her.

She was seated again, and bending forward she studied the sheet by the flickering light. Then she held out her hand for the book and pencil. She placed these on her knee, and glanced up at Ridley.

"What sort of a night is it going to be?" she asked. And so sent him to the window again.

Presently she called to him, and held out the sheet. A strip had been torn from either end. He could not have identified the place where he had inscribed his name.

"Have I written above, or below, your signature?" asked Quenride.

Again Ridley took the paper to the fire, and bent over it. His name was written there twice—the duplicate being so perfect that he could not tell which line his own fingers had traced.

"I do not know," he said, in reply to her. "It is—marvellous."

He handed the paper back to her, and stood upright. His face went into the shadows.

"It is terrible, you mean," she said. "Not the sort of accomplishment you would care for your sister to possess? I never intended to do such a thing again. I vowed that I would not. You compelled me to it. Has it served my purpose? Are you now convinced of my guilt?"

"It seems," said Ridley, with slow unwillingness, "that you could have done it."

She laughed—the low, harsh laugh of wretchedness.

"Oh, but I both could and did," she said. "Why do you doubt it? Others will not."

"Others?" repeated Ridley, with a sudden frown.

"The twelve good men and true who will try my case," she said.

Dreading lest she should fall back into her former wild bitterness, Ridley made haste to ask a question:

"How did you learn the trick?"

"It needed no learning. It is in my blood. A great-grand-uncle of mine was a forger. His craft has been transmitted to me."

Ridley's mind went back to the sun-baked attic in the constable Hutchins's cottage, and to the man's gossip on Chideock affairs.

"I have heard of him," he said.

"You have? Yes. He was not an ancestor to be proud of. He would have been hanged, only his sister saved him.

We Chideock women have the privilege of claiming King's Pardon for our male relatives, for any crimes except treason and murder. Strange, isn't it?—we may save our husbands and brothers, but not ourselves. But I doubt if the privilege will be granted again. It was only allowed in the case of my great-grand-uncle on the understanding that it was not to be claimed any more. They said, I believe, that the cases where it had been already granted were a mere following of precedent, without any legal obligation."

"I heard some garbled version of all this," said Ridley absently. He was more interested in the one before him than in her shady ancestor.

Quenride leant across and touched his arm.

"You believe that I wrote the signature to the will, do you not?" she asked.

"You press me very closely upon that point," he said.

"It means so much to me!"

Ridley stared into the fire. He found himself facing two alternatives. He must believe that this girl was the forger she declared herself to be, or he must recognise in her the most audacious liar he had ever met with. The situation was not a pleasant one for a man who was neither old nor warped out of human susceptibility. And there were difficulties—at least, perplexities—in either case. Why should she trouble to risk her life in order to concoct a will which she was afterwards—and only two months later—at such pains to keep hidden and ineffective? Had she once loved the savage Alaric, and so sinned for his sake, or was it conceivable that she had dared so tremendous a story in order to induce himself to suppress the document? There was the evidence of the sheet of paper still lying in Quenride's lap.

And so, with a strange unwillingness, Ridley, though groping still in the darkness as to causes and motives, came back to the conviction which had gripped his heart some minutes since.

The girl before him was a forger, one of a class of criminals which the law still held in the greatest abhorrence, and punished with death. Of recent years, the laws against forgery had been considerably modified, but for the forgers of wills there was still no milder penalty.

A cry from Quenride brought his gaze back to her.

"Why don't you speak?" she implored. "Have I laid bare my soul to you in vain?"

"If I say that I do not trust you, Miss Chideock ? " he asked.

"Then, as soon as the will is produced," she answered, "I shall tell my story again."

"Where ?   To whom ? "

"In the streets—on the housetops—in a Court of Law ! Oh, a judge and jury won't have your excuse for disbelieving me !   They will not say, 'She is lying in order to set aside the will and she trusts to my compassion not to let her suffer ! ' "

"You mean that you would carry the matter even to that length ? "

"I do.   Do you think that I would let my brother be robbed and tortured by that devil for the sake of saving my own poor body ?   Mr. Ridley, you know that I would not ! So surely as you let that forgery pass into my cousin's hands, so surely do you send me to take my chance of the scaffold."

There was silence in the shadowy room.   The man bent his head over the mantelshelf.   The truth was as ugly as ever a lie might be ; but he looked it in the face, and knew it for what it was.   Here was no trickery, no artifice, no insidious bid for sympathy—nothing but a tormented woman offering him an inexplicable problem in naked sincerity.

And there was more than the truth to be faced, since, of his own free will, he had disregarded her warning, and deliberately stepped into the affair.

"In God's name, Miss Chideock," he said, "why did you do it ? "

She answered him slowly, leaning back in her chair, her nervous fingers busy with the paper in her lap.

"Yes, you have a right to ask me," she said.   "It is not a pretty story.   But because it is my justification, I have also a right to tell you.   It concerns my cousin."

After saying as much, she sat silent for so long that Ridley ventured on a remark which he hoped might help her.

"When a woman does a thing like that for a man," he said, but with no great relish for the suggestion, "there is only one interpretation to be placed upon it.   Forgive me if I seem too personal.   It is the function of us lawyers to pry into private concerns."

Her eyes flashed up to him with spirit.

"You think that I wanted to help my cousin ? " she cried.   "That I loved him ?   Never !   I always disliked him. Now I hate him. Love ? I have refused to marry him three times."

Ridley, hearing her speak, knew that she had said the words which he would have desired of her.

"The Mohuns were never very friendly with the Chideocks," Quenride went on, "and the intermarriage was not popular on my side of the family. Alaric was never the one to lessen the antipathy, and some three years ago there was an open rupture. He and my grandfather quarrelled violently. Gilbert was always the favourite, and my cousin was jealous. My grandfather was not an even-tempered man, and it ended as I say—Alaric was forbidden the house. I suppose he felt that he had gone too far, for he then began his advances towards me. My grandfather was not so fond of me as he was of Gilbert, but I got on with him well enough, and, at least, I am Gilbert's sister. That counted for a great deal in Alaric's eyes, for my brother has always been sickly, with a slender chance of ever reaching manhood at all. Alaric, then, courted me because of the likelihood of my ultimately becoming the heir. But I spoilt his plans by refusing to have anything to do with him. And so, he set his wicked wits to work to hit on a scheme whereby he could both secure the fortune—and punish me."

She paused to glance up at the figure standing silent and attentive before her. Then she took up her tale again.

"At the end of last year, Gilbert had one of his bad attacks. He made a slow recovery, and was ordered away to Weymouth. My grandfather was also ailing, and I was forced to spend my time between the two places. Gilbert, I knew, was in good hands ; but as his health mended he depended on my company in his drives abroad, so that I was at Weymouth whenever I could get away from here.

"When the year turned, my grandfather seemed so much better, and Gilbert clamoured so insistently for my presence, that I left home, with the intention of spending a longer period at Weymouth than usual. It was at this time that I found my cousin installed in the town, or, rather, a little way out of it, for he had taken a furnished house standing in a lonely part of the downs.

"This house, I soon found, was being much talked about. At first, I did not believe the gossip, for with all his faults I had never thought of my cousin as a vicious man. But there was a woman in the town—a notorious woman— rumour linked her name with Royalty. They said that she came from Brighton ; you understand. Well, one day, I saw this woman in my cousin's company, and there was no doubt that they were on friendly terms. He came across to me, and suggested an introduction. Mr. Ridley, I could have struck him in the face ! He laughed at me ; and I knew then that a great deal of the gossip about the sort of company he entertained at that house was true. And I decided that Gilbert and I would return home as soon as possible. But the weather just then was bitterly cold, and I dared not let my brother face the journey.

" So we came to the middle of the month. The sixteenth. I was vexed that day with a bad headache, and rode out alone into the country. I got back to our lodgings in the early part of the afternoon, and to my surprise, Gilbert was not there. When I asked where he was, they told me that a gentleman had fetched him away in a carriage, and had left a letter for me. Such a letter ! Oh, Mr. Ridley, such a brutal letter ! "

She dropped her face into her hands, and for the first time Ridley spoke.

" Is it necessary that I should know all this ? " he asked, in pity for her distress.

Quenride braced herself up.

" Yes—it is the justification of my crime," she said. " You asked me why I had done it."

" Forgive me ! " he responded quickly. " Perhaps I should not have asked."

" I meant to tell you before you did. I cannot leave off now. I should like to feel that there is one man who understands, and pities me."

Her quiet confidence warmed Ridley strangely. Almost it seemed as though the bitter words which had passed between them had never been spoken.

" The letter," she resumed, " well, the letter, considering its object, was one which only a fiend could have devised. He said in it that he was taking Gilbert to his house. It was dull for the boy, shut up in a lodging-house sitting-room. He was of an age to begin to enjoy himself. He was giving a grand dinner to his friends that evening, and Gilbert should see a little of life. He should meet gay company, and hear good stories, and if he didn't understand them, then madame —the woman I spoke of—should explain them to him. And —oh, Mr. Ridley, think of it !—he wasn't turned fifteen then ! "

"What a devil!" said Ridley, between his teeth. It pleased him to think that he was to meet Alaric Mohun the next morning.

"It would have been bad enough," Quenride went on, "if there had been nothing behind it. But it was all a part of his plan. The lonely house, the scandal, that vile woman—they were all the pieces that went to make up his wicked scheme. And the letter was the bait to draw me into the trap. When I read it I took it for truth. I was horrified, and rode off as quickly as I could to save my brother from that pollution.

"Mr. Ridley, it was all a hoax. When I got to the house, I found only a deaf old crone, who took me into a room upstairs, and left me there. The instant that she had gone, I heard the key turned, and knew that, for some reason or other, I had been locked in. I began to be alarmed, but more on Gilbert's account than on my own. I thought that they had discovered my intention, and had taken these steps to prevent my rescuing my brother. Then, while I stood wondering what I should do, I heard my cousin speaking to me from the other side of the door.

"I demanded to know why I had been tricked, and asked where Gilbert was. He would not answer me. He went on speaking of other things, and as I listened I understood into what a villainous trap I had fallen.

"He told me that in a certain drawer in the room I should find a document. It was, he said, sealed, but the space for the signature was left uncovered. I was to write my grandfather's name, in his handwriting, in that space, and the names of two witnesses whom my cousin mentioned. I should find originals of all three signatures in the drawer, with the document. My cousin knew, of course, of my extraordinary skill in penmanship—I was rather proud of it as a girl, and had made no secret among my friends, of my perilous gift. Innocently used, I saw no harm in it. But, now, I was asked to put it to a use from which I revolted. I refused to agree to my cousin's request. From behind the door, he laughed at me. Then he showed me how utterly I was in his power."

Ridley made a movement. Quenride checked his interruption, and went steadily on.

"We were alone in the house, save for the old woman who had admitted me. And she was to leave the place in an hour's time. She was stone-deaf, and would not hear

me if I called. The house, I have told you, was in a very
lonely spot. I was in an upper room, thirty feet of bare
stone falling sheer to the ground, had I been able to escape
that way. But the window was barred, and I could barely
stretch an arm through. I have told you the sort of
reputation which the house had. Unless I signed that
document as he directed, I was to remain a prisoner in that
room, until the next morning, when a party of his
friends were due to breakfast. He swore that I should
be released in time to meet them. By nine o'clock, he
promised, the story should be all over the town. Could
I have borne that? I who had always been so proud!
The alternative was easy. If I obeyed his directions, he
would fetch my brother to the house within the hour, and
let us both depart.

"Mr. Ridley, I yielded. I did the detestable thing.
I opened the drawer, I studied the signatures, I copied
them on to the document, and flung it, otherwise unopened,
down to him, as he waited below. Was I to blame—oh,
was I so grievously to blame? At the time, I was ignorant,
even unsuspicious of the true contents of the document.
I believed it to be a matter of far less importance than it
proved to be. My grandfather was meditating the sale
of some land at Warminster; Alaric wanted it made over
to him instead, and I fancied that what I had signed was
a spurious deed for that purpose. And, poor fool that I
was, I thought that I would frustrate the plot by a frank
relation of what had happened as soon as my grandfather
could hear it. That, Mr. Ridley, is the first part of my
story. What have you to say?"

"This, Miss Chideock. It is a story which fills me with
shame."

"You!" She leant forward a little, striving to see his
face. "Why, you?"

"Because I share the manhood which your cousin has so
vilely abased."

"Ah!" she said, and her hands fluttered out towards
him. "But you are not such as he."

He took her hands, and held them for a moment.

"I hope not," he said gravely. "Miss Chideock, I have
spoken some very hard things to you. I am sorry."

"Hear me out," she urged, suddenly drawing away from
him. "I have a little more yet to say. It was not long
before Alaric made me aware of what I had done, and the

penalty allotted to such a crime. He tried to frighten me into keeping silence, urging, plausibly enough, that if a whisper of the fraud leaked out I could not prove the coercion. I had already destroyed even the lying letter which had taken me to the house. He declared that, if I told my grandfather, the rage into which he would fall would cost the old man his life. It was a strong argument, for he had an absolute horror of the thought of his kinsfolk waiting greedily for what he prized so much. That is why he would never make a will. He often threatened to give it all away in his life-time, so that no one should be waiting for his death. In a word, my cousin set before me the fact that I could not hope to get the will set aside without the case being made public, and myself prepared to take my trial as a confessed forger.

"Mr. Ridley, I pray God that you may never suffer as I suffered during that short time. But I returned home, resolved to tell my grandfather everything as soon as his health allowed of it. In that case, something might have been done. But my troubles were beginning—not ending. A month had elapsed before my cousin told me the truth, for I had refused to see him during that time, and also I had been anxious about Gilbert, who had suffered a relapse from the exposure Alaric had subjected him to on that day. And as I believed that Alaric would not attempt to enforce the supposed deed of gift until my grandfather's death, I saw no immediate reason for haste. But on the twenty-second of the month—it was February then—I left Gilbert at Weymouth, intending to get my business over before he returned. When I reached home, however, to my utter amazement I found that my grandfather had left Wareham the preceding day, journeying to Leicestershire, and taking my old nurse with him.

"In his state of health, it was madness—no less! I was thoroughly alarmed, and set off at once to follow him. Of course, I found him very ill. He lived for a fortnight, and then he died. In all that time, he only spoke one word—my brother's name. I do not think he even recognised me. How could I set right the harm I had so innocently done? There was my grandfather dead at an obscure country inn, and my cousin waiting to flourish the lying will in my face—the will that defrauded Gilbert of everything, save the entailed estates which even Alaric could not touch; and not only this, but placed him in my cousin's guardianship for several years."

" Why was that clause inserted ? " asked Ridley, in a low voice.

" Out of sheer malice—to punish me for refusing to marry him.   Do you know, Mr. Ridley, on the day when he released me from the locked room, I struck him, as I passed out—struck him across the face with my riding-whip. He has never forgiven me that blow.   I have always known that he would pay it back, with interest, to my poor brother."

And Ridley, recalling Mohun's look of hatred flung at the unconscious boy, could well believe it.

" You can probably guess the rest," Quenride went on wearily.   " I buried my grandfather in the village where he died.   He had never wished to lie with his relatives.   Everything was in order, and at first I had no idea of keeping his death a secret.   The fraud was a thing of growth rather than of deliberate planning.   At the beginning, I merely wanted time to think—to decide what to do.   You see, I had no one to turn to.   Even your uncle, I heard, had died suddenly.   I had to fight Alaric all by myself.   My whole life gradually turned to this one point—how to get hold of the will, and so save both myself and Gilbert.   My cousin went abroad, confident that my pride was too great, or my courage too weak, for me ever to tell the truth.   I came back here, quite resolved to hide my grandfather's death from him, and to wait for some opportunity of helping myself. The thing was not so difficult as you might think.   We arrived here late at night.   Who could tell in the town whether the old man was with us or not ?   I had sent away all the under servants—two were already under notice to go. This house and estate, you understand, is my own exclusive property.   My nurse, the housekeeper, the butler were all devoted to me, and these I trusted.   Gilbert was better kept in ignorance, I fancied.   Dolly Pouncey came to me after my return, though I had arranged for her to live here before that.   Her parents came to see me about it two days before I returned home from Weymouth, I was told.   Oh, you would marvel at the vividness with which every detail of that terrible time is fixed on my brain."

She had now come to what, as Ridley conjectured, must be the hardest part of her story to relate—the part which concerned himself.   He was wondering how she might be spared this, when she went steadily on.

" Then you came.   Before that, I had hoped unreasonable

things from the new attorney. But people began to talk about you, and I saw that I dared not throw myself on your mercy——"

"Miss Chideock!" The cry burst in rebellion from the man before her, and she smiled, very slightly.

"That was what I thought then," she said. "So I still waited, hoping for I scarcely knew what. Each day seemed to make my case more difficult and dangerous. I did not want to die, at least—like that. Then, at last, I fancied that I saw a chance. Oh, it was mad and desperate and wicked enough, as you told me last night, though it never seemed to me that you would be in any danger. And you must believe this—if there had been anywhere another woman, I would have tempted you no further. But from what I had heard, I thought that there probably was not. Well, you know how that chance ended! You were pitiless. I would sooner have been scourged than have listened to the words you said! If you still blame my confident arrogance, you must remember that I had no reason to believe in the finer susceptibilities of men. But you flung my proposal back in my face, and tore my self-respect to shreds. The only way to reinstate it was, it seemed to me, by humiliating you. I made you suffer, not for what you had done, but for the opinion which I thought you held of me. But even so, you had the best of it. I felt, all the time, that you were infinitely stronger than I."

"And so," said Ridley, "you hated me."

"Not so much last night, when you defeated my final scheme," she answered, her eyes seeking his face. "I was afraid of you, ashamed of myself, but very tired of the long fight—willing, perhaps, to give in. Only God knows, how I have suffered; how heavily the pride which amused and angered you has been chastised. Now, the end approaches, and whatever that end may be I think that, after all, I am glad."

Ridley took a step nearer. He was touching something which had never crossed his experience before, and the sight and sound of it all moved him to a quick emotion. His finer feelings rose up, responsive and alert.

"Can you doubt what the end shall be?" he asked.

She made no answer, but sat looking up at him, the fire-light in her eyes.

"The end was bound to come," he told her, out of his larger knowledge of men and things. "Such a fraud trembled

8

on the verge of discovery at every turn. Without my help this day was certain to come."

"Yes," she said, "yes; that's true. But are you proud of your share in it?"

"Not yet," said Ridley, with a hard settling of the mouth. "Perhaps I may be."

"What do you mean to do?"

"See your cousin, and ascertain his strength. Also, I think I shall destroy the will."

She caught his hands, and carried them to her breast. He brought them away wet with her tears.

"If," she whispered, "by any bad chance, he should be more powerful than I believe, and harm should come to me——"

"I should curse the day when I hastened on the event, even though it was bound to come. But, tell me this, Miss Chideock; you warned me not to interfere, yet, with me on your side, you say your cousin is comparatively harmless. Did you not trust me, then, that you spoke of shame and regret?"

"I trusted you so far that I felt that you would suffer if I came to a pitiful end. What I was not sure of, was whether you would believe my strange story—whether you would not, by your disregard, compel me to a more public and a more dangerous avowal. I had no right to claim your confidence in my sincerity."

"I do believe," said Ridley earnestly. "I do believe; before God I say it. Doubt me no more."

Quenride rose. A certain languor in her movements touched him to fresh pity.

"My cousin played a bold game to-day," she said. "He could not at first be certain of the motive of your visit. He feared that you had discovered something wrong with the will, but he was somewhat reassured by my willingness to take you into that room. He hoped that your errand was mere unimportant business, and he could not miss the chance, in spite of his probable reception, of getting at my grandfather again. He was anxious to see for himself how ill he was. And I think he wanted, if possible, to get a genuine will in his favour drawn up."

"I shall see him to-morrow," said Ridley, "and I will let you know the result at once. It may be possible to compromise."

"I trust to you," she answered, lifting her eyes with new-born confidence. "And when the will is destroyed——"

" You shall be present," he promised her.

" Thank you. And now," she said, " you have been here some hours, and have a long ride before you. I will see that you are served with a meal before you go. Good-bye."

She gave him her hand.

He held it for a moment, half bent towards it, hesitated, and let it fall.

" Good-bye," he said a little abruptly.

And she left him to his thoughts.

These were strange enough when, half an hour later, he stood once more in the quiet hall, ready for the second time to depart. Dolly's singing had ceased long ago, but the words haunted his listening ear. Had he done ill ? He was unwilling to believe it. But, as he left the house, he almost wondered at the man who had entered it in the full arrogance of self-conscious integrity, to condemn a sinner, and who had found nothing but a deeply-wronged girl whose natural sweetness had been sharpened by her sorrows, but whose piteous eyes still held a glimpse of something he had never seen before.

CHAPTER XXII

MOVE AND COUNTER-MOVE

RIDLEY came downstairs the next morning looking a little worn. The events of the preceding day had bitten deeply into him, and he faced the new conditions with a frank realisation of the fact that his interest was personal, and not professional. Moreover, the revelation had come about too suddenly not to leave some sort of mark on him. But, as yet, he was more angry and compassionate over what had happened than anxious as to what was to come.

Mrs. Channing looked at him shrewdly. It was Ridley's quality, in the rare instances when he attracted liking or affection, to do so with a thoroughness denied to more popular men.

" The lad Fiander was in, yesterday," she said, presently, " to ask after you, sir."

Ridley roused himself.

" Oh, Fiander," he repeated. " I'd forgotten him. I want to speak to him to-day. I'll walk down before I go into the office. If anyone calls, say that I'll not be away long. Anything else ? "

" Only that Mrs. Hibbs came."

Ridley questioned her in silence.

" She as I thought of, sir, as a likely person to make her home with the young woman Hoddinott."

" Ah, I remember. You said you'd try to find some one. The girl certainly oughtn't to be left alone with that old maniac. Well ? "

" She wa'n't ill disposed, sir. She said she'd get a lift Monday, and go over and have a look at the place."

" I hope the girl will be civil," said Ridley, with a half-laugh. " Tell me if anything comes of it, please."

After breakfast, he walked down into the town, and turning into a by-street entered a small shop. The jangling of the

bell affixed to the door brought Robin Fiander out from
the room beyond. He was slightly overawed by his employer's condescension.

"Good day, Fiander," said Ridley. "How is your
mother ? "

"Getting on nicely, thank you, sir. And—and—good
day to you ! "

"I'm glad to hear it."

"'Tis really most kind of you to call," stammered Robin
uneasily. "She'll be very pleased, sir."

"You can give her my compliments. I wanted a word
with you, Fiander. That's why I came."

"Indeed, sir ? "

"Take care of those cheeses. I don't fancy stock that
I may purchase rolling about all over the floor first. Now,
Fiander, look me squarely in the face. You've not done
it, for some time, you know."

Robin attempted it, and failed.

Ridley's voice grew a little sharper.

"Listen to me, if you can't look at me," he said. "Three
weeks or so ago, a lady called at the office while I was out.
Do you remember it ? "

The lad, shamefaced and crimsoning, muttered inarticu-
lately. Ridley brought his eyes up by a smart rapping on
the counter.

"For some reason or other, you forgot to report the
occurrence to me," he went on. "Now—attend ! If such
a thing happens again, I shall have seriously to consider
whether you are fit to be entrusted with the responsibility
which is yours in my absence."

The cheeses fell in all directions.

"Don't you send any of that stuff up to my house," said
Ridley. "I warned you, you know."

"You did, sir," cried Fiander. "Oh, you did ! "

"Very well. Think over what I have been saying. I
shall be glad of you up at the office as soon as you can be
spared. Do you understand ? "

Robin did ; and worshipped accordingly.

Ridley went away thinking of Quenride. A weaker man
might have tried to persuade himself that he had acted by
her influence alone. Ridley was too fair-minded for that,
but at least he had done the thing of which she would approve.

It struck him as a trifle ironical that a few minutes

later he was compelled, as it were, to step into Fiander's shoes.

Outside St. Peter's Church, he came face to face with the Governor. He saluted him, and was for passing on, but to his surprise the elder man stood still. Ridley came round, hat in hand, and waited.

"Good morning, Kenelm. We have not seen much of each other lately," said the Governor. "How is it?"

"Why, sir, I understood——"

"Of course you did. I meant you to understand. But since I saw you the other day I have thought that it was only right to give you a chance."

"A chance of what, sir?"

"Of offering the explanation which you are perhaps too proud or too ashamed to give without encouragement."

Ridley was silent for a moment, looking down the street. Then he said:

"I have nothing to explain, sir."

The lines on the other's face settled rigidly.

"The disgraceful story is true, then?" he said.

"Perfectly true."

"You were given seven hours of it?"

"I had seven hours of it," said Ridley, venturing on an amendment which would not be recognised as such.

The Governor looked away.

"You ought to be ashamed of yourself!" he exclaimed, with exasperated indignation.

"He'd be a happy man," said Ridley, "who had nothing in his life to regret."

Again he was thinking of Quenride. The strange part of the situation was that while he felt certain she would now be the first to exonerate him to his friends, the possibility of his justifying himself was further removed than ever.

"I wonder," he said, "whether it is the thought of the offence or of the punishment that distresses you so much."

A pair of hawk-like eyes flashed fiercely at him.

"Both, sir, both!" the elder man rapped out. Then a touch of the prison became apparent. "Without an offence there can be no penalty," he said stiffly. "And those who live by the law should at least know how to keep it!"

"We're all law-breakers under our best coats," said Ridley.

"Keep your jests for your—backers!" retorted the other sharply, and showed a disposition to move on.

Ridley was hurt and out of humour; all the more so

because, in his heart, he could not honestly blame his companion. The man had loved his mother, and had loved him. And all his prejudices ran in the well-tried grooves of law and order. To intimate that he himself had not been so culpable as it might appear was to suggest a statement which he could not substantiate by explanations. Therefore, he said nothing.

"Gad!" cried the Governor, looking at him again. "You hold your head high still! Well, I will ask you no more; only request you not to call upon me until I have first visited you! Good morning!"

But, in turning away, he glanced back to put yet another question.

"Has the practice suffered at all through this?" he demanded sternly.

"Not in the least!" declared Ridley, with defiant cheerfulness. "People have been curious to look at me, you see."

"It is nothing to boast of, sir!" cried the other tartly, and went his way.

Ridley returned home, smarting a little, but regretting no word of what he had said. In the passage, he encountered his housekeeper. He took off his outer things, and was about to enter the office, when she hastened after him.

"Excuse me, sir—a hair on your sleeve."

He looked down, and saw it—a slender filament of burnished gold. He removed it, shaking it from his fingers to the floor. It settled again across his knee. He took hold of it a second time, a little self-consciously, for the woman's eyes were on him.

"Looks like love-making, I suppose," he said, as he twined it round his fingers, with a man's wonder at its length. "But it doesn't stand for any such thing."

"I didn't suppose that it did, I assure you, sir."

"Oh, and why not?"

"Well, you're not that sort of gentleman."

"You can't say that of any man until he's dead," said Ridley, and passed into the office with Quenride's hair still coiled round his little finger.

He went over to the fire-place, and unwound it slowly. It caught the light brilliantly. He admired it as he planned its destruction. Then he loosened his hold once more. The draught from the chimney caught it, and whirling it upward, spread it across his breast.

He laughed to himself, and winding it up once again, laid it in a folded sheet of paper, and placed it inside her letter in the secret drawer.

"I'll keep it," he said, "until I've saved her, and drawn the fangs of that viper."

It was Quenride herself who found it, some time later, and looked at it through a mist of sudden tears.

Ridley had not been at work longer than an hour when Alaric Mohun was shown in. The young lawyer turned to meet him with a kind of cold gladness.

Mohun advanced confidently, and even made a pretence of holding out his hand. Ridley never dealt in half-measures himself, and openly ignored it.

"I've come," began Mohun. "You see, I'm a dependable man, Mr. Ridley."

"Most of us are, when it's for our own advantage. I had a client once who never turned up to time. He brought an action against his greatest enemy—and was waiting at the court two hours before the case came on. Let me see, Mr. Mohun, you don't like that chair, I think."

"Dash it, no ! Thankye, I'll stand. I'm fresh from the saddle, and I shan't be here long."

Ridley had risen while speaking, and the two men stood facing each other at a little distance.

"Well, since I am very busy, Mr. Mohun, I won't press for your company longer than is necessary," said Ridley, and fell into silence again.

It cost him an effort to maintain it. His tongue was swelling in his mouth as he looked at the man.

Mohun, thus forced to open the subject himself, glared unpleasantly, and began.

"You know what I've come about, of course," he said.

"It is your part to state your business," Ridley replied, "not mine to waste time in guessing it."

"Look here, sir, you'd waste considerably less time if you dropped your confounded habit of hedging round everything I say. Such conduct doesn't strike one as particularly discreet from a fellow in your position to a man in mine."

"I know my own position, sir. All I know precisely about yours is that you have chosen to take it up in the house of a man who doesn't stand insolence from anyone."

Mohun flung a glance at Ridley's immobile face, swore under his breath, but, apparently deciding that the time was not yet ripe for a quarrel, tried to look civil.

"All I meant was," he explained, "that no doubt you'd like to continue to administer the Chideock estate."

"It hasn't represented a particularly fat patronage hitherto," said Ridley. "But I'm interested in it, naturally."

"Just so. And probably, with a new proprietor, things will be looking up a little."

Ridley nodded.

"Not improbable," he said. "I've known it to happen."

"Just so," repeated Mohun, with a fair show of amiability. "That's it. You serve me and I'll serve you. We ought to get along together."

"No doubt about it," agreed Ridley, with fingers that ached for the other's throat. "Did I understand you to say *serve*, Mr. Mohun?"

Mohun's sanguine face flushed a deeper red.

"An unfortunate word, Mr. Ridley," he cried quickly. In truth he had used it without reflection. "What I meant was to suggest—delicately, I hope—that I look for pleasantness, perhaps even a touch of deference in anyone whom I employ. A man who tries to please me never has reason to regret it."

"That's very gratifying," said Ridley. "Interesting too, of course. I'm glad to hear of such pleasant relations existing between a man of quality—and his flunkeys!"

Mohun lost his temper.

"Curse you!" he cried. "I wasn't talking of flunkeys. And you know it."

"I beg pardon," said Ridley, with a bow nicely balanced between irony and contempt.

Mohun fidgeted on his feet. Half a minute later, he thought of what to say.

"You should leave that to me, sir," he began. "I feel that an apology is due to you. You have been shamefully treated by a member of my family—hoodwinked in the most outrageous manner."

"So I have," said Ridley, at once.

It had been remarked that in argument one never knew on which points he would differ or agree—a disconcerting state of mind for a dishonest adversary. Mohun endeavoured to cover his discomfiture with a short laugh.

"Glad to hear you say so!" he averred. "Now we shall get on. I don't think that I can do better, as my grandfather's legatee, than place my affairs in your hands. I suppose, for the sake of the thing, we must first go through the form of proving the old man's death before we prove the will, eh ? "

" The one," said Ridley, " will be done more easily than the other."

Mohun darted a glance at him.

" Oh," he said, with a jauntiness which sat ill upon him, " I don't anticipate any difficulty. I shall leave that to you. All you'll have to do will be to get hold of that slut at Wareham, and make her tell the truth, if she can ! If you put the screw on—and you're the right sort of fellow to do it— you'll find she'll answer to it right enough. She's afraid of you already."

" If you can't keep your tongue civil in this room," said Ridley, " you must go out of it."

" Come, come, sir, your by-play was very pretty yesterday, and came off just in time for the lady to appreciate it, a little amateurish, perhaps, but anyone can see you're not a woman's man. Still, as she's not here, 'tis scarcely worth while to air your gallantries for my benefit."

" Mr. Mohun, I'm not, as you say, a lady's man. I don't profess to know anything about gallantry. But if I wanted to learn something about the art I shouldn't come to you for instruction. If, however, it's a question of the proper way to speak of a woman, I don't need lessons from you or any other man."

" Well—well—I promise not to offend again. Though, after all, you might tolerate a little freedom of speech, when you consider the incredible wrong my cousin has done me."

" You damned liar ! " said Ridley.

" Sir ! "

Mohun was flustered, wrath growing upon him with every heart-beat. The lawyer had, in those three words, made it so convincingly plain that he knew everything.

" You're confoundedly insulting ! " he spluttered. " Is it nothing for a man to be kept out of his inheritance for six months ? "

" Your inheritance ? " Ridley flung the observation at him like a handful of dirt.

" Is it not ? " Mohun had stepped back involuntarily.

" You can't inherit under a forgery."

" A forgery ? " Mohun tried to laugh. Then a thought came to him. " If you're clever enough to know so much," he snarled, " perhaps you can lay your finger on the forger ? "

" Never in this world," said Ridley.

An unpleasant kind of smile lifted the corners of Mohun's mouth. He felt that he had probed the weak spot. He stood back, hands in pockets, legs wide apart.

"Then," he said, "since you've no accusation to bring against anyone, perhaps you won't object to hand over that will."

Ridley's fingers dived into his pockets also. He was standing even more squarely than his companion. Fully a head taller, his superior inches discounted the other's greater bulk.

"I do object," he said, "very strongly. In fact, Mr. Mohun, I'm not going to do it."

"You're not?"

"No."

"Why not?"

"Because I'm too good a lawyer to let a counterfeit pass for a genuine document."

"Bah! Because my cousin's got a pretty face and sweet manners, you mean!"

"You can take my reason, or leave it, sir. The facts remain the same."

Mohun was silent for a moment. Ridley grew hopeful. The man's attitude implied that Quenride's assertion was correct. He was savage, but baffled, and conscious of his powerlessness. He was looking round the room.

"Where is the damned thing?" he broke out.

"Where there's no chance of your getting at it. Do you think I keep valuable documents lying about?"

"You say it's not valuable." Mohun was fencing idly, to give an idea of some sort a chance of presenting itself.

"Well," said Ridley bluntly "it would be so to you."

"Perhaps," suggested the man who had tempted him before, "it might be made of value to you as well."

"Mr. Mohun," said Ridley, "I'm not for sale."

And there was a look about him which prevented Mohun's repeating the suggestion.

"She's won you over, that sorry hussy," he said. "And you're a party to collusion."

"It's as good a crime as—coercion, anyway," said Ridley. Then he warmed suddenly. "You hound!" he cried. "You should thank your cousin for your own immunity, and be grateful for what the law will allow you out of the estate."

Mohun's face twisted with contempt.

"A beggarly third!" he cried. "Less than that half-made limping brat, who succeeds to the entail! Cripples ought to be disallowed by law! By God, sir, I'll prove that will yet, and when the young devil's in my keeping he shall know what a birch means!"

Ridley's face never showed much colour. It was like a piece of ivory now as he crossed the room, caught Mohun by the collar, and conducted him in silence towards the door.

"Take your fist away!" ordered Mohun, in savage wrath. "I'll not submit to being mauled about by a dirty, countrified attorney!"

"I may be countrified," said Ridley, still holding him, "I certainly am an attorney. But if any man calls me *dirty*, I've only got one way of dealing with him. You'll apologise, Mr. Mohun, or I'll fling you out of the house."

The slim hand on his collar had plenty of strength in it, and Mohun found it impossible to free himself.

"I'd fight you if you were a gentleman!" he gasped.

"I doubt it," said Ridley. "You don't want to come under the law at this particular moment. Let me give you a bit of advice gratis—a thing, by the way, which I don't usually do—don't let me hear any more of such language, or you'll find a smart man applying at the King's Bench for a Criminal Information against you, on a charge of inciting to a duel."

"I always thought," sneered Mohun, "that you legal fellows had water in your veins instead of blood."

"I'm not a coward," said Ridley, "if that's what you mean. But I don't believe in duelling—I never did! And in the present instance, considering all the points, I don't recognise even a so-called obligation. Now, sir, are you going to apologise?"

"Take your hand away!"

"The apology first, please!"

"Oh, very well, if you like!" said Mohun ungraciously. "Take it as said. We've enough to quarrel about without this. You're right in one thing. Pistols can't be our weapons. But, damn me, if I don't fight you in another way! And perhaps, in the end, you'll find it hurt just as much, Master Lawyer!"

He took himself off in a vile mood. Ridley watched him from the window. Then he looked at his hands, and went upstairs to wash them. When he came down, he called to the housekeeper.

" I'd like the office cleaned out," he said. " I'll go into the other room."

" La ! sir, 'twas all done yesterday," he was told. " We took the opportunity while you was out."

" I'd like it done again, please," he said. " The gentleman who's just left brought some dirt into it."

And he gathered his materials together, and left the room.

CHAPTER XXIII

THE LAWYER PAYS

IN accordance with his promise to Quenride, Ridley
sent her a more or less detailed account of his interview with Mohun, and made a suggestion that she
should grant himself another meeting shortly. A
stiff little note came back in Dolly's writing : Miss Chideock
was much obliged to Mr. Ridley for his information, but was
far too unwell to attend to business yet. She would, however,
be glad to meet him at no distant date, and until then left the
matter in his hands with the utmost confidence. So ran the
first note from Quenride to Ridley. And then the more
important correspondence began.

The next day, the young lawyer received a letter from
Mohun. It made no reference to the manner of their recent
parting. It was, in truth, as the recipient expressed it,
" devilish civil." The gist of it was a proposal that Quenride, Ridley, and the writer should agree to meet in some
private place, where the affair might be discussed, and possibly
some terms arranged without too much bad blood on either
side.

Ridley, pressed with work, on account of the forthcoming
Assizes, yet found time to dash off a brief note, refusing to
entertain any thought of the proposition. Acting for his
client, Miss Chideock, he failed to see the benefit to her arising
from such an interview.

A few hours later, Mohun, who appeared to be staying in
the neighbourhood, sent a second letter. One sentence made
Ridley pause.

" You two confederates appear to be forgetting one thing,"
Mohun wrote. " You rest your case upon the assumption
that I cannot prove the existence of the will. *What if I can ?* "

There was a decidedly unpleasant flavour about those last
words. Ridley picked up a pen, and laid it down again,
frowning. From the written page, it was impossible to gauge

the sincerity of the statement; Mohun's face of flesh and blood would have been a surer index. But Mohun had kept away, and Ridley had no time to seek him out. The letters bore no definite address. The situation appealed to the instincts of the lawyer almost as keenly as the tremendous personal issues did to the man. If this was mere bluff, what was Mohun's game? If a genuine setting forth of facts, it was too important to be disregarded. Had Quenride missed, in her inexperience and distress, some point which this villain had seized upon for his own advantage? Ridley saw the possibility; and his eyes grew very grave. Then they brightened again. Mohun had hinted at no such thing during their stormy interview. No man would have omitted at such a time to show the strength of his hand. Moreover, rage does not make for successful dissembling, and there was no doubt at all that Mohun had been in a pretty rage before the interview had ended. Ridley grew almost complacent again, and had already flung the letter aside, intending to ignore it altogether, when it occurred to him that he scarcely had the right to act so without consulting Quenride. The situation was so delicate that no false step must be risked. He must chance alarming her, for the sake of ascertaining what light she could throw upon her cousin's innuendo.

He wrote in as comforting a strain as possible, setting before her his own estimation of Mohun's words. And he entrusted the letter, as he had done the previous one, to a particularly vigorous and trustworthy man, whom he occasionally employed.

When the messenger returned, he brought a tremulous reply from Quenride herself. It was evident that her caution had caught fire. Reticence had been the keynote of Ridley's letters to her; ambiguousness characterised the one sent back. But into it he read a palpitating fear—not remarkable in one who had lived on the rack for the past six months. Her anxiety prompted her to a decision. She thought, before any steps were taken in the matter, that they ought to hear what Mohun had to say. Would her good friend see her cousin and make the necessary arrangements? She left these entirely in his hands.

Ridley gave in, all the more willingly, because he read in Mohun's proposal a sign of weakness—the attempt at a compromise. It pleased him to think that, on this occasion at least, the hapless Quenride would not meet her cousin alone. Ridley was quick at detecting motives where scarcely any were apparent, and he was moved now by the certainty that Quenride was fearful lest he himself should suffer as her fellow-conspirator. In his present attitude of mind it was a danger to laugh at, but her anxiety was not without its effect on him.

The next day being Sunday, Ridley had some leisure to go down to the inn to which Mohun had directed his letters to be sent. After some delay, he caught his man, and the two exchanged a few brief sentences.

" Miss Chideock and I have agreed to grant you the interview," said Ridley. " She has authorised me to negotiate for her. You probably know the country round about better than I do. Can you suggest any likely place ? It must be not too far from Wareham. That I insist upon."

" You're getting devilishly gallant," said Mohun, with a grin.

" Do you ? " asked Ridley imperturbably.

Mohun appeared to consider.

" There's a disused shepherd's hut," he said, " not more than a mile or so out. How would that do ? "

" Are we likely to be interrupted ? "

" I shouldn't think so. I believe that half-mad witch girl uses it to leave dairy produce in, for the carrier to bring to market for her. If she comes prowling round, we can soon shoo her off."

" Is the place easy to find ? "

" Quite," said Mohun. And gave a few simple directions.

" Very well," said Ridley. " I'll let Miss Chideock know."

" When shall it be ? " asked Mohun. " I can come at any time."

" The Court opens on Wednesday," said Ridley. " It must be to-morrow or Tuesday, for me."

" To-morrow, then ? "

" If it suits my client."

" And if not ? "

" I'll let you know."

" Name your hour ! "

" I can't be there before the afternoon. The end of the afternoon, probably."

" 'Tis all one to me," said Mohun. " And you can tell my cousin I'll see her home, if you're in a hurry to get away."

Ridley looked at him.

" It won't be necessary," he said. " If Miss Chideock takes my advice, she'll not come unattended."

Mohun whistled a tune, staring ahead nonchalantly.

" She can bring a whole retinue, for all I care," he said,
" so long as they remain out of earshot."

" Very well," said Ridley. " That's settled, then. I
have nothing more to say."

Mohun followed him to the door. He was not lodging
at the place, merely using it as a house of call.

" It's a thousand pities you're not more reasonable, Mr.
Ridley," he remarked. " You'd save us both a lot of
trouble."

Ridley turned sharply. This was the first opportunity
which Mohun had given him of seeing into his face, though
he had made several attempts to do so. It looked unamiable—
and not quite honest. Ridley drew his own conclusions, and
indulged in a light laugh.

" Men of my profession take care to get well paid for
the trouble they are put to, Mr. Mohun. Possibly the bill
may be a high one—for you ! "

There was not much meaning in the threat, but Mohun
must have found it at least amusing, for when Ridley had
left him he grinned again, unpleasantly.

" No, you fool, for you ! " he muttered, after the
retreating figure. " This time, at any rate, the lawyer
pays ! "

Quenride received Ridley's letter at a later hour of the
same day. He had hesitated whether or not to ride over
and acquaint her in person with the arrangements which he
had made. Some reluctance went with the relinquishing of
this idea. But he was also unwilling to force himself upon
her unnecessarily—more especially at a time when she was
nervous and unwell.

Having despatched her answer, signifying agreement, she
spent a restless night, and got through the agitated hours of
the next morning as best she might. She was sitting alone
in the early part of the afternoon, watching the clock, her
habit already laid out in her room, her orders given, when
to her surprise a letter from Mohun was put into her hands.
It ran :

" DEAR Coz.—That damnation lawyer has failed us. He
pleads pressure of work, owing to the Assizes, as a reason for
breaking his appointment. I conclude that it's a genuine
reason, and that you know nothing about it. At any rate,
we shan't see him to-day. He says the delay is unexpected,
but unavoidable, and promises to be without fail at the place

at the same time to-morrow. He asked me to let you know, as his pen is otherwise engaged until this evening, when he will write to you more fully than this, and will instruct his man to bring back word from you as to whether to-morrow will suit you. The change of date makes no difference to your devoted kinsman,

"ALARIC MOHUN."

If Mohun's style was rather prolix, at least the purport of the letter was plain enough. Quenride was disappointed, but accepted his statement with no more suspicion that it was a lie than Ridley had that it had been sent at all.

At about the time that Quenride had opened Mohun's letter, Ridley was giving his final instructions for the day to Fiander, who was back at work again. Soon afterwards, he left the house, making his way by short cuts and by-roads towards the meeting-place.

It was not a pleasant day for a country ride. October was running out, and the weather had become wet and stormy. A damp wind, chilly and boisterous, raked the up-lands, and descended, with sudden scuds of rain, into the valleys. The open road was carpeted with sodden leaves, the hedgerows showed long thinning trails of bramble and honeysuckle. Here and there, where a late summer flower survived, it hung upon a broken stalk, or was denuded of half its petals. The pasture land was dripping with moisture, the ploughed fields were of a rich chocolate colour. The gulls came inland and flew low. For the privacy of the suggested interview no day could have promised better. But for an out-of-door expedition for a young lady, it left much to be desired.

As Ridley had said, it was towards the end of the afternoon that he came in sight of the appointed place. The hut, a small squat erection, stood in the corner of a large field adjoining the high road. Tall hedges neighboured it on two sides, and it had been turned with its back to the roadway, the entrance, from that point, being invisible. A more lonely place for the conducting of private business could not have been chosen. There appeared to be no habitation within a mile or so.

Ridley entered the field, and was a little surprised to find that he apparently had it to himself, neither man nor animal appearing in any part of it. The road was out of sight by now, but no approaching clatter gave token of the arrival of his promised companions. He scarcely wondered at Quenride delaying on such an inclement afternoon, but he had reckoned on Mohun being there in time.

Before long, the meaning of the empty field was made plain.

He had secured his animal under the lee of a hedge, and was engaged in placing over it a horsecloth which he had brought with him, when, without warning, a terrific blow caught him on the temple. Reeling under it, he had a sight of Mohun standing over him, then as he fell he seemed to be sinking into a field of full-blown poppies, very content to lie down among them, and so to fall asleep.

When he came to himself, feeling sick and dizzy, his first hazy impression was that he was in his own room. He was certainly lying on a bed. The glimpse of a white shirt told that part of his clothing had been removed. He was conscious of feeling cold, and by degrees discovered the reason. The shirt was open at the throat, and thrown back. He made an attempt to draw it over his breast, but found that he could not move either of his hands. They were flung up above his head, and consciousness growing stronger with every moment, he became aware of an unpleasant sensation at each wrist. He tried to raise himself to see what had happened, strained his muscles to no purpose, and was forced to understand that his body was practically immovable. He was lying on a low truckle bed—bound hand and foot to the four corners of it.

The discovery quickened his wits. At the same time, a fuller capacity for sensation animated his body to the realisation of fresh discomforts. He felt bruised and sore, and a sharper pain stabbed him in the back. It took him some time to determine what this might be. But at length he knew. Shifting his body slightly, the lacerating stab pricked him in another spot. He no longer wondered. It was caused by the wards of the small key which belonged to the chest in his strong-room. The slender chain which suspended it round his neck had snapped under Mohun's rough treatment, and both had been caught in the slack of the shirt at his waist, where the edge of the key was now pressing into the bare flesh.

The process of Ridley's thoughts had thus brought him round to Mohun, when the trickster himself opened the door of the hut, and came in. He brought with him the scent of poppyheads, and Ridley sickened anew at the odour.

There was no window in the hut, but it was suffused with a reddish glow; and though Ridley, lying flat on his back, could not ascertain the cause, he judged that a brazier was burning at the foot of the bed. Mohun walked in this direction, bent down for a moment, and came into view carrying a lighted candle. He held it to Ridley's face.

"Not quite come round yet?" he said, and, fumbling in his pockets with one hand, he pulled out a flask.

The spirit revived Ridley yet further. He began to think coherently. The anger which was already making his weakened body quiver gave place for a moment to anxiety for Quenride.

"Where's your cousin?" he asked.

"Safe at home," Mohun answered, "expecting to get a letter from you presently, explaining why the appointment was postponed. You needn't worry about her. You've got enough to do to look after yourself."

"So it seems," said Ridley. "What's the meaning of it all?"

"It means what you see—and feel. You've been caught napping for once, my friend. I told you that you were giving us both a deal of unnecessary trouble."

Ridley lay silent for a moment.

"How did you get me here?" he asked. "I'm no light weight, and you struck me down out yonder."

"I managed it," said Mohun shortly. The hut was rudely furnished. He had stuck the candle into a holder, and now he drew a stool forward. "After all, you don't run to bulk. It wasn't exactly easy, but I managed it."

"Have you got any similar designs upon Miss Chideock?"

"Let Miss Chideock alone! Damn her, I say. What has she to do with this? It's between us — man and man."

"What's your game then, as regards myself?"

"To teach you a lesson in reasonableness."

"I wonder what sort of a schoolmaster you'll prove to be!"

"Not a lenient one!"

"Are you going to kill me?"

"No. I'm a gentleman——"

"I'm always glad to pick up information," murmured Ridley.

"And I don't want your blood on my hands."

"Well, there I can understand you, Mr. Mohun. That's

precisely my attitude with regard to duelling. You've been
kicking me, however."

Mohun laughed.

" Found that out, have you ?   Well, perhaps so.   Didn't
I owe it you ? "

" You're an unspeakable scoundrel ! "

" Don't call me names, Mr. Ridley.   You'll not find it
pay.   Besides, you've brought this on yourself."

" What do you want ? "

" That you know.   The will, of course.   Have another
dose of brandy ? "

Ridley shook his head.   He was thinking quickly, seeking
for some hope of escape, and finding only the flimsiest possibilities.   One definite thought stood out—he was glad that
Mohun had not discovered the key.

" Wake up ! "   said   the   man   at   the   bedside   harshly.
' Did you hear what I said ?   I want the will."

" Well," said Ridley—listening in between the pauses,
and hearing nothing but the rain pattering on the roof—" I
couldn't give it to you at this present moment if I wanted
to, could I ?   I don't carry it about with me."

" Where is it ? "

" That I shan't say."

" You haven't destroyed it yet, have you ? "

" I'm not going to give information on that point."

" Curse you !   Why not ? "

" Because as long as you don't know you're kept in
suspense.   And that's the only retaliation I've got, at
present."

Mohun looked down at him gloomily.

" You're a cool fellow," he remarked.

" Yes ; I am.   You've half-stripped me, and your confounded cords are stopping my circulation.   I'm downright cold."

" I hope," said Mohun, " that you won't put me to the
trouble of—warming you."

" My head aches," said Ridley.   " I'm not in a guessing
humour.   You must speak out."

But this Mohun seemed unwilling to do.   He had the
uneasy air of a man who approaches a distasteful task.

" First," he said, " let's go back to the point—the will.
I didn't suppose that you had it in your pocket.   If you've
not destroyed it already, it's in your house.   I know you
have not been to Wareham since that day——"

" What ? You add spying to your other accomplish-
ments, do you ? "

" Silence ! You tempt me to lay hands on you ! "

" Go on. How much more have you found out ? "

" It's not likely that you'd entrust the thing out of your
own keeping—to send it to my cousin, I mean—therefore, if
it's anywhere, it's in your house."

" Very ably reasoned out ! We'll assume, for the sake of
argument, that it is in my house. Well ? "

" You must give me a sort of search-warrant to go and
get it. I've paper and writing materials. You shall write
a few lines instructing your clerk—does he sleep in the
house ? "

" No, he does not."

" Your servants, then—instructing them to let me have
free access to any part of the house. If you'll promise to do
this, I'll free your arm sufficiently for you to be able to write,
and I'll make you as comfortable as I dare before I go. You
shall also be released at the earliest moment consistent with
my object. What do you say ? "

" You can go to the devil," said Ridley. " I shall do
nothing of the kind."

" What's your objection ? "

" My duty to my client, for one thing."

" Duty to your client ! " Mohun was impatient and
irritable by nature, and now began to lose temper. " Are
you in love with my cousin ? " he asked.

" I shouldn't tell you if I were ! "

" It won't do. She'd never marry you—don't you think
it ! "

" I'm not thinking it."

" It would be like your insolence ! " retorted Mohun.
" She's a Chideock, and you—a twopenny scrivener ! Well,
you've heard my proposal, and you have refused it once."

" A hundred times, if you like."

" Then you'll force me to persuade you."

" Wherewith ? oh, most lying spirit ! "

Mohun rose. To his natural anger against Ridley was
now added the sulky rage towards one who compels the use
of doubtful methods.

He took a slender strip of metal from a shelf, and held it
up.

" You see this ? "

" Yes."

" And you see—that ? " He waved his hand towards the red glow

" No. I'm too low down. But I can guess."

" Just so, Mr. Ridley. Put the two together, and what do you get ? "

Ridley lay silent. He had lived singularly free from physical pain, and Mohun's words came with something of a shock. But his silence meant a mere bracing of the nerves, and not a dallying with temptation. Mohun watched him, saw him moistening his dry lips, and grew hopeful. For an instant he laid his hand over Ridley's heart, and found it pounding rather furiously.

" You daren't do it ! " said Ridley, then. " As soon as I'm free, I can get you indicted for malicious maiming."

" No, you won't," said Mohun confidently. " You've no witnesses, and you'd never risk all the talk that such a charge would be certain to make. What sort of an account could you give without dragging my cousin's little escapade to light ? I shelter behind her."

Ridley thought this over as well as his hazy wits allowed. Unwillingly he recognised the strength of Mohun's position and the weakness of his own. He said nothing, but lay supine, watching his companion with feverishly bright eyes.

" Well ? " asked Mohun. " What do you say ? "

" No more than I've said before."

" Hulloa—angels ! " cried Mohun coarsely. " Here's a candidate for martyrdom ! "

" I'm sick of the sound of your voice," said Ridley. " Get to your heating irons and be damned to you ! "

Mohun moved away with lagging feet.

CHAPTER XXIV

SOPHY'S HOUR

DURING the next hour, Ridley lay silent, and gradually found out several things—notably, that the quivering flesh has to be reckoned with, as well as the willing spirit. He discovered minor points of interest besides : that pain is essentially a thing of the present, and that, in his case, it was sharper than he had expected it to be ; that the time seemed very long, and the chance of rescue less imminent with every heart-beat ; that Mohun's eyes had a trick of glowing with a dull red light in the shadows ; that he himself was growing thirsty and very faint.

His sufferings at length forced him to speak, though in so low a voice that Mohun had to bend over him to catch the words. He did so eagerly, for he was growing a little sick of the business himself.

" You must give me something to drink if you expect me to keep on with this," said Ridley, gasping painfully.

Mohun brought out his flask.

" Not that. Something cool. Water."

" There isn't any. You'll have to go without. Why not this ? "

" Too personal. Water doesn't belong to anyone."

" I tell you there is none ! " Mohun bent over him, and wiped the sweat from his face. Then he raised the flask to his own lips. Ridley watched him with half-closed eyes.

" You don't seem particularly happy yourself," he said.

" That's true," admitted Mohun. " You don't suppose I like this, do you ? "

" Then why not end it—for both of us ? "

Mohun laughed—the nervous laugh of a man ill at ease.

" Becae I'usm not such a fool as you ! " he said. " I don't let a little tender-heartedness stand in the way of my own interest."

Ridley's head had rolled over on to its side ; the sheet

beneath his cheek had grown damp within the last hour. Mohun regarded him doubtfully. He was hampered in his villainy by the prejudices of his birth and breeding, and had some natural repugnance to the work he had taken in hand. He had scarcely expected it to last so long. But the squeamishness was rather a product of tradition allied to nerves than of principle combined with heart. He grew unreasonably angry with the man whose obstinacy made for the self-depreciation of a Mohun.

"Wake up!" he said, and drew a finger across Ridley's forehead. "You're not going off just yet, are you? Listen to me! You shall have it red-hot next time. On my sinful soul, you shall! What have you to say to that?"

Ridley had nothing to say, for he had not heard.

Mohun turned his face up, and thrust forward the flask. But the jaw was fixed stubbornly, and the mouth would not open. Mohun swore under his breath, and wiped his own forehead.

"Damn you!" he said aloud. Then he bent over the unconscious form. "I'll say this," he muttered. "I told you the other day that you had water in your veins. It's not that! It's blood, real blood, not blue, perhaps, but good rich red blood, and plenty of it! I'd sooner face a brace of pistols, than go through half of—that!"

Twenty minutes passed. Ridley did not stir. He scarcely seemed to be breathing. Again Mohun felt his heart—gingerly this time, for there was a raw wound near the spot—the pulsation was perceptible, no more.

Mohun walked back to the brazier, and raked the glowing mass together, not from any malicious sentiment, but merely because his irritated nerves forced him to action of some sort. At that moment, he would have welcomed a stinging lash from Ridley's tongue as a fillip to his own lowered vitality.

As he bent, glowering and discontented, over the hot cinders, he suddenly shot bolt upright, and alarm laid a chilly finger on his heart. Into the silence of the place a sound had penetrated—a sound which had its origin from nothing inside the hut. Mohun stood rigid, listening. The sound was faint in itself, and to a less agitated man, it might have seemed to be caused by no more than the dried heads of grass rubbing against the sides of the hut. But Mohun's apprehension told him that it was made by a human hand, passing over the surface of the door, in search for the latch.

Only a few seconds separated the first intrusion of the sound from the opening of the door. But Mohun lit on his course of action, and wasted no time. The first thing which he did was to put out the light. To be caught or recognised was too evil a chance to admit of dallying. He might compel immunity from his victim, but dared not face an interloper, however mean.

The door opened inwards, swinging back in such a way that anyone turning on entrance towards the bed would have his back to it. Mohun slid across the floor, and pressed himself against the wall in a line with the jamb of the door. If he could slip away in the first moments of the new-comer's entrance, he could draw breath with comparative confidence. There was nothing in the hut to associate him specially with the outrage.

Nothing—except Ridley himself. And the events of the last hour or so had convinced Mohun that there he had a powerful weapon in Quenride's name.

He had scarcely reached his hiding-place, when the door fell back upon him. Some one paused on the threshold. Mohun, enraged at the interruption, mortified at his defeat, and anxious about his escape, waited in an agony of suspense. As a last resource, he was ready to strike the intruder down, and make a dash for his liberty. But it needed not to come to that. The stranger paused for no longer than a moment. Mohun could see nothing. Every second, he expected to find the covering door dragged away from him. There was the sound of a creaking plank. Then he heard a long, low, wailing cry in a woman's voice. Mohun knew that the right moment had come. He drew out from his place of conceal-ment, and darted into the dark space made by the open door. He brought away with him the impression of a woman's form bending over the bed. When, just outside, he caught his foot in some unseen object, and came hurtling to the ground across a basket, he had little doubt as to who the intruder was.

"Curse the ugly little witch!" he muttered, as he raced towards the road. "Who the devil was to guess she'd come on a Monday? She'll not know him, of course, and perhaps he'll have the sense to hold his tongue."

But Sophy had already recognised the inert figure stretched upon the bed, recognised him more by her heart than by the suffusing glow from the brazier. Practical, as those of her class usually are, she did no more than lay her hand on his clammy forehead, uttered no more laments than that one cry, before setting about the work that waited for her. Conjecture could follow on the heels of succour ; wonder must give place to pity. Of Mohun's presence she had not been conscious, so silently had he slipped away, so intent had been her horror and surprise.

She found the candle, and lit it from the charcoal fire. Then she turned to the still unconscious man, and gently drew the shirt over the ugly wounds that scored his flesh in five red stripes. The fastening cords occupied her for several minutes. Mohun had been scientific in the knotting of them, and Sophy had neither knife nor scissors. She plucked at them savagely, and tore at them with her teeth like a wild animal. Her nails were broken, and her fingers smarting by the time that she had loosened them, and little coarse ejaculations had gone to the doing of the work. But at length she dropped the last cord on to the floor, and drew Ridley's limbs into a more natural position. Then she stood by his head again, and looked down yearningly. Desire burnt in her like a flame, and broke through the restraints of sex and station. She slipped her arm beneath his shoulder, and raised his head to her thin bosom. His lips drew hers. With a curious choking sob, she bent down and kissed him on the mouth.

" Oh, my dear, my dear ! " she moaned. " To think that I'll never get 'ee, but must leave 'ee to—her ! "

There was no line of demarcation for the passions in Sophy Hoddinott's sullen and undisciplined soul. Love and hatred were in her more than usually blended—she would have marvelled to know that the one could exist without the other. The danger lay in the fact that such an alloyed emotion was liable to be overbalanced at any moment, threatening her own spiritual shipwreck, since there was neither principle nor experience to guide her to the saner view.

When she had lifted her face, and laid Ridley back upon the bed, she saw a red stain upon the front of her bodice. Examining him more closely, she found his hair clogged at the temple with half-dried blood. She stood a moment in thought. The hut, she saw at a glance, would yield nothing either to alleviate or to remedy. For the ordinary medicaments of the physician, Sophy had unbridled contempt. Her creed, in all cases of ailment or accident, was to go to Nature—and herein sense and superstition mingled. In the present instance, she did the one thing possible.

She untied her apron, and, going out of the hut, spread it upon the sodden grass until it had absorbed enough moisture for her purpose. Returning, she laved Ridley's face and hands with the dripping cloth, and as consciousness returned even succeeded in squeezing a few drops into his relaxed mouth.

"Bide still ! " she ordered. "It's me—Sophy. You've been hurt a deal. You mustn't speak yet."

He lay still, with closed eyes, for some few minutes longer. Then he made an effort to sit up. Sophy lent her small strength to aid the attempt, and Ridley, white and shaking, brought his feet to the ground, and began to speak.

"Why did you come ? " he asked. He was holding her hand, and scarcely seemed to be aware of it.

"I brought my skim-cheeses for Dorchester market," she told him. "I leave 'em here for th' tranter to fetch. To-morrow I'll bring along the eggs an' butter. An'—an'— you ? "

"Oh, don't ask me, Sophy ! I've been a fool, and got my deserts. Did you see anyone here ? "

"Ne'er a soul. Only you—on the bed."

Ridley sat silent, gathering what remained of his strength together. He felt dazed and stupid, wondering what had become of Mohun—as if that were the one important point to be considered. Sophy stood a little back from him, and watched.

"You're not to tell," he said, in a stronger voice.

"About your being hurt ? "

"Yes. Promise."

"If you like. But," and her nails pressed into his palm, " I'd like to kill him ! "

"I shall be all right soon. It's—it's not as bad as you might think. How many marks are there ? "

"Five," she answered.

"Strange," he muttered, "that just five marks can hurt— I mean, can be so uncomfortable ! What does one do for a burn, Sophy ? I think the air ought to be kept out. Can you fasten it for me ? Wait a moment ! "

"Well ? "

"There's a key, slipped down inside, could you find it ? I'd get it myself, only——"

"I'll get en," she said.

The contact of her fingers with his unseen body moved her to no blushes, only to an emotional sense of intimacy.

She found the key, and brought her hand away tinged with
blood. Ridley took the key, with a gasp of relief that it was
still in his possession. Then he made shift to stand up,
and found himself clutching at the girl's shoulder.

"I'd like my coat," he said. "Where is it? It's turned
very cold, surely."

As a matter of fact, the wind had shifted at sunset, and
was blowing less keenly now.

Sophy, saying nothing, at once helped him towards the
corner where Mohun had flung down the clothing which he
had stripped from his victim. Ridley, assisted by the girl,
managed to dress himself.

"Sophy," he said, as she fastened the coat very gently
across his breast, "I wish I were at home. How am I to
get there? I've got a horse outside—at least, he ought
to be there—but I can't ride him, that's certain."

Sophy thrilled with joy.

"You'll have to come wi' me," she said, "an' bide the
night. To-morrow, I'll go——"

But Ridley, thinking of the girl's unprotected state, was
already objecting.

"That won't quite do, Sophy. Isn't there any other
place near?"

"No, there's not. Isn't mine good enough for 'ee?"

"It's not that," said Ridley gently, for the girl, in her
ignorance, seemed hurt. "You're alone, you see."

"There's girt-uncle."

"I'm afraid he doesn't count for much."

"An' a woman. What more do 'ee want?"

"A woman?"

"The lady at your house sent her, she says."

"Oh, yes. I seem to remember. She's there now?"

"Goin' to sleep there," said Sophy, wondering obviously
what a strange woman more or less mattered. "Will 'ee
come?"

"Yes; I'll come," said Ridley. "And thank you, Sophy.
How far is it? I shall have to go slowly—very slowly."

The words were as honey to the love-smitten girl. To
prolong the walk at his side, beyond the natural time-limit,
he leaning the while upon her shoulder, using her strength,
needing her help—what did the chilly night air, the sodden
grass, the wet roads soaking their moisture through her
worn shoes, matter to Sophy Hoddinott? Small and weak
as she was, she felt that there was enough warm blood in

her body, enough bone and muscle too, to lend strength to
him in this time of his need. But all she said was:
"It don't matter." And she spoke half-sullenly, with her
eyes on the floor.

Together they moved to the doorway. It was dark
by now, but the rain had ceased, and the sky was showing
a few stars. Sophy lifted her basket into the hut, and came
back to Ridley's side.

"Don't come here to-morrow, child," he said. "I'd
sooner you kept away."

She promised, easily. She would have promised anything,
and asked no reason. It was a time when to-morrow seemed
far off; when only the moment, with its infinitude of emotion,
mattered.

"The horse," said Ridley, in his low, spasmodic utterance.
"Can we find him?"

He called aloud, as well as he was able, and an answering
neigh came back. Sophy ran forward, found the animal,
and brought him to Ridley's side. Then, she leading the
horse, and guiding her companion's unsteady feet, they
moved across the field at a slow and laborious pace.

The cottage was more than a mile away. To Ridley,
time seemed to have been changed into eternity. There
were moments when, but for the girl at his side, who silently
urged him on, he would have been content to lie down in the
roadway, craving nothing but cessation from the painful
toil of the road. Frequent stoppages were inevitable. After
one of these, he perplexed Sophy by asking whether she was
Fiander. When the cottage was reached, she had to tell him
more than once that they were there.

She herself was panting and should have been exhausted,
but the ardent nature of her emotions gave her feeble frame a
plenitude of energy. She could have walked twice the distance, supporting and guiding him, and have felt no fatigue.
She pushed open the door, and peered into the faintly-lit
interior. The kitchen was empty.

This suited her mood better than anything. She drew
Ridley inside, and left him leaning against the door-post,
staring round with misty eyes, while she dragged forward
the one chair in the place, and set it before the fire. It was a
chair with arms, a relic of Amos's more genteel days; and
when she had pulled out a pillow from the bed by the wall
it was not uncomfortable.

Ridley lay back in it with closed eyes, feeling, in his more conscious moments, that he could not have performed the journey again to save his life. Sophy moved about, with unaccustomed alertness, her gaze never away from him for long. She lit a rushlight, and reaching up to her hiding-place at the back of the chimney brought out a bottle of Hollands, the payment in kind from a smuggler to whom she had given a charm against drowning. She gave Ridley a draught of the liquor, watching him, as he drank it, from under her heavy lids.

" Thank you," he said. " You're a good girl, Sophy."

Her cheek flamed with pleasure.

" I'm going to see to them burns," she said. " Then I'll make up a wood-fire, to get some warmth into 'ee—for you be mortal cold, in spite of 'em—then I'll put the beast in the cowshed, and find girt-uncle, an' tell him he must sleep in the dairy. You must lay down in his bed."

She did it all, save for the finding of Amos, who had taken to strange fits of wandering since the adventure on the bridge. Coming back from her search, she brought a bowl of milk with her, and poured it into a pot which she hung over the fire. Billets of wood were now making a blaze above the smouldering peats, and the kitchen seemed filled with light.

Sophy spread the table according to her simple knowledge, and then crouched down before the fire at Ridley's feet. The light played over her puny figure, and lent some kind of dignity to her insignificant features. Her black hair shaded her forehead mysteriously. She might have been some wild thing from the secret night outside ; some slave-girl, left behind by ancient Rome ; some half-clad savage from the Prehistoric Age ; some witch who had passed from the White Art to the Black. Something of all these did the firelight lend to Sophy Hoddinott that night, as she faced the glare, kneeling there at her companion's feet. And the hottest depths of the fire blazed no more fiercely than did that dangerous passion within her breast.

For some minutes she sat so—in the ecstasy of emotion that has passed beyond conscious thought, and can but feel, feeding upon itself. To her, it was a time of quiescence, pregnant with possibilities—though she could have named none—a time so delicate and intimate, that she had forgotten that a footfall on the threshold, a call from overhead, intruding upon it suddenly, might shatter it out of existence.

But Amos still lingered, and the woman upstairs made no sign. The hour was to Sophy alone.

Ridley lay so white and still, that the girl wondered whether he were aware of her presence. For awhile, she was content to have it even so ; but at length she spoke, in the low hushed voice of one facing mysteries.

" Feel better, don't 'ee ? " she questioned, wistful and yearning.

She had dressed the wounds in simple fashion by laying an oiled handkerchief across them, and placing a piece of flannel over it. Her desire for reassurance that she had done well, was apparent even to the exhausted Ridley. In spite of his pain, he made shift to answer her unasked question, and to minimise his sufferings.

" I am much more comfortable now, Sophy," he told her.

She gave a gasp of pleasure, which was intensified the next moment, when she felt his hand upon her shoulder.

" Ay ? " she said.

" There's one thing I must say," he began. " I'll tell you now, in case I—forget in the morning. If I can see to the matter myself, I will. If not, will you go to Miss Chideock's for me ? "

Sophy frowned, bending her heavy brows towards the fire.

" What for ? " she muttered.

" To take a message. Only this. Tell her that I said ' Don't go.' Do you understand ? You needn't say more than that. She'll know what I mean. And, Sophy——"

" Ay ? "

" You are not to tell her how you found me. Remember that ! And you must take something to let her know you come from me. My seals will do. Take those."

The task was not to Sophy's mind. She bit at the loose strands of her hair, and answered sullenly :

" I reckon ye'll not be able to go yourself."

" Then you will ? "

" Oh—ay."

" Thank you," he said. " You're a good girl, and I'll not forget you."

He was merely thinking of the imminent time when the old man's death would leave her without a home, and planning negotiations by which the roof might still be kept over her. But the words stirred the girl to madness. She turned slowly, and still on her knees looked up at him.

" Won't 'ee ? " she whispered. " Never ? Will 'ee hink of me—always ? "

In a more comprehending mood, he would have caught the alarm at that. As it was, he merely set it down to the ungracious gratitude which had always characterised her intercourse with him.

" I could never forget anyone who has been so kind to me as you," he said.

" Kind ? " cried the girl, her voice breaking on the word. Without rising, she moved towards him, and suddenly fell across his knee. " How can I help bein' kind," she moaned. " when I love 'ee so dear ! "

Had he heard the words alone, he might have fitted to them a less intense meaning than that which her gesture and half-sobbing tones threw into them. But seeing her so, listening to her rapid emotional breathing, he had no doubt as to their true significance. And this, no less because it was a revelation to him. He forgot his own pain in witnessing hers.

" Good God ! " he said aloud. " What a villain I must seem ! "

" There ! " said Sophy, raising her head boldly, " I've a-told you. You had to know—I always felt that. I only wonder you've not guessed it—weeks ago ! "

" Sophy," he spoke very gently, and not without some strange touch of shame, " I wish that you had not said it. God knows I did not mean this to happen ! "

" You don't want me to love you, I s'pose ? "

He shook his head.

" Why not ? It don't hurt 'ee—what harm can I do ? "

" A great deal—to yourself."

She made an impatient movement. She had raised her face, but her arms still hung limply across his knee.

" I don't care about myself," she said.

" Sophy," said Ridley, " I am very, very sorry. God is my witness that I never meant to do you this harm."

" 'Tisn't harm ! " she cried, with sudden passion that had a touch of angry resentment in it. " 'Tis the best thing I've got in my life. I wouldn't be without it for a crock o' gold. 'Tis all I care for, and I'd die afore I gave up loving 'ee. 'Tis all my good to think of 'ee, and see thee sometimes ! Don't ye think you've hurt me—you've given me more taste o' happiness than I thought there was in the whole world ! "

He put out a restraining hand.

" Hush ! Hush ! Some one may hear."

" I bain't ashamed of it ! " she cried recklessly, and flung

9

back her loosened hair like a wild thing. Her eyes burnt sombrely; her breast was heaving. She would have nothing of restraint, even from him.

From his heart, he pitied her. And though he knew that there was no justice in the accusation he blamed himself. The only chance of salvation that he saw for her was that the passion should burn out quickly, and leave her dead cold. A new experience had been thrust upon him, at a time when his weakened nerves were ill-fitted to bear the strain, and though his distress was genuine his words came haltingly.

"Sophy, my poor child," he said, "you are very young. This is all a mistake. If I have helped it at all, without meaning to, may God forgive me! Such thoughts were never in my mind, be sure of that. But now that I know, I must do what I can to help you."

In the pause occasioned by a sudden feeling of faintness, Sophy crept closer to him. Her eyes were hungry and hopeful.

"I will go away," he said, "as soon as I can. I ought never to have come. But I will go away, Sophy; and I will not see you again, unless it is quite certain that you have forgotten this folly, and no longer care."

"Go away? Not never see you again?"

She was startled, horrified, almost angry.

"It's the only way, Sophy—the only right wise way."

She seemed speechless—amazed. Then words poured from her, her reticent lips becoming a floodgate for her passion.

"But I love you! I love you! You'd said as you'd help me! 'Tisn't helpin' to go away, an' never let me see you no more. 'Tis the cruellest thing in the world. I must see you; I can't live without seein' you at times. I want to be near you, so as I can see you every day. Mayn't I come to you? If not now, when girt-uncle's gone. I'll have no home than. Mayn't I come to you then? Oh, say as I may come to 'ee then!"

"Sophy," said Ridley very firmly, "you may not."

She flung herself down again, tearing at her wild hair, and sobbing half-aloud.

"Why mayn't I come?" she wailed. "You've got a girt house, and I'd not be idle. Isn't there aught there as I could do?"

"Nothing," said Ridley.

"You be cruel to me!"

" I'd be crueller if I did what you ask."

She flung back her head to look at him.

" Why mayn't I come ? " she questioned, with some of the old sullenness.

" Sophy, if I took you into my house, do you know what people would say ? "

Something of his meaning dawned upon her, half-taught as she was. But she answered :

" No."

" Then," said Ridley, " it's not for me to tell you."

She bit her hair savagely. A little defiance was creeping into her manner.

" I don't care what they say ! 'Tis because you don't reckon I'm good enough. You be thinking of yourself."

" I'm thinking of both of us."

" 'Tis lies anyway," she averred. " There's a maid in your house already. Folks don't talk about her."

" That's very different. She's going to marry some one in the town. Sophy, how can I make you understand ? Don't you see ? You've told me something which, as I believe, a woman generally holds as her deepest secret. If you have let me know, presently you might let others know too, and because, my poor child, there are men who would take all that you have to offer, and—God help you !—would ask for more, people would think ill of you, who mean no harm at all. I like you too well to let that happen, Sophy. Blame me now if you will. But later on, when you are married to some honest fellow, you'll bless me in your prayers that I said *No* to you to-night."

There was no blessing in the glance which she turned on him. The alchemy of pain was doing its insidious work.

" 'Tis because I'm poor——" she began—Ridley shook his head feebly. He looked white and exhausted—" an' ugly ! "

" If I loved you, Sophy," he whispered, " I'd turn you into a lady, and marry you."

" You hate me ! And I so fond of 'ee ! "

He made no reply. Sophy worked herself up to fresh madness. She was on her feet now, trembling with mingled passions.

" 'Tis because of her ! " she cried. " That Chideock woman ! How I hate her—the fine madam that she be ! I'd like to spit in her face, an' claw her eyes out ! "

" Sophy," cried Ridley, stung into speech, " you

mustn't talk like this. I tell you, I should say just the same if Miss Chideock had never been born."

" But 'tis her, isn't it ? " persisted the girl. Her pale face was flaming

" You have no right to ask me that, Sophy. I shall not answer."

She laughed harshly.

" Them words your answer," she said. " 'Tis little thanks you've got to spare for me, wi' her about. Yet she'll never love 'ee—as well as I've done ! "

Ridley made a strong effort to deal forcefully with the situation. He spoke moderately, but with a show of firmness.

" Sophy," he said, " this must end. For your own sake, try to be reasonable. I like you. I'm grateful to you. But from my heart I wish this had not happened. You have been very good to me to-night——"

" Good ! " she interrupted. " I was so sorry for 'ee. I thought you might be kind. But you're not—you're cruel to me. An' I don't know as I want to be good to ye any more."

She spoke and looked at him with a kind of bitter sullenness. She had offered him of her best, and had been refused because the gift was not good enough—because he chose to take another from elsewhere. So, in her ignorance, she interpreted the history of this her hour, and the desire to strike back gave direction to her pain.

" I'm sorry, Sophy," said Ridley. " I would go away, if only I knew where to go to."

The milk was boiling in the pot. Sophy suddenly unhooked it, and set it aside, making no attempt to fill the bowl on the table. She faced round towards him. She was little and helpless ; a poor despised creature, with small power to sting, even when crushed underfoot. But there was one way in which she could assert herself, and punish him for the pain and self-humiliation which he had caused. He had taken her heart and wrung it between his hands. But he had placed her body in her care. She could make that suffer. And she would.

" If I'm not good enough for your home," she said, speaking very carefully, " mine can't be good enough for you. You'd best go."

" Do you mean that, Sophy ? "

" 'Course I mean it. You said you'd not come if I was alone. Well, then—I am alone. Girt-uncle be out, an'

there's no woman here. 'Twas a lie I told ye to get 'ee
to come, and I wish my tongue had froze up first afore I
brought you in."

"Sophy," said Ridley, with some sternness, "you have
done very wrong. I'll go at once. I couldn't remain, in
any case, against your wish." He stood up, bit his lip
suddenly, and seemed for a moment to forget what he was
saying. Then he swayed across the floor towards the door,
and, remembering, asked for his horse.

"'Tis outside," said Sophy, without moving. "I reckon
you can find it."

It was her last word to him. She heard him open the
door and go stumbling out into the night. She had no pity
for him—only for herself. Her raw passion was but changed
in kind, not in intensity. She turned by instinct to the
undying fire. The wood had burnt through, and now lay in
a red-hot heap on the surface of the more slowly burning
peats. The soft glare irradiated her face. She dropped to
her knees in its warmth and light.

"If he'd a-cared the littlest bit in the world," she murmured, "he'd not ha' minded folk's tongues no more than
me. But 'tis her—always her! 'Twasn't no harm I was
asking anyway—always her!"

It was Sophy's point of view, clung to with the tenacity
of her class.

After a long interval, she heard him leading the horse
away.

An hour later, Amos came in from his wanderings, and
crept into his bed. The girl was still crouching by the fire.

At midnight, a door opened overhead. A woman came
half-way down the stairs, and called to her.

"My dear, ain't you never coming to bed?"

CHAPTER XXV

A BUNCH OF SEALS

"I AM not to go ? " repeated Quenride. " Are you sure that is what the gentleman said ? "

"Certain sure, ma'am. As I were tellin' ye, he'd ha' brought his own message, only he wa'n't in no fit state to do it. And seein' as he'd be best off at home I made so bold as to jogtrot en thitherwards, so soon as med be."

"That was very wise of you, Jonathan," said Quenride. She sat down, trembling. In her hand was clasped a bunch of seals, which the messenger had just delivered to her. One of them bore a monogram; and, moreover, the man who had brought the token was well known to her. He was the dairy-man who had carried Sophy Hoddinott into Dorchester after her night on the bridge.

"And he gave you this ? " she said. The old fellow's story had been somewhat rambling, and she wished to hear it again.

"He did, ma'am. 'If I should go off afore we gets there,' says he, 'just you take this here bunch o' seals to Miss Chideock,' he says, 'and tell her that the man as sent 'em says she's not, on no account, to go.' And with that, ma'am, off he goes into the deadest swound as ever I see. So, knowin' as his tongue 'ouldn't be o' use if I brought en to your ladyship, I whips up the old harse, and sets out for Darchester at a tidy pace."

Quenride had drawn her brows together as if in pain. She was holding the seals very tightly in her hand.

"Did—did you know what was the matter with him ? " she asked. " Did he tell you nothing more ? "

"Well, ma'am, since I'm put to it like that, he did say as I wa'n't to alarm ye."

"Alarm me ! " repeated Quenride. She opened her hand with a little passionate movement, looked at the seals, and

closed it up again. " Yes. That is what he would say. Go
on. I am not at all—alarmed. When did he tell you that ? "
" A'most so soon as I found him," said Jonathan Burt.
" As I was a-tellin' you, Miss Quen, ma'am, I was goin' Carfe
way, an' happened to mind as I promised little Sophy Hoddinott to fetch her along a truss of hay for her beasts—Farmer
havin' said she med have it, if she could get it took away—
and havin' the cart empty, I pulled up at the rick-yard nat'ral,
and turned in."

" Yes ! " said Quenride impatiently.

" An' there I found en," concluded Jonathan, with rustic
sense of climax.

" How did he look ? " she asked.

" Bad, ma'am. There be no other word for it. Tar'ble
bad."

" But he was able to speak to you ? "

" In a sort of a kind o' way, ay, he were. But how he
got there, he couldn't hardly tell. He did say as he minded
leaning on a gate for a long time, an' he s'posed he must ha'
crept inside. Anyways, there I did find en, layin' under a
rick, like a rascal, and the nag aside en, without more harness
on it than a twist o' rope round its neck. Pretty come-to-
pass for a gentleman, thinks I ! "

" Didn't he tell you more than that ? "

" He told me, after a bit, who he were, an' where a' belonged to, and asked for a lift to his place. So, seein' as he
were so desprit set on gettin' home-along, I fell in wi's
notion. An' then, when a' couldn't speak no more, I thinks
to myself, ' Now, if I passes up Wareham way, an' planks
what's little better than a dead man down at Miss Quen's door,
'tisn't a pretty sight for such a dainty she.' So, I reckoned
I'd carry the man home, and come back with his message
a'terwards. Didn' I do right, ma'am ? "

" Yes—oh, yes," said Quenride. " But didn't you find
out what happened to him ? It is such a strange story,
you see."

Jonathan Burt stared past her through the window.

" He said as he'd met with a accident," he answered
unwillingly.

" What sort of an accident ? " she cried.

" Ma'am, he didn't say."

" You were a fool not to ask ! " she retorted sharply.
She stared helplessly on the floor, conscious of great alarm
and distress.

Glancing up to put another question, she surprised a certain look on her companion's face, and leapt to a conclusion, as her manner was.

" You can tell me more ! " she declared. " What is it ? "

" 'Tisn't pretty hearing for your ears, ma'am," objected Burt.

" But my ears will have it ! " she said. " What soft schoolmiss do you take me for ? Out with it ! "

" Well, 'tis so. As I were jogging along, I pulls up on the road for a drap o' cider, and the folk at the place, seein' what I'd got in the cart, must needs flock round. One of 'em was for loosening his neckerchief to ease his breathing, and when 'twas done we found his chest all covered up with greasy linen, and underneath—the cause o' the mischief, ma'am."

" What was it ? " she asked ; and heard the answer with parted lips.

" Just five bad burns," said Burt sympathetically. " All of 'em the same size, long an' narrer. If a man med say so to you, Miss Quen, ma'am, 'twas the same as if he'd fallen naked across hot bars. For there weren't a smell or sign o' scorching on any of his clothes."

Quenride sat very still, her hands clasping the trinket in her lap. She remained thus for so long that Jonathan Burt fell to wondering how a common man got out of a great lady's house when she appeared to have forgotten that he was in it. He had taken the first step in a self-effacing shamble towards the door, when Quenride roused herself.

" And you took him safely home ? " she asked, though she had been told this at the beginning.

" I did, ma'am. And the young chap there said he'd get en to bed at once, and fetch in the doctor."

" Thank you very much, Jonathan." Quenride rose, and handed him a coin. " I will tell the gentleman of your good services. Yes, you may go. Good day."

" Good day, ma'am."

" A very bad day ! " she murmured, as he closed the door. She looked again at the token which Ridley had sent. " Oh, dear heart o' me, a very bad day ! "

Then she set her mind to piece together the various happenings that she might discover for herself what the whole event had been. She did so fearfully, and with a troubled conscience. She could not forget that Ridley had been at first indisposed to fall in with her cousin's proposal, and had accepted it rather by reason of her solicitude than from much inclination of his own.

If, as seemed probable, harm had come to him on this account, the blame was hers. The thought had an extraordinary power to hurt her. She passed on to a consideration of the facts. Allied to her impulsive nature she had a clear head, and, though she usually sprang at her conclusions, her perception was seldom at fault. It guided her aright now. She recalled the plausible phrasing of Mohun's letter, and recognised it for a clever lie. Ridley's apparent neglect to fulfil his promise to write himself later in the day was now explained. The fact had surprised, even disappointed her, on the previous evening, but it had neither alarmed her nor aroused any suspicion. Regarded in the light of what she had just learned, it was plain that he had kept the appointment as originally arranged, and that, for some reason, Mohun had prevented her from attending. To this had been added, within the last hour, Ridley's own message—" *Don't go.*"

As to what had actually happened at the meeting between the two men, Quenride dwelt shudderingly on the facts laid before her. Her imagination, always too ardent for her own happiness, caught fire. She embroidered the plain words of Jonathan Burt, until she had before her a glowing presentment of the affair. And here again, her instincts led her aright. She could have suggested a fairly accurate account of what had taken place. The knowledge left her with a sense of shame.

Of Ridley's integrity, had such, in truth, been put to the test, she had no doubt. Of his courage, had Mohun's object gone no deeper than mere personal revenge, she was equally sure. The only uncertainties to her mind were, the reason of such a savage attack as Ridley must have endured, and the still more urgent question of how he was faring at this present time. These two points assailed heart and conscience alike. Neither would rest while the twin-doubt remained. Something horrible had happened to a man bent only on her service. Why had it happened? And, more persistently, what was happening to him now?—now, while she sat, idle and in comfort at home, saved perhaps from a similar fate by those gasping words of his, by the little token clutched so tightly in her hot hand.

She was not one to suffer emotion of any kind in quietness and silence. Sympathetic action was needed in times of stress by this intense soul. Sharp words and a spoiled temper had been the natural outcome of her long months of suspense and anguish. And, during that time, the four walls of a room had seldom witnessed her most despairing moods. She grew restless now, as this new trouble weighed upon her. She realised with more conviction, as each moment passed, that to wait until chance should provide the solution of her doubts was a thing impossible. It would be the easiest, as well as the most natural thing in the world, to bid her stolid Williams to ride over to Dorchester to inquire if Lawyer Ridley was much the worse for his accident. A formal inquiry—and a stiffly courteous reply. Surely the man deserved more than that ; certainly she desired a better reassurance.

"There's nothing strange in it," she told herself. "He's simply my man of business, who's engaged upon a delicate negotiation for me. He seems to have come to grief over it somehow, and I am naturally anxious—for myself. What more proper than that I should ride over in person—it being a fine day—to make inquiry, instead of trusting to a stupid groom ? If he were a private gentleman, and a friend of mine, the case would be different ; but he's not. Just an act of courtesy from a client—that's all he'll see in it, and that's all it will be. I'll go ! "

She was in her habit, and had the horses round at the door, before she had allowed herself to question again the propriety of the enterprise. Yet even the excitement could not keep the chill dread from her heart, and she would have bowed her head in the dust for very shame. Not for the daring which, as she well knew, lay in the present act, but for thought of the harm which he had suffered in her cause.

"Why didn't he listen to me ? " she cried inwardly, as she raced along, leaving Williams far behind. "Dear God ! why was I born to hurt all whom I care for ? I've done Gilbert a wrong that I thought I should hardly undo save with my life ; and now an honest man has come, against my wish, into the toils—to his own hurt and pain. Why didn't he take my warning, and keep out of it ? Am I worth saving at such cost ? "

And the clattering hoofs rang out the answer—No ! No ! No !

The message had been brought to her at the beginning of the afternoon, and the light had not begun to diminish by the time that the tree-girt town was reached. Before entering its streets, Quenride waited for the groom, and made a decorous canter of it, with the man in close attendance. She schooled herself to a matter-of-fact composure, and, slipping to the ground at Ridley's door, walked between the spiked railings with the self-possession of a great lady making a business call.

She did not carry this pose for long. She was too nervous and overwrought to maintain it in the face of the grave looks and hushed deprecatory manner of the woman who answered her gentle rapping.

"I heard that Mr. Ridley is ill," she said. "I have come to ask about it."

"Yes, ma'am. Pray to step inside."

Quenride was taken into Ridley's sitting-room. Its scrupulous order suggested the temporary loss of a tenant.

"I'm afraid I can't tell you very much, ma'am," said Mrs. Channing, in her quiet tones. "Mr. Ridley has met with an accident, and is suffering a good deal from shock and exhaustion, so the doctor says."

"How did it happen?" asked Quenride faintly, putting off the question which she dreaded yet longed to ask.

"That I don't know, ma'am. He has not told us. You see, men, especially young men, take a little shame at being laid by. The master's so hearty as a rule that he feels it a good deal. He's 'clined to worry too, I'm afraid, about its happening just at Assize time."

"Never mind that!" said Quenride, with feminine impatience at such a grievance. "He'll be present at the next. Was—was it a bad accident?"

"He's been severely burnt about the body, ma'am, and didn't get the attention he ought to have had at the time. He's taken cold from exposure, and the doctor says there's more inflammation than should be, ma'am."

Quenride drew a sharp breath.

"He—he is—is he in much pain?" she asked, at last.

"He has been in a good deal, I'm sorry to say. But he's a Christian gentleman, and knows how to bear it."

"Oh, I am sure of that," said Quenride, with an odd touch of pride. "Is he conscious now?" she added quickly, for she saw that the housekeeper was looking at her in a marked way.

"He was, when I left him," she was told.

"Asleep, perhaps?"

Mrs. Channing shook her head.

" Dear heart, I wish he could sleep," she said.

" Will you tell him that I called ? You know who I am ? "

" I remember you perfectly, ma'am."

Quenride's cheek burned a deeper rose.

" I want you to give him—this," she said hurriedly. She took out the bunch of seals, which she had placed in a small box. But she did not hand it over. Mrs. Channing waited. " I suppose," said Quenride, stumbling over her words, " that I could not possibly—see him ? "

" Indeed, no, ma'am ; he's a-bed, of course, and not fit to see anyone."

" Yes, I know," answered Quenride shamelessly admitting to herself that she had cherished this desire all the time, " but I have something of real importance to say to him. Something which, I think, he might be pleased to hear. It is of too private a nature to send by message—and there is something which I must ask him as well."

Mrs. Channing, as custodian both of the sick-room and of the proprieties in her master's house, looked doubtful. Quenride's eyes were wistful with appeal.

" It could not harm him," she urged. " It is really a matter of business—I mean, it is connected with some business which Mr. Ridley is conducting for me. And I am sure that he would care to hear it."

" 'Tis a pity, I think, to trouble him about business just now," Mrs. Channing said, regarding the visitor gravely.

Quenride smiled very slightly.

" Believe me," she said, " I have far too great a regard for Mr. Ridley to wish to trouble him about anything."

There was about her an inherent winsome quality which had become overlaid of late by the curtness and asperity born of her distress. It showed now, with unconscious charm, and Mrs. Channing was not untouched. She reflected that it was well not to offend the clients.

" If 'tis so very important, ma'am," she said, " maybe the master wouldn't object to see ye for one minute. I'll ask him if he feels fit."

She went away with a doubtful face, but when she returned she brought the permission for which Quenride longed. How could she go away, she asked herself, without learning how great an injury he had sustained for her sake—and what motive had prompted its infliction ?

She followed the woman up the stairs quite steadily. The proceeding was unconventional, of course ; but all the great moments of her life had been so, and she no longer hid from herself the knowledge that this moment held a greatness indescribable. Prudes might have shaken their heads at her. Quenride Chideock went on.

Mrs. Channing softly threw open a door.

Ridley was lying flat in the bed, the whiteness of his face merged into the whiteness of the pillow, his hair and eyes dark blots upon the whole. His hand came out from under the bed-clothes. The frill fell back, and showed the bandaged wrist.

" I must apologise for receiving you in such a way," he said. " But I am very glad to see you safe, Miss Chideock. You got my message, then ? "

" I did," said Quenride. She appeared less embarrassed than he, but her eyes had grown soft and pitiful. " I am grateful to you for sending it. Why did you trouble to think of me, in all your pain ? "

" It would have hurt me more to know that you were in danger," he said.

Mrs. Channing had moved to the window. Her partial deafness covered the sound of the low voices.

" It was my cousin," said Quenride.

" Yes. But don't worry. He has done no harm. Everything is quite safe."

The words told her more than he had intended.

" It was—for that, then ? " she asked. " To win your consent to the fraud ! Oh, I know, I understand. Such devilry is worthy of him ! And you — you — oh, I did not know that men were ever like that ! You shame me to the ground. Why don't you curse me as I deserve ? But for my weak fears, you would never have gone. He tricked me for the second time with his lies—oh, I was a fool not to know ! "

" Don't trouble about it," said Ridley warmly, moved by her distress. " You had something to tell me ? "

" Only this," she whispered, " and it seems so poor a thing to say: I am very, very sorry—from my heart I speak it—can you forgive me ? "

She bent forward, and in that moment Ridley saw in

her face something of the tenderness which he had once
tried to picture there.

" Don't ask it," he said. " There's no serious damage
done. I'll be about again in a week, I hope."

" I pray so ! " she answered. " Will you not prosecute
him ? "

" No. I think not. I couldn't prove the crime. And
the situation's too delicate to stand much handling."

Mrs. Channing approached.

" Yes," said Quenride. " I am going."

She had more questions to ask, many details to be enlightened upon, but the look of exhaustion creeping over
Ridley's face drove her away. His hand was lying on the
counterpane.

" I have to give you this," she said, and pressed into
it the little box containing the seals.

In spirit she did more. Very humbly, she laid her heart
there too. But, in actuality, she had never been more conscious of that tumultuous organ in her own breast than she
was as she preceded the housekeeper down into the passage.

" You will be good to him ? " she said, as the door was
being opened.

" I hope I don't need to be told my duty towards my
master, ma'am."

" No, of course not. I am sure you don't," said Quenride
eagerly. She passed outside. " Still, you will be good to
him, won't you ? " she asked.

The prim features of the housekeeper relaxed into a
smile.

" I promise you that, ma'am," she said.

And Quenride, with a flushed cheek, stared across the
road, wondering what right she had to exact it. Her self-
consciousness hurried her into further embarrassment.

" I will not detain you longer," she said, bringing her
eyes back to Mrs. Channing's face. " You will have plenty
of this sort of thing to do, I suppose—answering inquiries,
I mean ? "

" I don't know, ma'am."

There was a quality in the tone which appealed to Quenride. She raised questioning brows.

" Mr. Ridley's friends have not treated him very well of
late," explained the other, with reserve.

" In what way ? " asked Quenride.

" They do not call, ma'am."

Quenride guessed the truth, with a rush of hot remorse. But she did not spare herself.

" Why is it ? " she asked.

Mrs. Channing was not minded to spare her either.

" Since the trouble at Wareham," she said, " they seem to take shame at the thought of noticing him."

" The trouble at Wareham," replied Quenride hotly, " was none of Mr. Ridley's making. You can tell his friends so—with my authority. And I hope they will learn reason soon."

On the way home it pleased her, with a gaiety of spirit which she had not known for many months, to rehearse to herself all the reasons why Ridley should suffer disparagement in her eyes. After these, she set out the answering arguments :

" He's nothing to boast of in the matter of position. Just a practising attorney in a country town. What's that ? I should like to know ! If he earns food and raiment, that's all he does. He's a man of absolutely no connections. His knowledge of his ancestry probably stops short where most middle-class people's does, at his grandfather ! I dare say there was a cobbler in the family three or four generations back, if one only knew. And his Radical opinions are abominable.

" But he's nearer to the truth of things than the wine-sotted old Tories who don't even trouble to inquire what their opinions stand for. And his manners are as superior to most of them as his mind is to all. There's not a coarse fibre in him — he's a gentleman, to all intents and purposes. More than that, he's an honourable man. More than that— oh, much more !—he's the man I love. And, dear heart, how poor the rest of the world seems in comparison ! "

Back in the sick-room, Quenride herself had left a fragrant memory.

" That's a beautiful young lady, sir," commented Mrs. Channing tentatively, later on in the day.

" She's as fine as she's fair," answered Ridley. " You will please be very attentive to her, if she calls again."

It was the complement to Quenride's entreaty, " You will be very good to him." And Mrs. Channing recognised it as such.

During a restless and painful night, Ridley's mind also played with ideas. The tenor of his disjointed thoughts ran :

" A man can't suffer for a woman without feeling—something for her, I suppose. Or else he can't feel—something for her, without wanting to suffer for her sake. Which is it, I wonder ? "

And Quenride's face pressed upon him, in all its tenderness, from the shadows of the room.

CHAPTER XXVI

LOVE-LETTERS

"DON'T draw the shutters yet, Dolly. I never knew such a creature as you are for shutting out the daylight."

"There's not much left, Mr. Gilbert."

"That's just it. I want to see the stars. There! Leave it so!"

Gilbert, whether from instinct or assimilation, often adopted his sister's imperious manner. Dolly, who was engaged in embroidering muslin, gave in to him like the good-natured little soul that she was.

"Aren't they splendid?" said the boy, when presently the clear October sky deepened to dusk, and the first stars became visible. "Do you know how far off they are?"

Dolly twisted her pretty face up at the window.

"Oh, miles and miles," she said vaguely. "As far away as London."

Gilbert laughed at her.

"London!" he cried, in pleasant derision. "Why, that's less than a hop in comparison. The very nearest of them is twenty millions of millions of miles."

"Dear me!" said Dolly, in mild surprise. "I shouldn't have thought it."

"That's not quite fair, perhaps," added Gilbert. "The planets are nearer, though the nearest of them is an immense way off. Do you know, Dolly, if you were up on one of the stars, and looked down to the earth, what you'd see?"

"I'm quite content to be here, Mr. Gilbert, thank you. And I should think you'd need a very strong pair of spectacles to see anything at all, in the dark."

"It wouldn't be dark," said Gilbert.

"How could you see anything if 'tis as far off as you say?"

"Well, not really. But, for the sake of argument——"

265

" Young gentlemen of your age shouldn't argue," murmured Dolly, reiterating one of Quenride's reproofs.

Gilbert explained the theory of Light, and added a few other scraps of information. Dolly soon grew weary. The only sort of astronomical data which she would have appreciated would have been a favourable comparison of her eyes to the brightest orbs in the firmament. As this kind of thing was not to be expected from the youthful Gilbert, she endeavoured to change the subject.

" You're talking nonsense," she declared. " I can't think where you picked it all up."

" I'll tell you," said the boy. " I got it from Mr. Ridley. He knows a lot of interesting things like that."

" Then I'm surprised," said Dolly. " And I don't wonder that Miss Quen won't let you have anything to do with him."

" What's wrong, eh ? Though, for that matter, Quen has changed her mind. She's quite different about Mr. Ridley now. She says I can have him for my friend, if I like."

" Then she ought to be told ! Filling your head with all that nonsense ! "

" 'Tisn't nonsense. 'Tis what people have found out."

" Then," said Dolly, " I don't call it at all right. And I'm sure it was never intended."

" Who didn't intend it ? " asked the boy, with a smile.

" Now, Mr. Gilbert, you know well enough what I mean. And you preparing for Confirmation too ! Doesn't it stand to reason that, if we'd been meant to know such things, we'd have been born knowing them, without the trouble of racking our brains to find them out ? "

" We're not born knowing the alphabet," replied Gilbert, " but no one ever thinks it wrong to learn it."

" That's a very different matter," declared Dolly, at once. " If we didn't learn our letters, how could we ever read our Bibles ? "

" Well, isn't Nature just a big Bible ? " retorted the boy.

" Is that one of Mr. Ridley's sayings, too ? "

" Perhaps. I'm sorry you don't like him. He's very nice, and he knows a lot about things. I say, Dolly, didn't he talk about interesting things that day he kissed you on the bridge ? "

" Kissed me on the bridge, Mr. Gilbert ! You mustn't

repeat such tales about me. People might think very ill of
me indeed. It's a bad thing for a girl to get herself talked
about."

"Is it ? I wonder why they make people talk of 'em
then. Besides, Dolly, he did, didn't he ? "

"Well, perhaps so. But 'twasn't my fault, I'm sure.
And, after all, it wasn't much of a kiss either. I've had many
better ones. He only did it, as I told Miss Quen at the time,
to coax me into carrying a message to her."

Gilbert looked interested. He limped back to the sofa,
and allowed Dolly to close the shutters without further
protest.

"Was that it ? " he asked.

Dolly nodded.

"It's a strange thing," the boy went on, "a very
strange thing — talking of kisses made me think of it—
that neither you nor my sister has got a lover. You're
very pretty, and Quenny's quite the loveliest woman I ever
saw."

"Well," said Dolly, "it don't follow that we couldn't
have had them if we'd liked."

"I wonder ! " said the boy. "I was afraid last year that
Quen might marry Cousin Alaric. I'm glad "—he shuddered
perceptibly—" she didn't."

"He's a very pleasant gentleman," said Dolly.

"He's not, really. He'd have made it hell for both of
us."

"You mustn't talk like that ! "

"I can't help it ! I hate him—nearly. There's something about him that I can't understand. He always seems
to know things that he doesn't tell. Just as if he has some
power to hurt me that he keeps hidden, and means to put
into action some day."

Dolly looked up. Gilbert showed a white excited face
that alarmed her. She tried to reassure him.

"Don't be foolish, Mr. Gilbert," she said. "How fanciful
you are ! Miss Quenride isn't going to marry Mr. Mohun,
so there's an end of the matter."

"You—you don't think he'll perhaps make her ? "

"What nonsense ! How could he ? " cried Dolly. "And
she won't marry him from choice. She's just as likely to
marry Mr. Ridley himself."

"Well," demanded the boy, "and why shouldn't that
be ? "

" Because ladies in her position don't marry men like that."

" How silly of 'em. Dolly, he writes to her sometimes ! "

" Of course. He's her lawyer."

" Oh ! But she was deuced close about what was in the letter. Did that mean anything, should you say ? "

" I really can't, Mr. Gilbert. It might have been very particular business."

" Or a love-letter."

" Or a love-letter," said Dolly, to humour him.

Gilbert, whose interests were necessarily limited, followed up the point with some eagerness.

" I wish I knew," he said. " What fun it would be to find out, just to tease her for being so close ! " He raised himself, and looked round the room. Dolly had lit the candles by now. " I wonder whether she kept it ! I wonder if it's in her desk over there ! Dolly ! What a chance ! Look, my dear, look ! "

" Whatever's the matter ? " asked the girl.

" She's left the keys in the lock ! Give me over the desk, please. I'm going to hunt for that letter."

Dolly, rather curious herself, nevertheless protested.

" You'd never pry into your sister's desk, while she's away ? " she cried.

" 'Tisn't prying," said Gilbert, with a laugh. " If it is a love-letter, I'll stop reading the instant I find out. I promise that, on my honour. And I'll tell Quen all about it before I say my prayers to-night. Do fetch it, there's a dear, or you'll make me go for it, and you know how getting up hurts my back."

" I'm sure it isn't right," said Dolly, mentally rehearsing a number of reasons why she should obey. Gilbert was not to be unreasonably thwarted ; he was to be kept amused ; he must be humoured ; he ought to lie still. In half a minute, Dolly rose, and placed the desk at Gilbert's side. He scrambled into a sitting position, and took it on to his knees. The desk was unlocked with a little click.

Simultaneously, there came a peal at the outside bell. Dolly started guiltily, and Gilbert looked annoyed.

" That can't be Quen," he said, " because we didn't hear any horses."

The door was not opened immediately, and Gilbert looked into the desk. There were many letters there. He pulled

a few out, glanced at the signatures, and replaced them. The
bell rang again.

"Confound it!" muttered the boy, busy with Quenride's
property. "Oh, Barnes is going at last, and, see here,
Dolly, here's one." He held out a sheet. "I thought that
would be his writing from the style. And here's another.
Why, she's got quite a lot! Looks promising, doesn't it?"
Dolly answered from the door.

"Do be quiet!" she entreated. "It's—yes, I believe
it's Mr. Mohun."

"The deuce!" cried the boy, hastily placing the desk on
the stool at his side, and preparing to leave the sofa. "Are
you sure?"

"Yes," said Dolly, after a pause. "He's come in. Barnes
told him Miss Quen was out, and he says he'll wait. I think
he's asked for me."

"You're welcome to his company," muttered the boy.
"I don't want to see him; and I doubt if Quen does. Dolly,
if he comes in here, I shall go back to my room."

He scrambled to his feet unaided in his awkward fashion,
and in so doing allowed Ridley's letters to fall on to the
floor. His exclamation of annoyance and the sound of
Mohun's approaching steps reached Dolly at the same
moment. The boy called to her under his breath.

"The letters, Dolly!" He was coming towards her at the
door. "Pick 'em up, there's a dear. Put them back in the
desk, and lock it up. I don't think I'll look at them, after
all. It wouldn't be quite fair play. I'd hate to be mean—
like my cousin is."

"I'll see to it," promised Dolly. She had no objection
to entertaining Alaric Mohun alone, until Quenride's return.

Mohun had lingered a moment in the hall, talking to one
of the servants. He wished to find out whether Quenride
had kept the abortive appointment. Now they heard him
cursing the man for a fool at the moment when Gilbert had
opened the door, hoping to get away unnoticed.

His cousin caught him by the ear on the threshold.

"Hello, you young sinner!" was his greeting. "Still
idling about at home, eh? Don't you know that it's time
you began to learn things?"

"That's not quite fair, Cousin Alaric," said Gilbert, with
an attempt at good-humour. "I'm neither so ignorant nor
so idle as you make out. Quenny's teaching me French.
I know a lot of Latin, and I've started Greek. Parson says

I'm very good at Euclid and mathematics. I study with him two hours a day when I'm well enough."

"When you're well enough!" repeated Mohun, giving the ear a twist that made the boy wince, and pushing him away so sharply that he nearly fell. "When you come to live with me, I'll see that you're always well enough—do you hear? And if you're obstinate, I shall pack you off to a nice strict school, where they'll soon lick you into shape, you sickly little cub."

"Yes ; I expect you'd like to do that," answered the lad, with spirit. "But even though grandfather is dead you can't take me away from Quen."

"Can't I?" retorted the bully. "We shall see about that!" He smiled in a sneering way. "What if your late respected gran'dad left you to my care in his will?"

"He didn't," said Gilbert, flinching a little. "He wouldn't. He was fond of me, and he didn't like you."

"Well, my boy, you ask your sister about it, and see if she doesn't look uncomfortable. Watch if her pretty cheek doesn't flush, and her eyes snap fire. Well, she may fly into a tantrum, but that won't set the will aside. You're lawyer enough to understand that, eh?"

"I'll not believe it," said Gilbert, but with less confidence now.

"Well," retorted his cousin, "you wait and see. That's all."

And to this he would add nothing, entering the room immediately afterwards. Gilbert crept away, uneasy and miserable.

"You really shouldn't tease him so, Mr. Mohun," remonstrated Dolly mildly. "The poor child thinks you mean it."

Mohun had been taken aback at discovering his charming little acquaintance and petty informer behind the door. But Dolly Pouncey was exceedingly amenable to management, as Mohun had found out.

"My dear," he said, as they shook hands, "I didn't want him bothering us in here. I had to drive him away."

"Oh, he really was going," said Dolly, who never disbelieved anything that sounded like a compliment. "I didn't expect to see you this evening. Wait a moment! Oh, yes. Mr. Gilbert is all right; and it really is time he went to bed." She came back from glancing after the boy, who was now safe in the butler's care. "Miss Chideock is out, Mr. Mohun. I don't suppose she'll be long now. Will you wait ? "

" No hardship, I assure you, Miss Dolly," said the man, selecting the most comfortable chair. " I wish waiting for a relative was always made so pleasant. What have you got there—love-letters, eh ? "

" The idea of the thing, Mr. Mohun ! "

" Yet I'll swear they are, you dear rogue. Charming young ladies like you always get 'em by the shoal."

Dolly had gone so far as to collect the letters which Gilbert had dropped, but had not yet replaced them in the desk. She had been wondering how she could do so without being questioned. She looked at them doubtfully.

" Well," she said, with a laugh, " if they are love-letters, they're not mine. They belong to Miss Quenride."

" Indeed ! That's interesting too. Who's the swain ? "

" I'm told they're from her lawyer, Mr. Ridley. But, really, I don't know anything about it, and I think I'd better put them away."

" Wait a bit," said Mohun, rising, " all ladies are interested in love-letters, whether their own, or anyone else's. Now I can't tell you from the envelopes if they are such, but at least I can tell you if they're not. I happen to know the man's writing, and if this is the clerk's they're certainly not what you think. For no lover would let some one else address his *billy-doos* for him. At least I shouldn't, if I were writing to—well, we'll not say whom ! "

He held out his hand, his eyes on Dolly's face. Dazzled by his last suggestion, as he had meant her to be, she succumbed at once, and gave up the packet. Ridley, away at Dorchester, might have groaned at that moment.

Before letting his glance fall upon the letters, which he was now holding, Mohun said :

" Go and fetch me a pint of porter, my dear girl," his eyes having observed that there was already wine on the sideboard.

Dolly might reasonably have rung the bell and ordered in the refreshment, but the visitor's manner suggested flatteringly that he would infinitely prefer to receive it at her hands. She went away to the housekeeper's room. In less than five minutes she was back, bearing a silver tankard with a fine head on it. Mohun took it from her with a bow. There was a glitter in his cold eyes, and he seemed well pleased with himself.

" To Hebe ! " he said.

And Dolly laughed and blushed, bright and blooming as any Olympian cup-bearer might be.

Mohun threw a finger towards the envelopes lying where he had laid them down.

" 'Tis the man's hand right enough," he said. " But what's inside 'tis not for us to know. Though, from my cousin's carelessness in leaving them lying about, I shouldn't think they were important."

" She's usually most particular," murmured Dolly, who was not going to get Gilbert into trouble.

" Ha," said Mohun, finishing the porter with relish, " she's made a mistake this time, it seems."

The explanation was simple. Quenride had opened the desk to find the box in which she wished to place the bunch of seals. In her horrified imagining of what had happened to the owner, she had omitted to remove the keys after locking up the desk.

Some desultory talk followed. But Mohun seemed preoccupied, and paid Dolly no more compliments. Presently, he declared his intention of waiting no longer.

" I'll call again to-morrow," he said. " Give my respects to my cousin, Miss Dolly, and tell her that."

The desk stood back in its place.

A few yards up the street, figures on horseback went past him. Mohun turned to watch. The animals were stopped at the Chideocks' house.

" Ah, to-morrow, my lady, to-morrow ! " he said.

He slapped his breast pocket, and strolled easily on.

CHAPTER XXVII

WINNING ALL ROUND

THE next day, he was at the house again, forcing an entrance in spite of Quenride's orders that he was not to be admitted. A shamefaced servant carried the news of his arrival to Quenride, as she sat at work in a back room.

" Mr. Mohun, I am afraid, will have his trouble for his pains," she remarked icily. " I shall not see him."

" Good morning," said a voice over the servant's shoulder, and Mohun himself stood in the doorway.

" I only ask for five minutes, cousin," he continued, coming forward. " If, at the end of that time, you still wish me to leave, I give you my promise to do so, as peaceably as you could desire."

Quenride looked at him, and said nothing. She had come very near to hating the man. But, though her tongue burned to order him from the house, there was some quality in his demeanour that arrested her attention. Never a fool, he saw her momentary hesitation, and was quick to lay hold of it.

" Things have developed a little since yesterday," he told her. " You really would be wise to hear my latest views."

" Wiser, I think, to tell you mine," she retorted. " Do you wish to know how I regard you—now ? "

Mohun raised his eyebrows, with a glance at the servant.

" Oh," said Quenride, with a contempt that stung him in spite of his newly-acquired confidence, " I am not at all interested in shielding your credit. If you force your way into this house, you must not look for protection from me."

Mohun sneered at her openly.

" Your protection, Quenny," he said, " is a thing I'd be very sorry to have to trust to. As to forcing my way in, I wanted to talk business, so judged I'd a right to call. As I live, my dear, you take a little too much upon your charming shoulders."

"How dare you claim any right?" cried Quenride, with heightened colour; but she wavered a little, and turned to the waiting servant. "I will ring when Mr. Mohun is to be shown out," she said, and stood very still when she had finished speaking.

Mohun also waited until the door was closed. Then he sat down, while his cousin was yet on her feet. A little smile twisted his lips.

Quenride fell back into her chair, shivering.

"I wish I could tell you all that I think of you," she said, at length.

"We will waive that," he said. "Take it all for granted, my dear Quen."

"I knew you were a liar and a scoundrel," she went on, gripping the arms of the chair, and leaning forward to watch him. "But I didn't think that you were a cruel brute as well."

"Be reasonable!" said Mohun, at ease again. "Our legal friend has been telling tales, I see. Quenride, I congratulate you on your adviser. The man's a jewel. I'd admire him confoundedly if I didn't hate him so well. By the way, have you heard how he is?"

"Oh, you are intolerable!" she cried. "What had he done to you, that you should make him suffer so?"

"Done? He'd got in my way."

"It was brutal! It was fiendish!" she cried. "I'll not be silent, I don't care who hears or knows. If he had been twice as vile as yourself, you might have felt pity and have spared him that! And you could lay your wicked hands on him, he being what he is—the most stainless and upright of men! You could do it, and take no shame to yourself for as coldly cruel a deed as any man ever paid penalty for!"

"My dear cousin, keep calm." Mohun noticed her glowing face with interest. It seemed to please him. He looked like a card-player who, re-sorting his hand, finds an overlooked trump hidden behind the rest. "You don't imagine that I liked doing the business, do you? I felt a contemptible hound all the time, and I tell you I was fairly sorry for the poor devil before I'd finished. On my honour, I was."

"Honour!" Quenride flung the word at him, so that it seemed to cut him like a sharp-edged stone.

"And, after all, I did show compassion of a sort," Mohun

went on. " I spared his face. I said to myself, ' It's a
handsomer one than your own, Alaric, my boy, and it would
be rather a pity to spoil it.' "

Again a tremor ran through Quenride. A horror of what
might have been crept into her eyes. But in a moment she
had recovered herself, and was answering with spirit.

" You considered your own interests as much as his,"
she said. " You didn't want the outrage openly spoken
of."

" Well, well, at any rate, he gets the benefit. And his lady-
love, if he's got one, will still be able to kiss him without
shrinking."

" He will bear those marks always," said Quenride, in a
lower voice.

" Exactly. And 'tisn't every lady who can boast that a
presentable young man is going about carrying on his body
the proof of his devotion to her. The pair of you ought to be
rather grateful to me."

To the highly-strung Quenride it was intolerable that her
newly-realised tenderness should be handled in such rough
fashion. But her cousin's eyes were upon her, and she
succeeded in repressing her indignation, and said in a cold
manner :

" I have yet to learn what cause Mr. Ridley has to feel
grateful to you."

Mohun laughed.

" For getting him the sympathy of so very charming a
client," he said.

" Have you ever found me unsympathetic over a tale of
injury and wrong ? " she asked.

" Did I suggest it ? " replied Mohun at once. " It strikes
me, my dear Quen, that you're very anxious to justify your
interest in this young man. Why is it ? "

" He is my friend."

" Very good. Make him your friend at court by all means,
so long as you don't expect him to become anything else.
Because, you know, I should never consent."

" What right have you to dictate to me on any subject ? "
Quenride asked, in some confusion.

" I'm your kinsman," said Mohun doggedly. " To all
intents and purposes, your nearest male relative ; for in this
case, of course, Gilbert doesn't count. I should never, as I
say, allow my cousin to form an alliance with a pettifogging
lawyer."

" I think," said Quenride quietly, " that the stipulated five minutes must have passed. Will you kindly leave the house ? "

" No, I won't. I've not done yet."

" Then, you put me to an unpleasant necessity."

Quenride reached out a hand to the bell-rope.

" Going to have me put out ? " grinned Mohun. " On my soul, I'd like to see you try it."

" You shall." And she jerked the rope.

" Lost your temper, have you ? " cried Mohun. He sprang up, turned the key in the lock, and slipped it into his pocket. Then he came back to his seat, and nodded his head at her. " On second thoughts, perhaps I'm wrong. You'd better have him if you can. After the Weymouth affair, you can't afford to be particular——"

" Silence ! how dare you ? "

" And I dare say the lawyer's stomach's stout enough to digest the blemish, for the sake of marrying into a county family."

" That's a lie, a double lie ! " cried Quenride. " As foul a lie as you ever uttered. I will bear no more. Open that door, and leave the house."

While she was still making the angry demand, some one first tapped and then tried the door. Quenride looked at her cousin. He raised his voice.

" Yes, you're quite right," he said. " The lock is stiff. Some oil, I think you said. Bring us a little oil," he cried, through the panels. " The lock's got caught up. I can't open the door. Come round to the window."

" You shall go," said Quenride, " if they have to break the door in."

" You'll only damage your property," retorted Mohun. " Come now ! Let's talk business. Where's the will ? Surely you haven't been so ill-advised as to destroy it already ? "

Quenride made no answer.

" If so, it's a pity. A great pity, for the pair of ye."

" Oh, I know your brag and bluster," she said disdainfully.

" But perhaps you don't know this : I've got proof of the existence of that will. Irrefutable proof."

" You hinted at that before, and your own treachery proved it a lie."

" So it was—then," Mohun admitted coolly. " Things

have veered a little since. I am now in a position to demand the production of the will. And if Mr. Ridley isn't in a similar position to produce it—why, things will look very black against him. And, incidentally, against you too, I shouldn't wonder."

Quenride watched him, with gathering pain in her eyes. Across her inner vision there swept the memory of a pale face backed by a white pillow, and a nerveless hand which had yet given her the clasp of a friend.

"What proof have you ? " she asked, and it was noticeable that her confidence had failed.

" One moment ! " said her cousin.

He crossed to the window, took the jar of oil which was handed in from outside, and sent the bearer away. Quenride sat tense and silent, making no attempt to detain the servant.

" What proof ? " she asked, again.

" A letter to yourself, bearing on the subject, in Ridley's writing."

Quenride sprang up.

" A letter ? "

" Exactly. As I gather from it, he was good enough to object to a certain clause in Mr. Benjamin Chidcock's will—expressly so named, mark you !—and seems to have been trying to arrange an interview for the purpose of getting it altered."

Quenride remembered the letter. It was one of those which had passed between herself and Ridley immediately after his first return from Wareham. In new distress, she heard Mohun continuing :

" Of course, the date of the letter proves that Ridley at least was not concerned in the fraud of concealing the old man's death. But that won't help him much, for if he can't or won't produce the will. there'll be a very clear case of collusion against the pair of you."

There was an even clearer case than Mohun supposed. And Quenride shivered as she thought of it. There was the six thousand pounds still lying to Ridley's credit at the County Bank, and placed there, by herself, as the firm of Reeves and Frampton could testify. True, the money had, in effect, been refused. It had not been touched. But who, hearing the story as Mohun would tell it, would not believe that this apparent rejection was a blind—and the sum itself the price of Lawyer Ridley's honour ? Quenride's head bowed over her clasped hands. She lashed herself mercilessly for that gratuitous insult which she had laid upon a man who had not withheld his own body in her service.

"You seem dazed," said Mohun, who was watching her. "Even a little dull. Haven't I made my case clear? Properly speaking, I ought to have laid it first before the lawyer himself. But his present condition prevents him from attending to business, I imagine. I shan't commit the affair to writing, because I shall take warning by his own indiscretion. His letters will probably be opened by a third party. Altogether, I should prefer to deal with him by word of mouth. And I hope our interview will be more satisfactory, on both sides, than the last was."

"You are hoping——?" said Quenride, with dry lips, and paused.

"That he'll throw up the sponge," said Mohun. "In other words, that he'll produce the will, and let me claim my inheritance."

"And Gilbert!" said Quenride, with a shudder.

"Of course. Gilbert comes with me. It'll be the making of the lad."

"I'll die first," she said.

Mohun laughed.

"Well, you've got a choice!" he said. "You'll have to let something go."'

"Gilbert is no use to you," she protested, in deep distress.

"Oh, isn't he? He's the pledge of your good behaviour. For your own sake, of course, you'll not tell the whole truth. But a malicious woman's tongue is best gagged, if possible, and I prefer to make sure."

Quenride dropped her cheek on to her hand. All the fire seemed to have gone out of her. On the one hand—Gilbert; on the other—Kenelm Ridley; between the two—herself.

"If you have my letter," she said, "you must have broken open my desk, and have stolen it."

"Not at all."

"Yet you have read it."

"And have it put away in a safe place, true. If you doubt my word, go and get your desk, and look inside the envelopes."

"Open the door, then, and I will."

Mohun let her pass out. She went into the front room, which was empty, and found the keys dangling from the desk. The circumstance puzzled her. But searching her memory she had no clear recollection of removing them after relocking the case, and a bitter sense of her own carelessness smote her heavily.

She opened the desk. Ridley's letters, to all seeming, lay at the top. Her shaking fingers pulled the envelopes apart. In each case, there was nothing inside but a sheet or so of blank paper, obviously torn in haste from a pocket-book. She went back to the other room with the envelopes in her hand.

" Well ? " asked Mohun.

" Truth, for once," she said. " You have stolen my letters."

" I am not so reprehensible as you think," said Mohun. " As a matter of fact, the letters were put into my hands."

" Oh, I am not going to believe anything you choose to say, because you have told truth when I could wish it a lie."

" Ask your pretty little companion, Dolly Pouncey, what she knows about it," retorted Mohun.

" Dolly ? What had she to do with it ? "

" I found her fingering the letters. Don't ask me how or why she got hold of them. She wanted to know if they were addressed in Ridley's writing. I saw that they were, and thought there might be something interesting inside. So I got a peep at 'em while Dolly was out of the room, and collected evidence, as every man who's preparing to go to law should do. Oh, you needn't look so surprised and furious. It isn't the first time the girl's played you a trick."

" What else then has she done ? " cried Quenride, though her anger was already hot enough.

" I heard of secret meetings with the lawyer, a little time ago. Don't be unfair, Quen. You're as tricky as Dolly ; and she, at any rate, never means any harm."

" But she has done it ! " cried the impassioned Quenride, " and I'll bear with her no longer. She shall go—go back to her own people, and work her mischief there. Oh, if she only knew—only realised, the harm she has done ! "

" Well, she does seem to have put the game into my hands," agreed Mohun. " Poor little thing ! you'll frighten her with that temper of yours, Quen. I suppose I ought to marry her out of gratitude, eh ? "

He picked up his hat and gloves, and rose. Quenride faced him. He put out a mocking finger, and caressed her chin.

" So now you see how the case stands," he said. " Either you make up your minds to let me have what, in all probability, the old man intended me to have or you and Ridley go under.　You'll have time to get used to the idea, for as I said, I shan't move in the matter until Ridley's about again. He's not likely to go destroying wills so long as he's on his back, with witnesses about.　Perhaps you think he'll save the situation by indicting me on account of our recent interview. I fancy he's too good a lawyer for that.　He knows there's no evidence to build up a case on, and the facts which might help him are precisely those which he's moving heaven and earth to suppress.　So you see, I win all round ! "

With that, he left her.　She would have broken down after his departure, had there not been two things to be done. The first was the necessary interview with Dolly.

It was very brief.

" Since I find that you cannot be trusted not to meddle with my correspondence," said Quenride, " I am writing to tell your father to make arrangements to fetch you away to-morrow."

" To go home ? " gasped Dolly.

" Yes.　And at once.　What do you expect ?　Possibly you meant no harm, but you have done a great deal.　You must go."

Dolly was too honest flatly to deny her culpability, and Quenride was too angry to ask for explanations or excuses. Thus Gilbert's share in the episode did not appear until some time later.　Dolly had a genuine regard for the lad, and consequently a disinclination to lay the blame on his shoulders. A pride in this forbearance was the only prop left to her. Down in her foolish little heart was an intense surprise and mortification that the pleasant Alaric Mohun should have betrayed her innocent curiosity.　Lawyer Ridley at the bridge had promised to protect her from her father's wrath, and had done so, at cost to himself.　Even Robin Fiander, she reflected, would have died sooner than play her such a heartless trick.　She set about her packing in a very chastened mood.

Downstairs, Quenride wrote thus:

" I have seen my cousin.　He will presently seek an interview with you.　In God's name, do not grant it until I have seen you again.　Send me assurance of this, and I pray of you, cause nothing to be done in the matter yet awhile.

" You will think me careless of your suffering.　Believe me, I am very far from being that.　My greatest desire is for

your recovery and well-being ; my keenest regret is that
you should have been brought to this through your unhappy
friend,

"QUENRIDE CHIDEOCK."

The letter began and ended with a carefully worded
solicitude. The gist was in the middle. She dreaded lest
Ridley, learning of the new weapon in Mohun's hand, should
refuse to let her suffer alone, and by still declining to hand up
the will should wreck himself by her side.

To prevent this, she must induce him to part with the
document to herself, before he knew of this latest danger.
After that, must come the end.

It was a chilling thought. For yesterday she had dared to
look happiness in the face, and had found it very sweet.

CHAPTER XXVIII

HER PART

I N the meanwhile, she sent frequently to ascertain news of Ridley's condition. The impulse which had carried her in person to his house was now held in check, lest he should see through the thin disguise of natural concern down to the true spring of her anxiety. The tidings for which she waited so eagerly followed the ordinary course in such affairs. Ridley was recovering with the steady progress to be expected of his healthy constitution, and temperate habits. At the end of a week he had left all chance of a serious illness behind him. At the end of the next he was ready to spend part of each day downstairs, though the office door was still denied him by the orders of his doctor.

When Quenride heard that this stage of recovery had been reached she knew that the time to take action had come. Now that Ridley was on his feet again, and therefore no longer inaccessible, it was not to be thought that Mohun would delay his promised visit, beyond a day or so. With the self-consciousness which lent so deep a significance in her own eyes to her every action with regard to Ridley, Quenride would have shrunk from seeking her own interview in such haste, had the issue been a lesser one. To intrude, unbidden, upon a convalescent, when he had left his room only a few hours before, argued a lack of consideration, if not a disregard of manners. But to the distressed Quenride, the day for a seemly observance of such things appeared to have passed. She would have said that her capacity, if not her appreciation with regard to these, had left her in the moment when she knew herself to be trapped in her cousin's house on the Weymouth downs. She would be fortunate, she told herself, if she could accomplish her object, and leave behind her a man merely wondering at the indecorous haste with which she plunged him into business while the taint of the sick-room was still on him. At best, she would have but a poor excuse to make, a weak reason to offer. She regretted the impassioned style of the note of warning which she had sent. The thought that Ridley might discern a discrepancy between her urgent words and apparently feeble motive set her quivering with an emotion akin to anguish.

She had had time in which to prepare herself, to elaborate some plan. But she had not done so, leaving it to the impulsive incentive of the last moment. On the whole, it had been a time of quiescence, full of rich emotions, and of delirious glimpses of the impossible. A time, if not of development, at least of a deeper realisation. A breathing-space, in which a strange kind of happiness was snatched at, and only held by a defiant disregard of what should happen at the end. It was part of her bewildering experience that every breath which gave fresh strength to the man she loved must necessarily mean the quickening of her own pulses for the sacrifice. As he drew nearer to recovery, so her freedom, her honour, her pride—the things once so precious to her soul—all slipped further away, diminishing until the moment when she should lose them altogether.

On the day when, as she understood, Ridley would be able to see her in private, she drove in to Dorchester, arrived there in the afternoon, and went straight to the house.

At the opening of the door, she made her request in a casual way.

" Mr. Ridley is about again, I understand," she said. " Would it be expecting too much to ask if he could see me for a few moments ? It is not exactly an appointment, but he has promised me an interview as soon as possible."

Mrs. Channing hesitated. She had been given no warning of the beautiful visitor's probable arrival, but if matters were as she half-suspected she ran no risk of reproof by admitting her. Moreover, Ridley had certainly not suffered from a plethora of callers. During the whole time of his confinement, no one had been near him save his friend, Dr. Homer, whose visits, being purely professional, offered no real exception to the general rule. This neglect, especially in a particular quarter, had hurt him more than he cared to show.

He had therefore a dual pleasure in hearing Quenride's message, and expressed his willingness to see her at once.

Mrs. Channing brought her in from the little office where she had waited, and left them alone together.

There was no trace of a casual or perfunctory interest in Quenride's greeting. She moved swiftly across the room, animated and eager. Ridley rose from his place by the fireside, and held out his hand. Her eyes ran up to his face, her own grave and anxious.

" You are better ? " she asked, with a little play of emotion. " Oh, you are better, are you not ? "

" Very nearly well again," he told her. " I hope to be back at work next week."

She took the chair which he placed for her, glad to accept it, for she was trembling a little. She drew off her gloves, and leant forward to the fire. The red glow played over her. Ridley lay back again among his cushions, and found a strange content in the nearness of her presence. It came to him as a foolish fancy that he could wish her to warm her fingers at his fire for ever. Quenride returned his look openly. His face was partly in shadow, but she saw enough to trouble her. He had grown lean in his illness ; there was a super-delicacy about face and hands out of keeping with his sex and calling. He lacked his ordinary alertness of movement. His eyes looked very bright and dark in their pale setting. Quenride noticed all this, and thrust out her hands impulsively.

" Have you forgiven me ? " she asked.

" I have never tried to," he said.

" Then, you have not blamed me ? "

" Miss Chideock," he returned, with a quiet smile, " I have practised for five years, and have, I may say, been in touch with the law all my life, but my prejudices still run in favour of justice. Could I hold you responsible for your cousin's treachery ? "

" I wish," she said a trifle sadly, " that you had listened to me at the first, and kept out of this miserable affair."

With his newly developed sensibility towards her, he had detected the underlying sentiment before she had made the superficial thought known.

" Something fresh has happened ? " he asked. " Something that alarms you ? "

Quenride drew back from the fire-light, lest he should read things which she must keep from him. She answered with a truthful reserve.

" There is no real danger to you, I am glad to say," she

replied. "I was letting my mind dwell, rather foolishly, I admit, on what would have been possible, had I not the power to thwart my cousin's malice."

"Of course," said Ridley, "if his treacherous hint had not been the lie that it was, he would have had the game very much in his own hands."

Quenride shivered.

"But since his subsequent action proved the falsity of his suggestion," Ridley went on, "there is nothing to be alarmed at. We can snap our fingers at him, and dare him to do his worst."

Quenride sat silent. In her heart was a deep pity, not for herself—the last fortnight had taught her better things than that—but because this man's scarred flesh had suffered for her in vain.

Ridley was puzzled; not seriously disturbed by her manner, but conscious, in his super-sensitive state, of an unnatural depression in her. He leant forward, and touched her arm.

"You are worried and anxious still," he said. "Or is it that you have troubled more than you should have done—on my account? If so, I would ask you to forget."

"I shall never do that!" she exclaimed. "Never! As long as I live. Oh, do you think that I have no heart at all?"

"I think," said Ridley, "that the sooner the will is destroyed, and your mind set entirely at rest, the better it will be."

Quenride caught at his words eagerly. She had not expected the lead to come from him.

"That is why I am here," she said. "I have come to ask you to let me have it."

"To let you have it? Now?"

"If you please."

She held her breath, waiting for his answer. He did not give it at once, but lay back thoughtfully, shielding his eyes from the fire-light with his thin hand. Quenride watched him, sick with excitement. Undue eagerness on her part would ruin her plan of salvation. Yet the tension grew with each moment, until every nerve was throbbing with pain.

"Speak, my love, speak!" she would have cried. "Give the accursed thing to me—and let me save you!"

At length, Ridley broke silence, speaking more slowly than usual, and the words were not those which she was hoping to hear. Her request had apparently turned his mind to some side-issue of the matter.

"While I have been upstairs," he said, "I have been thinking a great deal of your affairs, Miss Chideock. I need not say that your cousin's conduct does not improve upon consideration, but I'm not thinking so much of that just now as of a certain curious point which has somehow become fixed in my mind. A sick man's brain, I suppose, must needs twist itself round something. Yet I am by no means certain that it might not have some bearing upon the matter in hand. Indeed, I am so much interested that I believe I shall try to resolve my doubts when I have time, simply for my own satisfaction. If I could succeed in doing this, and my notion should prove to be a correct one, it would make a very neat rounding-off to Mr. Mohun's discomfiture."

"I am afraid," she murmured, "that I am more interested in discomfiting him, than in providing an artistic ending to this most miserable affair."

Ridley laughed.

"Of course you are," he said. "Forgive me for my digression. As you suggest, the most important thing is to get the better of your cousin as soon as possible. And that being so, we'll take the easiest way."

"And that is—?" she breathed.

"To destroy the forgery. There's a good fire. There's no reason why it should not be done at once."

Quenride grew cold in spite of the leaping flames which held her eyes with a certain fascination. Her brain became dazed with seeking for some adequate excuse. If she could prevent it, Ridley should have no finger in this business, beyond the mere act of handing over the will. To keep his name clear, the document, she saw, must not be destroyed at all. It must be produced, to be denounced by herself. To make the confession after Ridley had, either actually or presumably, been implicated in the destruction of the forgery, would be to suggest that he had compounded a felony, and merely to ruin him in another way. As it was, Quenride was conscious of a certain flaw in her plan. But the irregularity of his parting with the will at all, was a clumsiness which she saw no way of getting over. He would never, she felt convinced, deliver it up to Mohun. She could only trust that Mohun himself, in his anxiety to persuade the world that the will, and every circumstance connected with it was in perfect order, would inadvertently shield Ridley here, by declaring that he had obtained it in a legitimate way. Ridley, she knew, for her sake, would not press forward to declare his knowledge of the forgery.

All this she had thought out, as it seemed, long ago. But the train of reasoning ran rapidly through her mind once again, in Ridley's sitting-room that afternoon. She saw him rise, as if conclusions had been arrived at, and still her pulses throbbed, and she could find nothing of value to urge.

" Not here ; not now, I think," she managed to say. " It doesn't seem to me—quite safe."

" We are alone," he returned. She knew that he had noticed her extreme agitation, and the consciousness increased it. " It will be done in a minute."

" Of course," she answered. " But it will leave traces." He smiled down at her.

" That won't harm us," he said indulgently. " I have been sorting out and destroying worthless private letters already. Mr. Mohun can't make much out of a few tindery ashes."

" I think," she said feebly, " that you had better let me do it—at home."

He shook his head, pleasantly yet resolutely, and said :

" I cannot consent to your leaving here with that document in your possession. A hundred chances might deprive you of it on the road. The risk is far too great. You might even meet your cousin."

" It is not likely," she murmured. " I happen to know that he left for Weymouth this morning."

" Forgive me, Miss Chideock," he said, " if I seem obstinate and over-cautious. But I have often thought that the law has been built up largely to guard against the unlikely happenings. The others are so obvious that we know how to avoid them by instinct. My traditions therefore lead me to a deep distrust of a possibility which, as a probability, does not exist. We will throw the will into the fire, and rejoice together."

Her lips opened to cry out " No ! " but the word was not uttered. Her whole figure drooped. Had she ever yet struggled against this man, and come out conqueror ? She saw him cross the room with his languid steps, which nevertheless had such a suggestion of resolution in them, and the tears of a despairing woman wet her eyes. She sprang up, and followed him to the door.

She heard him go into the office, heard the words with

which he sent the clerk out of the room while he opened the secret drawer that she remembered so well.

"Go and get a light, Fiander. I'm going downstairs. I'll give you those papers now."

A moment or so later, he said:

"Will you lend me your arm, Fiander? I'm afraid I can't manage those steps alone."

Quenride pressed her throbbing forehead against the door-post.

"Why didn't he ask for mine?" she thought. "Why didn't he ask for mine?"

She crept back miserably to her chair, and waited, staring at the fire. The only thought in her mind was a foolish wish that it would suddenly go out. It blazed at her in mockery.

Quick steps ran up from the cellar—Fiander, sent off again, with another excuse. Presently, she heard the clanging of the door down below. Ridley ascended slowly, pausing perceptibly when he reached the top. A murmur of voices at the office threshold. Apparently some exchange of papers. Then she heard him returning. She faced round with a quick glance. His hands were empty, but one was already slipping into a pocket.

"I hope I have not been long," he said.

"No," she said listlessly. Her manner of approaching the moment was strangely different from the anticipations of six months ago.

Ridley looked at her curiously as he went back to his seat.

"You are not well," he said. "You told me that you had seen your cousin. Has he been threatening you again? I wanted to ask you what your letter meant."

"No distrust of you," she cried, in haste, for she suddenly dreaded that it might seem so, and that he would be hurt. "I ask you to believe that."

"I never thought of such a thing," he told her. "We should be a poor pair of conspirators, Miss Chideock, if we couldn't trust each other. But you meant something, I think."

"I wrote under the stress of great excitement," she explained vaguely. "You are quite right. My cousin had been rather uncivil. I hope I did not alarm you. You must have thought me hysterical to write as I did."

Ridley considered her words, joined them to her manner, and came to a conclusion. Mohun, he decided, must have threatened further violence against himself. Quenride, with her natural impulsiveness, had wished to warn him against meeting Mohun again. Calmer reflection had shown her the frothiness of her cousin's threats, and she naturally shrank from explaining her own foolishness. So Ridley interpreted her reluctance to enlarge upon the subject, and dismissed the matter as easily as she wished him to do.

"I don't think your cousin can harm either of us any more," he said. "Now, Miss Chideock, with your permission, I am going to burn the document which has given you so much undeserved anxiety."

She held out a hand.

"Please, not here!" she said.

"Again, why not?"

Quenride suddenly laughed.

"For one thing, there's some one coming!" she said.

Ridley had heard the footsteps as soon as she. He was in the act of taking the will from his pocket. Now he thrust it back again.

"Come in!" he called.

Mrs. Channing came in, with a white table-cloth in her hand.

"You'll excuse me, ma'am, I know. But the master must have his meals regular. 'Tis doctor's orders."

"I was just going," said Quenride, at once.

"A great many of the doctor's orders," said Ridley, "exist, I feel certain, solely in Mrs. Channing's mind. Miss Chideock will take a cup of tea before leaving," he added.

"I hope that Mr. Ridley has been a good patient," remarked Quenride, with a smile, as the table was being laid.

Mrs. Channing turned an almost motherly look on her master.

"Fair, as gentlemen go," she said. "You see, ma'am, he's mostly so set on giving no trouble, that he ends by making extry work all round. How do you think he's looking, ma'am?"

"Not as well as I could wish. Though I'm sure he has had the best of nursing."

"She hasn't spared herself," said Ridley, when the two were alone for a moment. "I want to make her some return, and don't know how to do it. A present of some sort, I thought. But for the life of me, I don't know what."

"Try a black satin gown, Mr. Ridley," said Quenride. "There's no woman in the world would refuse that!"

So they talked with superficial lightness, hiding the deeper issues which neither had forgotten.

Then occurred a small incident which went sharply to Quenride's heart, and chilled her sense of their friendliness.

Mrs. Channing had filled a cup with tea and placed it at her side. When Ridley saw the tea-pot being lifted a second time, he checked the housekeeper with a look. And though he left his chair, it was only to hand her a dish of cakes, and to return immediately to his place by the fire. Quenride scarcely knew whether to admire the delicacy of feeling which thus robbed the hospitality of the intimacy of a meal shared in common, or to blame the lack of perception which kept him punctiliously on his own side of the barrier which, at the first, she herself had raised. In the end, she did both. And loved him as well for the one quality as the other. But he had pained her nevertheless, and would have been forgiven the liberty of drinking tea at that moment, had he attempted it.

That such thoughts were running in her mind, he was unaware, for he met her gaze with no sign of self-consciousness. As soon as they were alone, he pulled out the sheet of parchment with Amos Hoddinott's endorsement on the outside, and laid it on his knee. He glanced at her inquiringly.

There came the sound of the front door opening.

"It's only Fiander going out with the letters," said Ridley. "But he shouldn't have left those papers I gave him lying about."

He laid the will down on the table, and rose. Before he had reached the door of the room, it was burst open, and two figures appeared in the passage. The foremost, a tall soldierly-looking man ; in the background, Fiander, who had opened to the visitor as soon as he had caught sight of him through the window. In the slight confusion which now ensued, Quenride possessed herself of the will, and quietly slipped it into her muff.

"My dear Kenelm ! " cried the elderly man, striding into the room, with eyes for no one but the owner of it. "I've only this hour heard of your accident. Why, in Heaven's name, didn't you send to tell me of it ? "

"Why, sir, there were several reasons. It was scarcely important enough for one thing——"

"Not important ! But, good God ! you've suffered. I can see that in your face. What else ? "

"I thought you would hear of it from Homer, or one of the others."

The Governor shook his head.

" That was a shabby way of letting me know."

" Well, sir, to be quite frank, I had no right to believe that you would be interested."

The Governor, who had been holding his hand all this time, dropped it, and pushed him away.

" I'd like to order you a good flogging, Kenelm. You deserve it ; on my soul, you do. How did it happen ? "

" Entirely my own fault, sir. A little care would have prevented it. I ought to have known better."

Quenride was listening, with a flush on her face.

" Please introduce your friend to me," she said.

And so the pair looked into one another's eyes for the first time. The man made no sign of appreciation at sight of Quenride's ripe beauty, but his eyebrows moved slightly when he heard her name, as Ridley introduced her formally as one of his clients.

" Don't let me interrupt you, sir," she said.

" The intrusion is mine, madam," replied the Governor, with the stiff courtesy he used towards women. " But Mr. Ridley is a dear and valued young friend to me, and you will pardon my lack of ceremony just now."

" Very willingly," she returned. " All the more so, as I believe Mr. Ridley has had no reason to complain of his friends' attentions of late."

" Is that so ? " demanded the Governor, swinging round.

" I have not complained," said Ridley, " one way or the other, to Miss Chideock, or to anyone else."

He was watching the two with a quiet amusement, which took his thoughts off the awkwardness of the situation. A passage-of-arms between this man—set in as great authority as the Centurion of old—and the maiden chatelaine of Wareham town, was a form of entertainment which Ridley, of all men, was fitted to enjoy. The Governor turned back to Quenride.

" You think, perhaps, that I have been neglecting Mr. Ridley ? "

" I'd be sorry to believe that 'twas you who set the fashion ! " she returned.

He waved a hand.

" Sit down, Kenelm ! Madam, your servant ! " He handed her a chair, seated himself, and went on. " Allow me to explain. As I said just now, I have only learned, with deep regret, I may add, of the accident. I know no details of it, even now. I can only excuse my ignorance by reminding you that I have had necessary duties to attend to after the recent Assizes." He turned to Ridley. "I missed you in court, of course, but I said to myself, 'He's letting the practice go to the dogs!' and I was too angry at the time to interfere. Still, I meant to look you up sooner or later, and ask you to give an account of yourself."

"My cases went very well," Ridley reminded him.

"I know that. Counsel told me he'd never handled better work on the Western Circuit. There's the makings of a reputation in you—I always said that." The brusque tones softened, and he reached out his hand. "If I had only guessed—if you had sent for me—I shouldn't have allowed you to think all the hard things which you must have been thinking. Homer only let the facts out casually. I damned him for not acquainting me before, and hurried here at once."

"You are very welcome, sir. I hope you can spare me an hour. The evenings are very long."

"They have all left you alone, then?"

Ridley was obliged to admit that they had.

Quenride sprang up.

"Sir," she said, bright-eyed and indignant, "it is useless to pretend not to understand the reason why this gentleman has received so many slights from his friends. It is not a pleasant matter to discuss in his presence. But I wish to take this opportunity of publicly apologising to him for the wrong he suffered at my hands. Mr. Ridley, sir, was entirely guiltless of the rather vulgar offence with which he was charged. The real shame of the affair rested with the woman who, for private reasons—wherein, again, Mr. Ridley was in the right—allowed her sense of justice to go so far astray. My colleague, of course, was entirely influenced by myself. Mr. Ridley, I believe, has forgiven me, but the incident must have caused him great pain, since he was not in the position to clear himself without bringing discredit on me. I beg of you, very earnestly and humbly, to make these facts known."

The Governor stood stiff and silent for a moment when she had finished. Then he turned to Ridley.

"I ask your pardon, Kenelm," he said. "I should have trusted you more. It seems that a man may be in the right, and yet have his own reasons for not saying so."

As the two clasped hands, Quenride made hasty preparations for departure. There was nothing to keep her longer. She felt that things had happened very well for her purpose. Ridley could now do no less than fall in with her proposal to carry the will away. In her heart, she blessed the stern-faced disciplinarian whose coming had released her from some difficulty. Yet she shrank a little from him also, wondering how, and how soon they would meet again.

Ridley dropped the elder man's hand, and they both turned.

"I hope," said the Governor, regarding her with new interest, "that I am not driving you away."

"Indeed, no," she told him, meeting his keen gaze with courage. "My business with Mr. Ridley is finished."

"Would you not prefer to call again, another day?" asked Ridley himself, who knew well enough what she was holding inside her muff.

"I don't see the necessity," she answered. "I think we have settled everything."

"Or I will come over myself as soon as possible," he suggested. "Next week."

"I do not choose to wait till then," she said.

"I shall call, with your permission, all the same."

"By all means. Not too soon, I entreat, for your own sake. My brother has been asking to see you. He sent a message of sympathy by me."

"I shall be glad to renew his acquaintance," said Ridley, as he took the hand which she held out. "And I need hardly say how much your own kind solicitude has been appreciated. Very well. You will see me next week. Good-bye, Miss Chideock. You have your man with you, I think?"

"Williams is driving," she told him. "The road won't be lonely either. There will be plenty of market-carts going home with me."

So their hands fell apart. The sole expression of the thoughts in the mind of each was the lingering look that held their eyes as Quenride turned away. He had given her a very friendly handclasp, but she wished that she could have carried away the touch of his lips on her fingers.

"I trust that I may have the pleasure of seeing you again, madam," said the Governor, with his stiff bow.

"It is not improbable, sir," she returned, her dignity drooping a little under the reflection.

The Governor turned to Ridley, as the door shut her out. Her words had induced an erroneous train of thought. He found his companion standing on the hearth-rug, looking into the fire. A touch on the shoulder roused him, but he said nothing.

" Ah," said the Governor, " I beg your pardon. I'm too inquisitive, I see. You have nothing to tell me."

" Very little, I'm afraid, sir. I hoped for the news from you."

" Ah, my day is nearly over. You don't want to be told of prison cells, and convict ships, I take it. Kenelm, I suppose I was wrong. I thought, from finding the lady here, that some understanding must have bridged over your unpleasantness. And a foolish thought came to me that the understanding might be of a more intimate nature than appeared. The lady's last words somehow encouraged the notion."

Ridley rang the bell, and ordered in some fresh tea before replying. His manner had a quiet deliberation in it. It was plain that he did not resent the other's words.

" Miss Chideock is a client of mine, and a friend," he said, at length. " You must not imagine that she is anything more."

" It has taken you a long time to come to that conclusion," returned the other drily. " Well, I'll not force your confidence. I scarcely deserve it, after my recent treatment of you."

" Don't think that, sir. Very well, then, since you press me, you shall have it. I do love her ; but she doesn't suspect it, and I doubt very much if I shall ever tell her. So it's not interesting to anyone but myself."

A shade of anxiety set the Governor's stern features into even grimmer lines than usual.

" Is it as bad as that, Kenelm ? " he asked, his hand on the young man's shoulder.

" As what, sir ? I have told you precisely how the matter stands——"

" The lady's affections are already engaged ? Is that what you mean ? "

" That's a question I can't answer," said Ridley. " It may very well be so."

" But, if you are not certain, what, in God's name, holds you back ? I should have thought, with your damnably heretical notions about the equality of mankind, the difference between your families wouldn't have troubled you."

" It is not that, sir."

" Then what else can it be ? Surely you don't pay her the poor compliment of supposing she's inspired love that's not worth offering ? Don't let your diffidence ruin two lives. Your record is a clean one. No man can raise his tongue against you."

"That's perfectly true, sir. But you haven't touched my reason yet."

" I'd be glad to hear it then ! "

" The fact is," said Ridley, " I have had the happiness of being of some service to Miss Chideock, and dare not risk taking advantage of her gratitude. She is impulsive and very generous. Only a special dispensation of circumstances could induce me to speak to her just yet."

The elder man looked at him, with a slight lowering of the veil which habitually hid his more human sentiments.

" I don't say that you are not right from your point of view," he said, after a pause. " But don't wait too long. Give the girl a chance ! Your interests are very dear to me. I should be sorry to know that you had missed—your best desire ! "

Ridley, with his swift perception of incongruities, and his appreciation of them, was struck with a sense of the contrast formed by Quenride Chideock and her grim champion. But a short time afterwards, when a fuller revelation of the hidden irony of the situation came to him, the memory of the words set his own face into lines as rigid and suggestive as those of the man who had uttered them.

CHAPTER XXIX

TWO AND TWO ARE FOUR

TWICE Fiander had approached his employer with an open letter in his hand, and twice he had retired without saying a word. An hour ago, he had been dismissed to the smaller office, while a client enjoyed a confidential interview with the lawyer himself. The consultation, or whatever it was, had not been of long duration. At the end of fifteen minutes or so, the visitor had left the house, and the clerk had been recalled. Fiander was not given to speculating as to other people's business—being wisely content to attend to his own, and to leave the rest in his employer's hands—but on this occasion he did wonder what the florid-faced gentleman had said to make his late companion look and behave as he subsequently did.

Three-quarters of an hour ago, Ridley had taken his place before his table, and since then he had not raised his head. His hands were idle and empty, his gaze fixed upon a sheet of blotting-paper with an intentness which suggested nothing so much as concentration upon a page of cipher.

At his second attempt at communication, Fiander had a sight of the other's face. He crept softly away, honestly troubled—for only some great happening, he knew, could make a man look so.

Presently he left his place to mend the fire. Glancing over his shoulder as he did it, he found that the clatter had roused Ridley to some sort of appreciation of his presence. He dropped the fire-irons, rushed to his desk, and seized the debatable letter. This time he succeeded in detaching Ridley's attention for a few moments. The point was one easily settled.

" Anything else ? " asked Ridley.

" The letters are ready for the signatures, sir."

" Bring them here."

As Ridley put down the pen, he said :

" Don't interrupt me again, if you can help it. I am very busy this morning. Fiander, what do two and two make ? "

Fiander stared.

" Four, as a rule, sir," he said, at last.

" Ah, as a rule. But suppose, after all your adding, it comes out something quite different ? When I was an unbreeched youngster at a dame school, I had a firm conviction that it was *three*. But I was smacked so often for saying so, that I gave in at length to popular opinion, and have held it to be *four* ever since. It ought to be four ; everything points to it being four. And yet, supposing it shouldn't be ? "

Fiander went back to his work, and Ridley pursued his task of mental arithmetic uninterrupted.

Mohun had come and gone. The result of his brief visit had been to turn confidence into trepidation, security into alarm. The man had stated his case with brutal frankness. He had begun with a half-insolent assurance, and had ended with plain threats. Throughout the interview, Ridley himself had scarcely spoken more than a dozen sentences. From the moment when Mohun had made declaration of his proof of the will's existence, Ridley had realised the strength of his adversary's hand.

There was no chance that the man was speaking empty words. He proved his sincerity by quoting passages from Ridley's letters to Quenride. Accustomed to facing facts, and not to playing with them, Ridley accepted the situation in all its suggested hatefulness, accepted also the short reprieve which Mohun allowed him, and bowed his visitor out, with scant civility.

He had been given precisely two days in which to decide whether he would defy Alaric Mohun, and so bring ruin down upon his own head, or whether he would betray Quenride's interests, and by handing up the will place both the estate and Gilbert Chideock's welfare in Mohun's covetous grasp.

" I'm not prepared to make any statement at present," he had said firmly. " You must call again."

To which Mohun had replied by the offer of two days in which to make up his mind.

" You'll have to give in ; you know you will," he said. " But I'll give you two days to get used to the idea, because you're a sort of gentleman, and not the white-livered knave I pretended to think you, and because I'm so damned sure of

winning this case. There's no use in your putting your head
to my pretty cousin's to try to discover a way out. I've got
you both like—that! And Quenny knows it as surely as
you do. I've had a talk with her already. She knows she's
only got the house she lives in, and a beggarly thousand or so
of her own. I daresay she'd be glad enough to marry me now
for the sake of the fortune, and to be near that homespun
brother of hers. She's not without points, after all. I might
take pity on her—I shall see."

If he had hoped to rouse his companion by the suggestion,
he might have spared his pains, for Ridley heard him with
inflexible muscles.

"And do you start your courting at once, Mr. Mohun?"
he asked.

"Lord, no!" was the reply, given with a spontaneity
which suggested that the man was so far indicating his purpose
without deception. "She'll have to run after me before I run
after her. I'll not go near her until I've got something to
show the pretty dear. She'll be in suspense until she knows
what you're going to do, won't she?"

"So will you, I take it," said Ridley, who was now fairly
certain of what he wanted to know.

At this, Mohun had laughed, reiterated his expectation of
an easy triumph in the matter of the will, and had taken
himself off, with a quiet boastfulness. And Ridley sat down
to wrestle with the problem alone.

Like a wise man, he took encouragement by first thinking
of the few points in his favour. They were, in truth, very few.
But he had managed to get Mohun's assurance—which, on
the whole, he was inclined to believe—that he would not
attempt to see Quenride until after his next interview with
himself. And he had a couple of days, in which surely something might be done.

Mohun's reason for granting the breathing-space was not
hard to find. Ridley, grateful for it from any cause, knew that
it proceeded less from Mohun's appreciation of his adversary's
character than from his conviction that compliance would
follow upon a lengthy reflection. He apparently would prefer
not to be obliged to use extreme measures—not to have to
challenge the production of the will, but to have it put into his
hands in the ordinary way. Two days' consideration of the
hopeless position would reduce Ridley, then, to submission,
and save himself some trouble.

"Whereas," reasoned Ridley, "if I had made a prompt

refusal, as he fancied I might do, if pressed to decide at once, he would have been compelled to invoke the law to his aid."

It was clear that Mohun had no suspicion that the matter no longer rested with Ridley himself.

" Thank God for that ! " he said.

Quenride's whole action now lay before him in its self-sacrificing integrity. He understood both her motive and purpose. In this he was guided by the remembrance of her anxiety to convey the forgery out of his reach. Her agitated letter, never fully explained, was now accounted for. Ridley had no doubt that her solution of the new complexity was a full confession of her innocent guilt, and the possible sacrifice of her own fair body.

" But it shan't be ! " he said to himself. " Not if I can help it—no ! By God, it shan't ! "

And it was this determination which gave to his face the look that puzzled his clerk ; and set him to the putting of two and two together, in the hope that the result would prove to be the desired *four*.

But there was a little ground to be cleared before he could settle unreservedly to the task. What was Quenride doing ? Waiting, apparently, until Mohun should make his next move. A week had passed since she had carried off the will. He had heard of nothing. Therefore, she had not yet spoken. Ridley saw that, if salvation could possibly come to her, her strength was to sit still. Would she continue her silence for another two days ? He believed that she would, but lest a sudden impulse should sway her he sent an urgent message, desiring her to take no action until he had seen her again. He gave no specified reason for the request, merely stating that he believed he had discovered a weak spot in the other side, which he trusted to investigate shortly.

Then he plunged deeply into the real matter.

The point upon which he was building up his case was the ascertained fact that on the twentieth of last February, the day of his uncle's death, Mr. Benjamin Chideock had summoned the old lawyer to his house at Wareham.

By itself, the fact was paltry enough. But so a foundation stone may appear before an elaborate pile rests upon it.

Ridley had thought the matter over during his convalescence, finding in it not only interest, but a certain amount of convincing evidence. There being, until this morning, no absolute necessity for sifting it thoroughly, he had laid it by on the shelf of future possibilities. Now he carefully tested

every point anew. He laid the little diary before him, and
read once more the last entry :—

February 20.—*Very unwell. Should have been at Mr. B.
Chideock's, who sent for me. Deputed Hoddinott (sober for
once, being his annual holiday) to ascertain the message for me,
and to return at once if necessary. Bridge being repaired,
I hear—so warned him . . .*

Two factors stood out clearly. The dead lawyer had
linked them together ; the girl Sophy, in that strange story
of hers, had joined them so suggestively that new prominence
was given to them in the written words. Amos Hoddinott and
the bridge.

Had the old fellow retained his wits sufficiently to fulfil his
errand to Mr. Chideock ? Had he returned, as provisionally
instructed ? Much hung upon that. Fortunately, the means
of ascertaining the fact was at hand. Ridley sent for the
housekeeper.

" You remember the day when my uncle died ? " he said.

" Perfectly, sir."

" Was the clerk Hoddinott here at the time ? "

" Not in the house, sir. He'd left the same morning, to
go on his holiday. He'd been giving the master a deal of
trouble with his ways, and I think he was glad to be quit of
him for a while."

" He'd not returned, later in the day, and left again ? "

" Oh, no, sir."

" You're quite sure of that ? "

" Positive, for he couldn't have done it without my
knowing. I'd no maid in the house then, so I'd have had
to let him in myself. He came back as soon as he heard the
news, but not for a day or so. And then he was half-dazed
like."

" He'd been drinking a good deal about that time, I understand ? "

" More'n usual," said the housekeeper, " no sense left in
him at all."

" Scandalous ! " said Ridley, with unusual vehemence.
" Thank you, Mrs. Channing, that is all."

He plunged anew into his calculations.

Whatever message had been sent, whatever business
conducted, no word of it then had ever reached the old lawyer.
The diary, though suggesting as much, was not conclusive,

since there might have been much to add to the unfinished entry. Now, which was it—had a mere verbal message been given, or had anything more tangible passed between client and clerk ? If the former, then Quenride was hapless indeed. But if the latter—what ?

Another entry in the diary showed that, a fortnight or so before, Mr. Chideock had consulted his lawyer with regard to the sale of some land at Warminster ; the very land which had aroused Mohun's cupidity, and the ownership of which Quenride had believed herself to be tampering with, when she signed the spurious will. Ridley was alive to the possibility that Hoddinott's interview with the old gentleman might either have represented a mere instruction to sell or a yielding to the grandson's importunities, evidenced by the preparation of a deed of gift.

" It's more than possible," he told himself honestly. " It's most damnably probable. But there's just a chance that it was a little more important than either of these suppositions. Now, how do I make that out ? "

If Mr. Chideock had merely desired to instruct Thomas Ridley to place the land on the market, there was no urgent, or even very apparent need why he should have sent for the lawyer in person. A written authority would have sufficed. Again, at the time, he was on unfriendly terms with his grandson, even to the extent of forbidding him the house. Could such a state of things be reconciled with a wish on the old man's part to bestow on Mohun the gift he coveted ? If a genuine pacification of the elder man's anger had been established in Quenride's absence, she would have heard of it from her faithful servants. After a little more sifting of the facts, Ridley thought that all these hypotheses might be dismissed as untenable. Cleared of encumbrance, the case stood thus : Hoddinott had gone to Mr. Chideock's on some important business ; he had not returned to fetch the lawyer himself, either he had managed the business alone or his fatal habits had once more interfered with his duty.

This last was exceedingly probable. Ridley would have admitted it as fairly well evidenced fact, but for two circumstances. If Amos had drunk himself ill anywhere between Wareham and Dorchester, he would have been conveyed back to his employer's by friendly hands. And he had not been so conveyed. The inference was that he had left the house with no intention of postponing his holiday, and that, however much he had subsequently indulged, he had retained his w.ts sufficiently to enable him to proceed as originally arranged.

The second circumstance was more interesting still. It brought Ridley into touch with personal experience. His mind ran back to the day of Sophy's blackberrying. Mentally, he looked again at the sunny garden, the bench under the apple-tree, where he had waited while the girl prepared the meal. At the other end of it, Amos Hoddinott, maudlin and drink-sodden, striking feeble hands on the seat, and crying out, " I can't find it ! I can't find it ! " with the mournful reiteration of the doting.

The cry, so Sophy had assured him, had been ever in the old man's mouth since he had left his employment. Apparently, the implied loss was one which had occurred during his time of service. Since he was hardly the type of man to have any interests beyond those of his master's office, it might be presumed that the loss had relation to these.

By itself, this hypothesis would have formed no very clear evidence that Amos received from Mr. Chideock some letter or document on that last day of the old lawyer's life, or that he had subsequently lost or mislaid such a paper.

But again Ridley was helped to an assumption by his personal knowledge of later facts.

What was it that had drawn the old man to Wareham Bridge on that evening when his grand-niece had followed him ? What connection was dimly recognised by his crazy old brain, as he swung his lanthorn along the wall ? What had occasioned his lamentable cry at the end of his scrutiny ?

Surely a man might grasp at a solution without incurring the charge of romanticism ? Surely there was more to guide him than his own desire and eager imagination ? Ridley pulled himself up, and very cautiously allowed that imagination to reconstruct the case. Seen through that medium, it was slightly fantastic, but by no means improbable, considering the nature of the circumstances. Thus he reasoned : Mr. Benjamin Chideock, threatened by repeated illness, and being on very bad terms with his elder grandson, decided at length to make his will. He summoned his lawyer, but was served only by the clerk. The document, nevertheless, was properly drawn up, signed and witnessed, and delivered to the lawyer's representative, who might, or might not have left the house with the intention of conveying it at once to his employer. In either case, he had not done so. He had lingered in the town to indulge his favourite vice of drinking, had muddled his wits sufficiently to retain only a dim sense of his responsibility, and had set off for the cottage near Corfe. Passing by necessity over the bridge, at that time undergoing repair, a crazy notion had occurred to his mind, probably appealing to him as a very brilliant one. The disordered masonry had suggested a means of ridding himself of his encumbrance at no cost to its security. Taking his opportunity —perhaps the workmen were at dinner in an adjoining meadow, or were absent altogether that day—he secreted the paper in a cranny formed by the removal of some of the stones, unmindful of the fact that by the time he returned that way the stones would be replaced, and the paper inaccessible.

With his return to comparative sobriety, all remembrance of the performance became obliterated. His mind had been filled with the news of his employer's death ; then had come his own retirement, and the cessation of all interest in legal matters. He had sunk, as far as his faculties were concerned, into premature decay. But across his darkened intelligence there glimmered, at times, a distressful sense of something left undone, finally resolving itself into a fixed appreciation of loss. But without some outside stimulus he was incapable of realising more. For months, that stimulus had been wanting. But with his discovery of Quenride's locket the link was supplied. Here was another treasure of value lying in his hands. Too precious to keep, too priceless to lose, what should he do with it ? Where hide it, that his niece might not, in her turn, spy it out ?

As a man under the influence of somnambulism will involuntarily repeat a former action, so Amos Hoddinott had recalled, in his misty way, the previous hiding-place. Some association had been touched. He babbled of the Chideocks all day, and at night set out for the bridge that he might lay the new treasure with the old responsibility.

Had Ridley been aware of the portrait within the locket, exposed by Sophy's wrenching open of the lid, he would, at this point, have grasped his connections even more forcibly than he did.

The bridge offered no hiding-place this second time. Search as he would along its surface, there was no crack nor cranny which might hold his prize. His bitter disappointment had culminated in an abandonment to grief. The loss of the locket had been accidental. The shock of his defeated

expectations had been too much for his weak wits, thereby
proving his salvation to some extent. After the first strain
of endurance had passed, a numbed blank had ensued. He
had returned quietly home, and had probably forgotten
locket and document alike by now.

"And is there anything at all unfeasible in all that?"
Ridley demanded of himself. "Should I care to carry such
a case into court? Would I stake my reputation on the
issue? Am I sound? So far, I've got no actual proof. But
even that ought not to be impossible. The document, whatever it was, was a finished one when Amos went off with it.
Otherwise, Mr. Chideock would scarcely have set out for
Leicestershire the next day. And I had it from Quenride that
he did. For she returned on the twenty-second of the month,
to find that he had left home the preceding day. Now, a
signed document means witnesses. So, who were those witnesses?"

The servants naturally were suggested. At such a time,
a man reasonably would select the most trusted. The lower
domestics probably could not write. But how was it the
knowledge of such a transaction had not come to Quenride?
All three of the upper servants had been in the secret of the
old man's death—a fact in itself conducive to confidence
towards their young mistress. Yet Quenride knew nothing.

It was at this point that Ridley's calculations threatened
to work out to the undesired answer. Quenride's ignorance
was a stumbling-block, a more serious one than Amos's
apparent neglect, when asked to draw the genuine will, to
mention the spurious one. Being always more or less in
liquor at this period, he was unlikely to retain any clear recollection of the work he managed to do. And his share in
the former will had not gone beyond the endorsing of the
cover.

But those witnesses? If they had, in truth, been chosen
from the subsequently dismissed servants, how long, in
Heaven's name, would it take to hunt them up? More than
two days. And the first one was nearly gone. He looked
up with a start, to find that it was growing dusk. He had
wrestled with the problem for the greater part of the working
day.

Fiander was lighting candles at the other side of the room.
The rays illuminated his face, and showed it to be unusually
grave, even sorrowful. Ridley might have been thought
scarcely in the mood to take heed of lesser interests than those

which had held his brain for the past hours. But the brain
itself was tired, for his ordinary work still came a little hardly
to him. He was ready for the relief afforded by a momentary
change of thought. Moreover, the lad had won his regard.
He threw a careless query across the room, asking what was
wrong.

"Nothing," said Fiander. "That is—well, 'tisn't my affair,
sir."

"What isn't?"

Fiander showed a pink countenance over the candles.
But he needed no second questioning.

"'Tis about Miss Pouncey," he said.

"Well? What's happened? Going to be married?"

"I don't think so. But she's gone home. I heard of it
down town at dinner-time."

"And that's what's making you look so dismal?"

"She's gone there for good, sir."

"The best place too, I should say! Do you mean that
she's left Miss Chideock?"

"Yes, sir. Just think of her at the farm. She'll hate it
horribly, after being so long with gentlefolks."

"Don't worry," said Ridley. "She'll soon settle down.
After all, she's not been at Wareham very long, has she?"

"She went on the third of April," said Fiander, with a
lover's accuracy.

Ridley's mind fell into the old habit. The third of April.
That must have been soon after Quenride's return from her
grandfather's deathbed. He remembered that the girl's
residence had been decided upon before that date. Quenride
had declared that even the trivial incidents of that time were
fixed in her memory. She had said—good God! what had
she said?

The next moment, Fiander was surprised by a tremendous
blow struck upon the writing-table. He glanced round to find
Ridley risen to his feet, with a look of exultation in his eyes.

"I've got it!" he cried, aloud. "Fiander, the old school-
dame was right after all! Two and two are four! There's
not a piece that doesn't fit. The case is as perfect as it
possibly can be. There's good work for you!"

He walked to the window and stared at nothing. Quenride's words rang through his head.

"Her father and mother came to make arrangements
two days before I returned from Weymouth." On the day,
in fact—since Quenride had returned on the twenty-second

of February—when Amos had visited Mr. Chideock, and
witnesses were required at the signing of a document.

Pouncey was a tenant on the estate, respectful where the
family were concerned, and on good terms with his landlord.
His opportune arrival would render gossip among the servants
unnecessary.

" I'm a worse lawyer than I think myself," said Ridley,
inwardly, " if the Pounceys weren't called up to do the
business. But I'll go over to Medley's Croft to-morrow to
make sure ! "

CHAPTER XXX

HIS SHADOW

THE next morning found him riding towards the farm with a greater zest in life than he had felt since his illness. There was some courage in this, for at the back of his mind there lurked a shadow which for the time he refused to face. A shadow ugly enough to have made some men pause ; but Ridley went on.

Medley's Croft lay a few miles further up the valley of the Frome. It was a prosperous holding, situated snugly in a rich dairy country. Generations of Pounceys had rented it of innumerable Chideocks, but, since the predecessors of each tenant had not tried to make it personal property, the successor had no desire to possess it for his own. Like father, like son, was more than a truism in rural Dorset. It was a religious principle.

It was a mild dull day of early winter when Ridley first set eyes on the place. Moisture hung upon the denuded branches of the trees, and caked together the sodden leaves under his horse's hoofs. A half-melancholy, half-pleasant stillness was in the air. More placid than the drowsy hush of midsummer noon, it was the quietude of a no less gracious mood. Nature was quiescent, but wakeful still. The year was declining softly, in a mild grey haze that deepened towards nightfall, but was perceptible at far distances in the middle of the day. As, with the rising of the sap, fresh activities come into prominence, so thought rather than action befits this season of the year. Yet, impressed with this consciousness, Ridley pushed forward to the consummation of the most stirring episode of his life.

The farm-house itself was a decadent manor-house, and, as such, presented an appearance superior to what Ridley had expected. A short double avenue of elms led up to the front door, ending in a small paved yard, formed by the two projecting wings that ran out on either side of the main block.

The windows were mullioned, the roof high-pitched, the lintel an ornamented one of carved stone-work. Dairies, stables, and other outposts of a farmer's residence were invisible from this quarter; and, as a consequence, no one was in sight.

Ridley rode up and rattled on the door. It was presently opened by Mrs. Pouncey herself. The young man in the porch was a stranger to her. She began to draw down her sleeves and to pull off her apron in his full sight.

" Mrs. Pouncey, I believe ? " he said.

" Yes ; I be."

" Can I have a few words with you ? " asked Ridley.

He had dismounted, and, throwing the reins over a hook set for the purpose at the side of the door, now stepped forward to enter.

" Who med you be ? " inquired Mrs. Pouncey, and then turned to peer into the obscurity behind her, with a " What's that you say, Dolly ? "

" What name, if you please ? " she asked, then.

But before he could reply, Dolly herself darted past her mother, holding out her hand.

" Please come in, Mr. Ridley," she cried. " You've taken us rather unaware. But who was to expect callers so early in the day ? "

" Is't a friend o' yours, my dear ? " asked the mother timidly, as Ridley came in to the large flagged hall.

" Yes ; and of Miss Chideock," said Dolly, pleased to make the addendum.

" Then I'm sure we be pleased to see you, sir," said Mrs. Pouncey. " 'Tis the master you'll be wanting to speak with, I reckon."

Dolly, who had succeeded in heading her mother off from the kitchen, now piloted the visitor safely into the best parlour —a chilly apartment savouring of leather and disuse. Behind his back, she frowned at her mother a little aggressively.

" I wanted a word or so," explained Ridley, " with both you and your husband, if you please."

" Oh, certainly, sir," murmured the abashed woman. " You'll—you'll be Miss Chideock's cousin, won't 'ee ? Him as my Dolly has talked of. I didn't rightly catch the name."

" I'm sorry," said Ridley. " No. I haven't the honour you suppose. I'm Miss Chideock's lawyer—that's all. My name's Ridley, of Dorchester."

Mrs. Pouncey turned a blank look on her daughter.

" The gentleman who took your father's twenty-five pounds ! " she stammered.

Ridley laughed, chiefly because Dolly was looking so confused.

" It's only information I want this time, however," he said. " Perhaps we needn't trouble Mr. Pouncey, after all. It's a very simple matter."

" I—I dursen't go into law business without the master knowing," she protested. " He's terr'ble strict."

" You can tell me what I want to know, and no harm done. Some time last February, I understand, you and your husband went to Wareham to arrange about this young lady's acting as companion to Miss Chideock ? "

" Yes," she admitted uneasily.

" Don't be a goose, mother," muttered Dolly. " Of course you did."

" The lady was from home," pursued Ridley. " Now, whom did you see ? "

" Several folk."

" Including Mr. Benjamin Chideock himself ? "

" Well, sir, I'll not deny it. But I do wish——"

" Oh, you're not compromising yourself, I assure you. Was Mr. Chideock alone when you saw him ? "

" I s'pose I must answer ? "

" Indeed, you must. Was he alone ? "

" Not—exactly."

" Now we're getting at it ! " exclaimed Ridley, with inward satisfaction. " Not alone. Then who was with him ? "

But the farmer's wife was shrewd enough to see his relish for what she was saying, and ignorant enough to be suspicious of it. She found herself in an awkward position, and was not strong enough to endure it alone. On one side was her daughter, frowning at her apparent incivility ; on the other a prejudiced remembrance that her questioner was a man whose rascality, as her husband affirmed, had cost her a store of household linen and a new silk dress. Not another answer could Ridley get out of her. In truth, he scarcely tried. It was never his way to waste time on one ineffective method when another was at hand. In this instance, Mrs. Pouncey took the words out of his mouth.

" Dolly," she said, " run and fetch your father—do ! He'll be able to answer the gentleman better nor me."

Dolly moved off slowly.

" I'm sure, sir," went on her mother anxiously, " I don't

want to seem uncivil, but I shouldn't like to vex the master. And, seeing as you're my Dolly's friend, we'd take it as an honour, I'm sure, if you'd stay and have a bite with us. 'Tis close on dinner-time, and there's a nice bit of boiled brisket and taties you couldn't beat in all Darset. And Dolly'll fry you up some pancakes, if you do say the word."

Dolly breathed heavily, and threw an appealing glance at the visitor. She knew how that dinner would be served up. Moreover, she had no intention of scorching her cheeks over the fire for his benefit. Before she went to call her father, she had the satisfaction of hearing Ridley excuse himself from accepting the proffered hospitality. Mrs. Pouncey sat on the edge of a chair and said nothing. The young man waited expectantly by the window. The farmer came in, slightly ruffled from an altercation with his daughter —who had been worsted—regarding the wearing of a coat over his bare arms.

"Well," he demanded, when he saw who his visitor was, "what d'ye want? My house be for honest men, not for rogues like ye."

"I've come like an honest man, haven't I?" said the other, reassuring Dolly with his eyes.

"Ah, all the better for ye. If I'd ca'ght ye sniffing round, ye'd ha' left less smug than ye came. What? Squinting at my maid, are ye? Think I'm a warm man, I reckon, and would like to feed your starved money-bags wi' my guineas. Pretty son-in-law you'd be!"

"Father!"

"Be off, baggage! Out wi' you! 'Tes no manner o' use——"

"Listen to me!" interrupted Ridley. "I came on a matter of business, and since my presence annoys you so much it's to your interest to help me to get through it as soon as possible."

"Speak out, then. I can't waste all day over knaves of your kidney."

Ridley then put to the farmer the same questions that Mrs. Pouncey had already been asked. When he came to the one whereat she had stumbled, Pouncey replied:

"No. He wa'n't alone. That wold starvecrow of a Amos Hoddinott was wi' him. Sober as a judge, an' as solemn as a owl. And half a hour a'terwards so mizzy as a weathercock on a starmy day."

"Ah!" said Ridley. "Now, how came you to be

there while Mr. Chideock was engaged with some one else ?
Wouldn't it have been better manners to wait ? "

Pouncey flared up—much as his questioner had intended.

" Be you come then," he demanded, " to l'arn manners
to me, as had my hands harned from the plough afore you
knew your mother from your daddy ? Manners, says he ?
I tell 'ee, I shouldn't ha' been in wi' the Squire and
Amos if me and the mis'ess hadn't been told to. ' Tell
Mr. Pouncey an' his wife,' says the wold gentleman—
Mr. Pouncey, mark ye, not Pouncey, nor Farmer Pouncey,
but Mr., same as he'd ha' spoke o' you—' to step up for
a moment,' says he. So up we do step, and where's the
harm done, pray ? "

" That depends," said Ridley, " on what happened next."

" Seems to me," grumbled the farmer, " that you want
to know too much."

" Not at all," said the other, with an irritating easiness.
" I am only wondering whether, by any chance, Mr. Chideock
called you both in to witness his signature to a paper of some
sort."

Pouncey stared. The suggestion had been made so unexpectedly that the notion of refusing to give any information
slipped out of his mind. He looked at his wife.

" Lard love 'ee ! " he gasped. " How do the man know
that ? "

" Of course you didn't refuse ? " Ridley went on at once.

" Why shouldn't we oblige a gentleman in such a simple
way ? " asked the farmer. " Yes, we did sign for en ;
though the mis'ess, she made a rare to-do about setting her
slammicky writin' alongside gentlefolks'."

" Oh, she's too modest," said Ridley. " Now, Mr.
Pouncey, after you'd all signed, did you see what was done
with that paper ? "

" Ay. Amos Hoddinott grabbed it, and stowed en away
next his lean ribs. That be all I know."

All ! Yet surely it was enough. Ridley felt the blood
rising to his face, and breathed with parted lips. All ! Yet
so much. Here then was the last link set in its place. The
strength of the whole chain might now be tested.

" There's just one other thing," he said. " Did you
happen to notice what the paper was about ? "

" No, I didn't. I don't set up to be a scholard, an' I
bain't ashamed o' it. I can write my own name, an' read
t'other chaps' on the tilts o' their waggons, an' that be all.

An' there bain't a better farmer going, whatever you med say. As to all this readin' an' writin', 'tis sendin' the country straight to the Wold Un. Tar'ble little bit o' good in it that I can see! Look at our maid there! If I'd had my way, she'd ha' gone to school in the dairy, an' l'arnt her letters in the henhouse. But the mis'ess must have her eddicated, and her head filled wi' book-l'arning nonsense. Finishin'-school at Weymouth, an' all the rest o' it! And what do the result be? Her feyther and mother bain't good enough for she; an' she bain't good enough, it do seem, for the gentry. Here she be, turned back on our hands, no good for naught. Turns cream sour if she do set a finger on the churn, and spoils every batch o' bread she do bake. As for her pies—a man med swaller 'em an' never feel a bit the fuller for all he'd crammed down his gullet. Give me some'at as I can stick my teeth into like a Briton! Eddication be danged!"

"For my part," said Ridley, not without sympathy for Dolly, who seemed as much at home here as an exotic in a cowshed, "I look forward to a day when every child will be taught to read and write by law."

"Do 'ee now? One thing's sure, I reckon. You'll not live to see it!"

"Oh, I hope so."

"No. No, ye won't. Ye'll be hanged for a rogue long afore that day!"

Ridley laughed, but only after a slight pause.

"Ay," said the other, "ye'd better ha' been scaring crows at five an' hoein' turmuts at ten, same as I were, than bein' eddicated up to lie an' cheat, like as ye hev' been. It pays to be plain an' honest in the long-run, and so ye'll find."

Ridley turned to the woman.

"Did you read anything of the paper, ma'am?" he asked.

"Me, sir? No! Leastways, I hope it wasn't wrong just to peep——"

"No harm at all! What did you see?"

"Not much," murmured Mrs. Pouncey faintly. "Only, I can mind just reading young Mr. Gilbert's name."

"Thank you," said Ridley, with a heartiness which was a poor exponent of his inward feelings. "I'm much obliged to you both, and I'll not keep you any longer."

He bowed to each in turn, and the farmer escorted him to the door of the house. Dolly, driven off by her father, had not returned. But Ridley was not much surprised to find

her waiting for him at the end of the avenue. He reined
up, and looking at her saw that she had been crying. There
was no doubt that the girl was miserable.

"I heard you'd left Wareham," he said a little awkwardly, for Dolly did not speak.

"Yes."

"Got tired of it?" he suggested.

"I'm tired of—this!" she burst out. "I wish you
hadn't come!"

"Oh, you mustn't mind that. I go into all kinds of
homes. You ought to be happy here."

"Happy! Would you be? No one to speak to but
farm-hands, and all the things you know counted as nonsense,
and all the hateful things you can't do thrown in your face at
every turn! Oh, it's horrid; and I'd as soon be dead!"

"Not yet, I think?" said Ridley.

"Almost," amended Dolly.

"You wish you were back with Miss Chideock, then?"

"No, indeed, I don't! I wouldn't go back for anything,
after the way——"

"Sure it wasn't your fault?" he insinuated.

Dolly looked down.

"Of course not! You're rather unkind. Everybody's
unkind to me; I don't know why. Well, at any rate, I
really wasn't so much to blame as she thought, only she
wouldn't hear reason, and I couldn't get other people into
trouble, could I?"

"Oh," said Ridley thoughtfully, "it's like that, is it?"

"Well?" said Dolly.

"It's a pity you don't want to go back, because I might
have been able to manage it for you. Still, what's to be
done?"

"I don't know," said Dolly miserably.

"Why don't you get married?"

"Mr. Ridley! As if I'd ever thought of such a thing!"

"I beg your pardon. That's my mistake. There's
Fiander, now. An excellent young fellow. He'd eat your pie-
crust, and think it was made in Heaven. He's devoted to you."

Dolly stared away across the misty fields.

"He doesn't seem very devoted at present," she murmured.
"He hasn't been near me. I call it most unfeeling."

"He's only just heard that you're here," said the peace-
maker. "Besides, your father hasn't precisely encouraged
him to call."

11

Dolly answered with spirit.

" I don't think much of a young man who wants en-couragement from a father when he knows—some one else would be pleased."

" Ah," said Ridley, " but does Fiander know that ? Have you ever told him ? "

Dolly was silent. The horse moved forward of his own accord. She walked at the side. When a few yards had been covered, she spoke.

" I couldn't marry Robin," she said. " He's not earning enough."

"Three-and-twenty shillings a week I give him," said Ridley. " And I should increase it, of course, if he married. But you're both so young that he'll be earning much more by the time you ought to think of it."

" What ? And I stay here, till then ? " cried Dolly, dismayed. " I don't see that Robin's too young," she added thoughtfully. " He's a full year older than I am."

" It's a matter for yourselves," said Ridley tersely, staring ahead.

" I suppose," said the girl, then, " you wouldn't like to speak to Miss Quenride for me ? "

" I've no liking, one way or the other," said Ridley. " But I thought you said——"

Dolly sighed.

" You're as unkind as the rest ! " she exclaimed pettishly. " And I won't go back—there now ! "

A smile began to quiver at Ridley's mouth.

" Perhaps, on the whole, you'd better not," he said. " It wouldn't be judicious, I think, for me to help you."

" Why not ? " she asked.

" On Fiander's account ! " he said.

He set his horse to the trot, and rode off laughing without any formal leave-taking. But presently he looked back to wave a farewell, and saw Dolly standing there as if still wondering what his last words meant.

The laugh died in his throat. He pushed forward alone. Dolly's little pseudo-tragedy would work itself out to a happy ending. For himself, the black shadow was coming very near.

He reached home as Fiander was returning to the house for the afternoon's work.

" You look tired, sir," said the lad.

" Yes. I am ; a little. Come here, Fiander."

They went into the office together. Ridley sat down at his

table. Fiander waited. There was a long pause. Ridley passed his hand over his eyes, and roused himself.

"You've had a busy time lately," he said. "I daresay you've found me a sharp master, but I'm not insensible to the fact that you've served me well. I wish to make a slight acknowledgment of this while I can."

He opened a drawer, and took out a cheque-book as he spoke. When he had filled in one of the leaves and detached it, he handed it to Fiander, saying:

"Take it to the bank at once. You'll find a use for it. You'll be marrying some day, probably. But don't be in a hurry. You're full young yet."

Fiander looked at the sheet. It made him the possessor of fifty pounds. He began to stammer thanks that were half apologies. Ridley stopped him.

"Go and put it away in a safe place—never mind all the rest!" he said. "Wait a moment before going out, and send Mrs. Channing in to me, please."

When she came, he had a similar cheque ready for her.

"I've given you a deal of trouble," he said. "A friend of mine suggested a satin gown as a suitable return. I've no notion what such a thing costs, but I think this will defray the expense. I would, perhaps, have preferred to offer it in a less blunt fashion, but that you must please overlook, for I cannot help it."

"But, dear heart, sir," cried the astonished woman, "it won't take all this—— !"

"Never mind!" he interrupted. "I wish it. Say no more. Fiander is going down to the bank. I should advise you to ask him to deposit it for you."

After Fiander had left the house, Ridley went to his sitting-room, dined, and then sat down by the fire. And now, at last, he turned, and looked the shadow squarely in the face.

His reasoning was short and simple; but he found it very convincing.

To-morrow, at noon, Mohun was coming for his answer. His own response must be the production of a later will. Only so could his beloved lady be saved. That will lay secreted in a crevice in the interior of Wareham Bridge. Only himself was aware of this. He might make his discovery known, and apply in the proper quarter for permission to examine the bridge. Mohun, learning of this, would use all his influence against such a proceeding. The law would move forward with its customary delays. The suspense would be agonising to the woman who had already borne so much. It might even tempt her into premature confession. Should the boy Gilbert, during the delay, be assigned into Mohun's guardianship, assuredly she would speak.

And in the end the application would probably be refused. Fantastic indeed was the story he would have to tell—resting at best upon the evidence of so poor a witness as Sophy Hoddinott, who might even, in her latest inimical attitude, refuse to speak at all at his bidding.

" I'd have laughed at such a claim as a very weak fabrication—a year ago ! " he said. " Dare I then risk her happiness and honour to the chance of others believing it ? "

No. He did not dare.

It must be done — this night — by himself. Secretly, because the bridge was a sacred thing, protected by Government ; inviolable ; not to be tampered with. If a man should so offend, he must do it at his peril.

But, oh, the feebleness of an earthly Law to hold back a man who wrought for the sake of justice and of love! Surely, were the risk ten times as great, such a one must needs go on.

Ridley knew that he would go on.

He blinded himself to nothing. The risks, the chances—he looked at them all. He neither exaggerated nor minimised either.

And if the danger of discovery outweighed the possibility of escape—his determination suffered no change. The words had no power to alter that.

DORSET

ANY PERSON WILFULLY INJURING
ANY PART OF THIS COUNTY BRIDGE
WILL BE GUILTY OF FELONY AND
UPON CONVICTION LIABLE TO BE
TRANSPORTED FOR LIFE
BY THE COURT

7 & 8 GEO 4 C50 S15   T FOOKS

" Oh, my dear, my dear," he said to the absent Quenride, " do you think that I would love you at no cost to myself ? "

And the shadow rolled back, to trouble him no more.

CHAPTER XXXI

THE PASSER-BY

THE short December day was closing down rapidly. Sophy Hoddinott stood in the desolate garden, idle and alone. She had fed her poultry and stalled her cows. A milk-pail dangled from one hand. There was no more outside work to be done. She loitered in the open air, not from inclination, but from lack of it. Desire moved her in these lesser matters not at all. Indoors or out, a sick distaste for life, and all the trivial details of it, possessed her soul. She lived, in these days, in a blank world, lit solely by a great passion which fed upon itself, moved towards no set purpose, and coloured her outward existence to no appreciable degree.

Sophy herself never gave the passion a name. She was not sure whether she still loved the man who had turned away from her entreaties ; she only knew that she hated him. Yet the look of him haunted her ; and every remembrance of him was pain — unsatisfied pain, as burning as love, as tenacious as hatred. Small wonder that she could not have named it for either. It was, in truth, the continued concentration of the bitter mood which had held her in the moment of his last departure. No. In her ignorance and inexperience, the girl was right. The passion was complex. It had no name.

In this curious negation of any dominating elemental principle, there lurked a considerable amount of danger to herself. Given the opportunity, it was impossible to tell towards what actions she would be swayed, and equally difficult to anticipate results. And since such a foreknowledge is the sole safeguard to an unprincipled nature when in the stress of strong emotion, Sophy, lacking it, was at the mercy of her own sensations when the time for impulsive action should come.

But, meanwhile, there was little sign in that slight spare

frame and apathetic face of such direful possibilities. She went about her work as usual, and the few strangers who encountered her noticed no change. She had always been unfriendly—one who gave the small gratuity of civil words with reluctance—a silent brooding maid. As she had never gone far afield, save on fair-days, her even closer confinement to her own area occasioned no comment. If her brows maintained their sullen expression permanently, the only one who was constantly in her company was incapable of observing the fact.

The deepening shadows had absorbed her, making her one with the mystery of night, before she moved. When she did, it was with a heavy intaking of the breath, and listless movements. She threw open the cottage door, and passing through the tiny dairy entered the kitchen. Only the glow from the hearth was visible. And this was but in a partial degree, for her uncle was seated before the fire, obscuring its radiance.

Long familiarity with her circumscribed abode had rendered the girl capable of finding her way, and performing any simple duty, in the dark. She bolted the farther door, fetched the meal-bag, and filled a pot with water.

"Sit back, girt-uncle, do!" she ordered petulantly, as she advanced to hang up her pot. But the old man did not stir. "Bad luck to 'ee then, for a thirtover wold man!" she muttered, as she fetched the billets of wood with which to make a blaze.

Presently, in crossing over for the meal, she stumbled against his feet. Scolding angrily, she thrust out a hand to recover balance, and happened to clutch one of his. Something unusual in the feel of it silenced her. She took hold of the arm above it. But the limb was irresponsive, and Sophy's hand dropped to her side.

"Be you sick, girt-uncle?" she questioned. "Can't 'ee speak to me?"

The figure of Amos neither answered nor moved.

Sophy lifted down the rush-candle from a shelf, and got it alight. She thrust it against the old man's face. His head had fallen forward, and she had to stoop to peer into his features. Two words came from her, uttered with commonplace calm.

"He's dead."

She stood the light aside, and proceeded with her preparations for supper, making only one variant from her usual habit, in the lesser quantity of meal which would now suffice. While the porridge was cooking, she crouched down before the blaze, in her old position, and thought.

Sorrow for the death of her last known relative, she had none. But regret there was, and it stabbed her sharply. It did more. It found its way into the heart of her passion, and gave it fresh fuel. Amos having represented the last life in the tenure of the cottage, the girl, by his death, had lost place and roof-tree. She dwelt upon her situation with bitterness.

"A homeless wanderer I be," she said, gnawing at the loose strands of hair. Since her disappointment she had fallen back into her former untidy ways. "I'll be forced to trapes from fair to fair for a livin'. They'll be wantin' to sell the wold place, I reckon, an' if they don't however be I to pay 'em for it? There's the bit o' pension money gone too. A beggar—that's what I'll be. A deal he'll care if I starve! An' I—I'd ha' died for him, an' he reckoned me worth just naught at all, so as he could get courtin'—her!"

She clenched her hands, and bit yet more savagely at her hair, until it was tumbling all about her shoulders. Her bitter humour distorted Ridley's honourable desire to avoid all possibility of scandal, and to help the girl to conquer her attachment, into the cause of her present unhappy condition. Had he allowed her to find shelter under his roof, her future would not have been rendered precarious by her uncle's death. So she argued in her own unlettered way. And the strength of her present attitude towards one who had thought for her when she would not think for herself was augmented by the intrusion of a more material grievance against him.

"I do hate him!" she moaned. "But if he'd only be kind, and forget her, how I'd love the dear body of him again!"

The billets of wood flared out. Underneath their white ash, the fire burnt dully as usual. Sophy gazed at it with sudden apprehension. Then she stretched out her hands to it with a little cry.

"An'—they'll put—you out! You, as ha' been burning for long afore girt-uncle were born! I—can't abear to think on't—my dear, my pretty! Oh, oh, how it do hurt me to know it!"

The old man's passing had left her unmoved. But the thought of the cold hearth touched the human chord, and made a sentient thing of her. Almost fiercely she rose, and fed the threatened fire with fresh fuel, as one might thrust food upon a starving child, taking pleasure in the act. Had she at that moment been forced to witness the extinction of the fire, she would have fought for its life, and, failing, would have shed the tears which her bereavement had no power to produce.

It was long before she roused herself to a sense of present need. The past and the future, both circling round the object of her hapless love, shut out all consideration of the moment. She pushed the chair across the room, succeeded in dragging the old man from it, and having laid him upon the bed pulled forward the concealing curtain, and hid the still form.

" A girt silly ye were," she said, before returning to the hearth, " to go an' die an' leave me wi' naught. The beastës'll fetch a trifle. But the sticks med so well be made into a bonfire for all the vally they be."

If Amos had ever saved, she knew nothing of it. She saw no prospect before her but a precarious livelihood, snatched from the credulity of her neighbours, no roof to cover her but an occasional one, no place of her own to hide her sorrows in. It was a cheerless outlook. But the misery of it rose chiefly from her sense that, had Ridley not rejected her, such a much better state of things would have freed her from discomfort and anxiety.

She took her supper with a country girl's appetite. The near presence of death aroused in her neither repugnance nor dread. It was one of the facts of life, and, as such, acceptable. She was alone in the cottage, therefore there was no need to hasten over the spreading of the news. The woman who had found a temporary residence with her had some reason for not staying beyond a week or so. Sophy, in the first revulsion of feeling towards Ridley, had no wish to take from him a lesser benefit than the one for which she had pleaded in vain. She had found it an easy matter to drive the woman away.

But though there was at hand no human being with whom to share the tidings that a soul had gone out of the world, there remained her superstitious belief that the bees must be told. For luck's sake, the duty must be performed.

She left the hearth, drew a cloak over her head, and went

into the dairy. A lanthorn hung there, and when she had
lit it she went out into the garden, and visited the hives,
one by one.

"Girt-uncle be gone!" she said to each, bending low
over the hive like a sorceress repeating a charm. And so to
the end of the row, her breath floating out on the chilly
air across the lanthorn rays. Then, back again at the cottage,
she glanced up at the sky.

It was a fair night, now advanced, as the position of the
stars told her, to between eight and nine o'clock. It was
windless and misty, but not actually cold. Whatever her
hand came into contact with, was damp and clammy. Sometimes, a drop of moisture would fall from the tiles of the
roof, and make a solemn splash in the silence. Nothing else
stirred. But close at hand a soft sibilant sound, continuous
and placid, indicated where her cows slept in their stall.

Sophy grudged them their happy oblivion. She herself
had no thought of sleep. She stared wide-eyed into the night.

Of correct procedure in the case of sudden death, she had
no knowledge. But, true to her class, she distrusted the
unusual. Fearful of little else, she had a vague but genuine
dread of the law. She was intelligent enough to guess that
the old man would have to be *crowned*, and a dim foreboding
that she might be suspected of having a hand in his death
now took hold of her. The only way of averting this, would
be to act straightforwardly, and to act at once. She must
tell of what had happened without delay. Painfully anxious
to have everything done in order, it seemed wisest to her to
fetch in a doctor. That meant going at least to Wareham
—which was visited by a practitioner from Dorchester twice
a week. If the morrow did not chance to be one of the specific
days, she would have to go on to the larger town.

"Deal o' trouble for naught!" she complained, as she
went indoors. "Nobody can't do the wold man any good.
Still, I'll have to go, or they'll be sayin' that I killed en!"

She jerked the door to viciously, and went up to her
own room without further entering the kitchen. Here she lay
down without undressing, and passed a few wakeful hours.
When midnight had turned, she fell asleep, waking long
before it was light, to peer from the casement at the skies.

She judged it now to be nearing three o'clock. Sleep had
left her for good. She waited for another half-hour, then
groped her way downstairs, wrapped herself in the hooded
cloak, and left the cottage by the back way. She carried the

lanthorn with her—but rather for emergency than guidance, since it was not alight—the tinder-box being held in her other hand. Her intention was to go to her acquaintance Hutchins, learn from him whether the doctor could be found at Wareham that day, and, if not, to command the constable's help in getting to Dorchester as soon as possible. Easy walking, she calculated, would bring her to Wareham at about daybreak.

Mile after mile she trudged forward, her mind still brooding, her heart still in revolt. An unreasonable anger against Amos for dying so soon alternated with her former jealous resentment towards Ridley for denying her desire. Neither the presence of death nor of love had the power to soften her in either direction.

She walked on, suffering nothing by reason of the darkness, guiding herself to a certain extent by the starlit sky, and conscious of neither loneliness nor fatigue. Now and again, supposing herself to be approaching some landmark, she went forward more cautiously, and endeavoured to identify it by touch as she passed.

And so she came in time to Wareham Bridge.

Guessing that she must be nearing the river, which formed the southerly boundary of the town, she listened to catch the sound either of the water washing against the arches of the bridge or of the withered flags rustled by the light wind. She heard both in a faint degree, but she heard also another sound, which, emanating from the same direction, had no connection with either. It was a succession of sounds—low, but clear and regular—each following rapidly upon the preceding one, but perfectly distinct from it. A series of dull blows, wood on wood, it seemed, some thirty in all; then a pause. While she waited, the sound recommenced.

Sophy Hoddinott was possessed of much of the superstition of her class, though her own mild frauds had given her a bias towards reasonableness in such matters. But here was something which could neither be explained nor reasoned away. Her thoughts turned to death-watches and kindred subjects. Almost against her will, she crept forward, fearfully, and at no great pace. Suddenly her heart leapt into her throat. A few yards ahead, she having already stepped on to the bridge, a light shone out. It moved slowly along, with an action closely resembling that of her uncle's lanthorn on the memorable night. Sophy clutched her breast with fear. She hugged the further wall in her stealthy glide

forward. She could see the travelling patch of light moving
across the opposite blocks of stone. Still drawn involuntarily onward, she came almost abreast of the thing. Straining forward, without advancing her feet an inch nearer to the
object of her superstitious dread, she found an added horror
in the fact that the light, swinging round, showed itself to be
supported by a hand and arm. The next moment, its rays
partially revealed a man's figure, as the lanthorn was raised
and lowered again.

"'Tis girt-uncle ! " thought the girl, hot with fear. " He
be come back. I'll never dare cross the bridge by night
again."

For the time, her limbs shook to a degree that made flight
impossible. While she stood there, panting, the light disappeared, and the tapping started anew.

In spite of her terror, there was a human suggestion about
the sound that steadied her nerves. She found strength to
pass the opposite figure, and still keeping on her own side of
the bridge she looked back. This proved to be a better
vantage ground. The light, raised at intervals and then set
down, now threw the figure of the other into partial illumina-
tion. With her ideas still in confusion, and her will almost
in abeyance, Sophy watched. And, by degrees, she found
some sort of sequence and consistent resolve in the movements.
The tapping was continued at more or less regular intervals
for a long while. And now at length, she identified the
sound. From out her childhood's recollections, there swam
up a memory. Some one long ago had taken her to Port-
land, and she had stood within a stone-mason's yard. The
noise of it came back to her. She realised that the din of that
place had been caused by an aggregate of similar sounds to the
one now in her ears. She knew that this one was also produced
by the mallet and chisel of one who works on stone.

The light was again set down. It shone upon a highly
glazed Hessian boot, and the skirt of a dark coat. The foot
was planted firmly, the coat swayed to and fro. There was a
rough grating sound, and though some yards separated them
Sophy heard a very human gasping coming from the figure
near the light. A sudden agitation of the whole was followed
by a heavy thud, a suppressed cry of pain, and the vigorous
stamping of the illuminated foot. Then the light was whirled
up once more and thrust close to the wall.

It showed to the girl two things. A damaged bridge and
a man's face.

She drew the hood more tightly round her own, and shivered from head to foot. Unconscious of the fact though she was at the time, that moment of the lanthorn's revelation had placed Kenelm Ridley in her power.

At sight of him, speculation failed, and wonder ceased. The virus of her passion swept through her whole being. In her madness she regarded him as the man for whom she would have willingly given up her life, but who had left her to starve. A look, a word from him at that instant, would either have driven her to frenzy or have drawn her sobbing to his feet. She herself could not have told which. But he never raised his head. Intent upon his occupation, he had shut the door of the world upon himself, and Sophy was left on the other side. Her hot breath was lost in the space between them, and never touched his cheek.

And now her desire was to get away unobserved. His very absorption lent her a sense of insignificance, of shame. She was so poor a thing in his eyes already. Were she discovered, he would have the right to order her away. And she, being small and helpless, would be forced to creep off at his word. At their last parting, it had been she who had sent him from her, and that fact had kept her from utter humiliation and preserved a rag of self-respect. She loathed the thought of giving him the opportunity of taking that poor satisfaction from her.

He did not hear her go.

From the further end of the bridge, when darkness had once more covered him, she set her face in his direction, and whispered words aloud.

"Why wasn't ye kind to me?" she said. "I did love 'ee so. An' now I'd like to hurt ye if I could, an' make 'ee suffer, same as I'm a-doin' now."

But the words never reached him, and she passed on her way, disregarded from first to last.

CHAPTER XXXII

TO HAVE AND TO HOLD

RIDLEY had already put in a good night's work when Sophy passed by.

He had left Dorchester early in the afternoon, had approached Wareham circuitously, and avoiding the town had reached the bridge before dusk. Here he had made a careful scrutiny of the wall on his left hand, which happened to be the one which bore the sinister notice-plate. He read it now without any weakening of his purpose.

This left-hand, or westerly wall, claimed his regard, for Sophy had, in her narration, intimated that it was on this side of the bridge that the locket had been lost in the river. A close observation of the wall enabled him to determine, with tolerable certainty, which of the stones had been placed there more recently than their neighbours. A purer colour, and a less adhesion of extraneous matter led him to his conclusions.

He noted the positions of such very carefully, jotting down the memoranda in his pocket-book. Then, since nothing more could be done until nightfall, he left the bridge, satisfied to think that, so far as a man might be sure on such a matter, he had made his observations unnoticed by any.

He made his way back to a certain quiet spot where he had tethered his horse, and opening a small valise, which he had not let go out of his hand, he took from it a few provisions and a flask of spirits. He made an uncomfortable meal on his feet, and remained in retirement until darkness was falling. The clock of St. Mary's was striking six when he regained the bridge.

He hung about in the vicinity for another hour, lest a chance wayfarer should pass that way, a precaution the needlessness of which emboldened him to begin his work rather sooner than he had intended. But for the first three hours he wrought fitfully, with eye and ear ever on the strain. The lanthorn he kept closed when not in actual use, and the distant.

rattle of a cart at the other end of the town rendered his hand unsteady.

By degrees, a greater stillness prevailed and gave him confidence. The nervousness natural to a man engaged in surreptitiously committing felony left him entirely, to be replaced, after a certain interval, by physical weakness, deepening, as the hours fled by, into actual pain.

Of necessity, he was clumsy at the work, one result being that some damage was done to the stones themselves. Corners were split off, and one, placed without sufficient care on the coping, overbalanced, and falling on to those already laid in the roadway split itself in half, and made enough noise to imperil the whole undertaking.

By midnight, Ridley was working in a silence and solitude so profound that detection seemed the least imaginable thing. He no longer divided his attention between the work and the watching, but gave himself whole-heartedly to the task. He had removed some five or six of the stones, and was beginning to feel the effects of his labours in strained muscles and an aching back. Healthy, but without any superabundance of strength, the exertion told on him after his recent illness. The sweat lay clammy on his forehead and round his throat. His breath came in gasps. He loosened his neckcloth, and wiped his face, resting for a short time against the wall.

Six stones removed. And as yet, no sign of what he sought.

" And yet it's here ! " he muttered, striking the top of the wall with his hand. " I'll swear it's here ! It must be. It is ! Only the cunning old fox has done his part a little too well."

And so the chisel and mallet went to work again, the blows throbbing more or less regularly into the still night. Now and then he exposed some tiny fissure between the stones on the inner side, but on the whole the structure had been put carefully together, and such crannies were bared less frequently than he had expected. That they did exist was an encouragement to go on.

All through the night he worked, now energetically, now with signs of fatigue, but always with the purpose set steadily before him. As the hours passed—and pass they did, with an ever-increasing celerity to the man on the bridge—he went at his task with a kind of desperation. The hair clung to his forehead with the heat of his exertions, he had bared his throat completely, the muscles of his neck stood out hard and tense, his brows had been concentrated in a perpetual frown. The necessity for breathing-space became of more frequent occurrence.

By now—it was drawing on towards five o'clock in the morning—he had no sense of caution left. All through he had been undisturbed ; he expected to remain so until daybreak. That moment, he was aware, was perilously near at hand— near, at least, in the light of what still had to be done. As well as an exhausted man might labour, he stuck grimly to his task. Small wonder that, in such a state of mind and body, he had no consciousness of human feet sliding along behind him, and was never aware that human eyes, fiercely intent, beheld him at his work.

The last stone, in falling, had he vaguely realised, injured his foot to an appreciable degree. But he set the matter aside, as one to be investigated at a more convenient time, and turned the lanthorn once more on to the freshly bared portion of the interior of the wall. What the light revealed sent him hanging over the cavity, with the blood pounding at his temples. Without a doubt, there was a crumpled piece of paper thrust in between two of the stones, packed into a small hollow formed by the defective shape of one of the blocks on the inner side.

Whatever natural tendency to demonstration of feeling Ridley might have possessed at the outset of his career, had been checked and smothered by the career itself. But he could have halloed aloud this night on the bridge, when he saw before him the justification of his deductions and labours. The exultation was as unselfish as it was dearly bought. He thought not with pride of his own acumen, but with passion- ate tenderness of Quenride's salvation.

With fingers that shook between weakness and excitement, he drew out the paper very carefully, and succeeded in re- leasing it without damage. Sitting down upon the pile of dislodged stones, he drew the lanthorn towards him, and smoothed out the crumpled document, bringing his blood- shot eyes to bear upon it a little fearfully.

There were a few lines written across the outside, it being a large single sheet of paper, folded into half. Three words stood out, and sent the blood to his cheek anew.

Deed of Gift

" Good God ! " he gasped. " Have I risked so much for a thing like this ? "

And for a second or so he sat staring at the paper. The notice-plate at his left side seemed to scorch his shoulder. The quintessence of all that he had borne during the night was gathered up in that moment. He felt a coward's reluctance to turn the page.

He did so at last. The inner sheet drew his eyes down. And then joy came to him, the relief that stabs as keenly as any pain.

He read it through, thanked God for the brain which had led him to the discovery, and then pored over it until he had the thing by heart.

It had been drawn up by Hoddinott. If the phraseology was not such as the lawyer himself would have employed, at least there was no irregularity to invalidate its purpose.

This Indenture Witnesseth that I Benjamin Chideock now of Wareham in the county of Dorset gentleman being of sound mind and intention do hereby give absolutely and irrevocably all and whole my property in furniture and pictures silverplate horses and carriages farm stock and appurtenances at Wareham where I at present reside and elsewhere together with all and several Bonds in East India Stock monies lying at my Bankers and secured in investments to my beloved grandson Gilbert John Chideock for his own absolute use and benefit whatsoever

And I do also hereby express my most earnest desire that the said property shall be held in Trust for the said Gilbert John Chideock during his minority by Mr Thomas Ridley attorney of Dorchester or in the event of his decease by his successor or successors in conjunction with my granddaughter Quenride Chideock

And I direct and charge the parties herein named to act well and honestly by the donee of these presents

And I hereby revoke all previously expressed wishes with regard to the disposition of my property

In witness whereof I have set my hand and seal this twentieth day of February in the Year of Our Lord One Thousand Eight Hundred and Twenty Eight

(Seal)

BENJAMIN CHIDEOCK

JOHN POUNCEY Witness
   Farmer Medley's Croft
SARAH POUNCEY Witness
   Wife of the foregoing

It was to Ridley's credit that, in these first moments, his exultation had less of the personal element than circumstances warranted. He had released Quenride from her perilous situation, and there was as yet no room for the thought of Mohun's helpless rage. Later, the mood came, and the delicate irony of the position appealed to his mental palate with infinite relish. Such a subtle triumph over the man who had insulted and tortured him was an achievement in itself not to be despised. He allowed himself to enjoy it because he knew that it was merely incidental. No such consideration, by itself, could have led to such a result. It had been—For Quenride ! always.

He folded up the paper and put it carefully away. Then, since his present position was sufficiently hazardous to demand practical attention, he rose, and swinging the lanthorn around, surveyed the debris which his exertions had caused. There was a great deal of clearing up to be done. And though he was now worn-out, and had no longer the incentive of the search, his own safety necessitated that the task of repairing should be carried out with as much thoroughness as he had brought to bear upon the work of spoliation.

In itself, this part of his labour was by far the easier of the two. But his injured foot was paining considerably, and his whole body was aching and strained. He worked slowly, and when the first few stones had been raised and set in place he grew contemptuous over the performance, telling himself that the bridge must inevitably show signs of having been tampered with. He had brought a quantity of cement in his bag, and mixed it now with the water from the river. But the supply, he found, was insufficient, and the last layers were necessarily thin and inadequate. The broken stone seemed to stand out from the rest accusingly. All were heavy, and, to his unskilled labour, difficult to adjust in the right place. Here and there, they showed a streak of blood, for his hands had suffered by the work. He cleansed the marks away, cleared up the fragments of mortar and stone that littered the road, and packed up his tools. The sky was lightening, morning was at hand.

He flashed the lanthorn for a last survey of his work.

" A bad bit of bungling ! " he pronounced. " Certain of detection. But I've got all I want, and the rest is of very little importance. Good Lord, how tired I am ! "

There was no more to be done, and everything possibly to be lost, by remaining longer on the spot. He put out the lanthorn, and dragged himself away.

At noon he was to meet Alaric Mohun. Before that, he must see Quenride. It was as yet barely seven o'clock. There was therefore time for him to rest and make himself presentable before seeking her with his good news. He went first to release his horse from the shelter of the thicket where he had left him snug enough, and then rode by lonely ways until he came to a small posting-house. He knew the place, having used it once or twice when his clients' business carried him far afield. He ordered breakfast for half-past nine, and asking for a room threw himself upon the bed, and slept.

He came down a couple of hours later, looking white and worn, but beyond this, and his perceptible limp, showing no sign of having spent the night in any unusual way. His rest had lasted longer than he had intended. Mohun would be kept waiting. The certainty of this caused Ridley to smile.

The morning was well advanced when he entered Wareham at the upper end, and approached the Chideocks' house. In spite of his fatigue, there was an air of easy confidence about him, as he slid from the saddle, and walked up to the door. The rest had freshened his mind. To such an extent, that when he had been admitted, and was taken into Quenride's presence, her expression of alarm at his appearance surprised him.

She came forward, holding out both her hands.

"Oh, Mr. Ridley," she cried, "something terrible has happened! You are ill!"

"I am very happy," he said, looking down at her.

Her eyes hung upon his. These were bright and excited, and, as was usual in such moods, the inequality of brilliance was more marked than at other times. Something of his spirit fell upon her. She felt as if a hand had been laid upon her throat.

"Is it a happiness which I may share?" she asked, beginning to tremble.

"It is your happiness—I hope—I believe," he said. "That is why I have come."

"You bring me good news?" she whispered, as one who hopes and fears.

"The very best!" he told her. "Mohun is worsted—utterly done for! He may gnaw his fingers with rage, but he cannot harm you now!"

She caught at his hands.

"It is your doing," she said.

Ridley released himself as quickly as possible, and hid his lacerated hands behind his back, regretting his thoughtlessness in having removed his gloves.

Quenride drew back, flushing a little. Was this man, after all, nothing but her lawyer, come to inform her of the successful termination of a certain case which she had entrusted to him ? Was his repressed jubilation due merely to professional satisfaction, and not to some deeper and dearer feeling ? Of late, in her loneliness, she had begun to dream dreams. Was the hour which brought her back to peace and freedom to close the door on happiness, or did he only keep behind the barrier because he did not understand ? Surely, in that case, he would not have repulsed her advance so decidedly. She turned aside, with a slight change of manner.

" I am quite ready, Mr. Ridley," she said, " to hear all that you have to tell."

Ridley was hurt. A little of the exultation died out of his eyes. His manner also became more normal.

" May I sit down ? " he asked.

" Of course," she said. " You must be cold after your long ride. Come to the fire."

He had been standing near the door. Now he moved forward, dragging his left foot slightly as he came.

" Something is the matter ! " she exclaimed, at once. " Your foot is hurt ! "

Ridley sank into a chair.

" It is nothing," he said. " I assure you. Miss Chideock, I am quite well. But I did not come to talk about myself. I have something to show you."

Quenride glanced at the valise which he had carried into the room with him, not being minded to let so much incriminating evidence out of his sight.

" Oh, the bag," he said. " No. That's not it. It is here."

" You have not come straight from home, then ? " she asked, in some surprise.

" No, I left home yesterday." He had opened his coat, and now took out the pocket-book. From the flap of the inner lining he drew out old Hoddinott's paper. " Where is the will, Miss Chideock ? " he asked, the light coming back to his eyes.

Quenride drew nearer. Again she caught his mood. Her voice thrilled excitedly as she replied.

" The will ? What of it, Mr. Ridley ? "

" Why did you carry it away ? " he asked, bending upon her a gaze which was at once a challenge and a command.

Quenride sat very still, her hands clasped upon her knees. Ridley kept silent until she spoke.

" I did not think it right," she said, at length, " to leave it with you."

" Will you tell me why you thought that ? "

He spoke very gently, but again there was a pause before Quenride answered him.

" I do not choose to be cross-examined like this," she protested, " in my own house."

Ridley laughed softly.

His look startled and impressed her. She had never yet seen him in a gay mood. And there was no doubt that she was gazing into the face of a happy man. Her own grew a little bewildered.

" I do not understand," she answered, with an appealing wistfulness. " Am I to do so ? It is certain that you have something to tell me, but I cannot guess at what it is."

" Will you bear with me for a moment ? " he asked. " I promise that I will not be tedious."

She sat silent, waiting. As she did so, her eyes naturally turned to the paper which he was still holding. He had again forgotten the condition of his hands, and so she discovered it. She checked the inquiry that sprang to her lips, and leant back, with a smile, very faint and tender, at her mouth. This, then, was why he had appeared to repulse her a few minutes ago.

" In looking over my late uncle's papers," he began, " I found much that bore upon your affairs, and a great deal of suggested matter. As I told you last week, a certain idea was the product of my investigations. I amused myself with piecing together several disconnected incidents, but not until I understood the terrible necessity for some great step being taken did I set to work to get my evidence thoroughly in order. Miss Chideock, you cannot hide from me what your intention was in carrying off the will. And I say that no woman ever did a finer, a more generous action than yours. It put me to private shame, when I recalled the manner in which I had treated you."

" It need not have done so ! " she said quickly. " Had you borne nothing for me ? And why should you be dragged down because of my misfortunes ? Surely, if I suffer, it is enough."

"You are not going to suffer any longer," he said. "Let Mr. Mohun have the will—give him the precious document which he has schemed so vilely for. Give it to him, I say ! I will prove it to be no more than waste paper, yet you may hold up your head, and laugh in his face. For, were it as genuine a document as ever man signed, here is one which, by superseding it, would render it absolutely valueless."

He placed the paper in her hands as he spoke. She took it, but looked at him.

"Another will ! " she breathed.

"No. But what is as good. Since the day before yesterday, I felt convinced that such a document existed, if I could only lay my hands on it. Like yourself, I expected to find a will. I found this instead. Look at it, Miss Chideock ; read it. I think you will be satisfied."

She opened it, and bent her eyes on the page. She read it so slowly that he rose, and came to read it also over her shoulder. Then he saw the large drops falling ever more quickly down her drooping face. He took the paper from her, and laid it by, standing there at her side a little awkwardly. Her head drooped still lower. She covered her face with her hands. He saw nothing but the glory of her hair.

He walked to the window and presently spoke without turning round.

"Is it all as you would have it ? " he asked, at length.

"It is just as I would have it ! " she declared, with a little passionate catching of the breath. "There is nothing now unappropriated save the few acres at Warminster. Alaric will say that I have defrauded him of his share of that all these months. Well, he shall add my portion to his own, by way of compensation." She fingered the paper lying in her lap, and went on, in her exhilarated tones, "The whole thing is most characteristic of my grandfather. I have told you, I think, that he used often to say that he would give away his property in his lifetime, so that his kin could not be greedily anticipating his death."

"Yes," said Ridley. "You told me. I ought to have remembered it. It would have taught me what to expect. There is a certain clause which seems to suggest that Mr. Chideock had, of his own accord, made a previous disposition of his property. Yet, to your knowledge, he had never made a will."

" I do not think so.   I should surely have heard of it."

" Then," said Ridley, " either his sickening brain must have fancied that a revocation of any spoken wish was necessary, or Hoddinott's bemused mind recalled the circumstance of the will, and he inserted the phrase as a matter of form.   We cannot get nearer to the fact, I fancy, than that."

Silence followed his words.

" It is wonderful," he heard her say, then, in a voice still gasping with emotion.   " I can hardly believe that it is true."

Ridley laughed in his quiet way.

" Oh, it is quite genuine," he said.   " Not a doubt of that, Miss Chideock.   Both Pouncey and his wife remember the circumstances perfectly."

" Tell me everything! " cried Quenride, coming towards him.   " What made you think that there was such a paper ? How did you find it ? "

Ridley turned.   The light from the window showed very plainly all the strain and stress of the night.   It showed her something more in the half-minute which he allowed to pass before he replied, something which had risen to the surface all unknown to himself.   It sent her back a pace, into the shadow of the curtain.

" It is rather a long story," he told her, " and I don't think we need to trouble ourselves about it just now.   The most important thing is that the deed is found."

" Oh," said Quenride faintly, from her place among the shadows, " you have done so much, borne so much for me. The thought of my deliverance is so sweet that I am become a fool, and cannot thank you as I should."

She swayed slightly towards him, but he mistook the tenderness in her voice for the expression of her gratitude, and did not yet understand.   Again she broke into weeping, the hysteria of relief and excitement, and again Ridley turned away.

" Were the circumstances different," he said, " you would have little reason to thank me, I fear.   I have made you a poor woman, Miss Chideock."

" You have made me a happy and a very grateful one. And besides, I am no worse off than I was before my grandfather died."

" No," he said thoughtfully.   " That's true.   And presently, no doubt, you will——"

" Will—what ? " she asked, when he had paused so long on the unspoken word that it was plain that he did not intend to utter it.

She saw a wave of colour sweep over his pale face.

" Forgive me ! " he said quickly, with a bright smile. " I was giving speech to a thought which should have remained only in my mind. I was about to say that some day, no doubt, you will marry."

" Do you think so ? " she returned. " You who know everything ? Could I, as an honest woman, give myself to any man without telling him the truth ? And it would need some courage to tell him such a history as mine, would it not ? "

He looked down into her frank eyes. His own grew hazy with troubled thoughts.

" Heaven grant," he said, then, " that you never fall in love."

" I shall not do that—now."

" Don't be too sure," he said. " It is a thing of which no one can say, ' I will,' or ' I will not.' "

She returned to her shadows, and answered him from there. Answered him with a question which had a sweet breathing like a laugh in it.

" Are you speaking from your own experience ? " she asked.

He turned and caught her in his arms. She rested there like one who, out of many wanderings and distresses, had come to a shelter at last, where she might abide for ever.

" Quenride ! Is it true then ? "

" With all my heart and soul ! " she told him. " But why do you make me speak first ? "

" If I have not told you yet of my love," he answered, " it is because I dared not force it on you at such a time, lest your own generosity should have you at a disadvantage. You believe that, my Quenride ? "

" I believe all that you tell me. It is that which makes my love so perfect a thing. And you ? — you trust me now ? "

" In everything ; with everything. For ever and ever," he said. " You are not afraid to be my wife, Quenride ? I am not the man you should have chosen, I fear."

" I am a proud woman," she answered. " I have chosen the man I love. No one else is good enough for me."

The next moment she was moving away from him, but still with the glad serene light in her eyes. Their hands

fell apart lingeringly. He caught her back, and pressed kisses
upon her mouth once more.

"Hush ! " she said. " There is Gilbert. He ought to be
told of his fortune. Shall I call him in ? "

The door opened before she reached it. Gilbert came
forward, with a look of glad surprise. Half-way across the
room he stopped, and turned from one to the other.

" Dear," said Quenride, " Mr. Ridley has something very
important to tell you."

" He needn't," said the boy, beginning to smile. " I
know. You and he are going to be married. Mr. Ridley has
just asked you, and you've said ' Yes.' "

" You dear rogue ! " cried Quenride, with an arm thrown
round him. " That's quite true, and I hope you're pleased——"

" Of course I am ! I always wanted it."

" But it's something much more interesting that I
mean. I'll leave Mr. Ridley to tell you all about it, and when
he's finished you can both come to me and let me know
how you like it."

She left them together, and went away with a glad heart.
Her last glance was radiant.

" I didn't know that there was so much happiness in all
the world," she thought.

And in that same hour—somewhere down in the town—
Sophy Hoddinott laughed.

CHAPTER XXXIII

THE WAY OF A MAID

IT chanced that Amos Hoddinott's death had coincided with the visit of the Dorchester doctor to Wareham. This much Sophy learned from Hutchins, who, mistaking the girl's strange manner for bewilderment at her sudden loss, offered to accompany her on her errand. She had nothing either way as regarded the proposal, but must needs wait until far into the morning before communication was possible. The doctor seldom arrived at the town before noon. Sophy passed the time of waiting at the Hutchinses' cottage. She was in no hurry to return to her own home.

"Pore maid! She be fair dazed-like!" said the kindly constable, as he went about the duties of his multifarious calling.

But Sophy was not dazed. Her brooding mind was perfectly clear. She was merely cherishing her wrongs, feeding them with bitterness.

Soon after twelve o'clock, the constable looked in to say that the medical man had arrived, and the two set off up the street together. As they went, a neighbour called across the road to Hutchins, with a grin:

"Hev' the Passon sent for 'ee yet?"

"Not he!" returned Hutchins.

"Then a' reckon 'twon't be so very long afore he do," came the answer. "There be a job waitin' for 'ee, so I do hear."

"Where to?" asked Sophy's companion, standing still.

"Down at the bridge," cried the other, passing on.

"Whatever do the chap mean?" questioned Hutchins.

Sophy said nothing.

They reached the house, where the visiting doctor had already established himself, without any more words passing on either side. The girl sat down in a corner to wait her turn. Hutchins was called away by his friends already assembled, and stood gossiping with them until Sophy was summoned to the inner room. He then accompanied her into the physician's presence, where he remained by the door, unnoticed until the conclusion of Sophy's business.

"The pore maid be a-feelin' her loss tar'ble bad," he remarked, with customary sympathy, as the doctor dismissed the girl.

"Oh, is that you, Hutchins? 'Pon my soul, I didn't notice you. How do you come to be dawdling about here? And what's all this talk about the bridge being knocked down?"

"Why, to tell ye the truth, sir," responded the constable gravely, "I've only just heared on it."

"Oh, it's your business, surely? There's not been a fellow come to me who hasn't mentioned it. I thought the whole town must be a-gog with the story."

"From what I do make out," said Hutchins, shaking his head, "'tis not ezackerly knocked down, sir."

"Knocked about, then. It's the same thing, I take it, from a legal point of view. It's been damaged, within the meaning of the Act, I understand."

"'Twould seem so," agreed Hutchins. "But I'll ha' a look at it myself as I go to churchyard. An' I'll step up, if 'tis proper, and drop a word to Miss Chideock."

"Very good. She's got her lawyer there this morning; so I heard, when I looked in to see how Mr. Gilbert is going on. Mr. Ridley, from Dorchester, you know. If there's anything wrong, he'll be able to put you in the way of what to do. It'll mean transportation for some poor fellow if he's caught, I suppose."

"I reckon it'll mean that—pore feller!" agreed Hutchins regretfully.

"Well," said the other, with a jerk of his head, "it's not my business, thank God! I heal men's bodies, and you ruin them, and their souls as well, as often as not! And I hope this lad, whoever he is, won't be found." He turned to Sophy. "Now, my girl, don't fret any more. I'll attend to your affair, and make the necessary arrangements."

Sophy scarcely heard him. She went away without a word of thanks, her mind being set on other things.

Outside the house, she spoke.

"What does trans—transportation mean?" she asked, raising her heavy eyes to her companion's face.

" 'Tis the punishment by law for felony," he said.

" What's that ? "

" A crime, my dear, o' a tar'ble serious natur'."

" A—crime ? "

" Breaking the law," he explained. " Same as stealin' an' murder, and such-like wickedness."

" An' how do 'ee do it ? "

" In a-many ways," said Hutchins vaguely. " Just ye see, now. You did hear Mr. Garland talking about the bridge being damaged. That's one sort o' felony. Forgery I b'lieve, be another."

" And t'other thing — the punishment. Does it hurt much ? "

Hutchins looked grave.

" It hurts a deal, I reckon," he said.

" Men's bodies ? "

" Ay, an' as doctor says, their souls too—pore fellers ! "

Sophy walked a few yards in silence. Then she said :

" Tell me just what it is, an' then, maybe, I'll tell you something."

" Transportation, maidy ? It means sending overseas to Australy. That's a place a long way off, where 'tis all cruel hot sunshine all day and the nights so warm as midsummer all the year round. A topsy-turvy sort o' a place, too, where they do have their cold weather in the summer and their hot weather at Christmas. So I'm told, leastways."

" Go on. I don't see as that can hurt a man."

" Ah, it don't stop there. If they'd only to reckon wi' what God A'mighty has done, no doubt they'd get used even to such heathenish ways, in time. But there's other things."

" What ? "

" They be all under Gov'ment out there. Like bein' in gaol, 'tis. Or if a man do get hired out, there's no wages at the end o' week, an' if he do work ill or answer back to his master, as a-many do, in their shame an' misery, 'tis fifty or a hundred lashes at a standing for him. Or maybe he'll be set to work in chains, and have to wear 'em day an' night. Ah, 'tis a cruel life, for sure."

Sophy gazed at him questioningly. Her sombre eyes seemed lit by some fire from within.

" An' how long do it last ? " she said, at length.

" That depends on what term a man do get. This matter o' the bridge, now—if he be a-ca'ght, they'll send him overseas for his nat'ral life."

" So as he'd never come back ? "

" Never no more," said Hutchins, with due solemnity.

Sophy looked round at the wintry landscape—fair, even so, to her nature-loving eyes.

" Reckon it'd hurt a man to leave all this," she muttered, her curious strain of refinement prompting her to the perception. " 'Specially if he left some one as he was fond of along with it."

" That's truth, my dear. But don't ye go a-frettin' about he. We hasn't ca'ght him yet."

" Who ? " she asked quickly.

" The lad as ha' damaged the bridge. I can't say who. Why, how queer ye look, maidy ! "

Sophy, who had been staring ahead, with a hard set look on her face, halted suddenly, and said :

" Is it true—all as you've been tellin' me ? "

" True as gospel," affirmed her companion.

" About the way they serve 'em, out yonder ? "

He nodded, wondering at her.

" Common folk, I s'pose," she went on.   " If a gentleman, now, went against the law, they'd never put him in gaol for ever, and make him work hard for no pay."

" Ay, sure, they would."

Her eyes brightened evilly.

" An' put him in chains — an' thrash him, as you said ? "

Hutchins took her arm, and led her on, explaining.

" Look 'ee here ! " he said. " This be the law. If a man, gentle or simple, do commit felony, and be ca'ght, and get convicted, he be transported, and do become a convict, subject to all the laws for such. It don't matter what he was afore. Once he's a convict, he hasn't got money, nor rank, nor rights. If he were a lard afore, 'twouldn't make a ha'p'orth o' difference to en then. They sarves 'em all alike."

" But s'posing he was in the law himself. They'd let him off then, I reckon ? Being of their own sort, like."

" No. No, they wouldn't. 'Twould be such a scandal, as it would fair turn their stomachs, and he'd get a extry hot dose o' everythin', just to l'arn en his dooty."

Sophy asked no more. She walked on with the strange glittering light still in her eyes. She was conscious of sensation ; scarcely of thought. She had made up her mind what to do. That at least needed no thinking over. For the first time in her life, unlimited power was hers. She meant to use it.

By betraying the man whom she had once loved, she could gain a two-fold end. She could punish him for his coldness towards her hot passion, and she could effectually prevent his union with her rival. Either consideration would have been sufficient. The two together would have swept her on, even to her own ruin.

Her body moved quietly along at the constable's side. Her imagination ran from the past to the future, and back again. Ridley's face and figure were ever before her. Her sensations became abnormally acute. She forgot nothing : the well-favouredness of him, the tones of his voice, his quick glances and sudden smiles, his hard speeches and strange ideas of things.

" Don't you mind pain ? " she had asked him once.

" Not much, as long as I get what I want," he had replied.

Ah ! but the pain which devastates, which takes all away and leads to nothing but suffering ? When the aching heart throbs in a weary body, and neither may rest ? Could pain such as that be borne without anguish of soul ?

And it was in her power to inflict this pain. Small and despised, she had only to stretch out her roughened hand, and he would bleed and groan, where none should pity him.

A little cruel smile twisted her mouth. Her mind ran back to the moment when she had searched for the key which had fallen from his neck. The smooth silkiness of his skin —she pictured it reddened and lacerated by the lash. Stripe for stripe, and burning for burning ! Well—why not ? He had given her pain enough.

She was pitiless, now that the opportunity had come. And in her pitilessness she forgot nothing.

That odd jingling rhyme of his floated into her mind.

> " *And the Day shall have a sun*
> *Which shall make thee wish it done.*"

It was very hot—out there ; Hutchins had said so. Given to work all day with chains upon his limbs, a man might well learn to hate the sunshine, and to long for the brief respite of night.

" *Don't you mind pain ?* "

" *Not much, as long as I get what I want.*"

It never came to the impassioned girl that he would have given the same answer even now.

In such a fashion had her formless thoughts run on, while all the time her bodily eyes were fixed upon the bridge which they were approaching. She roused herself, as the constable touched her arm.

" No need for 'ee to come furder, my dear," he said, in his kindly way. " Nip up-along to the mis'ess, an' tell her what I be about. Ye'll ha' a bite wi' us afore gettin' home-along, I reckon."

" I want to see the bridge," she answered steadily.

There was a little group of townspeople on it, staring hard at Ridley's handiwork. Now and again, one reached out a finger, and prodded the soft mortar.

" Hands off ! " roared the constable. And the rest fell back before him.

Sophy stood apart. Given other circumstances, and a different nature, she might have been said to be amused by the remarks and conjectures that were tossed to and fro. In her taciturn way, she hugged her secret knowledge to herself, and to these made no sign.

Hutchins made a business-like examination of the damaged wall, detected on the ground a few minute chippings of stone, and an infinitesimal quantity of cement in powder ; and finally came to the conclusion that the mischief done was enough to warrant a report being made.

" 'Tis a pure wanton bit o' wickedness," he pronounced. " Wi' no sense in it at all. Though I'm not sayin' as the punishment bain't a thought too hard."

Questioned by the others, as one whose legal knowledge was indisputable, he explained the case to them, much as he had done to Sophy. Faces brightened with interest as they listened. Important crimes were rare at Wareham. The whole assemblage showed a disposition to congratulate itself on having done something to distinguish its town from its neighbours. And this no less, because respectability held the field. Hutchins, enjoying his position of authority, held forth at some length, until reminded, by an envious neighbour, that while he was talking the criminal was probably getting clear away.

When he quitted the bridge, Sophy followed him.

" Why did they make such a law ? " she asked.

" Why, 'tis quite a new one," he said. " I doubt if a' has ever been broke afore," he added importantly. " Why did

they make en ? Well, now, there's a question, for sure ɪ
Why, I reckon 'twas along of these here recent mobs round
about—the rioting an' damaging o' property, on account o'
the new machinery. Ay, that'll be it. But whether or no,
there 'tis, and I've to help to see as folks respec's it."

" What are you goin' to do ? "

" Step in to Parson's, or up to Miss Chideock's, and tell
'em what have happened."

" An' what'll they do ? "

" Well, nobody can't do much," admitted Hutchins, " till
we know a little more about it. Parson'll maybe put up
an *Information Wanted* notice, with a big reward, and then
somebody'll be coming forward."

" An' what ought they to do ? "

" Go straight to Parson or Miss Chideock, and tell 'em
ev'rything."

Sophy turned a slow glance upon her companion.

" I'll tell," she said.

" What ? Tell what ? "

" Who broke the bridge."

Hutchins stared at her.

" But ye can't tell what ye don't know ! " he expostulated.

Then it was that Sophy laughed—an angry, bitter laugh
that impressed even the man at her side unpleasantly.

" I'll tell," she said, again. She leant towards him. " I
do know," she said.

" You mean you know who's knocked the bridge about ? "
cried the constable, round-eyed with incredulity.

Sophy nodded, a little defiantly.

" Why, what can a scrap o' a maid like ye know con-
sarning such things ? "

" You're a fool," said Sophy, with contempt. " I came
over the bridge last night. He was on it then."

" The man was ? "

" Ay."

" And what med he ha' been doin' ? " demanded the
astonished Hutchins.

" Chippin' out girt stones, an' layin' 'em in the road."

" Well, to be sure ! This do fair take my breath away.
You must come afore the justice, that's sartain."

" I'm ready," said Sophy brusquely, beginning to move
on. " No. I'll not tell 'ee no more, Timothy Hutchins.
You're a fool, as don't believe what I say. Take me to some
one as will."

Hutchins followed her, whistling softly.

"You'll get into trouble," he warned her, "if you go a-makin' up a story."

Sophy's eyes flashed round at him.

"What should I make it up for?" she demanded, with sudden passion. "I tell 'ee, I do know the man!"

"But, my maidy, how'mever could ye see en in the dark?"

"He'd got a lanthorn. He held it up, and he turned his face."

"Well, I'm danged! 'Tis a pretty ugly state o' things anyway," commented Hutchins, in real distress. "But there! 'Tis my dooty to march ye up-along to the nearest justice, to tell your tale on oath. Will ye go afore Miss Chideock, bein' o' your own sect, an' not so likely as Parson to swear at ye if you're stupid?"

Sophy turned sullen, and obstinately refused to lodge her information in the manner suggested. With no great heart for the task, the constable accordingly escorted her up to the house of the parson, and sent in the necessary message.

The parson, who had heard nothing, was not pleased to be called upon to drop his clerical capacity in order to assume, at a moment's notice, his magisterial duties. At the time of the interruption he was sermon-writing in his study. He gave the order for Hutchins's admittance irritably.

The constable ushered Sophy into the room, and stepped forward to state his business.

"Well, what is it? What's the young woman been doing?" he inquired sharply. "Ah, Sophy Hoddinott, isn't it? We've had her up before us already. Let's see— what did she get last time?"

Hutchins hastened to explain the meaning of Sophy's present appearance. He began by reporting the damage done to the bridge. The parson pushed aside his *Commentary on St. John*, and grew more alert. Never, in all the time that he had helped to dispense local justice, had so serious a crime as felony fallen to his ruling.

"Is that all?" he asked, when the constable had brought the first part of his rambling account to an end. "What have you brought the girl here for?"

"That's all I know," said Hutchins. "The maid do say as she can tell 'ee more. Please the Lard, she's mistook, whatever she may think. I'd be sorry to get a pore feller sent overseas for the matter o' a few stones, myself."

I 2

" It's the law," said the parson sharply. " If the girl knows the guilty party, she's bound to speak. And if the man's caught, he must be punished. That's as I see it. No case for pity at all. Now then, my good girl, what do you know ? "

Sophy came forward. There was neither haste nor leisure in her movements ; neither eagerness nor a reluctance to speak. She listened while the parson warned her of the enormity of false swearing, and intimated that she understood.

Then she told her story. Of her uncle's death, and of her own resolve. Of her night journey ; of the strange noises on the bridge. Of the dark figure ; his work, and his utter absorption in it. Of the raising of the lanthorn and the illuminating of his face. And at the last—she told his name.

The parson sat back in his chair.

" Good God ! " he said in surprise.

But Hutchins was red and blustering.

" Whatever be thinkin' of, I can't tell, he said, " to pitch up such a tale against a gen'leman as was kind to ye, when ye was in trouble. My mis'ess was right after all, do seem ! You're a wicked maid, Sophy Hoddinott, an' I didn't think it of ye ! "

The parson, who by now had completely sunk the cleric in the magistrate, called him sharply to order.

" Don't alarm the girl ! " he said. " She's done quite right. You've no reason to assume that she's not telling the truth, simply because you don't like it. Prejudice is positively criminal in legal affairs. The matter must be attended to at once."

He began searching for his mislaid pen. Sophy followed his movements furtively. Hutchins ventured on a mild remonstrance.

" But, lookye, sir," he said, " do it sound likely as a gen'leman, same as Mr. Ridley, an' him in the law too, would go knocking down bridges in the middle o' the night ? "

" I can't help what it sounds like," was the other's reply. " It's my duty to act on the girl's information. And it's yours to see that my orders are carried out."

" Ye're never going to have him arrested ! " gasped the constable.

" I am. On a charge of felony. Why not ? "

" But it bain't possible as he's guilty."

The parson had found his pen, and was busy using it.

" You're prejudiced, Hutchins, as I said just now," he

remarked. " To my mind, it is not only possible, but extremely
probable. Such an act of wilful damage entirely coincides
with what I hear of this young man. He's an advanced
Radical, and an ungodly person, if not a downright infidel.
The sooner he, and all such as he are sent out of the country,
the better for it. Such fellows are the poison of society.
That's all I've got to say about him, until I see him." He
held out the paper which he had been engaged upon. " Here's
your warrant," he continued. " Go after the man, and bring
him back at once. I'll retain the girl until you return, and
you can charge him without delay."

Hutchins took the paper reluctantly. Like his superior,
he had not yet enjoyed the distinction of being mixed up in
a criminal case, but, unlike him, he shrank from the responsibility. He muttered something about letting Miss Chideock
know.

" There's no need to trouble her," said the parson tartly.
" My authority is sufficient. Do as I tell you, and if you're
sharp you'll have the young man in Dorchester Gaol before
night."

The truth was that he had been held under Quenride's
dainty thumb hitherto, in most matters of public business.
Now that he had got a case to himself, he was resolved to
carry it through alone. A Tory of the extreme school,
he held all advanced opinions in the greatest abhorrence.
Reform was anathema to him ; Radicalism was of the
devil. Ridley's reputation, as a holder of such tenets,
had swept round the country-side. Moreover, he was also
the impious disturber of a certain Sabbath-day's peace ; the
sacrilegious intruder who had unsettled the parson's congregation at a time when he had flattered himself that he had
them well in hand. Duty, demanding the instant apprehension of the godless law-breaker, appealed very pleasantly
to the parson this day.

Hutchins was edging slowly towards the door, with a
black look for Sophy, when the other called him back.

" You'll probably find the fellow at home," he said.
" Get in outside help, if he makes any resistance. And I'll
give you a search-warrant. There'll be plenty of inflammatory
literature, if nothing more incriminating, I'll go bail."

Hutchins slouched off at last, in an ill-humour. To set
a drunkard in the stocks, or even to inflict a light chastise-
ment upon a thievish gipsy, was all in the day's work. But
to help to bring a well-nurtured young gentleman into peril

of transportation, all on the word of an unreasonable little wench, was a task which took away his appetite.

Remembering that Ridley had been heard of at the Chideocks' house, he found in the circumstance a justification for disobeying his superior by calling there. His honest faith in the great lady of the town was unbounded. She would advise him what to do.

To his disappointment, she was not at home. She had gone out driving with her brother. The visitor, he was told, had also left the house a short time ago. There was nothing to be done but to follow Ridley to Dorchester.

Sophy crouched in a corner of the parson's study. That gentleman himself settled anew to the composition of his sermon. It was an erudite piece of analysis, which none of his hearers would understand. At the head was written: " *Blessed are the merciful, for they shall obtain mercy.*"

CHAPTER XXXIV

COMMITTAL

R IDLEY, with the prospect of the interview with Mohun before him, had not lingered at Wareham, even to contemplate his new-found happiness as Quenride's accepted lover. She herself, longing ardently for the moment when her cousin should know himself to be hopelessly beaten, had not urged a delay. The long years stretched out before her, sweet with love and content, bright to the end of Time. And beyond was the mystery of Eternity, illumined by the continuity of that same pure passion grown more perfect and more radiant still. She let her lover go without a backward call, because there were to be so many glad to-morrows.

And the morrow saw her on her knees, weeping alone.

Ridley rode away in a buoyant mood. Last night's work had justified his existence. He defied his fatigue, and held up his head and laughed. Mohun was no longer to be feared. He might bluster and rage, but the forged will was in ashes at last. A less exalted judgment had convinced Ridley of the advisability of destroying it without allowing Mohun to lay a finger upon it. By its destruction Quenride had full immunity from exposure, should Mohun desire to carry out so fantastic a scheme of revenge.

"He can't bring forward witnesses to prove that they didn't sign a will that doesn't exist," said Ridley, " and that's the only tittle of power left to him. Here it goes ! "

And he dropped the forgery into the fire, even as he had already destroyed his uncle's diary, with its incriminating statements as to the forgery's existence.

" Not that I believe that he would have attempted much," he added. " He's cold and cunning. Such natures are always cautious. He wouldn't care to risk incriminating himself."

Now the work was over, and the consummating moment

of Mohun's discomfiture was at hand. Small wonder that Ridley rode as a victor. He had saved the woman whom he loved, and had won her for his own.

"It's too good to be true!" he told himself, as the leafless hedgerows flew past to his quick rise and fall in the saddle. "To think of her caring for a fellow like me! It's wonderful!"

He knew that he could have bared the whole of his life to her pure eyes without shame. But there was no pride in the thought; only a strange uplifting and a desire for a still better order of things.

This mood held until the constable Hutchins, who had been pursuing him almost from the beginning of his ride, caught him up, tapped him on the shoulder, and called upon him to halt.

Ridley looked round with a start.

"Beg pardon, sir," gasped the constable, whose little nag had had considerable difficulty in overtaking the better mount, "but I've a-been a-hollering and a-waving of my arm till he do fair achy, and ye wouldn't never look round."

"I'm sorry," said Ridley. "What is it?"

"You see, sir, 'tis this way. Parson do send 'ee his—comp'iments, and would take it very kind if ye'd just step back along o' me."

Hutchins spoke apologetically, and looked on the ground. Ridley, suspicion working within him, stared over the hedge at the fallow land beyond.

"It's an odd sort of a message," he said, at length. "I'm in a hurry, and I don't know that I can oblige the parson."

The constable threw an appealing look up at him.

"Why, sir," he said, "to speak plain—you see, 'tis like this. There's been a little bit o' a mistake. You mustn't feel put-about, sir, for 'tis only a trifling matter. But there! you do know what parsons be. Get a notion into their noddle, and there a' do stick till Judgment Day. These here arkward little affairs will happen times to the best o' us, and no harm done."

"Well?" said Ridley drily.

"Why, sir," cried the distressed officer of the law, slipping his hand into his pocket, "here it be. 'Tis my dooty to warn 'ee, as anythin' ye may say'll be used against 'ee. Just cast your eye over this paper, sir, an' remember that I'd a-spared your feelin's, only you wouldn't let me."

He unfolded the warrant, and spread it, flapping in the

wind, before his companion's eyes. Ridley looked at it, motioned to Hutchins to put it away, and wheeled his horse round without a word.

On the way back, Hutchins, who evidently considered that all unpleasantness was now at an end, chattered garrulously. Ridley heeded none of it. He was nerving himself for the new position, and the man who returned to the town, at the constable's side, was a different being from the one who had ridden out of it in the pride of coming victory, with his lady's kisses on his lips.

He spoke no word at all until they were at the parson's door. Hutchins was shocked then at the change in him.

" Help me down," he said. " I've got an injured foot. It's swollen ; I can hardly put it to the ground."

" I—I only done my dooty, sir," murmured Hutchins, as he assisted his prisoner into the house.

" That's all right," said Ridley, with a poor sort of a smile.

At the door of the room he pulled himself together. His first glance at the man behind the table stimulated him. The severe set of the face, the cold eyes and hard mouth, the curt acknowledgment of his entrance, all induced a spirit of antagonism, very useful to support a man at such a time. Ridley bowed in silence.

" Any trouble, Hutchins ? " inquired the magistrate.

" Come along like a lamb, sir."

" Very good. I'll attend to you in a moment. Stand there," turning to Ridley, and indicating the precise spot which his feet were to cover.

The parson had used the time of the constable's absence to ascertain a few more facts about the prisoner. Consequently the sermon was still unfinished. To this task he now bent himself, while Ridley, chilled by anticipation and with physical weakness gradually overmastering him, waited cheerlessly enough.

But at length the *Mercy* sermon was completed, and the writer was free to bring his mind down from abstract virtues to painful mundane affairs.

Very reluctantly, Hutchins formally charged the prisoner with committing felony on the previous night, by wilfully damaging the County Bridge at Wareham.

" You have witnesses to prove this ? " asked the parson.

" I've got a witness," amended Hutchins. " You know I have. But danged if she bain't lying."

" Produce your witness ! " ordered the parson. Then as the slow-footed Hutchins moved off to fetch the girl, who had been dismissed to wait in another room, he said, " Stay a moment ! Has the accused been searched ? "

" Not by me," declared the other, with more than usual stolidity.

" Then do it now, in my presence," was the reply.

" There's no need ! " said Ridley sharply, stepping back a pace. " I'll show you all I've got upon me."

He emptied his pockets, turning them inside-out with little contemptuous gestures, and filled the constable's hands. He threw back his coat, and the parson, running his eyes over the slim figure, could detect no secretion of property beneath the tightly-fitting garments. He examined the articles which Hutchins laid before him. Here was nothing incriminating, he was bound to admit. A watch with ribbon and seals attached ; a handkerchief ; a penknife ; a pocket-book, containing what seemed to be irrelevant matter ; a small leather bag holding a couple of guineas and some silver ; and the key which Ridley had slipped from his neck.

" H'm ! " said the parson. " Is this all ? No saddle-bags, or anything of that sort ? Come now ! Don't attempt to conceal it ! Was there ? "

" The gen'leman did have a bag, sir."

" Bring it in ! What are you thinking of to leave it outside ? It's monstrous behaviour ! One might almost believe that you are in league with the prisoner."

Hutchins fetched in the valise, and dumped it down with a slightly defiant air. It was an old one, and the lock had been broken long ago. The parson had only to unstrap it, and throw it open.

" Ah ! " he said, with a different intonation altogether.

He took out another set of articles, and made a second heap.

A stonemason's mallet and chisel ; a trowel, with a little dry mortar adhering to the edge ; a soiled handkerchief ; a flask, with a little brandy in it ; a small can ; a dark lanthorn ; a tinder-box.

" The whole paraphernalia, in fact ! " commented the parson, with a sour smile.

" It looks like it," said Ridley, strung into retort.

" Silence ! " commanded the other, and turned to the discomfited constable with a look almost of triumph in his cold eyes. " Bring forward the witness," he said. " Let the accused hear the evidence against him."

While Hutchins went off on his errand, the parson chose to put a few questions to Ridley, and carefully noted down the answers. His object apparently being to twist the offence into a political crime, he was at much pains to extract such admissions as should prejudice the prisoner in that direction, when the case came on for trial.

" You are an avowed Radical, I believe ? " he began.

" I have heard it so stated," Ridley informed him.

" Straight answers, please. Are you not an admirer of the pernicious author of *Political Justice* ? "

" No."

" You have been heard to praise Tom Paine ? "

" I once said that he was a clever arguer. Not a reasoner, mind."

" You are a follower of William Cobbett ? "

" I was brought up on his *Grammar*."

" I am speaking of his political opinions."

" Ah !—I'm not."

The parson frowned, and shifted ground uneasily.

" You have unorthodox tendencies, I believe ? "

" I'm not answerable to you for my opinions."

" Answer me plainly. I know you for a Sabbath-breaker. Do you deny that you are a blasphemer as well ? "

The suggestion was outrageous enough to be an insult. Ridley's mouth grew obstinate.

" I don't choose to reply to that," he said.

The parson looked at him keenly. Then he began again.

" Is it not true that your father was a notorious evil-liver ? "

" Oh, come," said Ridley, with a dangerous smoothness of manner, " he wasn't so bad as all that."

" Nevertheless, he died from——"

" Apoplexy."

" At thirty-eight, after a drinking-bout."

Ridley came a step nearer.

" Can I supply you with any further details of my private history, sir ? " he asked. " Would you care to know what caused my grandfather's death ? Or what was my great-grandfather's precise attitude with regard to the Athanasian Creed ? It might all come in useful, to prove that I really did damage the bridge last night. No one knows better than I how exceedingly damnatory the most innocent statements may become, if properly handled."

The parson sat back.

" You're insolent," he said.

" Not yet. But I can be, to a Jack in office, who grossly abuses his authority."

" A most dangerous fellow ! " commented the astonished magistrate ; and signed to Hutchins, who was waiting at the door.

And now came what was to Ridley the bitterest part of the affair as far as it had gone. He had sufficient command over himself not to show either surprise or recognition when Sophy was brought forward. He remained quiet while she told her story again. But the malignity, apparent to none but himself behind the dull words, hurt him almost as much as the girl herself could have desired. To be struck down by one whom he had tried, in all sincerity, to befriend, added an irony to the situation, wellnigh beyond bearing.

" Can you swear," asked the parson, at the close of her recital, " that the man whom you saw on the bridge was the same as the one before you now ? "

" Ay."

" Look at him ! "

With extreme reluctance, she did so. Ridley's face might have been carved in marble, for all the colour or emotion it displayed. Only he saw the venom in her eyes.

" Ay. 'Tis him," she said, and turned sullenly away.

" How often have you seen him ? " she was asked then.

" A few times—three or four."

" Your uncle was his late uncle's clerk ? "

" Ay."

" Well, you're a good girl, and a very honest one, to come forward and tell the truth boldly, without respect of persons," pronounced the parson. "That will do. Stand down."

And Hutchins added :

" Reckon she'd not ha' been so ready to speak if the wold man 'd been still alive to take the gen'leman's pension-money."

" Silence ! " The parson again took up his pen, and looked at Ridley. " I have no option," he said, " but to commit you for trial at the next Assizes. You will be removed to Dorchester Prison immediately."

Ridley bowed.

" I have friends in the town," he said. " Will you allow me to communicate with them ? "

" Certainly not. You will be conveyed to the county town without delay. The lock-up here is not an adequate place of confinement for a lawless ruffian like you. Hutchins, what is the girl waiting for ? Make her understand that she must be ready to appear when called upon, and that she can go now."

Hutchins led Sophy away, explaining as he did so, but not in such language as the parson intended.

" An' now," he concluded, " ye'd best make yourself scarce. Ye've done enough mischief wi' your wicked tongue for one day, I'm thinkin'."

Sophy hung on the threshold to look back. What did it mean ? They were going to take him off to gaol. He ought to look sad. Instead, he looked—nothing ! Surely the pain had begun. Why did he seem to be taking it as if it was giving him some great good that he longed for ? He had no right to look like that ! It was, she vaguely felt, as though he had taken the shame of it all, and laid it upon her shoulders —and sent her off with a fresh humiliation to bear.

Meanwhile, the parson rang a bell. Hutchins and a servant came into the room together. A closed chaise was ordered, and the constable instructed to convey the prisoner into safe custody. " He must go handcuffed," was the concluding direction. " It's not advisable to run risks with a dangerous character such as he. Fetch out the irons, and put them on at once."

" That bain't necessary," expostulated Hutchins. " Mr. Ridley, I take it, bain't the sort o' gen'leman to try to do a bolt."

" Do as I tell you ! "

" Sir," said Ridley, " this is extremely painful. I would ask to be treated with the consideration due to my position."

" Consideration ! Position ! " snapped the parson. " You've no right to the one, and you've forfeited the other. Moreover, you have been in the stocks already. You ought to be as hardened to ignominy as you are to vice. I'll do my duty, though the heavens should fall."

" 'Tis only the thought o' the thing, a'ter all," consoled the constable, in a whisper, as he reluctantly obeyed. " Lard love 'ee, sir, your wrist be so small as a lady's, an' they'll never pinch ye a scrap. An' I'll have 'em off the moment his danged wold back's turned."

He kept his word, as soon as the wheels of the carriage began to move. Ridley thanked him, and lay back in a corner with closed eyes.

" Be feelin' more comferble-like, sir ? "

" Why, to be sure, Hutchins," he answered, " I'd sooner
be going home to bed than to a cell in the prison. But that's
not your fault. I wonder——"

" Yes, sir ? "

" This thing has come upon me very suddenly," Ridley
went on. " It's a hard thing to be hustled off to prison without arranging one's affairs to some extent."

" 'Tis true, sir. I do feel for 'ee——"

" To the length of allowing me to inform my people of
what has happened ? "

" An' how med that be done ? "

" Let me have three minutes in my own house before you
take me to the prison. I give you my word that I shall
attempt no escape."

" I don't reckon you would. Still, 'tisn't quite the thing,
be it, sir ? "

" I won't deceive you—it is not."

" Still, maybe it med be done. Once in a way, an'
Parson not to know nothin' about it."

" Thank you. Three minutes. I'll not ask for more."

Neither spoke again until Dorchester was reached. Then
Hutchins, at Ridley's direction, ordered the post-boy to pull
up before the specified house.

" Now, sir ! " he remarked, as the carriage came to a stop.
And he helped his companion to his feet.

Fiander had the door open before they reached it. At
sight of his employer he gasped, and ran forward.

" Oh, sir, what's happened—whatever has happened ?
Are you ill ? We thought you'd have been home long ago.
There's been a gentleman here. He's gone now—cursing
something awful ! Take my arm, sir. Oh, what is it ? "

They went into the office, for Ridley said :

" Let's get inside. I don't want a crowd here.
Fiander, something serious has happened. Don't speak.
Listen to me. I've been arrested, and am committed for
trial. That means, of course, that I must lie in prison till
next March. I shall try to arrange for the practice to be carried
on by Reeves and Frampton during my absence. They will
probably retain your services. If not, don't hang about at
home waiting for my return. Get another situation. There,
lad, don't look so grieved. It can't be helped, and I've
done no wrong."

" I'll swear that ! " cried Fiander, who had tears in his eyes.

Hutchins turned aside. Seeing which, Ridley's look grew

extraordinarily keen. He made an almost imperceptible sign
to the youth at his side, compelling attention.

" I should like to see my housekeeper, please," he said,
then, turning to Hutchins. " Will you bring her here ?
She's a little deaf. You'd better go into the kitchen for her."

The instant that the constable had left the room, Ridley
strode to his writing-table, though the effort twisted his face
with pain. A quick touch opened the secret drawer, and in a
moment he was thrusting Quenride's first letter into Fiander's
hand.

" Take it to Miss Chideock ! " he said. " Hide it away !
some one might find it—they're going to search the place.
Tell her what has happened—but she'll probably have heard—
and say that I'll write as soon as I can. Thank you, Fiander.
You're doing me a great service, and no harm to anyone.
I'm not secreting evidence. That paper is a private one :
so private that I cannot prove my words to you, but must
ask you to trust me in this."

" I do, sir, oh, I do ! " cried Fiander earnestly. " I'd
trust you against all the world," he added, his voice all husky
with emotion.

" There, there ! " said Ridley. " Bear up like a man.
You can come and see me sometimes. Come now—I didn't
know you cared so much for me."

Fiander turned an expressive look on him.

" There's another thing," said Ridley. " If you should
be subpœnaed by the Crown, don't be afraid to speak out.
Nothing that you may say can do me the least harm."

He left Fiander to recover himself and turned to meet the
housekeeper, who, awkwardly prepared by Hutchins, showed
signs of the most distressful consternation. As this leave-
taking also threatened to be a painful one, Ridley endeavoured
to keep to matter-of-fact subjects, and to make the interview
as brief as possible. He entered into no details of his situation, concerning himself chiefly with a few commonplace
directions. At the last he said :

" I should like you to remain here during my absence, and
to carry things on in the usual way, against my return. If I
do not come back——"

" Oh, for God's sake, sir, don't say that ! " she cried,
crying openly now.

" Why, we have to face these things, Mrs. Channing," said
Ridley. He paused, and ran his eyes round the office, then
walked silently across the passage to the sitting-room. **A**

fire blazed, the arm-chair was drawn before it, his shoes were placed beside. The table was laid for his belated meal. "Ah, it will be a long time, I am afraid," he said, "before I am ready for it!"

He returned to the passage. Hutchins was looking uneasy. Ridley laid his fingers on the door.

"I have been very comfortable, I may say, very happy, here," he told them. "I—I should like to think that I am coming back to it all again—later on."

He held out his hand to the sobbing woman. Afterwards, she recollected a score of questions, commiserations, injunctions, which at the time so rioted in her distressed mind that she was too bewildered to utter them. She blessed him, and let him go. Fiander, too, was scarcely less agitated, when Ridley turned to him.

"Time, sir," said Hutchins respectfully.

And in another moment the old life was left behind. For better, or for worse, the old order of things, so broken into and set aside, can never be taken up again in precisely the same way. It was Ridley's tragedy to know that it would probably never be taken up at all.

.   .   .   .

"Good God!" said the Governor, some half-hour later. Then, very sharply, "Officer! look to the prisoner—he will fall!"

"Not yet," said Ridley, "not yet, sir—if you will only— lose no time."

"Cell Fifteen is unoccupied," said the Governor, at the end of a few minutes. "Put him in that, and let him have the usual privileges, if he chooses to pay for them."

Outside the door, Ridley collapsed in the turnkey's arms.

The Governor, hearing the slight commotion, half-rose to his feet, checked himself sternly, and sat down again.

That night he made entries in a ledger. It was a large book, and in it were records of many sordid tragedies, and a few pitiful ones.

He turned a leaf, and wrote, with a steady hand, under date December 6, 1828:

"Kenelm Ridley, Attorney of Dorchester, charged with committing Felony at Wareham, on the 5th instant. Age, 29. Height, 6 ft. 1 in. Complexion, pale. Hair and eyes, dark. Latter, very bright. Features, regular. Slightly

built. Walks with a limp at present, due to an injured foot.
Five parallel scars across the breast. Has the address of a
gentleman. Admitted, 3.45 p.m."

When he had finished, he closed the book heavily, and
clenched his lips. His face looked grey, and much lined.
He stared across at the whitewashed wall. Memory drew a
picture for him on the dreary surface.

His mouth relaxed. The lines settled yet more deeply
into the grey face. He passed his hand across his eyes, and
looked again. Nothing but a cheerless stretch of whitewashed
wall.

" Harriet ! " he muttered. " God forgive me ! Oh—
Harriet ! "

In Cell Fifteen, the cry was much the same :

" Quenride ! Oh, my God, to lose her now ! Quenride ! "

CHAPTER XXXV

MANY TONGUES

THE news of Ridley's downfall took but a short time to reach the ears of those to whom, for some good or bad reason, it was a matter of interest. The prison doors had closed upon him, but it seemed as though such inaccessibility had given him a popularity never accorded to him while he moved freely among his fellow townsmen. There were even found a few who asserted belief in his innocence—which circumstance lent the savour of argument to what else would have been mere discussion. Idlers with nothing better to do, went to stare at the house where he dwelt no longer, and took note of trivial details impassively passed by hitherto. If Mrs. Channing, still at her post, went in or out, curious eyes watched her progress. It was to her credit that she had had the foresight to get the few necessaries, which Ridley had asked her to send to the prison, conveyed there at night-time. Hutchins, making a perfunctory search of the premises, had been practically escorted in and out by would-be helpers.

" A body med a'most b'lieve as ye was glad ! " he said, in disgust.

The supposition defined the attitude of many with much exactitude. In or out of his station, Ridley had made few friends. The commoner people made no attempt to subdue their satisfaction. The better sort shrugged shoulders and compressed lips, as the gossip grew.

" Young Ridley ? Ah, he's done it now, it seems ! Been getting into trouble pretty deep this time. Too much damned Radicalism about him to please me. I never did trust him, sir. No, I can't say that I ever caught him doing a dirty act. But there's no doubt he'd have done it if I hadn't been too smart for him. Actually preferred port to brandy-punch ; and Madeira to both ! Dashed newfangled notions, sir ! "

Before the town had got used to the thought of a respectable member of its society lying in the gaol like any common rogue, market-day came round, and the consequent influx gave a fillip to the scandal.

Foremost in such matters was ever Farmer Pouncey. On this occasion, his heartiness and loquacity outdid all previous achievements. Only his strong head was answerable for the fact that he went home sober. As he emptied pint-pot after pint-pot, so in proportion did his old enemy's character suffer, until it might have been said to be hanged, drawn, quartered, and dissected before the public gaze.

" I always know'd as the gallus was a-waitin' for en ! " he averred. "Why, neighbo'rs, what did I say to en, last time as 'twere my onluck to clap eyes on the lanky figur' o' en ? ' 'Twon't be in your time,' says I—he bein' rarely took-up wi' the tomfool notion o' ev'ry manjack o' us bein' l'arned to spell by law—' 'Twon't be in your time,' says I, smart-like. ' For why not ? ' says my gen'leman, starin' hard. ' 'Cos ye'll be hanged for a rogue long afore that day,' says I, to his face. An' if you'll trust my word, neighbo'rs and frien's all, the man ha'n't got a word to say, but takes his hook, wi' his tail atween his lags, so mum as ye please. Ah, I reckon he felt so small as a plucked chick'n, a'ter I'd cut his comb for en that fashion ! And why,—neighbo'rs all ? 'Cos he knowd 'twas the truth I'd telled en ! Danged if his hand didn't go up to his throttle, as if a' felt the rope there a'ready."

" Ah, you'm a wise man, tew be sure," came the slow but gratifying response. " Martal sight too smart for he."

A day came, following close upon Ridley's committal to the prison, when a stranger sat in his chair, and examined papers at his table. Fiander re-entered the office, and took up his usual work. There was a mingled gratification and pain in this resumption of the old occupation under changed conditions. The junior partner of the firm of Messrs. Frampton and Reeve was one of the old-fashioned school, slow, punctilious, and courteous. He accepted his clerk's service as a favour conferred, not as so much hired labour, which had been Ridley's point of view. But nevertheless, Fiander would have counted a year's salary well lost for the sound of the sharp word, the curt phrase of approbation, the crisp clear order, which had been his working accompaniment hitherto. His depression in the office was followed by a gentle kind of melancholy during his hours of leisure. He gave up all his usual mild relaxations, and spent his spare time in helping his mother in the shop, and in writing long letters to his late employer—which he had not the presumption to send.

Over at Wareham, in these first days, a woman wept, and wondered, and wept again.

The weeping blinded her eyes with pain. The wondering led her along much such a line of reasoning as Ridley's own, and brought her, as himself, to the marvellous truth. For her additional guidance there were his own subsequent actions. Of chief importance here was his repeated evasion when pressed by Gilbert and herself to describe the actual finding of the deed. At separate times they were told that it was a long story, not of any real importance, a matter which might be more conveniently related when he had greater leisure. No, he could hardly blame himself for not having discovered it before. Oh, yes ; it certainly was a good thing that Mohun had not found it ; but he was not likely ever to have done that.

"It is martyrdom !" said Quenride, in her impulsive way, when she had come to her conclusions. " Martyrdom —for me ! "

She clasped her hands, and sat very still, rehearsing once more the various facts which had tormented her brain in those moments, when her eyes could weep no longer. Facts connected with Ridley's situation, which, if her better knowledge painted in a less lurid light than that which had tinged Hutchins's descriptions to Sophy, were still ugly enough with possibility to set her shuddering.

If the worst befell, it did not follow that Ridley's life would necessarily be one of acute physical suffering. Such talents as he possessed would have their value, even in a Convict Settlement. The system of Assignment held opportunities for a cultured and educated man. His legal knowledge, and all that it stood for, would almost certainly save him at the first from being sent out to do manual labour. But the principle at the root of the system was that of slavery. Even should he school his independent spirit to endure such a position, who could tell what pitfalls might not entrap him in the shape of a dishonest master ! He might subdue himself to obedience ; he would never yield himself to fraud. Many of the settlers were ex-convicts themselves. What honour, what mercy, could be hoped for from men who, as a class, comprised the most vicious and infamous of England's criminals ? Ridley would be flung over to any foul-mouthed, evil-living ticket-o'-leave man who chose to bespeak his services. What if he passed on in his degradation to the scourge and the chain-gang ? Norfolk Island, that lurid hell upon earth, rose up before her heated brain. She buried her face in her hands.

" No," she told herself presently, as she had done a dozen times already. " He'd never get there. They'd kill him long before."

She made an effort at calmness, and at length succeeded in restraining her perfervid imagination, and tried to set her thoughts in order. Then she declared :

" He shan't be left to bear it alone! I'll go out too. I'll be a rich Colonial lady who needs a secretary. He shall come to me. The biggest rogues often escape their punishments so. Why should not an honest man ? "

But looking up, she saw her brother's lips quivering.

" Yes," he said earnestly. " Do that. Go out and meet him there. Never mind me, Quen ; I've often thought that I shan't live very long."

And immediately she was on her knees with her arms round him.

" Dear," she sobbed, " I want you both! What am I to do ? "

Then, out of the haze of her natural stupefaction, had come a thought born as soon as the knowledge of his motive had revealed itself. All that she might do to save him now was to urge the extenuating circumstances supplied by the truth. To confess this, and to hope for a merciful considera-tion of his crime in consequence, was all that was now left to her.

Her way seemed plain. Had the issue been less tragic, she could have smiled at such a pitiful end to all her scheming. If, by sacrificing herself, she could win her lover's immunity, Gilbert would have a friend still. If she ruined herself to no purpose—God help them all !

Yet she dried her eyes, and with deliberate design set her mind on her brother and his present needs. The news, which had wellnigh shipwrecked her, had given the lad a shock from which he had barely recovered. She found him studying alone, and bending over him, she kissed him lightly, and said :

" Do you find it hard to get on by yourself ? We must make inquiries about another tutor for you."

The parson, Gilbert's master hitherto, had received his dismissal.

"It's not very interesting reading alone," said the boy. "Quen, I saw the parson this morning."

"Did you ? I hope you only acknowledged him and went on."

"I couldn't. He stopped and spoke to me."

"Indeed ! What had he to say ? "

"He asked me if it was true that you had promised to marry Mr. Ridley."

"What impertinence ! "

"I told him that it was—and that the arrangement had my entire approval."

Quenride smiled sadly.

"He ought to have been impressed by that, dear."

"He wasn't ! "

"What did he say then ? "

"Oh—you'd be angry."

"You must go on now you've begun," said Quenride, with quiet authority. "That's the rule, you know."

"Well then, he said that he was very happy to know that, under Heaven, he'd been the means of saving you from a bad husband."

Quenride showed a bright spot on either cheek.

"The man's insane about Heaven ! " she cried. "If he gets a cold, he fancies Providence adjusted the wind specially for his respiratory organs. It's strange that God is often blamed for man's own dispensations. But, at least, I wish he'd keep such cant out of my most miserable affairs."

"Well, I thought it rather silly," said Gilbert. "And the rest of it was a lie. So I told him that I begged to differ, and he said that in that case I was in a very dangerous state, and I was afraid he was going to offer to pray for me. But I suppose he thought I was beyond that ; for he didn't, only looked very sour, and marched on."

Quenride took a chair by the fire and became thoughtful. The next day was to be the occasion of her first meeting with Ridley since his apprehension. It had been formally intimated to her that such interviews would be permitted at regular intervals. She had had one letter from him—a letter obviously hampered by the knowledge that it would be subjected to official inspection before it reached her. It was not in the nature of things that Kenelm Ridley would be a demonstrative lover at any time. His first love-letter left out nearly all the love. Quenride, for her part, was equally characteristic. She set down her thoughts unreservedly. And with her, to think was to feel. The cold eye of officialism might scan her pages—but she loved, and was not ashamed of it. As it proved, her impulsiveness was better justified than his reticence. The Governor glanced at the superscriptions and signatures, and let the rest pass between the lovers unread.

But such as it was, his letter was infinitely dear to Quenride. She had carried it about with her since its arrival, and took it out now, though she could have repeated it word for word. She even dwelt upon some parts of it with a sad kind of satisfaction.

" You must not think of me as being subjected to any particular discomfort," he wrote. " God knows, our Prisons are in crying need of Reform, but my friend is an honourable and a humane man, and as far as lies in his power he endeavours to comply with the recently passed Acts. I feel convinced that many others would do the same, only they are prevented by the criminal reluctance of the local authorities to provide the necessary funds."

And again :

" I have a cell to myself, for which I am infinitely thankful, and the use of the yard for exercise, in common with the rest. I am allowed lights and books. I have asked for a set of carving tools, not because I suspect myself to have any special skill in this particular, but because it seems the proper occupation for a prisoner."

There was much more ; directions about her own affairs ; inquiries about Mohun, whom she had not yet seen; and at the close a most precious message that seemed to defy surveillance itself.

" Quen, dear, are you going to put it with the others ? "

She looked up. She had almost forgotten Gilbert.

" The—others ? "

" Yes. Ah, you didn't know that I knew."

" Knew what ? "

" That you used to keep all Mr. Ridley's letters. Oh, Quen, why do you look at me like that ? What have I said to hurt you ? "

She was gazing at him with an expression of intense pain. Gilbert came to her side.

" What do you know about my letters ? " she asked.

" Nothing, dear. Only that you kept them. I wondered about the one you wouldn't show me, you know. And when you happened to leave your desk unlocked, I looked for it, and Dolly said I oughtn't to, but I wasn't going to read it, really——"

Quenride was on her feet, gripping him by the shoulder.

" You ? " she said. " You ? "

" What do you mean ? Quen, you're hurting me ! "

Her hold did not relax.

" Tell me the truth, Gilbert. You took those letters out of my desk ? "

" Yes."

" What did you do with them ? "

" Nothing. I thought I wouldn't be so mean after all. So I just told Dolly to put them back again. I couldn't stop to do it myself, for Cousin Alaric had called, and I was trying to get away before he came in. Oh, Quen, what have I done ? "

For the first time in his life Gilbert Chideock saw his sister's eyes turned upon him in hot anger.

" Done ? " she cried. " You've wellnigh broken my heart, that's what you've done ! If you weren't as you are, I'd have you punished for this ! "

He shrank back, flushing painfully. Never before had she touched his infirmity with an ungentle hand. Boy as he was, he realised that only some great upheaval of her nature could render the thing possible. He waited motionless, as though she had struck him.

" You ask what you've done ? " she went on, heedless of his distress. " Oh, I can't explain—'tis too terrible. But I'll tell you this, your wicked curiosity has sent Mr. Ridley to prison. It may even cost him his life ! "

" Oh, Quen—dear Quen, not that ! Not that ! "

He flung himself upon her. She pushed him away. He leant upon the table, and watched her with awe-struck eyes.

" I do say it ! " she cried, merciless to both herself and him. " How long do you think he'll live—out there ? "

Gilbert had nothing to say. He held on to the table, white-lipped and trembling. Quenride left him and re-mained away for an hour. A long brooding hour, wherein she studied the irony of human events, as exemplified by her brother's conduct.

At the end of that time she sought him again. He lay

across the table, his face hidden in his arms, his delicate
body shaken by the sobs, not of a child, but of a man. Quenride touched his shoulder. He was all she had ; all that she
might ever have. Upon him she had lavished an affection
which had the protective instinct of maternity in it. For
him she had struggled and suffered. If he had repaid her in
very ill kind, at least he had not known.

"Gilbert," she said, "the mischief is done. There is no
use in your going on like this. You will only do yourself
harm. Don't you think that I have enough trouble to bear,
without having you ill on my hands ? "

" I wish I was dead ! " he muttered in reply.

But presently he sat up, and tried to recover himself.
Quenride drew a chair to his side, and took his hand.

" Does Mr. Ridley know ? " he asked.

" He knows nothing about your part. If he did, he would,
I am quite sure, not blame you more than you deserve."

" And will you forgive me, Quen, and believe that if I'd
only guessed that I was harming anyone in the least degree,
I'd have had my fingers cut off before I'd opened the
desk ? "

" Yes ; I'll believe that, and I do forgive you. You and
I have to be very brave, Gilbert. And we can't help each
other by quarrelling."

The boy leant across and kissed her.

" You're the dearest dear in the world," he said. " Quen,
when I'm a man, do you know what I shall do ? I shall give
you half the money, as soon as I can ; you'll be married by
then——"

" Gilbert ! " It was a cry of pain.

" I'm not going to suppose ugly hateful things," he went
on resolutely. " It's all got to end happily, just to spite
that—that damned old parson. Quen, it's going to end like
that, isn't it ? We're all going to be happy together, aren't
we ? "

" Oh, my dear, I don't know. I don't know."

" And there's Dolly," Gilbert ran on quickly. " Was it
because of this that you sent her away ? "

Quenride suddenly remembered.

" It was," she told him. " Mr. Ridley saw her the other
day. She said that she was not so much to blame as I supposed. She spoke of trying to keep some one else out of
trouble. I thought she must mean Alaric ; I never guessed
that it was—you."

"I'm sorry," said the boy, in a shamed voice. "You'll let her come back now, won't you?"

But Quenride shook her head.

"She was not free from blame," she answered. "We must wait and see how things turn out."

"Quen—dear Quen!" For she had sighed, and sighed heavily.

"Well, then! She'll probably be married before long to that quiet-mannered young man who called the other day."

"I like the thought of that," said Gilbert. "Can I have some of the money to buy her a wedding present?"

"As much as you like, dear."

He took her hand, and caressed it in silence.

"I wish it was for you," he said, then.

Quenride looked at him with her beautiful eyes full of a quiet courage.

"We're going to be very brave, remember," she said.

CHAPTER XXXVI

THE SECOND TIME OF ASKING

THE next day, she paid the first of many visits to the prison. Apart from the mutual happiness derived by the lovers from the short interview, the visit was of importance to Quenride herself. Though she spent no longer than an hour within the gloomy walls, in that time one cherished plan was overthrown, and another erected on the ruins—only to be in its turn ruthlessly demolished. And this by the one whom it was designed to save.

Rarely, if ever, had such radiant young beauty been frowned upon by the dismal pile comprising, at this time, Dorchester Prison. She had schooled herself into comparative cheerfulness, and wore the subdued tints that suited best her rich colouring.

" I'll not go to him sighing," she had said. " He shan't think that he has chosen a poor-spirited dowd. No—I'm going to see my lover, and I'll look at my best."

So that it was a daintily-garbed and serene-mannered lady who left her carriage at the entrance of the gaol, and stepped inside with the dignity of an empress entering a throne-room.

Ridley's letter had in a measure prepared her for a mitigation of the evils still rife in prisons as a whole. In this department also, Reform was at work, but moving with characteristic slowness. As Ridley had suggested, Acts passed for the amelioration of prisoners' unnecessary sufferings were constantly being ignored and evaded. Only in the hands of a humane and conscientious Governor could a better state of things obtain.

Ridley's friend was a strict disciplinarian, and a somewhat rigid pietist, but he carried a humane heart beneath the strait-waistcoat of officialdom. Long ago, the young man had found his way into it without much seeking on his part. In their present curious relations, the natural embarrassment had been covered, on the Governor's side, by a sharpness of manner in public, which bestowed a favour as if it were a penalty; and, on Ridley's, by the assumption of a light ironical humour, which was also useful in saving him from becoming the butt of his companions. But occasionally the Governor visited Cell Fifteen, and then both prisoner and gaoler looked into the wounded heart of the other man.

The Governor raised his head and regarded the bright-eyed woman who stood before him.

" I believe, madam, that we have met previously," he said, when he had made her his stiff little bow.

" We have, sir. At Mr. Ridley's."

" I remember," he said. The grim face told her nothing.

" I have come to see him," said Quenride. " Shall I—shall I—I hope I shall not find a great change in him ? "

" You shall judge for yourself," said the Governor, and turned to give the necessary order.

" One moment, sir," said Quenride. " I should like to speak to you in private before—he is brought in."

" Wait outside with the prisoner until I ring," ordered the Governor, at once.

Quenride drew nearer to the table which divided him from her. She took some books from her muff, and laid them before him.

" I brought Mr. Ridley these," she said. " May he have them ? "

The Governor glanced at them, and set them down again.

" Certainly. If you wish it," he said.

" Thank you. I should like to ask you a question, if you please."

There was a note of proud humility in her voice that, added to its natural sweetness, made it very wistful and full of charm.

" I am willing to hear it," said the grizzled officer behind the table. " I cannot promise to answer it."

" Sir, I know you to be a great—I may even say, I think, a dear friend of Mr. Ridley. In your opinion, has he any chance of acquittal ? "

The Governor looked into her pleading eyes, and lowered his own. Had Ridley concealed the facts from him, he would have guessed them then.

" Miss Chideock," he said a little less formally, " I am concerned with the safe custody of my prisoners. It is no part of my duty to anticipate their future."

" But, as his friend ? " she urged. " This is surely not a common case."

" I pray God not, madam."

" You have known him, I think, for a long time ? "

" Twenty-nine years," he said.

" All his life ! " she said, and stood looking at him for a while. Presently, she returned to the point. " I should accept your opinion in this matter," she said.

He shot a keen glance at her, and saw, not her beauty, but her courage.

" Can you bear the truth ? " he asked, after a pause.

She answered :

" Yes."

" He has only the shadow of a chance," he told her. " The evidence is dead against him. His profession is certain to make things go hard with him."

" But," said Quenride, bringing her shining eyes still closer to his, " if there was a witness who could swear to his utter integrity in the matter—oh, if I am making a mistake in speaking thus openly, I entreat you to bear in mind that I speak only to his friend, and not to the Governor of Dorchester Prison—if there were such a witness, who, while not disproving his guilt, could set the action in so clear a light that it should be a virtue instead of a crime, who could plead the most extenuating circumstances for the illegal act, that would make some difference, would it not ? "

And now a sudden glow fired the steady eyes that met her impassioned gaze, and there came a thrill into the voice which had hitherto answered her so quietly.

" If such a witness there be," he said, leaning forward towards her, " let him keep silent—unless he wishes to damn Kenelm Ridley utterly ! "

Quenride stepped back with a low cry, her hand at her breast, her lips parted under the shock of surprise.

" I have said," went on the other, still with the strange quiver in his voice, and still bending across the table as she drew away, " that from the Bench he can expect no mercy, as the evidence now stands. From the jury, especially if they be drawn from his associates, he will get little sympathy. The defence can and must rest solely upon one hypothesis. A weak one, but the only one we have. In the hands of a clever counsel, it may serve our purpose. To bring forward such evidence as you suggest, would be to tear that one frail chance from him."

" I do not see—I do not understand," cried Quenride faintly. " I thought——"

" That you could save him. By silence you may do so ; not by speech. To suggest a plausible motive will be to settle the belief in his guilt still more firmly in the minds of both judge and jury. What we must endeavour to induce them to believe is that Kenelm has deliberately assumed the guilt of an unknown person—that he is willing to suffer in order to shield some one else. The chief witness against him is an ignorant country girl, who admits that it was dark when she saw him on the bridge. We shall endeavour to get her evidence set aside as unreliable, and shall discredit the rest in the manner which I have indicated."

The excitement left his voice. He sat back, rigid and inflexible as before. Quenride bent her head humbly.

" Thank you," she said. " I am so very inexperienced. You have saved me, it seems, from making a very great mistake."

" I hope so," he said.

" You have spoken," she added, with the wistfulness very marked in her tones, " entirely on your own initiative ? "

" Who should prompt me ? " he asked.

" I should like to have your word," she urged. " If you can give it, indeed I shall be far more ready to take your advice."

" On my sacred word of honour, Miss Chideock, the thought is my own. Should I, after conferring with the gentleman who will undertake the defence, see any reason to alter my opinion, you may rest assured that I will communicate with you."

" Thank you," she said, again.

" All this," said the Governor, " is very much out of order. I detest irregularities. Perhaps we had better say no more at present, on the point."

She signified her submission, by withdrawing from the table, with a bow, and retiring to the seat which had been placed for her. The Governor stayed his hand in the act of ringing the bell at his side.

" You would prefer, no doubt, to sit nearer to the fire ? " he said.

" Thank you, I am not at all cold," she told him.

" It will be more comfortable," persisted the Governor, and, advancing, took hold of the chair.

" You give yourself too much trouble, sir," she protested. " There is a chair there already."

"Indeed, madam ? You will need somewhere to lay your furs."

He stirred the fire into a blaze, and walked back to the table with hand outstretched.

"You had better wait where you are, Miss Chideock," he said, for she had moved as though to go towards the door. Then he rang the bell. Her bosom strained forward a little, but her feet remained motionless. And when, a moment later, Ridley was brought in, and she held his chilled hands in hers, and felt his cold kisses on her lips, she blessed the stern disciplinarian behind the table for the kindly thought. When she looked round, he was deep in his books, and even the turnkey was gone.

"God !" said Ridley, as he looked at her, "what a scoundrel I am to have brought you here ! "

"No," she said. "What wickedness must be mine, to have sent—you to such a place ! But now we have an hour of happiness, and, oh, we can't afford to spoil it by a lovers' quarrel. Let me look at you, Kenelm ; let me see how they treat you here."

There was at all times a quiet orderliness about him, which lent distinction to the plainest raiment, and, when he chose, enabled him to dress more modishly than his neighbours without them finding it out. But for a certain worn look about the eyes, and a harassing cough, there was nothing to suggest that he had not stepped out of his own office, instead of from a prison cell. Quenride sighed, remembered her resolution, and grew, to outward seeming, cheerful again. Ridley appeared to have formed a similar resolve ; his manner retained all its ordinary characteristics, with his newly expressed tenderness towards her added thereto. The Governor, glancing up presently, saw them sitting by the fire, hand in hand, and cheek by cheek, laughing together. Their voices reached him only in a low murmur. And the man who detested irregularities, went on with his books, and let them be.

By and by, he became aware of a change. Ridley's face he could not see. Quenride was addressing her companion with great earnestness, her eyes grown eloquent with pleading, and a heightened colour in her cheek. Something indefinably sweet and strong and pure about her arrested the Governor's gaze, and he unwittingly watched the pair for a while. From time to time, Ridley's dark head was shaken with a resolute gesture familiar to the elder man. Once he raised the fingers lying on his arm, and kissed them. But Quenride's forehead was drawn and lined with the earnestness of her entreaty, and her very lips were prayers. And still Ridley shook his head, and when at length the Governor had a sight of his face he saw that it was set rigid with refusal.

At that moment, Quenride, brought apparently to the point of despair, happened to catch the other man's eye. Something flickered in hers. She got to her feet, and with the colour flaming anew in her cheek, sent a look across to him. It was like a signal for help. He obeyed it immediately.

" Sir," she began, at once, " have you any authority over your prisoners ? "

" Over this one ? " he replied. " Not much, I regret to say."

Ridley had also risen.

" If Miss Chideock hopes to enlist your sympathies, sir," he said, " I must warn you both that, in this present instance, you will have no authority at all."

" What is the point under discussion ? " asked the Governor, looking from one to the other.

" Miss Chideock "—Ridley spoke unwillingly, and obviously only answered at all in order to save Quenride from doing so— " for reasons of her own, has been endeavouring to persuade me to consent, with your permission, sir, to an immediate marriage. In the circumstances, I hope you will agree with me that the suggestion is rather an absurd one."

" It is surely an unusual one," returned the Governor bluntly, not sparing her. " It must be also, I should say, embarrassing for any man to have to say *no* to such an offer from a lady."

A little bubble of nervous laughter came from Quenride, at the unconscious appositeness of the remark.

" Oh, I assure you," she cried, " he doesn't mind— refusing me, in the least."

" I think," said the Governor stiffly, " that you had better wait."

" Oh," was her piteous answer, " but you do not understand."

Ridley laid his hand on the other's arm. He spoke with an air of quiet determination, all the more impressive because it was mixed with great tenderness.

" You are aware, sir," he said, " of the deep affection which I have for Miss Chideock. But not even to please one whom I so love and honour can I consent to take the risk of making the woman for whom I would give my life—the wife of a transported felon. That, sir, is my first and last word upon the subject. I think you know me well enough to understand what that means."

Quenride spoke with a passionate intensity.

"Kenelm has not told you the reason of my strange request," she said. "I am not urged to it by any mere caprice, nor even by the desire to prove to the world my belief in the man to whom I have promised myself. It is to save him, at least to try to save him from future suffering that I speak. Believe me, no less a consideration could move me to make so unseemly a proposal, at such an ill-fitted time."

"I fail to see," said the Governor, "how marriage can effect his salvation."

"It cannot, and it would not," said Ridley. "At any rate, the risk is too heavy to be taken by any of us. This is how the case stands. Miss Chideock is possessed of what she believes to be an ancient prerogative, whereby the women of her house may claim immunity from certain crimes for such kinsmen as have so offended. The right, I understand, has been allowed in past times, but, in my opinion, it has merely been a matter of following a precedent, with no legal obligation at the back of it. Miss Chideock herself tells me that the authority was questioned on the last occasion, and warning given that in future such claims would be disregarded."

"That was not in the present reign," said Quenride. "Other ministers may regard the matter differently. If it fails, it fails. But surely it is worth trying."

There was a moment's silence. The Governor was gazing across at the whitewashed wall beyond. Ridley spoke.

"I can go into transportation," he said, "with a mind tolerably at ease, if I know that my downfall affects myself alone. But, if I felt that my fate had injured one I love, the horror of the situation would be unbearable."

"You are trying to persuade us that you have a selfish reason," said Quenride sadly.

"I speak the truth," he answered, with no sign of giving way.

She went close to him, and wreathed her arms round his neck.

"Dearest," she whispered—for the Governor still gazed at the opposite wall, and said nothing—"I could bear it, if it had to be."

He caught her wrists, and looked down into her face. Then again he shook his head.

" I will never bind you so, my Quenride," he said. " I do not doubt either your love or your strength. But it must not be."

Thus he refused her for the second time.

" Sir," she said, appealing to the Governor in his abstraction, "have you no word to add to mine ? "

" *I have sent for you to ask if you will be a friend to my boy. He will need one very often as the years go by. His father—I may say it now, without disloyalty—has nothing to give him. I can die in peace, if you will only promise me this.*"

" *I do promise it, Harriet. And may God forget me, if I fail in this my sacred trust.*"

The Governor brought his hawk-like gaze back to her face, turned it slowly from her to Ridley, and kept it there for a long time. Then he said :

" Madam, you ask too much. Before God, I dare not tamper with another man's conscience."

Ridley's hand shot out.

" Thank you, sir ! " he cried. " There spoke my friend indeed ! "

But Quenride, though in her heart she knew, as well as the Governor himself, that no word would have turned Ridley from his resolve, sorrowed because her second plan had failed, and she had nothing left to offer save her unprofitable love.

CHAPTER XXXVII

COLD COMFORT

AFTER the failure of her latest attempt to aid her
lover, Quenride knew that she would need all her
courage to live through the months that must elapse
before the next Assizes—that solemn function at
which she had once lightly averred, Ridley should not fail to
be present.

In order to keep her spirit as brave and unflagging as she
wished it to be, she resisted the brooding impulse, kept much
with Gilbert, and entered with interest into their joint affairs.
These were now safely in the hands of the lawyers who had
taken up Ridley's practice, and she anticipated no more
trouble in that immediate quarter. Mohun still kept away,
but from time to time she heard disturbing rumours, from
which it appeared that though defeated in his schemes he
was not idle. He had, she first learned, made a final attempt
to obtain the forged will. Messrs. Reeves and Frampton, knowing nothing of the matter, applied to Ridley for information,
which information was duly conveyed to their client, who
might then be supposed to have bitten his nails in ungovernable fury—a frame of mind which found its outlet in an
organised and at the same time an insidious attack upon his
now helpless antagonist. How much of the truth he had
reasoned out, Quenride had no means of knowing. She received no letter from him, no open threats reached her, she was
given no warning—there was nothing tangible in his revenge.
Ridley had gauged his character accurately when he had
doubted the probability of his daring even in a scheme of
vengeance. But, coldly and cautiously, Mohun was at work.
She felt the bane of his influence around her whenever she
drove into Dorchester, and this she did frequently, even on
such days as the prison door was closed to her, making tender
little excuses for the melancholy pleasure of lessening the
distance between herself and her lover. With a growing

consternation, she became aware that the original prejudice against Lawyer Ridley was slowly deepening and spreading. It was evident that, by the time he was tried, he would have come to be very generally regarded as a most unscrupulous and dangerous man.

And within the prison itself, Ridley was not careful to give the lie to such convictions by a perfect rule of conduct while under restraint.

A genuine principle was at the back of the affair. But the jarred nerves had as yet had no chance of recovering from the result of Mohun's rough handling, and the self-control which he exercised in public had a trick of exacting a heavy penalty when he was alone. Such conditions, acting upon his peculiar temperament, needed but a favourable medium to throw him into a mood at once obstinate and daring. Such an opportunity was presently afforded by the contumacy of a fellow-prisoner.

It was on Christmas Day that Quenride heard of the affair. As a special concession, she had received permission to visit the prison on that day, and at her request Ridley was not informed of her intention. She had but small scope for indulging in such little tender acts of playfulness, and antici-pated with much happiness his glad surprise at her unlooked-for coming. But, in the event, the surprise was for herself—and had no pleasure in it for anyone.

At first she suspected nothing amiss. When the ordinary usage was not followed, she set it down to a praiseworthy relaxation of rules in honour of the season. On the two previous occasions of her visiting the prison, she had been conducted to the bare whitewashed room in the main build-ing. Now, she was asked to accompany her guide to a differ-ent part of the gaol, which she soon learned comprised the Governor's private lodgings. On her arrival, she was shown into a well-furnished room, which good taste and comfort, combined with a certain homeliness, made a cheerful and pleasant place. From before a blazing fire, the owner of the room rose up to salute her, unofficial and courteous.

" Miss Chideock," he said, " I owe you a sincere apology. I am sorry that I have brought you here for no purpose."

" For no purpose ? " she cried.

" I would have let you know in time to prevent your com-ing," he went on, unmoved. " But I decided that the matter could be explained better in person. If I seem discourteous, you must please set it down, not to lack of good manners, but to a desire for explicitness. I live by rule, as you are aware, and any departure from exactitude does not satisfy my notions of regular behaviour."

"I quite understand your position," said Quenride, with some impatience and much anxiety. "But what has happened? Am I not to see Mr. Ridley to-day?"

"I regret to inform you that it is impossible."

"Impossible? He is ill, then?"

"He is as well as when you saw him last."

"What is it, then?" she demanded a little haughtily.

"I have been obliged to place him under punishment."

Quenride looked at him. Her lips fell apart a full second before she spoke. The Governor expected her to ask "What has he been doing?" But he did not yet understand Quenride Chideock. What she said was:

"I thought you were fond of him!"

He met her gaze steadily.

"Have I said anything," he asked, "to indicate that I am not?"

"Tell me all about it," she said—all the friendliness gone out of her voice—"since that is why you have brought me here."

The Governor bowed, and marched straight into his story.

"There was a man flogged in the yard yesterday. Perhaps you are not aware, Miss Chideock, that the subject of prison discipline is a favourite study with Kenelm, or that flogging is a form of it which he strongly condemns. I have discussed the point with him many times, for while he had his freedom I had, of course, no objection to a friendly argument with him on the subject. But at present the circumstances are somewhat different, and you will readily see that I could not submit to being reprimanded by one of my prisoners. I reproved him sharply for such a breach of discipline, and gave him to understand that I expected an apology."

"Surely," cried Quenride, "you didn't punish him for a trivial thing like that?"

"I did not, madam. I hoped, though I scarcely expected, to hear no more about the matter. But there has been a distressing sequel. To be brief : this morning Kenelm followed the lead of the first culprit—and committed the same offence."

Quenride's eyes were wide with horror.

"You didn't—did you?" she gasped.

The Governor looked at her, steady-lipped, master of himself.

"I did not," he said. Then, after a pause, "I think I have told you that I am—fond of him."

Quenride leant back with relief in her face. She was beginning to like this stern-mouthed veteran.

"Please go on," she said.

"I couldn't do—what you suggest," the Governor continued. "But I was bound to take notice of the affair."

"What was the offence, sir?"

"It begins," responded the Governor grimly, "with a refusal to attend chapel, and ends with knocking down a turnkey. Insubordination with violence, we call it. He was brought before me to answer for his conduct. He admitted the charge at once, and waited, almost smiling, to hear his sentence. It was a very unpleasant moment — for me."

"And how did you contrive to get out of it?"

"By making the state of his health an excuse for remitting the severer penalty. I was almost justified, but not quite."

"And you sentenced him to—what?" asked Quenride.

"Solitary confinement on bread and water and suspension of all privileges for three days."

"And that means that I may not see him," said Quenride wistfully.

She leant her chin in her hand, looking at him.

"I wonder," she said, "that you can bear to think of Kenelm lying there cold and half-starved——"

"I'm not in the habit of half-starving any of my prisoners, Miss Chideock."

"Still, on Christmas Day!"

"If," said the Governor, "there is one custom more absurd than another, it is that of celebrating a religious festival by an extra amount of eating and drinking."

"I entirely agree with you. At what hour do your guests arrive?"

"At six o'clock, madam," he said.

And Quenride Chideock became his personal friend from that moment. She bent forward, and put her next question so suddenly that he answered it in the same spirit.

"Doesn't it cost you a great deal to be so hard?" she asked.

For a moment the mask fell, and she saw before her a worn old man, with a lined face and anxious eyes.

" It costs me far more than I should care for anyone,
even him, to know."

She stretched out her hand, and laid it, with a winning
gesture, on his arm.

" By and by," she said, " you will remember this. And
then perhaps it will be too late to take him by the hand and
tell him that you are sorry that you didn't make—his last
Christmas in England a little—pleasanter for him."

" Yes ; yes, that is true, unfortunately for me," he answered
her. " But what I think of is this. Supposing he shows
to others the same spirit of wilful obstinacy which he has
shown to me "—he leant forward and touched her, very
earnest in his manner—" what's going to happen to him
out there ? I am trying to show him that to set his private
opinions against recognised authority cannot benefit anyone
in his present situation."

Quenride raised her head with a gesture of great dignity.

" Will you tell him," she said, " that I am very glad and
proud to be able to share in his punishment ? "

" I will tell him," said the Governor. He turned to the
fire, and seemed to fall into a fit of abstraction.

" He has never missed a Christmas Day in my company,
since he was sixteen," he continued, at length, in a strangely
softened tone. " I remember this time last year. Kenelm
spent the day with me. We took the Sacrament
together."

Quenride rose, and coming to the side of the man who
had ever set duty before inclination laid her hand on his
shoulder.

" I think," she said, with a strange sense of pity, " that
you will go to him—presently."

The Governor straightened his back with a jerk, and
recovered himself. He also rose, and looked her squarely
in the face.

" I shall not," he said.

She sighed a little, and began to fasten her cloak. Then
she gave him her hand in silence.

" You would like to send a message ? " he asked.

" Only what I have already said," she answered, a little
drearily, " and my love. He will know all that I mean
by that."

The door opened and closed. A lonely old man was left
to his thoughts.

Presently he seemed to remember something. He rose,

and crossed from one room to another.   Here a table was set
out with elegant silver and napery.   Candles were already
lit, and a servant was arranging nine chairs down the sides of
the board.   The Governor nodded his approval, and stood
watching.

"Spread the chairs out more on that side ! " he ordered,
at last.   "You make it look like a vacant space at the end."

"Nine's such an awkward number, sir."

The Governor went out.   It was four o'clock.   He mounted
the stairs half-way, and came down again.   It was full early
to dress for his guests.   He stood drumming his fingers on
his waistcoat, thinking.   Then he opened the outer door, and
looked across the yard.   The cold air stung his face.   He
took down a heavy cloak, and stepped out.   Reaching the
prisoners' quarters, he threaded his way along the dismal
passages until he stopped outside Cell Fifteen.   Inside, it was
growing dusk, and struck very cold.

CHAPTER XXXVIII

THE GOVERNOR'S TOAST

RIDLEY was finishing his supper when the door opened, dipping the dry bread into the mug of water. At sight of his visitor, he rose, and after a quiet greeting, pulled the stool towards him, and took up his own position on the side of the bed. The Governor sat down and looked at him.

" Why did you do it ? " he asked.

Ridley smiled.

" I wanted to test the System," he said. " A man must do something in gaol to amuse himself."

" A pity, surely, that you couldn't find a better thing to do, than to play such a trick on an old friend ? Don't you think that my authority has suffered ? "

" There was a way to preserve it," said Ridley, with the humorously malicious smile still on his lips.

" Ah, you mean——"

" That I ought to have been flogged."

" I'm afraid there can't be two opinions about that," retorted the Governor.

" Well, sir, surely it rested in your own hands. Your excuse was the most miserable shuffling I ever heard. You knew perfectly well that I could have borne it."

The Governor rapped out his answer very sharply.

" Probably ! But could I have done so ? "

Ridley's smile faded. He sat looking at his friend.

" Well," he said, after a pause, " I should like to think that my experiment hasn't been wasted. I'm not denying that I enjoyed the situation ; I did, hugely. But, after all, there is a serious side to it."

" For you, undoubtedly." The Governor's tone was very dry.

" I should like to feel that in future you will remember this episode, and temper your justice accordingly. It

was good of you to come. I suppose you're entertaining
to-night ? "

" Yes. The usual ones."

" Who's going to sit in my place, sir ? "

" No one."

" Thank you. Well, I shall be thinking of you all.
I should like to believe that you'd remember me at your wine.
But your guests wouldn't care for that toast, would they ?
They never were very fond of me. I lashed their foibles
too severely. Perhaps I was wrong. After all, a man may
do worse than cherish foibles ; and be worse than a fool.
If I could come back, and sit with you all again to-night, I
think I'd try to teach my tongue better manners. Homer
will tell a few good stories, new ones, I hope. I always
enjoyed Homer's stories——" he broke into a laugh, which
turned suddenly into a cough, but when he was able he went
on, speaking with a kind of nervous excitement, which
his companion had not noticed in him before to-night
—" and Tregonwell will sing ' Hearts of Oak,' just as
usual. And Garland will trump his partner's best card,
and revoke five times in every rubber ! And they'll all be
very much merrier because young Ridley isn't there to spoil
the fun."

" What have you been doing all day ? " asked the
Governor, after a pause.

" Working out an imaginary murder case. It was rather
interesting."

" I should have thought——" began the other, and paused.
Then he held out his hand. " Forgive me, Kenelm," he said.
" It was brutal of me to think of saying that."

Ridley laid his hand in the outstretched palm.

" You're cold to-night," said the elder man, shivering
at the touch. He placed his other hand over Ridley's, and the
two sat so in silence awhile.

Presently Ridley turned to his companion with a little
shake of the shoulders.

" Don't forget your guests, sir," he said.

" I'm not forgetting," the other answered. " It is my
curse to remember. There'll be an empty place at my
table to-night. And I wish you were not so cold."

" Don't worry about me," said Ridley, in a lighter tone.
" I shall go to bed, and get warm there."

The Governor came to his side, and stretched out a tentative finger and thumb to the single blanket and counterpane

which comprised the regulation covering. He turned sharply
to Ridley.

"You can have your extra blankets back!" he said,
much as though he was ordering him three dozen lashes.
And Ridley knew better than to thank him.

"Good night, sir," he said. "It was very good of you to
come."

"It was not altogether a personal matter," answered the
elder man, with all his habitual stiffness. "I have a message
to give you — from Miss Chideock. She had been given
to understand that she would see you to-day. Naturally,
she was much disappointed."

Ridley set his lips hard. The fingers which the Governor
was still holding twitched a little. Then he said :

"I wish I'd known. Did she blame me, sir ? "

"I'm afraid not," said the Governor. "On the whole,
I think she understood." He repeated Quenride's message,
adding, "She and I are very good friends."

"Of course, I'm glad of that," said Ridley. "Very glad.
Still——"

"Well ? " asked the other man.

"I'd sooner have had fifteen minutes at the triangle than
that this should have happened ! "

The Governor made no comment. He did not even
point out the desired moral to the culprit. He merely took
Ridley's unresponsive hand, bade him good night, and left
him.

Whether the subsequent dinner-party, with its eleven
covers at table, was a success or no, depended entirely on
the separate point of view of guests and host. To him, the
viands were flavourless, the wine without bouquet. There
had been after all too great a space left between the last right
hand chair and the end of the table. The talk and merri-
ment of the others jarred on the man who sat stiffly at the
head of them. Always, he had in his mind the remembrance
of another meal, at which bread was dipped in cold water,
and swallowed with an effort. At length, his tongue found
utterance.

Dr. Homer sat on his left hand. He had just finished
one of his good stories, and under cover of the applause which
followed the Governor addressed him.

"Homer, there's something come into my mind," he said.
"You make your rounds to-morrow ? "

"Oh, yes."

"There's one of the prisoners undergoing special discipline."

The doctor was aware of the fact, but said nothing.

"I'd be much obliged if you would find the treatment detrimental to his health ; and report the case to me in the usual way."

"Certainly ; if you wish it. Only——" the doctor hesitated. "You know what you're doing, I suppose ? You'll weaken your authority."

"Damn my authority ! " said the Governor savagely.

"Oh, of course. If you look at it in that way. Still, I doubt whether the object is worth it."

"Speak out, Homer. What is it you mean ? " The hawk-like eyes shone from under a frowning brow.

"There are a few—rumours going about, I've heard," began the doctor.

"There are a good many lies," corrected his host.

"I've recently been told a very queer story, sir ; on the best authority."

The Governor looked grim, but did not interrupt.

"From a patient of mine. That is, he came to me with a slight ailment t'other day. And when we'd finished the consultation, we got into general conversation. Quite a gentleman, nice manner and all that. Name of Mohun. Ever met him ? Well, it seems that he knows our young friend quite well. Told me a devilish queer yarn about him, in confidence of course. Still, we're all friends here, so——"

But the Governor raised his hand and spoke.

"Pray don't spoil it, Homer," he said. "I hate hearing a story twice over, particularly if it be a good one. Kenelm Ridley was praising your stories to me a short time ago. He's not with us this evening. But that's no reason why he should not share some of our good things. Therefore, I propose that you should keep your story till to-morrow, when he and I will enjoy it together."

Homer shrugged his shoulders, and held his tongue. But the Governor was too influential a friend to be lightly quarrelled with. Presently he relaxed, and touched his host's arm.

"Very well. I'll see to that matter, sir," he said. "After all, it's your affair."

The other man bent his head ; then he filled his glass and rose.

"Gentlemen," he said boldly, "there's an empty place

at our board to-night.   But I would have you all remember
that he who should have filled it will never lack a place in
my heart, or in my prayers, as long as God wills me to live.
My friend—Kenelm Ridley—God bless him ! "

He drank off his wine, and resumed his seat, careless
whether the toast was honoured by the rest or not.

Later, left alone, he followed his usual custom of going
the rounds in person.   Wrapped in his long cloak, and
attended by a turnkey with a lanthorn, he passed noiselessly
along the dark corridors.   Inside the cells, all was silent.
Coming to a certain door, he paused there longer than usual.
Then he drew back the bolts very stealthily, turned his key
in the lock, and taking the light from the other's hand
went in.

Beneath his restored blankets, Ridley lay fast asleep.
Shielding the candle rays very carefully, the Governor raised
the lanthorn, and looked at him.   His face, in slumber, had
taken on a more youthful expression than was permitted
by the anxieties of his waking moments.   He lay with one
hand thrust beneath his cheek, breathing like a child.   So
the Governor had often seen him lie, in his boyish days.
Memory went deeper still.   For even so had Harriet looked
in her last sleep.

Still shading the light with his careful hand, the Governor
bent low over the bed, where Harriet's son lay and dreamed
of freedom and of love.

" God bless you, my dear lad !   God bless you and keep
you, and give you peace wherever you go ! "

CHAPTER XXXIX

LOVE GOES A-MARKETING

IT chanced that Dolly Pouncey had first gladdened her parent's eyes with the sight of her undeveloped charms on a certain morning in mid-January. On the twentieth anniversary of that day, there happening to be the weekly market at Dorchester, she induced her father to tolerate her company into the town. The reason for the desire on her part, was vaguely described as " shopping," and, as soon as might be, she slipped out of her father's charge, and made her way to an establishment, which in the Wareham days she had frequented with fair regularity.

Having purchased, among other things, a beaver bonnet, and seen it set in its proper place with the cherry-coloured ribbons matching her own ripe lips, she stepped out into the street again. It was a fine frosty day, made for adventure of some sort. The town held its usual ingathering of villagers and farmers, and Dolly, as her father's daughter, was well known to all of these. But the market did not attract her. It was countrified and vulgar. She despised the country, and hated vulgarity. Farmers, even farmers' sons, were essentially uninteresting. Moreover, they were hardly to be credited with a capacity for appreciating a new beaver bonnet, even with her face inside. They nibbled at straws, or stuck their hands into the pockets of their corduroy breeches, and simply stared at her. Sometimes they yawned, and were too stupid even to admire. The present state of the wheat market, the possibilities of a harvest which was not yet sown, were matters of utter unimportance to her. And her father's society she could enjoy any day.

The upper end of the town was but little affected by the bustle and stir of market-day, and in this genteeler neighbourhood Dolly wandered awhile, a pretty, rather solitary little figure, turning her blue eyes about almost as though she were looking for some one.

388

At two o'clock, she was to meet her father at the *King's Arms* for dinner.   With what might have been an exemplary desire not to keep him waiting, she turned her face down street at a quarter to one.   Coming back into the busier parts of the town, she stared for a long time at the iron poles, which, set up on the roof of one of the churches, had once supported the grisly mementoes of the Bloody Assize.   A little extra colour came into her face, and rather deliberately she left the High Street, and turned into a narrow road running at right angles with it.

It still wanted an hour to dinner-time.   Though for that matter, she was young enough to be able to demolish sticks of barley-sugar at any hour of the day.   It was a desire for that confection among other things that drew her into the narrow side-street now.   For, of all the possible places where such a dainty might be obtained, there was none to beat Mrs. Fiander's modest shop at the corner of the road.

Dolly reached the shop in question, and, twisting the beaver bonnet this way and that, peered over and between sundry bottles and jars that obscured the interior from the foot-way.   Presently, still with the colour rather deeply staining her cheek, she entered.   Her handling of the closed door proved to be so delicate that the bell attached to it failed to sound the usual note of warning.

Dolly sat down in the only chair, arranged her position rather carefully, and regarded the row of sweet-bottles with an attention which kept her engaged until the bell jangled under a hasty hand, and a lanky young figure blocked the door-way.

" Oh—Miss Pouncey !   I—oh !   Good morning."

Dolly turned, surprise in her well-opened eyes.

" Good afternoon," she said.   She was always precise in such matters.   " It's quite a long time since we met, isn't it, Mr. Fiander ? "

" Ages," he said.   " At least, it seems so to me.   You don't come in very often, perhaps."

" No," sighed Dolly, " not now.   You see, father won't buy a gig like some of the others.   He insists on using the rickety old waggon, because his father always drove in to market in it.   It nearly shook me to death this morning I vow."

Fiander looked apologetic, closed the door, which he had been holding all the time, with great caution, and threw a

glance at the half-glazed partition which led into the adjoining room.

"Well," said Dolly, "since we have met in this accidental way, I suppose we may as well shake hands."

She held hers out, prettily gloved, and looked at him
from inside the new bonnet. He took her fingers for a
moment, then finding his face so near to hers his cheek
suddenly grew red, and he stood away.

"I came in," Dolly remarked rather coldly, "for some
barley-sugar." She ran her eyes along the bottles. "But
I don't see any."

"Oh, I'm sure there is some—fresh made—only last
night. Have you been waiting long?" Fiander spoke quickly,
his gaze wandering all over the shop, and settling anywhere
but on his companion.

"No one came to me," said Dolly, in her plaintive voice.
"I think the bell didn't ring."

"I expect mother's busy in the kitchen," he said. "She
didn't hear me come in, you know."

"I want sixpennyworth," said Dolly.

"Oh, yes. I'll be sure to set my hand on it in a minute."

Dolly rearranged her skirts as she again occupied the only
chair.

"I've got to meet father at two o'clock," she remarked,
when the search had gone on unsuccessfully for some three or
four minutes.

"It's not much after one," said Robin.

"But perhaps I'm detaining you?"

"Not at all! Mr. Frampton let me go early to-day."

"Do you like working under him?" asked Dolly, after
a pause, as her companion appeared to have nothing more
to say.

Fiander turned round, with a box of hard-bake in his
hand.

"Well," he said wonderingly, "of course, not as much
as when—as I used to."

"Is he a disagreeable gentleman?" asked Dolly, not
because she was in the least interested in Mr. Frampton's
disposition, but because, unless she talked, Fiander would
apparently devote his whole energy to the discovery of barley-
sugar.

"Well," he said, staring at the hard-bake, "I shouldn't
like—no, I certainly couldn't call him that. In fact, he's
much pleasanter in his speech than—no, I don't quite mean

that. Yes ; he's really a very nice gentleman, but, of course, it's not the same."

" I'm afraid I am disturbing you," said Dolly, at the end of another three minutes.

" No ; indeed you're not, Miss Pouncey. I'll be certain to find it soon, or, if you like, I'll step inside and ask mother."

Dolly frowned and pouted behind the assiduous youth's back.

" Please don't disturb her," she said, in a small voice. " Perhaps, after all, I'd better go elsewhere."

That brought Fiander round with a start.

" Of course," he said reproachfully, " if you'd sooner—— But I know it's here."

" Well, I can wait just a little longer," she conceded.

And the search began again, the obtuse Fiander persisting in keeping on the wrong side of the counter.

" Do you ever see Mr. Ridley now ? " asked Dolly, presently, for lack of a more personal subject.

" They let me see him last week. That was the first time."

" I hope he's keeping well ? "

" Yes—that is—he says so. And he always was rather pale, wasn't he ? "

" Genteelly so," averred Dolly. " And rather good-looking; almost handsome, I thought."

" Oh," said the impercipient Robin, with exasperating readiness, " quite ! "

Dolly nearly rose from her chair. But, if her head was flighty, her heart was a warm little piece of throbbing mechanism. She had a genuine liking for the object of Fiander's admiration, and saw the indecency of using, as a lever for a tardy wooer, the attractions of one who lay under so heavy a cloud of misfortune as the young lawyer.

Unconscious of all this, Fiander went on:

" He was very kind. But changed, I think, a little."

" Of course," said Dolly, " anyone would grow sharp-tempered, shut up so."

" That's just it ! " cried Fiander, distress in his voice. " He wasn't sharp at all. Only — very kind. He even wanted to know——" and Fiander very nearly came from behind the counter.

" Well ? " asked Dolly softly, with a clear remembrance of her last meeting with Ridley.

" Whether I'd seen you ! "

" Oh, and I suppose you said——"

" That I hadn't !   And then he asked——"

" Well ? " said Dolly even more softly than before.

" Oh — nothing — nothing much ! "   And   Fiander, hot and stammering, secured himself behind the counter again.

" If you really can't find that treacle-stick——"   said Dolly, with a coldness of demeanour at once dignified and instructive.

" Treacle-stick ? " cried Fiander.   " And all the time I've been looking for barley-sugar.   There's plenty——"

" I see there is," remarked Dolly.   " And it's the other I want after all."

" I think I'd better ask mother to come ! "

" Well, just as you like, Mr. Fiander.   I've no doubt I am a great trouble, keeping you from your dinner like this."

" As if I minded that ! " he cried, but without showing the sense to look at her.

Dolly sighed during the next pause.

" I heard from Miss Quenride the other week," she said. " Quite a friendly letter.   She's extremely sorry I don't like the country."

" Then you'll be going back to her, I suppose ? " said Fiander hopefully.

" Oh, not yet, of course.   Poor young lady, her affairs are woefully unsettled, owing to Mr. Ridley's trouble.   You've heard that they were going to be married, I suppose ? "

" Mr. Ridley told me that they would have been, if only——"

" Yes, I understand," said Dolly, quickly.   " Mr. Gilbert wrote too ; he wanted me to promise that I'd go back if Miss Quen asked me.   Unless, of course—I don't know what put such an idea into his head ! "

" Unless what ? "

" Unless I was married by then ! "

Fiander laid down the box he was holding.   He came slowly nearer, and looked at her with great earnestness across the counter.

" And are you likely to be—married, by then, Dolly ? " he asked.

" Dear me, how should I know ?   What odd questions you do put to one ! "

His face brightened.   Dolly had dropped one hand upon the counter.   She waited for him to speak.

"I suppose," he said, beginning to edge away again, "it was silly of me."

Dolly almost gasped. She withdrew her hand as sharply as if it had got itself on to the counter without leave.

"It was silly," she exclaimed, "downright silly! Because, how do I know when *by then* is?"

"Oh," said Robin thoughtfully. "Then you mean that you may be married, perhaps."

"It's not altogether improbable," declared Dolly, looking down.

"Soon?" he inquired, with growing earnestness.

"That depends," she said.

"On what?—if you're not angry with me for asking."

"On several things," said Dolly airily.

"On yourself, that means," he said.

"Partly; yes, I suppose it does."

"I hope you will be very happy," said Fiander, in his simple way.

Dolly scarcely looked it, at that moment. Had he been on the right side of the counter, he would have seen that there were tears in her eyes. She said nothing.

"Is it," asked Fiander, "the gentleman you told me about before?"

Dolly flashed an angry look at him, her cheek no less vivid than the cherry ribbons.

"How dare you mention him to me?" she cried, in a flutter of real indignation. "He's a wretch! And I hate him!"

Fiander looked at the pretty glowing face, took courage, and leant across the counter.

"Dolly! has he made you unhappy?" he asked. His hands went out at last, and caught hold of hers. "Oh, Dolly dear!"

"At any rate," she asserted, "I quite hate him."

"Perhaps—oh, Dolly, did you care for him at all?"

To that she gave no answer. He let fall her hands and looked at her very humbly.

"I oughtn't to have asked it?" he said.

"Why not?" said she.

"Because I hadn't any right to."

"Oh, as much right as anyone, I suppose."

"No. Not now you're going to marry somebody else."

"It was you who said that," replied Dolly, regardless of accuracy.

"No! You!"

"How dare you contradict me? I say it was you!"

"Very well, then. I suppose I did. Anyhow, it don't matter much which of us it was since it's true," sighed Fiander.

"That's you again," Dolly pointed out.

"I? What?"

"Saying it's true!"

"But—isn't it?"

"How should I know?"

"But I thought——"

Dolly shook her head as if she gave up the whole situation.

"I really can't help what you thought, Robin," she said. "Somehow, you always do seem to think the wrong thing."

"I'm afraid I'm very stupid, Dolly dear."

"I don't know how Mr. Ridley managed to put up with you for so long," she retorted, in a tone of gentle complaint.

"Oh, Mr. Ridley." Fiander grew suddenly thoughtful.

"Such a clever man," said Dolly.

"Yes; of course." Fiander stared hard at the counter. "He told me something the other day. I've been thinking about it ever since."

"Oh!"

"Yes. I thought he must be wrong. It didn't seem possible somehow. Dolly, Dolly dear, is it true?"

"If I knew what you're talking about——" she began.

"He said he didn't believe you didn't care——"

"I shall never understand that!" said Dolly. "Can't you put it plainer?"

"Well, then, Dolly dear—'tis this—do you care?—just a little—not much, you know, I wouldn't expect that, of course. But just a little! Do you, dear?"

"Care?" repeated Dolly, in a tone of wonder. "For what?"

"For me!" said Fiander, with a gasp.

"Of course I do. We've always been friends, haven't we? What a lot of words you use over nothing."

"'Tisn't nothing!" he cried. "Oh, Dolly dear, I love you so well, and I'll always love you, all my life long! I know I'm not nearly good enough for you. But if you cared enough to—to marry me, I'd spend the rest of my life in trying to make you happy, indeed I would! Oh, Dolly dear, do look at me and say you will!"

" I can't look at you such a long way off," she murmured.
" I don't know how you can expect it."

" Expect you to marry me ? "

" To shout an answer across such a wide counter ! "

Then Fiander happened on wisdom at last, and came round into the body of the shop. A pair of alluring lips gleamed from out the beaver bonnet. Suddenly, they broke into a smile.

" Dolly ! Dear ! "

" There ! that'll do. You're crushing my ribbons," said she, drawing her head away a minute later. " And I'll not say whether I like you, because probably to-morrow I shan't, and then you'll bother me by reminding me of my word. And I don't promise anything. Perhaps I'll marry you, and perhaps I won't——"

" Dolly ! "

" But if I ever do, you'll have to make things very nice for me."

" Of course I should ! "

" I won't live in the country, mind ! "

" Of course not."

" And you must let me manage everything ! "

" As if I should want to interfere ! "

" And do things in my own way ! "

" I'm sure they couldn't be done better."

" And never have anything ungenteel ! "

" Dolly, dear Dolly, indeed you should have everything as you liked. If you served up the meals on the floor, I'm sure I shouldn't mind, with you at t'other end of the table."

" I don't know what you're talking about," remarked the prospective housewife. " But, anyway, that's a promise."

" There's only one thing," said the lover, venturing near again. " You wouldn't mind mother coming, now and then ? "

" Of course not," said Dolly, " if you wouldn't mind father."

" Oh ! Well, I suppose he couldn't say much, once we were married."

" I don't know about that," said Dolly sagely. " But, at any rate, you'd have the right to order him out of the house if he got very excited."

" Me ? " gasped Fiander. " Me order your father——? "

" Well," she returned, with unfilial alacrity, " if you wouldn't, I should have to."

"Of course," protested Fiander manfully, "if it had to be done, I'd do it. But I'm hoping he'd be reasonable."

"He won't be if I stay here much longer," said Dolly. "I really must go. He's ordered dinner at two."

"It wouldn't be right to keep him waiting," was Fiander's opinion, given with a virtuous sense of self-denial.

"Oh," said Dolly dubiously; "I don't think he'd be waiting. No! You'd better not come. It wouldn't be very pleasant for either of us, if he started on you at once."

"Good-bye, then, Dolly dear. And you'll let me see you sometimes?"

"I'll write. Yes. That'll do, I tell you. Well—what are you looking at so hard?"

"And it was behind your chair all the time!"

"To think of that now!" said the unblushing Dolly. "Perhaps, if you'd only come round to the right side of the counter, you'd have found it long ago!"

.   .   .   .

"Fiander writes to me," said Ridley, later on, to Quenride, "that he has at last succeeded in persuading Dolly Pouncey to engage herself to him. Though, from what I know of them, I fancy that I ought to put it the other way."

"I know, dearest. Dolly wrote to tell Gilbert. Considering how anxious she's always been to see a wedding-ring on her finger, she's made a really great sacrifice."

"In what way? I shouldn't have expected such from her."

"Nor I! But she declares she won't be married until—I am."

The pitiful pretence of confidence and cheerfulness had become a recognised code between these two, since their first interview.

"That's probably," said Ridley, after a slight pause, "because she wants to copy your wedding-gown."

"My wedding-gown!" Quenride repeated the words softly. She slipped her hand into her lover's, and leaned towards him, as she whispered, "Shall it be a pretty one?—oh! shall it be a very pretty one?"

"Whatever gown you wore would be that," said he.

"Oh, Kenelm," she breathed; "that's the first fondly foolish thing you've ever said to me."

"Is it? Ah, I'm a clumsy lover, I fear, my Quenride. You ought never to have chosen me."

"Hush! Listen to me, and I'll tell you a secret. When

we women bring our hearts to market, we don't like to carry
them home again."

"But you have made such a very bad bargain, my
Quenride."

"Ah," she said involuntarily, "it is you who are paying
the price."

And the day which should determine how heavy that
price must be, drew steadily nearer, with its darkening
shadow, and its grim menace.

CHAPTER XL

A CLAPPING OF HANDS

RIDLEY'S case was undeniably the most popular one in the calendar of the next Assizes. As the time drew on, although he could scarcely be said to have a friend left in the town, there were many, inside and out, who took a keen interest in his unhappy affairs. The day before the Court opened, the inns and taverns began to fill with a mixed concourse, drawn hither on his account. There was hardly a county family, in a shire well stocked with such, which did not send at least one representative. To take a share as an unofficial witness, to see how the prisoner bore himself, to ascertain how the verdict would go—such considerations were set before business and pleasure, alike by the browsing squires and the young provincial bloods round about. Wagers were offered freely, but were seldom taken up, since the betting was mainly on the one side. In manor-houses, in farm-yard corners, at mercantile counters, from landed gentry, pluralist clergy, farmer and shepherd alike, whenever the chances of the forthcoming trial were broached, at the close of the discussion came the inevitable words : " He's certain to be convicted ; absolutely certain."

That the beautiful Miss Chideock had a tender personal interest in the affair formed one reason for the widespread attention afforded to it by the neighbouring gentry. Her concerns had been much talked of during the winter, when sporting topics failed. Her concealment of her grandfather's death had rendered her a little conspicuous. To this was added the report of her betrothal to the young Radical attorney, now lying in gaol, under so serious a charge.

She was considered by many to have compromised her dignity, beyond pardon, by contemplating such an alliance. To permit the relations to continue now that her lover was little better than a convicted felon was no less than an outrage to society itself. Quenride was shunned accordingly. Yet her proud head was held as high as it had ever been, and her composure in public suffered no change.

As the days went by, and in fragmentary fashion she watched his case slowly assuming shape, seeing it prospectively as it would ultimately appear in the hand of one of the cleverest members of the Bar, her heart grew sick and heavy with dread. There seemed so little, so pitifully little, that could be urged on his behalf. And every hour the prejudice against him deepened, until she wondered wearily where there could be found, in all the judicial boundary, twelve unbiased men to try his cause. So little to say ; so few witnesses who cared to come forward to attest to his honour and integrity—she herself relegated to the other side.

Ridley's case was taken on the second day of the Assizes. The court was full. Not for many years had such a select assembly of spectators crowded itself into the dismal place. Quenride, glancing feverishly round, thought herself beset by well-known faces. She picked out the most significant, and studied each with a painful intensity. Anything, anything to keep her sick brain from dwelling too earnestly on the probable issue of the day ; anything, anything, so long as her thoughts did not set their mark too indelibly on her features, for, at least, she hoped to show her lover a high courage that should equal his own.

She therefore ran her eyes round the crowded court-house with a deliberation that seemed rather to seek than to avoid the curious glances which met her on all sides. She recognised many of the better sort of spectators : Welds, Strangewayses, Matraverses, Trenchards—and the rest. Some with looks of pity, others superciliously marvelling, the remainder merely curious or indifferent. She acknowledged her friends with more than customary hauteur, and was bringing her gaze back to the benches nearer at hand when she caught sight of a new arrival. It was Alaric Mohun, taking his place with a roving glance, that seemed to collect the whole spectacle and bring it to a focus on her face. In spite of her resolution, she shuddered and shrank back in her seat. Though separated from her by the width of the court, Mohun seemed aware of her revulsion. He bowed to her, and smiled. But the bow was an insult, and the smile, a mockery. A passionate bitterness swept the blood into her cheek. Mohun had the confident air of one who had triumphed at the last.

Nearer to her she saw Fiander's face, nervous and anxious-eyed ; beyond that, one who she was told was the attorney who had first instructed Ridley in his profession ; and others of whom she had no knowledge. She looked around at the more formidable array of witnesses for the prosecution. A medley collection these, where broadcloth rubbed shoulders with fustian, and dignified composure sat alongside rustic self-consciousness. She guessed rather than knew, the particular mission of each—save in the single case of Sophy Hoddinott.

The girl sat crouched in her place, with bent head and drooping shoulders. She hugged a worn shawl tightly across her pinched breast, and seemed either alarmed or stupefied. Her pale insignificant features, her sombre eyes, her slight figure wrapped in the tattered shawl, all had borrowed, for this one day, an importance that lifted her, ignorant cottage girl as she was, above the most finely dressed lady there. For it was her hand which had gathered them all together, to hear the momentous question decided, whether Kenelm Ridley should be cast out like an unclean thing from among them or not.

And now the court was full to overflowing, the air already, despite the crisp March breeze, growing warm and fetid. At the back, the hands of the clock were slowly coming to the hour of ten. A momentary faintness seized Quenride. She closed her eyes, grew aware of a sudden stirring throughout the court, and opened them upon the filling jury-box. She found herself gazing at Farmer Pouncey's heated visage. She felt her own grow pale. Beneath her cloak, her fingers worked apprehensively.

But she had short time for the indulging of emotion. Recollecting her need for composure, for confidence, for courage, she braced herself up, controlled the trembling nerves, and showed again the calm proud beauty of her face to all who cared to see.

But for the moment, interest in her had flagged. There were other and more important things at hand to chain attention and to excite eager curiosity. Her own gaze became fascinated by the scarlet-robed figure taking his place on the Bench. She kept her eyes upon him as if endeavouring to learn from the immobile features what manner of mind lay behind. Before she had well withdrawn her look, with a deep breathing almost like a sigh, the court fluttered again, and, turning, she saw the prisoner entering the dock.

Heads were thrust forward to look at him. A very faint whisper was felt rather than heard, as comments, born of curious interest, were given bare utterance. He had grown thin in prison, it was alleged, under the breath ; he looked as insolent as ever ; he had the air of a man who knew that his cause was hopeless ; he showed an indefensible lack of emotion, amounting to immorality in one in his situation. So the faint whispers averred, in the infinitesimal interval before they were repressed.

The truth was that Ridley, having bowed to the court, and sought out Quenride's face, was now waiting with a demeanour of quiet firmness for the trial to begin. His natural pallor had become intensified by the months of confinement, and a certain delicacy was accentuated by the sombreness of his attire. But his hands rested quite steadily on the rail in front of him, and there was no suggestion of flinching in the voice with which he presently pleaded *Guilty* to the charge.

There was a perceptible stir in the court. Eyes ran from the dock to the Bench, as the judge, intervening at this point, turned to the prisoner's counsel, and asked whether he had been prepared for such a plea.

" I had reason to suspect it, my lord," was the reply.

" Of course," continued his lordship, who seemed displeased, " the prisoner is aware of the consequences of such pleading ? "

" No one better, my lord," said the other. " But may I suggest that your lordship should exercise your discretion, and order the plea to be withdrawn ? "

The judge, after a moment's consideration, directed that a plea of *Not Guilty* should be entered, the court settled back again, and Ridley—whose desire to spare Quenride the ordeal of witnessing against him was thus over-ruled—had no choice but to submit. The trial thereupon proceeded.

The facts of the case were well known. Neither examination nor cross-examination could elicit much fresh evidence. From the first, the trial went against the prisoner. It ran on orthodox lines, and was scarcely capable of much dramatic surprise. Only at two points did the general interest warm into anything like excitement.

The first of these occurred during the cross-examination of the principal witness for the prosecution.

Sophy Hoddinott had repeated the evidence which she had delivered before the magistrate. Her manner of doing so was in no way remarkable. She spoke in short sentences, as her manner was, and kept her eyes fixed on the counsel's face. Throughout the time of her speaking she never once looked at the prisoner. Her voice held all its usual ungracious tones, and the only sign of emotion lay in her apparent awe of her surroundings. At the close of her evidence, there was a look on the barrister's face which suggested a belief that the prisoner was as good as transported already.

Then came the surprise.

" Take a good look at the prisoner," she was advised by the other side, " and say whether you are prepared to swear that he is the man whom you saw on Wareham Bridge, at five o'clock, on the morning of December the sixth last."

Sophy shifted her eyes, wavered, and let them fall to the ground. No answer. The question was repeated more sharply. She raised her head, slowly, unwillingly. The court thrilled a little.

" I—I can't see—him," she muttered.

It was a fact that Ridley had his shoulder turned slightly towards her. Those who cared to notice had already observed that the witness-box might have been empty for all the heed he took of its occupant.

" Perhaps the prisoner will have the goodness to let you see his face ! "

Ridley turned with a readiness which dispelled any notion that he was reluctant to meet her look. But even so, though he was now facing her squarely, he gave her no more than a set of expressionless features, and a pair of eyes focused on some point beyond and above her head.

" Look at him well ! " came the order. " Can you swear that he is the same man ? "

Sophy shivered. The court was very warm. Yet she shivered, and pulled the ragged shawl across her bosom. A great scarlet stain rose upon her pale cheek, and spread to her forehead. But her eyes were coming up slowly, as if against volition, and presently they found the prisoner's face.

" Now ! " said the counsel, leaning forward with index finger raised. " You saw the man on the bridge for a few moments only, by the light of an expiring lanthorn. You see the prisoner in full daylight, and may look at him as long as you please. Take your time. The court does not wish to hurry you. Then tell us if he is the same man."

And now her gaze, having fixed itself upon Ridley's face, hung there for so long a time that the counsel himself showed signs of impatience, while the spectators craned forward, and a little human interest animated even the judge's countenance.

The jurymen fidgeted, the prosecution looked uneasy. The prisoner never moved his regard from that distant point above the witness's head.

Sure of it ? Of a truth, she was sure.

She could have laughed the whole court to scorn for its doubt of her. And yet—and yet.

"*It's quite possible to be happy even while you're miserable—and it's a much better state than being miserable while you're happy.*"

So he had told her once, long ago ; and had added the wish that no such tragic experience might darken her lot. From the low standpoint of human vindictiveness, this girl should have been happy. Yet, in this moment—compelled as she was, less by order of the law than by some subtle nameless force, to look again at the man whom she had loved and betrayed—she knew that she was miserable.

Her lips fell apart. Her eyes never left his face. She saw it sharpened and streaked by the prison discipline, and she grasped the truth that it was her hand which had set such marks upon it. Her pitiful scheme of revenge for a fancied slight had succeeded well. She had brought him very low. And yet, humiliated as he undoubtedly was—even her crude perceptions showed her that—he gave her his face with the cold serenity of a conqueror and it was she who was ashamed.

Never a look, never a sign, while the court waited for her to speak.

And now this girl, whose half-sullen, half-resigned attitude towards the circumstances of life had given a curious lack of fear, began suddenly to tremble. Very slowly her head drooped ; very slowly her hands came up to meet it. She covered her face, dry-eyed, and numbed beneath the power of an agony keener than any pain which she had yet known.

Dully she heard the often-repeated question drumming in her ears, " Is he the same man ? " She looked up with a baffled hunted expression, which made her strangely repellent, as she gave the answer in a low thick voice.

" I don't know."

The counsel glanced round with as much satisfaction in his manner as he might permit himself, and bade her stand down.

The incident produced some sensation, and stimulated interest. Undoubtedly, the weakening of Sophy's evidence was a point in Ridley's favour. Quenride's spirits rose, and

she regarded her lover with a cheerfulness not wholly as
sumed.   Upon Ridley himself, the episode had a different
effect.   He became thoughtful, even abstracted in his bearing,
and appeared to pay little heed to the next few witnesses.

As he himself had foreseen, the aim of the prosecution was
to twist the crime into a political offence.   Having traced
with tolerable exactitude the prisoner's movements immediately before and after the alleged commission of the crime,
a number of witnesses were called to attest the dangerous
nature of his avowed principles.

Quenride was still slightly shaken from her own ordeal,
wherein she had been forced to admit no more than the
fact of Ridley's visit to her, with the valise in his possession,
on the morning of the sixth of December.

She now listened with a growing horror, as from this point
onward the case blackened against him.

It was idle to demand, with inward passionateness, what
political opinion had to do with the present charge.   Trusting,
in her inexperience, to those better fitted to be her guide for
good or ill in this matter, she sought out faces here and there,
that she might judge by these.   She found the Governor
looking more than usually hard-featured and stern of mouth.
The jurymen showed disapproval without exception.   The
counsel for the defence conducted the cross-examination
with a slight loss of temper.   Heads were nodded with an
air of terrible finality ; and in his far corner Alaric Mohun
was smiling openly.

When the court adjourned at midday she had an agonised
word with the Governor.   He looked grave, and bade her
be prepared for what might happen.

" But the girl broke down ! " she urged.

He admitted it, without admitting anything else.

" And the defence is yet to come ! "

The Governor could not deny it.   But Quenride saw that
he was not hopeful.

There was worse to come.

When the trial was resumed, and Ridley stood again in
the dock, she dared to make him the supreme criterion of
his probable fate.   Here, she felt, was a judgment clear and
keen, one to which she herself owed everything ; a mind
so evenly balanced and withal so delicate, that, given the
opportunity, it could not fail eventually to gain for him a
high place in his profession.   Surely, it might be trusted now.

She looked at him.   In the same moment, he met her

gaze—met it with a little shock of pain agitating his features, the first sign of emotion which he had shown. And though, an instant later, he made shift to smile at her, it was little more than a spasmodic movement of the lips, and hurt her accordingly. From that minute, fear clutched at her heart, fear all the more terrible because she must needs hide it from him.

She saw too that his manner had changed. Undoubtedly, he looked more worn.

His self-control was not as perfect as it had been. He now kept his hands out of sight, or gripped the edge of the dock with unnecessary firmness. He sought her face more frequently, and regarded it always with that look of distressed wonderment.

More ground was lost. It was the Governor's lot to provide another, though a smaller sensation. After testifying nobly to the prisoner's high principles and unblemished reputation, it was demanded of him whether he had not had occasion, during the prisoner's period of detention, to inflict punishment for a serious misdemeanour.

The Governor was observed to flush a dull red, and to pause noticeably before answering.

" Of so severe a character that it was subsequently remitted by the doctor's advice ? "

" At my own request," amended the Governor.

" Is that your usual practice ? "

" The case was exceptional."

" Was the offence an act of insubordination followed by violence towards an official of the prison ? "

" It was. But, in my judgment, the act was rather one of wilful daring than of deliberate lawlessness."

" The fact, however, remains, that the prisoner, while in your charge, did not conduct himself with the regularity compatible with a genuine regard for established authority, as vested in yourself. Is that so ? "

" It is. But the circumstance can be explained," said the Governor obstinately.

" The court, sir, asks for facts, not for explanations. That will do."

The Governor left the box, knowing that Ridley's credit had gone down several points since he had entered it.

The afternoon wore away. The prosecuting counsel spoke. The speech was a bitter and rather unscrupulous attack upon the prisoner. His public principles and private morals were slandered with a disregard for the decencies of honest argument, only possible in an age when the utmost licence was indulged in by the leading literary organs. At the end of twenty minutes, Kenelm Ridley, late attorney of the town, was shown to be a danger to society, an unmitigated liar, a blasphemous infidel, and a law-breaker of the most daring type.

The calumny was so audacious and monstrous that even the prisoner's pale cheek reddened under the violence of the attack. While the voice went on, continuing the work of defilement, he remained motionless, the centre to which the general attention was turned ; but when, at length, the peroration came to a dramatic close, he was observed to lean against the side of the dock as though physically exhausted by the tirade.

The speech for the defence was a no less remarkable piece of work. It even revived Quenride's fast-fading hopes. It was brilliant in delivery, and audacious in argument. In it was pointed out that there was no particular reason why any man should be standing his trial on account of Wareham Bridge. The bridge still spanned the Frome. Whatever damage had been done, had been adequately repaired. But if it was alleged that, in effect, the law for its preservation had been broken, then there was no proof that the deed had been committed by the prisoner. There was only one person who had observed anyone on the bridge during the time when the crime was supposed to have been committed. And that witness had signally failed to identify the prisoner with the alleged culprit. That the prisoner was absent from home during that night, proved nothing. He had a widespread practice, and had, on other occasions, spent a night abroad. And so on—and so on, leading gradually, and with perfect good-humour, up to the assumption that Ridley was the vicarious sufferer for a criminal whom he generously desired to shield.

Quenride flashed grateful glances at the speaker when he had ended. In the short pause which followed, each one heard his neighbour's breathing.

The summing-up showed very clearly that his lordship had taken alarm. His address was brief, but pregnant with antagonism towards the prisoner. If the jury, in their minds, held him to be guilty, let them look to it that no considerations of false sentiment tempted them from their obvious duty. It was not for them to criticise the severity of the incurred penalty but merely to return a verdict for or against the man in the dock.

At five minutes to four the jury retired. At four o'clock, they re-entered the court. A great hush filled the place.

" Are you agreed upon your verdict ? "

They were so agreed.

" Do you find the prisoner *Guilty* or *Not Guilty* ? "

" *Guilty*, my lord."

The court drew a deep breath, and craned forward a little more.

The damning word went like fire through Quenride's brain. In the moments that followed, even her lover's face was blotted from her vision.

When she recovered, she heard the judge speaking. Listening, with an infinite effort, she gathered that he had seldom presided at a trial presenting so many painful features ; that the fact of the prisoner being an avowed exponent of the law, which he had outraged and defied, was a circumstance conducive to the utmost horror in all well-ordered minds ; that his lordship owed gratitude to Heaven that it was in his power to inflict an exemplary punishment upon one who had so criminally betrayed his profession.

The prisoner had nothing to say.

Sentence was accordingly pronounced.

Transportation for Life.

In a distant corner of the court, arose the sound of a clapping of hands. Glancing in the direction from whence it came, the curious noted a florid-faced man, who was a stranger to the town.

Nearer at hand, came the noise of a falling body. A whisper ran round that one of the female witnesses had fainted. Natural enough : the place was certainly hot.

In the jury-box, Farmer Pouncey wiped his forehead, and offered his broad palm to his colleagues with the air of a hero.

There was a slight stir eddying towards the dock. Something, a scrap of paper, was passing from hand to hand. Presently it reached Ridley, who stood exchanging a few brief words with his counsel.

" I'm sorry, Mr. Ridley, I did my best. But you gave me no chance," said the one.

" That doesn't prevent my being deeply grateful to you. Your speech was the finest thing I ever heard. It would have given me a great deal of pleasure, at another time."

"Well, you have my sympathy, sir, and my good wishes, if a petition should be raised."

"That would be a popular proceeding, I take it!" said Ridley, with a strange sort of smile.

As he was leaving the dock, the scrap of paper reached his hand. He crushed it mechanically between his fingers, and dropped it unheeding to the floor.

If he had looked at it, he would have seen only three words: "*I'm sorry. Sophy.*"

They stood up to watch him pass, an eager curious throng, all at gaze upon one who went out from among them a convicted felon, yet none the less the honest lawyer and the man of honour that he had always been.

And Quenride Chideock kept her eyes upon him to the last, drawing her strength for this hour from the look which he had given her in the supreme moment.

The court began to empty. A touch on her arm roused her. Turning, she saw Fiander at her side.

"Is there anything that I can do for you, ma'am?"

"I should have liked," she told him, "to speak to the Governor. But I see that he has gone."

"You might catch him up, ma'am, if you make haste. This way, please, ma'am."

She followed the lad blindly, and thus overtook the Governor not many yards from the entrance. He turned upon her rather than to her. At another time, she would almost have quailed before the subdued ferocity of his manner.

Before she could speak, he was answering her.

"Not now, madam, not now!" he said, barely pausing in his stride. "For God's sake, have some pity on him, and spare him that!"

"I will," she said. "I did not mean—that is, I did not hope—— But you are going to him, are you not?"

"Could I leave him alone in his hour of shame?"

"Will you take a message from me?"

"What is it?"

"Only this," said the agitated woman at his side, "tell him, that when he stood there, disgraced before them all, his name dishonoured, his worldly goods taken from him, judged only fit to be thrust out from among honest men, tell him, in that moment, I knew him to be a better and a greater man than any who sat in judgment on him, or feasted their curiosity on his humiliation. Tell him, that I saw his honour clear and unsullied still, in spite of the lies which

have been flung at it this day. And, oh, sir, in pity tell
him that it is my pride in him no less than my love for him
which keeps my heart from breaking in this hour."

" I will tell him," said the Governor, and so was gone.

Quenride set forward again, with Fiander half a pace
behind. The rest were passing them now, a chattering,
noisy-voiced crew. The streets were filling rapidly. The
recent jurymen went by in a stream. With a swift gesture,
Quenride detached one of them, and spoke.

" Mr. Pouncey," she said, " you will receive notice to quit
on quarter-day."

He gaped at her. She was for passing on, when he
stretched out a broad expostulating palm.

" To quit ? Quit Medley's Croft, ma'am ? "

" I said so."

" But—I were barn there ! An' my feyther afore I ! "

" I'm not responsible for that, Mr. Pouncey. As my
brother's trustee, I think it advisable to make a change."

Again she passed on. Out of the fast thickening crowd
about her, a face suddenly drew near to hers—a highly
coloured face, mocking in its complacency.

" Well, Quenny, so it's to be single-blessedness, is it—or
are you for my arms, after all ? "

At her full height she was a trifle taller than he. On
occasion, she had the trick of turning this fact to great advantage. It was such a moment now.

" Sir," she said, " if you presume to address me again, I
will lay upon you an insult that will make you hate me a
little more than you already do ! "

With such words, and with so fine a bearing did Quenride
Chideock make her progress from the court-house to her inn.

14

CHAPTER XLI

THE THIRD TIME OF ASKING

IT was not a time for many words. The two men clasped hands in silence.

"There's very little use in saying that I'm cut to the heart, Kenelm," the Governor began, with an unusual huskiness thickening the incisive tones. "It's bad, very bad, for all of us."

"It's about as bad as it can be," said Ridley, after a long pause. "I used to wonder why, when men were given the choice, they often preferred the rope to the settlements. I know now."

"That's a hard saying, Kenelm."

"Do you think so?"

The cell had grown perceptibly darker when the elder man spoke again.

"You have frequently said that you were prepared for —it."

"Ah, you remind me of that?"

"You have said so."

"I must have been boasting, then!"

"Surely not."

"Ah, well! I thought I was prepared. I know now that —I was not."

The Governor laid his hand on the bowed shoulder.

"Kenelm——" he said, and caught his breath on the name, and so said no more.

Presently Ridley raised his head.

"Tell me again," he pleaded, "what she said to you."

The Governor searched his memory—which seemed less clear than usual—and once more repeated the purport of Quenride's words. Ridley listened thoughtfully, and kept silent for some moments after the other had ceased to speak.

"She said that? Why, do you know, sir, in that moment, I was like a drowning man. All my life rose up before me, and remembering the things I wished undone I felt that the sentence was an absolutely just one."

The Governor shook his head.

"You judge yourself too harshly. Great offences have no place in your life."

"There are the lesser things."

"Very little, in your case."

Ridley looked at him with a kind of shudder.

"What a brute they made me out to be! I suppose every one believed it," he said; and dropped his face again into his hands.

"The opinion of the crowd has never troubled you much as yet," said the other. "You're not yourself to-night."

"Can you blame me for that?" asked Ridley, with a sudden passion, which rose and fell in an instant.

"Did I say so?" replied the Governor, with a mildness born of his unspoken pity. "But to-morrow, I think, you will forget the unessential things. There is no state in this life so hopeless that nothing can be saved. And I know you for a brave man, Kenelm."

"If she had died," said Ridley, presently, "if I had lost her in that way, I should have known that her pure body was at rest, and her innocent soul in safe keeping. But to part from her like this!—to leave her alone in a world where the best woman has the hardest time, where the worst man is usually so strong."

"She will never need a friend while I live," said the Governor.

"I know that, sir. I was sure of it. I am not ungrateful, but——"

Silence fell again. The elder man rose to his feet a little heavily. The bowed figure at the table did not stir. Twice the Governor made as if to speak, and still the silence held. He touched the drooping shoulder very lightly.

"God give you strength to bear it," he said, then. "For your own part, you can do no good by weakening your body for what is yet to come. You have fasted all day; you need food and rest. See that you take both. And, though the Lord forbid that I should help you to false hopes, remember that your friends will not be idle."

Ridley raised his head, with a strangled sort of laugh.

"My friends!" he cried bitterly. "Oh, my God! where are my friends? Didn't you see them in court to-day?— the men and women who have taken my hand and broken

bread with me a score of times ! My fault, you will say. I
didn't take enough care to make myself liked. True ! I'd
have admitted it yesterday—a man can't spend four months
in prison without learning something—and I'd have called
upon you to witness that I passed from your charge a better
man than when I came into it. But to-night, with the memory
of those curious mocking eyes stabbing me, it's fatally easy
to forget new resolutions, and to long to strike back, with the
weapons one best knows how to use."

The Governor caught the unsteady hands held out to him,
and looking down with his quiet bright eyes said never a
word. But, by and by, the nervous fingers ceased to shake
in his clasp, and the excited voice grew calm.

" I must ask you to excuse me, sir," said Ridley. " You
were right. I am overstrained, tired, and rather illogical,
I'm afraid. I've admitted the justice of the sentence on
private grounds. I have no right to quarrel with others for
looking at it in the same light — but I wish I could remember one sympathetic face among all those that stared
at me when I left the court. That is all."

Soon afterwards, the Governor went away. He himself
seemed to have aged somewhat since the morning. He
walked heavily, and a turnkey who addressed him in the yard
had to speak twice before an answer was returned.

The Governor completed his official duties for the day, and
dismissing his servants shut himself up in his private room.
And there, throughout the long night, he laboured, like the
king of old, to deliver his friend from the fate which the law
decreed.

A long night. A night of doubt and distress, of heaviness
and hesitation. A night when this man found himself face
to face with the most stupendous problem which had ever
opened out before him, a problem of such tremendous issue
that he might well pray for the right judgment, lest he should
decide amiss.

For to the Governor, grieving in his secret way over the
impending calamity, light had come. But the light had a
horror of great darkness behind it, so that he clasped his
twitching hands, as he paced to and fro, and told himself that
he dared not do this thing.

Across the yard, behind the locked doors, lay those for
whose safe keeping he was answerable. He drew the shutter
once, and looked out. All was very quiet and still. The
prison house gave no sign. The prisoners slept. Even the

exhausted Ridley had found a temporary peace at last, and
would awake in the morning with a saner vision and a calmer
courage to endure the ordeal of the coming days.

And still across the way the Governor laboured to deliver
him.

A night of darkness and sudden rain ; of weary wrestling
and mental toil ; of doubt and fear. A long night—and,
at the end, a haggard-faced man, with the strength of a
great determination in his eyes.

For the Governor had come to his resolve, bitter with
desperation though that resolve was. Because of the light,
the darkness must be forgotten, since it was possible that the
light might win. Possible, but no more. God of Heaven !
he dared claim no more. An intense hope carries ever an
intense fear in its skirts. But those who fear the most, hope
in the highest degree also, and gather courage from their
very dread.

Yet, by himself, this man could not stand. Not to him
alone was the task in which he was now ready to bear his
part—a part which, safely carried through, could scarcely
fail to earn censure, or worse, for himself. Such considerations had not thrown an iota of weight into the balance
during the night, and in the morning he went no less steadily
forward.

He worked in his own way. And a silent, grim, uncom-
promising way it proved to be. Even a hard or cruel way,
some humanitarians would have affirmed. For though on
the next day, and on other subsequent days, he encountered
the woman who was to be his co-partner in the attempt, he
said no word to her of the project in his mind.

The days, two, three, even four, passed by. And still he
made no sign. Quenride showed to him an agonised face
with an everlasting question written there. He shook his
head at her, and said nothing. To Ridley himself he said
little more. It was evident that the younger man expected
nothing. It was understood by the lovers that the Governor,
as he had promised, was not idle ; but while Quenride watched,
and the elder man waited, Ridley had fallen into a resigned
mood, which indicated, with sufficient clearness, his acceptance of his position, as one without hope.

In his new condition, as a convicted felon awaiting the
carrying out of his sentence, changes were inevitable. The
Governor, throwing regulations on one side, offered him
some slight amelioration of the necessary hardship, but this

Ridley refused, submitting to the present order of things, without rebellion or complaint. The only change in his manner was an increasing reticence. Of what lay behind the whole affair, the Governor had no knowledge. He was never one to force any man's confidence, and reserve was a quality which he could both respect and appreciate.

On the fifth day, he dared wait no longer. He sent for Quenride, who had not left the town since the day of the trial. She came immediately, and, as before, questioned him with her eyes. And again he shook his head.

"You wished to see me, sir ? " she said, then, checking a sigh.

"I did. I should have come to you. But what I have to say is of an exceedingly private nature, and is best said within these walls."

"Yes, sir," she said, with a patience new to her.

"I have heard nothing from London," the Governor went on. "When I do hear, I do not expect the answer to be favourable. To the ordinary mind, it is not a case for sympathy."

"Did you send for me—— ? " began Quenride indignantly.

But he checked her impetuosity with upraised hand.

"I have thought the matter well over," he said. "I lost no time about that. And it seems to me that there is one chance, and one chance only."

"Then, in Heaven's name, sir, why don't you take it ? " she cried, a new light on her face. "Why do you hesitate so long ? "

"Not without reason, Miss Chideock. The chance is a poor one, I must tell you——"

"But anything that is a chance at all is worth trying ! "

"And it carries with it a great risk."

"Of what ? "

"Of failure."

She was silent for a moment. Then she began to speak with a steady confidence.

"That must be said, I suppose, of all chances," she answered. "But at least we should be no worse off than we are now."

He regarded her very steadily.

"That is where you are wrong," he told her. "If we succeed, we do succeed ; if we fail, we thrust a double portion of suffering upon him."

She went a little white at that, and sat silent, with clasped hands.

" I leave the choice with you," the Governor went on, in calm level tones. " For myself, I am willing to sanction the attempt. But it needs courage ; for your own sake ; even more, for his. I do not doubt you, Miss Chideock. But, for your subsequent peace of mind, it is only right to point out the risk to Kenelm himself. Our responsibility is all the greater, because he must know nothing until we have either lost or won."

She looked at him piteously.

" For his sake," she made reply, " I would dare anything, I would lose anything, except my woman's honour, for which I am answerable both to my God and to the man I love. But the risk is not one to be taken lightly, it seems. Will you tell me what your scheme is, that I may the better judge whether I dare consent to it or not ? "

Then, in a few brief sentences, he unfolded his plan to her.

She heard him in silence, desire and dread alternating in her expressive eyes. When he had finished, she still said nothing.

" You see the cruelty of it," he pointed out. " At present, by God's help, he has come to a spirit of resignation, and expects nothing. Believe me—before you decide—the second state will be worse, far worse, than the first. I saw him immediately after he was sentenced. And then he had been, in some measure, prepared. To raise him now to the assurance of release, and then to thrust him back to his despair with a new regret, is a possibility which only a very brave woman dare face. And yet, only so, can we hope to gain his consent to the marriage which shall entitle you to claim, on his behalf, your ancient privilege."

Quenride sprang up.

" It shall be done," she said. " I have the courage, even for this."

" Have you thought of yourself ? " the Governor asked her. " If you fail——"

" I shall not fail ! He has no faith in my power, I know. But I think that my petition is more likely to obtain a hearing than yours. Surely precedent must count for something ! "

" If you fail," the Governor said again, as if she had not spoken, " you will be the wife of a transported felon. You have thought of that ? "

Quenride flung back her head, almost with a laugh.

" I shall be the proudest wife in all England," she said.

" You have decided, then ? " he asked.

" Certainly, I have. Why did you not ask me before ? "

" Because I wished the event to appear natural. Because I feared you might unconsciously raise his suspicion by something in your demeanour."

" You are very thoughtful, sir."

" You are very brave," he said.

" No, I am not," she answered, with a quick look of dread. " There is something which I cannot do."

" What is that ? "

" You must tell him—everything. I will do my part faithfully. But you must prepare him. Say that it is my wish—my earnest wish—oh, say whatever you please ! Anything that will bend his will to ours, and induce him to consent. But until that consent is won I will not see him. Not until the very moment of its fulfilment. For I dare not look into his honest eyes with a lie on my lips. I should break down, and he would guess the truth—and so we should lose all."

" Miss Chideock," said the Governor gravely, " I shall not ask it of you."

She put out her hands.

" Thank you, oh, thank you ! And do you trust yourself ? "

He bowed his head.

" For the sake of my friend—yes, I can do it."

" When ? "

" Now."

Quenride shivered.

" May I wait ? " she asked.

" It will be best," he said.

He left her then, and made his way to the cell where Ridley was confined. He went resolutely, as to a stern task. His look was the one which he habitually wore on what were known in the prison as " hanging mornings." It might be that he himself saw no great difference, from a moral point of view, in the two duties.

He entered the cell alone, and closed the door behind him. Ridley looked up with the smile to which the elder man had grown accustomed in these days. As the Governor came forward, he sprang up, and his expression changed.

" You have come to tell me something ! " he exclaimed.

" Yes."

" The ship——"

" It is not that."

" I am to be removed, then ? "

" No. The order has not yet come."

" What is it, sir ? "

The Governor sat down heavily. Ridley leant on the table, watching him. The place was so poorly lighted that it was not easy at a short distance to distinguish much play of expression. Furthermore, the visitor was now shielding his face. He nerved himself to the task. He had seen much, and done much, this grizzled veteran, but the self-imposed duty came very hard.

" You have borne bad news, Kenelm," he said. " Do you think that you could bear to hear good tidings, as well ? "

" Good tidings, sir ? "

And the Governor almost flinched before the trembling note of joy in the other's voice.

" Good—tidings, sir ? " repeated Ridley, with the strange sweet thrill still rising in his tones. His hands, resting on the table, suddenly began to tremble. " For God's sake, tell me what you mean ! "

Almost, in that moment, the Governor repented him, and turned aside from his purpose. The dawning relief and happiness in the haggard young face opposite to him was the cruellest sight he had been called upon to bear. He drew his hand over his eyes, as if to shut it out.

But now Ridley's fingers were clutching at him, and his voice, grown strong and eager, was plying him with questions, so that the Governor groaned in his heart, and thought of the woman waiting out yonder, to goad himself on to the task.

" Surely it can't be true ! " he heard that earnest young voice saying, with an almost painful iteration. " Is it—is it—a pardon—a—release, sir ? Oh, my God ! it can't be true. In mercy, tell me, sir—is that what you mean ? "

The nervous fingers had plucked his hands away, and Ridley was looking at him now—such a look as Quenride truly could not have borne. Before the intensity of it, the other man was struck dumb. The spoken lie died on his lips, scorched into silence by that ardent and honest gaze.

To carry the deception into the brutality of speech, was a thing too heinous, while Ridley laid bare his own soul with such a passion of sincerity, revealing its hitherto unacknowledged suffering and its present longing for the confirmation of its desires. To bow his head in silence, was all that he could do.

For a moment yet, Ridley continued to look at him, then, with a curious soft cry, he withdrew his hands, covered his own face, and was still.

Heavily the Governor rose. Only half of his task was done. What remained must needs be approached with extreme care. He therefore took up a position behind the bowed figure, and spoke from there.

" There is something else," he began, his tone not so firm as he could have wished.   " Are you attending, Kenelm ? "

Ridley looked up, a little moisture clinging to his lashes.

" I am listening ; yes."

" Miss Chideock——"

" Ah, yes.   Does she know ? "

" Everything.   It is her wish—that is, she has a wish, a very natural, a very womanly wish, and I hope that you will not refuse to grant it.   I think that she deserves to be humoured, to be allowed her own way in this."

" Can you doubt me, sir ? " returned Ridley readily. " I, who would give my life to serve her.   Tell me the least thing that I can do to give her pleasure, and it shall be done."

" Is that a promise ?   For, indeed, she is strangely set upon this thing."

" Here is my hand, sir ! " said Ridley, with a quick smile.

" It is—not a difficult thing," replied the other more hopefully.   " It is, in effect, merely the anticipation of what would come about in the ordinary course of things.   Miss Chideock is a warm-hearted and impulsive young lady.   Loyalty is a passion with her.   You are a fortunate man to have won her love."

" I hope you don't think it necessary to tell me that, sir."

" And being what she is "—the Governor's voice had steadied somewhat now—" you cannot wonder that she should desire to show to the world a substantial proof of her faithfulness to you."

" It would be like her to desire it, sir."

" And it is your duty to allow it.   Miss Chideock, then, wishes, and wishes very earnestly, to be united to you in marriage before you leave this prison."

Ridley was startled into sudden gravity.

" To marry me—here ? " he questioned.   " Why, what strange idea is this ? "

" A very natural one," persisted the Governor.   " Taking all the circumstances into account," he added, with a substratum of truth, " the most natural one in the world."

"But surely," said Ridley, "we had better wait. I shall be free—when, sir?"

The Governor avoided the question.

"I thought," he said, "that I had made it plain that Miss Chideock's wish is to be married to you in the prison?"

"To prove that she attaches no importance to the stigma, I suppose?"

"Well," said the elder man drily, "it would appear so."

"But marriage with me, in any case, would sufficiently prove that."

"It would seem not to be her idea."

Ridley fell into silence. His companion watched him anxiously.

"You have no foolish thought of breaking your engagement, I hope?" he asked, at length, with some sharpness.

"I would, of course, have pointed out the disadvantage of a union with such a man as I must henceforth appear. But, since my conscience is clear in this matter of the felony, I don't see the necessity of making her miserable from a mistaken sense of honour. It seems to me that it would be a poor return for her devotion of these months to cast her from me now."

The Governor nodded approval.

"I'm glad to hear you say so," he answered. "I hope you will go a little further, and agree to make her your wife before your formal release."

"She has won you over to her side," said Ridley, with a half-laugh. "Frankly, sir, I don't much like it, and I scarcely see how it is to be done."

"By means of a special licence and with the aid of my permission!" retorted the Governor. "The one is as easily obtained as the other."

"It is not the wedding she ought to have," said Ridley, after another long pause.

"It's the wedding she wants," said the elder man shortly.

"You are certain of that?"

"As certain as—you are."

"Well," said Ridley, at length, "if the matter ended there, I would sink my own feelings, and let my dear one have her way. But, you see, sir, when all's said and done, I am still a discredited and dishonoured man. My career as a lawyer is at an end. I don't choose to skulk away in a corner. No!"—his eyes grew suddenly hard and fierce, and

he brought his fist down on the table with a bang—" No!
I'll face them all! I'll live it down, by God, I will! and teach
'em to forget what I shall always remember, That's to be the
way of it, and I know it would be Quenride's way too, God
bless her! But how can I ask her to share such a life as that
from the beginning?"

"The affair is hardly as hopeless as you think," the other
man pointed out. "If you cease to be the boy's trustee, you
can become the salaried agent to the estate. Mr. Frampton
has proved himself your friend already. He is not likely to
fail you at such a critical hour. If he should, I can offer you
employment as you leave the prison door."

Ridley seemed impressed, but still refused a decided answer
until he had given the matter further consideration. The
Governor went back to Quenride, and the agitated pair were
kept in suspense throughout half the day. At the end of
that time, Ridley, having looked at the matter from all
points of view, admitted the soundness of his friend's arguments, and though still personally opposed to the suggestion
from sentimental reasons, gave his consent.

Two days later, they brought her to him, a somewhat
wistful bride, who regarded her lover with a shy timidity not
wholly due to the occasion. To her, the change which the
deception had wrought in him was pitiful, for by it might be
judged the inverse process, should the scheme fail. He took
her into his arms very tenderly.

"It is your wish, my Quenride?" he said.

"Kenelm, I have asked it. You will not refuse me—
for the third time?"

"You understand whom — what you are marrying?
The Governor has told you all?"

"Everything," she said.

"And you still desire it?"

"With all my heart; my love."

He took her hand, and led her forward.

"They are waiting for us," he said.

So they were made man and wife.

.   .   .   .   .

Outside the door, the Governor turned to her.

"God help us," he said, " if, between us, we have broken
his heart!"

"God help him!" she whispered back.

"I have done my part, Mrs. Ridley," the Governor went
on. "It is for you to do yours. Lose no time. I cannot,

in actual fact, keep him here much longer. And the Lord knows how I am to account to him for the detention."

" You must account for it," she said firmly. " He must suspect nothing—until I return to take him away ! "

There were tears in her voice, but she pressed his hand bravely enough, gave a last lingering look at the closed door and suffered the chaplain to lead her away.

CHAPTER XLII

" AND THE DAY SHALL HAVE A SUN——"

A BRIGHT breezy day at the end of March—a day of brilliant sunshine and sharp winds, when departing winter and advancing spring join hands. The atmosphere was so clear that distant objects stood out in detail, and gradations of colour were perceptible to the most casual eye. In Sophy Hoddinott's garden, the eternal life of plants was springing up, but the weeds were suffered to grow apace, and last year's dead leaves still littered the ground.

Sophy herself moved with heavy limbs, when movement was necessary. At other times, she sat crouched before the fire in her old attitude, scarcely lifting her eyes from the smouldering sods.

She was alone in the cottage, and had been so since the old man's death. Permission had been granted her to continue in the home until she had made some plans for the future. She had taken full advantage of the concession, but had made no plans. It might, she decided at such times as she thought at all about the matter, be possible to stay on permanently. Living cost little enough ; she could pay her way and rent the cottage besides. The loneliness of such a life troubled her not at all. She had missed Amos at the first, but without regret. Decently *crowned* by the Mayor at Wareham, and buried at the adjacent town of Corfe, the old man had passed out of her life, and had rapidly become a mere memory. She had lived much in the somnolent state of a hibernating animal throughout the winter, faculty and emotion alike suspended, her mind holding only the one thought that had sprung into being when she crossed Wareham Bridge on a certain December morning.

But, now, she had been stabbed back to life. Every emotion of which she was capable was stirring, and setting to one sure focus—that of pain. A moral sense, feeble and

struggling, had awakened in her at last. And it dated from
the moment when, against her will, she had been forced to look
again on the face of the man she had wronged—and looking,
realised, in a dual sense, what she had done. In that wild
instant, she understood that she had not only ruined him,
but had killed the kindly sentiment which he had once held
towards her. His cold averted gaze was a thing to remember
always.

She did remember it. It had moved her to ask a fellow-
witness to pen for her the words which Ridley had failed
to read. Her sudden fainting-fit had prevented her from
seeing the fate of her simple *apologia*. She had hoped for
a sign, a message to reach her, in some inconsidered way.
As the days passed, and none came, she said to herself that she
had certainly killed that which she had once had. He would
not forgive.

It was a week after the trial. Sophy had lain before the
fire all night, moaning at intervals to it as to a sentient thing.
In the early forenoon, she rose wearily, unhasped the door, and
looked forth. The brilliant world outside mocked her misery.
The sunshine was a hateful fact. Why could it not always be
night ? Then at least one could hide.

> "*And the Day shall have a sun
> Which shall make thee wish it done.*"

He had said it. What wise things he knew. If she could
only cry, maybe the sun would hurt her eyes the less. How
the light pained and scorched her.

She thrust the door to, and crept upstairs. In the tiny
room above, fragrant memories leapt out—lasted so for a
moment, then turned bitter and acrid. But, nevertheless,
the purpose which had drawn her to the place still held her
there. Very slowly she moved forward, and fell on her knees
beside the chest which held her scanty clothing. She lifted
the lid as one might draw back the sheet from a beloved
face.

She laid aside her own paltry garments, and removed the
strip of linen which was spread beneath. A moth flew out.

With a sharp cry, she drew the coat from the box, and
examined it carefully. Her lap, as she knelt, was bestrewn
with the crumbling fragments of the sweet herbs which she
had laid among its folds last year. One sleeve was riddled
with tiny holes. Even so, had she suffered her love to become

despoiled. There was no art in either case to restore the former order of things.

Sophy's perception missed the analogy, but she saw the material damage, and grieved over it with a sudden rush of tears. Weeping bitterly, she knelt there for a long time. And, without, the sun still shone.

She was almost glad now that he had not looked at her. She had a strange fancy that she could not have borne it, and lived. Her shamed head sank lower and lower, while remembrance stabbed her through and through.

" An' I'll never hear him say, ' You're a good girl, Sophy,' no more ! "

There was nothing to live for. She had done her worst, and repented. But the harm still remained. And he had not forgiven her. How dare she hope for that ? Even this pain was less than she deserved.

She did not wish to live. And so presently she resolved to die.

Noon was far past when she left the attic, and hugging the coat in her arms went down to the kitchen. Her simple plans were made, and she set about effecting them in a quiet determined manner that was true to her purpose. She fed her poultry and released them, to scatter over the neglected garden. The cows she had sold in the early days of her calamity. Returning indoors, she laid the small store of money in her possession on the table to be claimed by the first comer. Then she lifted the coat, held it to her breast, kissed it many times, and finally laid it, but with caressing fingers, on the heap of smouldering peats. Beneath and between the slabs of fuel she thrust sticks and taper ends, building up the whole, and fanning the embers into little streaks of flame. When these ran up, and seized upon the thicker sticks that formed a network round and above the garment, she turned away, and looked no more. If complete destruction was not possible, at least she would prevent the coat from serving as a covering for any who otherwise might have desired it.

The same half-unconscious sense of fitness guided her towards her ultimate action.

Three minutes after the first scorching of the coat, Sophy was walking towards Wareham Bridge.

She reached it far too soon for her purpose—regarding that purpose from a practical point of view—otherwise, the time was long, to one who had ceased to care for life, and had no desire but to end it.

It was late afternoon when she once more approached the spot where she had passed him on that early December morning. The sun, in its westering aspect, was as brilliant and unclouded as at noontide. And still the radiance of it mocked her cruelly. She turned her back upon it, leaned forward against the wall of the bridge, and wondered dully whether he would ever know.

Shadows grew longer, the light more mellow. In another half-hour it would be time.

Footsteps occasionally passed along the bridge behind her. She never turned her head. Presently came one unlike the rest, one which halted in its going, with a little dragging sound. It drew nearer, and ceased suddenly, at her side. Anger moved the girl. She waited for it to pass on. It did not pass. Instead, a voice struck into the silence, and addressed her.

"Why are you waiting here?" it asked. "I've been watching you for ever so long."

"Go away," she muttered. "I can stand here if I like, can't I?"

"Of course. But why don't you go home?"

"'Cos I want to bide here. Go away, I tell 'ee—ugly lame brat!"

"I can't help being lame," said Gilbert, after a pause. "Do you think I like it?"

"Reckon I don't think about 'ee at all."

"What are you waiting for?" he persisted, with an odd gentleness. His youth seemed to touch hers, for in truth there was but a short span of years between them, and to give him grace to minister to her need.

"For the night!" she answered, with a note of defiance.

"Why?"

She made no answer. After the first glance, she had turned back to the wall, and now kept her gaze fixed on the river beyond. Her whole attitude was one of abandonment to despair. Even the innocent boy beside her knew that his experience had never touched anything quite like this before. Repellent as was her manner, to his mind her recent history was far more so. She moved his wonder as well as his dislike. But her obvious distress appealed to him, at this moment, with a force which conquered prejudice, and though she offered no inducement to stay, he still lingered. Save for themselves, the bridge and road were empty.

"You're unhappy," said Gilbert.

" What's that to you ? "

" Well, I think you deserve to be. You've made many others unhappy. I suppose you're sorry now ! "

" Sorry ! " she echoed, with a heave of the slouching shoulders.

Gilbert came nearer, and also leant against the wall, trying to see her face.

" What made you do it ? " he asked.

" I don't know—must ha' been mad, I reckon. There ! 'tis all over now. I'll kill myself ; I will. An' then folks'll know as I was sorry, when it were too late ! "

" Kill yourself ? " cried Gilbert, with a look of horror.

She nodded down at the river.

" 'Tis what I be waitin' for," she said, " if you'd only let me alone."

Gilbert clutched her arm.

" You mustn't be so wicked ! " he exclaimed. " Why, what good can that do ? Come away at once ! "

She merely threw a glance at him, then resumed her previous crouching attitude.

" Reckon you don't know what pain be," she said.

" I think I do," Gilbert answered in his odd wise way. " I've had so much of it, all my life."

" Anybody med see as you be made all wrong," she muttered.

He flushed under her careless scrutiny.

" I'm better than I was," he averred, and his delicate face grew sharp with eagerness. " They say I shall be stronger by and by. I do so hope it's true. I want, oh, I want so much to live ! "

" I want to die," said the girl.

" Why ? Because you've harmed Mr. Ridley ? "

" An' he hates me for it ! "

Gilbert looked thoughtful.

" What makes you say that ? " he asked. " I can't imagine Mr. Ridley hating anyone."

" He hates me now ! "

" I can't think so ! Why do you ? "

She told him, in her reluctant way, of the unanswered message.

" Perhaps he didn't get it," the boy suggested. " Perhaps you've not got his."

" It don't matter now. I'll show folks another way."

" Don't be wicked and foolish ! In any case, he'd not

wish that. I feel certain of it. Of course, you've done a very bad thing : if Mr. Ridley, or anyone else did touch the bridge, 'twasn't your place to go telling tales. Still, if you're sorry, that's something——"

"I be sorry ! " she interrupted, with passion. "So sorry that I'd not mind nothin' now, if he were only free an' safe again. I'd not mind him not carin' for me as loves him so dear. He med marry her, an' I'd not cry out, so long as he were happy an' well. Oh, I'd not mind nothin' now, I tell 'ee, if only that were true ! "

So far forward had she crept to higher things, through her sin and suffering.

Gilbert Chideock listened amazed.

"Do you mean that you—love him ? " he said, pressing forward.

In her uncouth way, Sophy jerked out a correct account of the emotional situation. To no one but this gentle-mannered lad could she have spoken of such things. In the face of her abject wretchedness Gilbert kept his censure to himself. Moreover, he was growing alarmed at her fixed determination to end the miserable episode by self-destruction.

"Listen to me," he said, with something of his sister's manner. "You don't want to die while there's a chance of his being saved, do you ? "

She was startled into turning, and he noticed that she straightened her body as she did so. The red sunset light fell upon her face.

"Because there is a chance, you know," the boy went on, his own eagerness supplying all the necessary colour to his entreaty. "My sister has gone to London to see a great man. In a few days we shall know. I want this very much too— quite as much as you do. You see, my sister has married him ; he's my brother now. And I want them to be happy more than anything else in the world. Won't you wait with me ? Let's hope together, Sophy ! Won't you go home now, and wait until I let you know ? "

She made no sign of assent, but her eyes had brightened somewhat. She plucked restlessly at her shawl.

"If you go home now," Gilbert went on, "I promise that I will let him know how sorry you are. And if you'll be here at this time the day after to-morrow, I'll give you his answer. Oh, I'm sure he doesn't know ! And if you come each day, I'll come too, and tell you directly there's any news."

"Will 'ee ? " asked Sophy, after a long pause.

" I have promised it," said the boy, with dignity.

" But if 'tis bad news ? "

" It—won't be," he said.

" But if 'tis," she persisted sullenly, " I'll do for myself, just the same."

Gilbert was wise enough to leave that to the future. Even his inexperience recognised the truth that a mood generally depends on a certain set of circumstances, and that such a concatenation is seldom repeated.

" Well, we won't talk about that now," he said. " Go home, and don't trouble about anything until I see you again. Oh, Sophy, it will soon be dark—the sun has gone—look ! They'll be missing me up at my house. And I want to see you leave here before I do."

But the shadows had deepened still more before the boy gained his point. Sophy fought against yielding, as against an interference with her plan. But Gilbert, acting out of sheer simplicity, had used the greatest art. He had given her a hope, and in so doing had induced the willingness, if not the wish, to live a little longer.

While he watched and waited, she suddenly shivered, jerked her shawl round her shoulders, and without a word began to move away.

It was dark when she reached the cottage. The kitchen was a mere void of blackness. She groped her way to the corner where the rushlight stood, and grasping it went forward to the hearth.

But there was to be no light for Sophy that night. After a minute or so of anxious examination, she sat back, amazed, stupefied, inert. The fire had gone out.

The facts were simple enough, and a saner mind would have foreseen them. The heavy coat, by excluding the air, had smothered the blazing wood, and extinguished the glow beneath. Not a spark remained, and the coat itself was barely singed.

Sophy lay by the desolate hearth all night, like a stricken thing.

But she was on the bridge at the appointed hour long before Gilbert Chideock came in sight.

" It was just as I said," he told her, at once. " Mr. Ridley never read your message. He has sent one back. He says, ' Tell Sophy Hoddinott that I forgive her, and that she mustn't, on any account, think of doing such a wicked thing as take her own life.' "

Sophy's face went white.

"Did he—did he—truly say them words?" she asked, with a heave of the breast.

"On my honour, he did."

Her head fell forward on to the parapet of the bridge.

"He'm a good man!" she sobbed.

"I haven't heard any news from my sister yet," said Gilbert, presently. His own face was growing pinched with anxiety. "Come again to-morrow."

She went the next day, and the next after that.

The same brilliant sun still mocked her suspense and misery. She longed, as she waited on the bridge, for the cool grey of nightfall, knowing well enough that as yet it had brought her no rest.

The boy was late in coming, or so it seemed to the heart-racked girl. But at length, at the sunset hour, she saw the halting figure approaching, with a quicker motion than usual. Some instinct led her to move forward to meet him, a thing which she had not done before.

He waved a hand in the air, and greeted her with a smile.

"It's all right!" he cried boyishly. "He's saved! My sister has gone to him! He'll be free by now. I couldn't come before because they wouldn't let me. And I'm not supposed to be out now. Oh, Sophy——!"

She raised her tear-sodden eyes to his face.

"Be they comin' here?" she asked unsteadily.

"She's going to take him into Devonshire," said Gilbert. "They'll be on their way by this. I'm to join them later on."

She seemed not to be listening. For a long spell her gaze fixed itself on the grey river beyond.

"Reckon 'tis best so!" she muttered. "An' now, I'll be gettin' home-along an' light up the fire!"

CHAPTER XLIII

FOR EVER AND EVER

QUENRIDE went down High West Street at a gallop. It was early afternoon, and there were many towns-folk to mark her progress. But her errand was all unknown. Since the previous evening, she had been on the road, posting from stage to stage, whirled through the darkness behind the flying horses, to the tune of rattling wheels and the creak of straining leather. And "faster! faster!" had ever been her cry. She had no thought of rest or refreshment until her goal was reached, but she had paused a few moments on her arrival at Wareham, and changed her mode of transit. It seemed to her that she could cover the remaining seventeen miles more swiftly on her own saddle-horse. Ten minutes after springing from the chaise, she was so mounted, and dashing away as wildly as her heart bade her, leaving much joy and a series of incoherent orders behind her.

At the point where the four chief roads crossed, a little knot of men was gathered together in talk. Quenride would have passed them without noticing that a familiar face was among the group. But it happened that, at the moment, her passage was impeded by a couple of wains, and she was forced to draw rein. While she paused, with the horse still quivering under her, one of the loiterers detached himself, and strolled into the roadway. A companion or two were interested enough to follow him. Mohun bowed to his cousin with a slightly offensive air. Then he spoke.

"Proud to see you, Quenny," he said. "Going down to the gaol to help your felon lover to pack up? I hear he sails in a day or so. I'm for London Dock to give him God-speed on the voyage."

Quenride turned slowly. Mohun was lounging at her elbow. She leant down a little, reaching out her bridle-hand, and laid it on his shoulder.

" Sir," she said, speaking very clearly, " you are a liar and a scoundrel, and if your friends are likely to forget it, perhaps this will help them to remember."

Quick as thought, she raised her whip and brought it down twice across his face, then sat back very quietly, looking at him while he writhed and gasped.

" Damnation! You shall pay for this, you——! " he sputtered, with a foul epithet, as he drew his arm across his cheek, and left a red stain on the sleeve.

Quenride flushed at the insult, but was unmoved by the threat.

" These gentlemen, I think," she said, " will bear witness that the provocation was yours."

And the way now being clear, she went forward again, confident that Alaric Mohun would henceforth leave her and hers alone.

" I wish to see the Governor! " she cried, at the prison gate.

She was brought to him immediately.

" Thank God! " he said, when she had told her news. And he kept silent for some moments.

" Take me to him! " said Quenride, holding out her hands.

" You are only just in time," he said. " To-night, I should have been compelled to tell him all. This has been a very bitter day for me."

She looked at him with a laugh and a sigh.

" There is the order for his release," she said. " The Pardon itself cannot be far behind. And, oh, I have done more than you think! I have obtained the promise that his professional credit shall remain untainted. I think that he will be very pleased at that."

The Governor took her hand, with his stiff old-fashioned courtesy, and in his heart he blessed this beautiful young wife, who, by the exercise of her ancient privilege, had brought Harriet's son out of darkness to the light of happiness and freedom.

" Take me to him! " said Quenride, again.

So the Governor led her once more along the dreary passages, and stopped before a certain door. He swung it back, and entered on her heels, but when he got inside she was already laughing and crying in her husband's arms.

" The door is open, Kenelm," said the Governor, presently. " But never until this moment. She, and she alone, has unlocked it for you. Don't you understand ? "

Ridley looked at him ; took in the meaning of the words, and of the strange new regulations of which he had heard so often of late—and realising the depths of the devoted courage which had dared the risk caught her to him with a low cry.

" We're going to be happy," she said, " for ever and ever."

" Amen to that, my Quenride," he answered.

The Governor was holding the door open.

" Come ! " he said crisply. " Come ! "

Ridley went forward, and, with Quenride at his side, turned to take up his task of teaching others to forget that which he himself must always remember.

But Quenride, looking through the open door-way, thought only of the happiness that could not fail.

THE END

www.ingramcontent.com/pod-product-compliance
Lightning Source LLC
Chambersburg PA
CBHW020503020726
47493CB00001B/165